CLASHING WITH THE CEO

clashing

with the

ceo

Published by
Westwell Press
New Zealand

Cover design by Sylvia Frost at The Book Brander

Paperback ISBN: 978-0-473-71865-7

saramartinauthor.com

For the romance connoisseurs who appreciate the delicious agony of a good slow burn.

Chapter One

The moment I'd been dreading all night had arrived.

Leon and I stood outside my building, the air thick with tension. He tilted his head, blond hair falling artfully across his face, and arched an eyebrow.

My heart raced. I couldn't mess this up—I'd been burned too many times by guys who just wanted a casual hook-up. Our date went well, and Leon seemed different, but I needed to set the tone from the start.

Leon folded his arms. "Well?"

I forced myself to look past his ridiculously handsome features —the mesmerising blue eyes, the sharp cheekbones, the lips just begging to be kissed. Keeping a level head was crucial. "Thank you for walking me home. I had a nice evening."

"Me too." Leon stepped closer. "I was hoping we could... keep it going?"

Subtlety wasn't his strong suit, apparently. Still, my knees went a little wobbly at the suggestion. I let out a nervous laugh, hoping it didn't sound as unhinged as I suspected it did. "I like you, Leon. But I want to take things slow, so let's call it a night."

For a torturous moment, I braced myself for the wounded-ego routine—the pout, the outburst, or some other childish display.

But to Leon's credit, he just sighed and raked a hand through his hair. "You sure?"

"Yes." I aimed for an apologetic, yet resolute tone.

Leon tensed for a second, but then he shrugged, regaining his composure. "All right then. Bye, Milly. See you around, I guess."

"I'll text you." I cringed inwardly, hating how it came out more like a question than a statement.

"Sure."

With that, he turned and sauntered away, hands shoved in the tight pockets of his black skinny jeans. I watched him go, letting out a giddy exhale. Despite his obvious disappointment, he seemed to take the rejection well. Or maybe he was just trying to play it cool?

No. I refused to second-guess myself. I did the smart, practical thing by turning him down. No more wasting time on the wrong guys.

I entered my apartment building feeling satisfied this would pan out just as I intended. Leon would get over the slight blow to his ego, and a second date would be on the horizon.

* * *

I boggled at the notification on my phone the next morning. A message from Leon so soon? I unlocked the screen, biting my lip to stop myself from grinning like a lunatic in front of all the other train passengers on their morning commute.

> You were so fuckin sexy last night. Sorry had to leave early. Let's do it again sometime?

I blinked. *What?*

Something was off about the message. It didn't quite align with what happened on our date. In fact, it sounded like he was talking about a different experience. A weight sank to the pit of my stomach as I reread the message, but before I could process it further, it disappeared. Leon had deleted it.

The truth hit me like a bucket of ice water. The message wasn't meant for me. Leon must have seen someone else last night. No wonder he was so calm about the rejection. He had a backup plan all along.

That jerk!

He never cared about me. He was just like all the other dud guys I'd ever had the displeasure of dating.

Agh!

The train doors jolted open at Britomart Station, passengers spilling out onto the platform. I hurried along with the throng.

How could I have been so blind? Looking back, the signs had been there all along. He had only talked about himself, he was whiny when I wouldn't order a second drink, and he couldn't walk me home without asking to come in.

I quickened my pace, weaving through the other pedestrians on my way to work.

The Luxmore Appliances head office was a twenty-floor tower on the corner of Hobson Street and Customs Street. I barged through the double doors into the lobby, then marched straight to the lifts. I stood with my arms crossed, foot tapping an agitated rhythm while I waited.

I can do much better than him anyway. I'm an intelligent, attractive young woman. I have my own apartment and a decent job. Any straight, single man would find me desirable. I bet the next available man I see wouldn't turn me down if I gave him a chance.

Right on cue, the lift door opened. Its occupant: one man.

Startled, I looked away, heat flaring in my cheeks. The man didn't exit, and I was the only person waiting to get on. Reaffirming my little bet with myself, I gave him a once-over as I stepped inside. What I saw made me pause.

This man wasn't my type at all. He looked much older than me, and he wasn't handsome. A far cry from pretty-boy Leon and his ilk. The man's black hair was immaculately groomed, and he had shrewd, dark eyes. A defined jawline led to stern lips and down his throat to a prominent Adam's apple peeking from his crisp shirt collar. He wore a suit which screamed tailor-made and expensive, not to mention the Rolex on his wrist. He exuded an aura of power.

Must be in upper management.

I looked at the keypad. Sure enough, he had selected the twentieth floor. All the top executives had their offices on the twentieth floor—the highest level of the building. He either worked there, or he was a visiting businessman from another company.

As I pressed the button for the fifth floor, I could feel the man's intense eyes boring holes into me. I wondered if he was checking me out.

Maybe he really is interested in me?

I didn't know what to make of it. He was too old for me, and he wasn't my type at all. Then again, he was far from decrepit— early forties at most. He looked fit and well-groomed, and he was probably intelligent and ambitious if he held a high position like I suspected. Maybe it was time to broaden my horizons. Besides, I could use the confidence boost.

Mind made up, I turned on my charm offensive and flashed him the sweetest smile I could muster. "Good morning."

His jaw tightened, and the veins in his neck flexed. He left me hanging for a long beat, an inscrutable expression on his face.

The corners of my mouth twitched, unable to hold up the smile much longer as awkwardness set in. Our eye contact was on the verge of unbearable when he finally spoke. "You're..." His voice was low, and he had a hint of a posh English accent.

What's this? All I had expected was a simple "Good morning" in return.

Is he actually going to hit on me? I can't believe it.

He cleared his throat and continued. "Your top's inside out."

Huh?

"My..." I looked down and examined my blouse while feeling

behind my neck for the tag. Sure enough, the seams were showing, and the tag was on the outside. A fresh surge of heat burst onto my face. "Oh!" I spluttered. "Thanks for telling me."

He didn't say another word.

I hurried out as soon as the door opened onto the fifth floor, nearly tripping over my feet on the way. I didn't know what was more embarrassing, an upper-management staff member seeing me with my top on inside out, or several strangers having witnessed the same thing during my commute.

Whut's wrong with me today?

I headed straight to the bathroom before anyone else could glimpse my wardrobe malfunction. In the safety of a vacant stall, I shrugged off my overstuffed bag and hooked it on the back of the door. My blouse came off next. I checked it was the right way around, then slipped it back over my sweaty head.

Properly dressed, I emerged from the stall and double-checked my appearance in the mirrors above the row of immaculate white basins. My forehead was shiny, and my cheeks were pink, but apart from that, everything was in order. I smoothed a hand through my hair.

Okay, so it's been a shitty morning. That doesn't mean that the rest of the day has to follow suit. Forget about Leon. Forget about that man in the lift. I've got more important things to think about.

I left the bathroom with my head held high, vowing not to let anything else rattle my self-composure.

An arctic blast from the air conditioner made me hunch my shoulders as I entered the communications department. I walked along the uniform row of wooden desks to my designated workstation and placed my phone, diary, and pen case into position. I had the tidiest desk on the entire floor, earning me the title of Resident Neat Freak among the staff. My neatness extended to the digital realm too, leading to my second nickname: File Management Nazi.

Brooke arrived shortly. She was wearing a green dress today, and her long dark was loose and straight. "Hey, Milly," she said, taking her seat at the desk next to mine.

"Hi, Brooke."

She leaned in close. "Sooo… How did your date go?"

I felt the colour drain from my face as the sting of Leon's text message resurfaced.

She cringed. "Not good, I take it."

"Correct."

"But he sounded so promising…"

"Long story short, it turned out he was a jerk."

"Okay, spill. I want all the juicy details."

We moved to the break room to continue our conversation over morning tea. Brooke set down two mugs of hot tea on a table opposite the window. I pulled out a chair.

"So, what happened?" Brooke asked.

I recounted the story of the date with Leon up to the text message he accidentally sent me this morning, and the realisation he was seeing someone else.

Brooke grimaced. "Yikes. What a douche."

"I shouldn't have got my hopes up. Think I'm ready to swear off dating apps for good."

"How old was the guy?"

"Twenty-seven. Same age as me."

"Maybe that's your problem. Boys in their twenties are too immature. Why don't you age up a little?"

"Most guys in their thirties are already taken, and the ones that aren't… well, they seem to be single for a good reason."

"Oof. I know what you mean. But there are some decent men out there. You just have to—"

Something in the background caught my attention and drowned out the rest of what Brooke was saying. My focus shifted to the window behind her.

The world slowed down. All I could hear was the blood rushing in my ears and my beating heart.

Something was falling. No… *someone*. A body soaring straight down outside the building.

My mug slipped from my grasp and hit the table, splashing the remnants of my tea. I shrieked.

Chapter Two

A month had passed since the CEO jumped from the roof, but the haunting image lingered in my mind. I avoided the fifth-floor break room, opting to use the kitchen facilities on the sixth floor instead. No one questioned my change of routine.

I came back downstairs after putting my lunch in the fridge. As soon as I pulled out my chair, Brooke descended. "Have you seen the latest article in the Herald?" she asked.

"No. What article?"

"Well, apparently, Alex was being audited for financial discrepancies in the business at the time of his death. That's why the police closed the case, ruling it as suicide."

I let her words sink in, mulling over their implications. Something didn't sit right. "Why steal money from the company? He was already rich enough."

Brooke rolled her eyes. "Duh. Greed, of course."

Ellen stuck her head through the gap between our monitors from the other side, joining our conversation. "I wonder if that means the other rumours aren't true."

"You mean that he was having an affair with an employee?" Brooke asked.

"Yeah. And the one about the rickety railing up on the roof—that maybe someone had tampered with it."

I threw up my hands. "I'm sure what the police have concluded is based on solid evidence. They would have noticed a so-called rickety railing if there was one."

Ellen and Brooke exchanged unconvinced glances. I was about to turn my focus back to work when Brooke changed the subject to a related tangent. "I wonder when there's going to be an announcement about who's going to replace Alex as CEO. It's been a month already."

Mike, who had evidently been listening in on our conversation from the row of desks behind ours, rolled up in his office chair. "You guys are way behind. Catch up."

Brooke narrowed her eyes. "What do you mean?"

"Management has already chosen a new CEO—and get this," he leaned in and lowered his voice, "mass layoffs are on the cards."

His statement struck me like a slap across the face. "What?" I spluttered. "Where did you hear that?"

"I know someone who knows someone who works on the twentieth floor. Apparently, Alex left the company in a state of financial difficulty, and the person who's going to fill his shoes has got a big ol' mess to clean up."

"Mess or no mess, layoffs so soon after such a big tragedy… That's just evil."

Brooke eyed Mike doubtfully. "If what you say is true, you don't sound too concerned about it."

"That's because I've got my exit plan all sorted out," Mike said.

"And what's that?"

"I'll take voluntary redundancy."

"Really?" I asked.

He shrugged. "Yeah. Maybe."

"How can you be so calm?"

"I'm twenty-three, and I've already gone through two redundancies in my brief career. What's a third?"

"He lives with his parents and doesn't have to pay any rent," Ellen explained.

"So what? Being a full-time gamer living in my parents' basement is a valid plan," Mike said.

"Not if you want to get a girlfriend," Brooke countered.

"One day I'll meet the gamer girl of my dreams. Just wait and see."

"I believe you," I offered with a smile. "Just don't forget about personal hygiene."

Brooke snickered.

As farfetched as his plan sounded, I knew Mike was smarter and more determined than he looked. I wouldn't be surprised if it worked out for him.

Ellen sighed. "I hope this isn't true. I like my job just the way it is."

"Me too," Brooke agreed. "Whoever the new CEO is, they can get fu—"

Brendon swooped in to break up our conversation. "All right, everyone, I know it's been difficult to focus lately, but work still needs to be done. Speculating won't achieve anything. Besides, tomorrow there's going to be an announcement and a question-and-answer session, and I have it on good authority that we'll find out what's going on then. Let's wait and see what management has to say."

Mike rolled away while Brooke grumbled under her breath, shaking her mouse to wake up her monitor.

I checked my emails, but my mind was still on what Mike had said. Could it be true? Was my job in jeopardy? I swallowed a rising sense of foreboding.

* * *

The conference theatre buzzed with anxious murmurs, twitching, foot tapping, and knee jostling.

This was our chance to get some answers—about what happened to Alex Patterson and what was going to happen to the business going forward.

Staff members crammed the conference theatre, spilling along the aisles and overflowing out the door. Brooke and I had secured two seats near the back right-hand corner.

David Green stood at the lectern in the centre of the stage. He was a middle-aged man, dressed in a snazzy pink shirt, grey trousers, and a black bow tie. He looked out to the audience through tortoiseshell-rimmed glasses, the stage lights bouncing off his shiny forehead and lenses.

I sat on the edge of my chair, hands clamped at my sides, body rigid. Were we finally going to get worthwhile answers? What if the rumour about layoffs was true?

"Thank you all for coming," David said. "I know you have busy schedules, but this shouldn't take too long. For those who don't know me, my name is David Green. I'm the Chief Operating Officer of this company, second in command to the CEO." He paused, surveying the room. "I'm sure you're all aware of the tragic loss we've suffered in recent weeks with the passing of our CEO, Alex Patterson."

A sombre hush fell over the crowd.

"I want to offer a personal apology for the lack of clarity about the situation. I know you have been left with unanswered questions and rumours going around. The truth is, there has been a lot to work out behind the scenes before the business can move forward. But with those rumours spreading, I felt it was important to call this meeting, to set the record straight and provide you all with the information you need to know."

Brooke leaned in, whispering beside me. "This sounds promising."

I nodded, my fingers tapping an anxious beat on the armrest.

David continued. "The last few weeks have been difficult for all of us. I hope each of you has taken the time you need to recover from this tragedy, and I want to remind you that our on-site counsellor is available if anyone needs additional support."

He took a deep breath. "I know there has been a lot of speculation about the circumstances of Alex's death, as well as the future of this company. I'm here today to provide you with the facts—to the best of my knowledge—and to address any concerns you may have."

The room fell silent, the anticipation palpable. All eyes were fixed on David, waiting with bated breath for the revelations to come.

"I'll start off by confirming recent media reports. Zelthia Group—our parent company, based in Singapore—ran an audit which exposed financial discrepancies in the business. The police believe stress and mental illness were a prominent factor in Alex's death. Let's trust this outcome and leave the matter to rest. Please consider his family, who are still grieving, and withhold from speaking to the media.

"Secondly, I can now confirm that Zelthia Group has selected a new CEO. Someone with a very high position in Zelthia will take over here. Final arrangements are still underway, but we can expect the new CEO to take up the post early next month. Meanwhile, I will remain in charge. Please bear with me during this difficult time.

"Now, I'd like to invite anyone who has questions or concerns they want to share to raise their hands, and I'll do my best to answer them."

Several hands shot up. David picked someone, making eye contact and aiming a nod in their direction. An assistant passed a microphone down the row.

"I've heard the new CEO doesn't have any experience in this sector. Is that true?" a man asked.

"He has a broad range of experience, but no, not in household appliances and whiteware specifically," David explained.

"So, the new CEO is a man?" someone else asked.

"Correct."

David pointed to another person in the crowd with their hand raised.

"Was Alex Patterson stealing money from the company?" a woman asked.

"We are still reviewing the findings of the audit, but I'm afraid it looks that way, yes. We will release more information once we have all the facts straight."

More hands shot up, stretching towards the ceiling in a bid for David's attention.

He picked someone else.

"What was the reason for the audit in the first place? How come we never heard anything about this?"

"Profits have been in decline for some time now, so I suspect that's what caused our parent firm to investigate."

The next person didn't wait to be chosen. He yelled his question without the mic. "What Alex did must have been pretty bad. Is the company in trouble because of him?"

Someone else cut in before David could answer. "Why is Singapore getting so involved all of a sudden? Luxmore is a New Zealand business."

"Yeah!" someone shouted.

"That's right!" others chimed in.

The questions and opinions started coming thick and fast.

"Is Zelthia going to take control of the company?"

"Are they going to take our jobs?"

"There's going to be a big restructure, right? That's what I've heard."

"I think it's about time we got new leadership. A new CEO could do us a lot of good."

Just like that, the organised manner of raising hands and waiting turn devolved into a free-for-all.

All I could do was watch on. I had the same questions everyone else had, and my voice wasn't powerful enough to cut through the chaos, especially from my position near the back of the theatre.

Beside me, Brooke seemed much more relaxed about the situation. Her uncle was high up in the management team, which must have afforded her a sense of security. If job losses were around the corner, she would likely be safe.

David was turning redder and redder, trying but failing to restore order among the staff. I thought he might give up and storm off, but then a sudden atmosphere shift took place. The tone of questioning changed from frustrated outbursts to murmured enquiry.

"Who's that?" someone asked.

"Is that him?" another person echoed.

I looked around, trying to see who they had noticed.

I heard the footsteps before I saw him. Leather soles thudding on the wooden stage, even and deliberate. He emerged from the shadows and approached the lectern.

I recognised him at once.

The man who walked across the stage in a flawless black suit was the same man I had seen in the lift on that fateful morning. I flashed back to that awkward moment, his penetrating eyes on me, his humourless, straight-faced remark.

"Your top's on inside out."

I slid down my seat in an aftershock of embarrassment.

Why is he up on the stage? He can't be… can he?

The man made a shooing gesture, and David Green stepped out of the way like a meek underling. He took the stand. Under the harsh stage lights, he looked even more severe than I remembered. Hard eyes, clenched jaw, sharp nose, pursed lips.

"Wow. He looks sinister," Brooke said.

"He does," I agreed.

The man commanded attention with his pin-straight posture and his stern expression. He scanned the audience as if sizing us up, and he didn't look impressed with what he saw. He clearly wasn't going to tolerate our behaviour and wouldn't speak until everyone had settled down. His fingertips drummed the side of the lectern. His jawline was stiff, his brow creased.

A hush fell over the audience like a blanket smothering a fire. All eyes were on him.

He tapped the microphone, causing a screech of feedback. Then, at last, he spoke. "How is it that so many people are gathered here? Who is out doing the work, running the business?" His voice had a low, luxurious timbre that made me shiver.

Confusion and nervous laughter rippled through the room.

"Anyone?" he pressed.

A woman near the front spoke with a slight tremor in her voice. "A few staff members from each department have stayed behind."

"But coming here to argue and complain is a productive use of your time?"

"Staff aren't machines. They're human beings. Trust and transparency go a long way in business."

"How wise." His words dripped with snide sarcasm. "Your name and position?"

"Clara Evans. Head of HR. And you are?"

He smirked, dark eyes glinting. "How rude of me. I haven't introduced myself." He turned his attention to the audience at large. "My name is Neil Kingston. I'm sure most of you have put two and two together, but for those who are a bit slow, I'll spell it out. I am going to be the new CEO of Luxmore Appliances."

Fresh gasps and murmurs broke out.

Just as I suspected. That man, Neil Kingston, was the new CEO. I slipped further down my seat, mortified. I had tried to flirt with the CEO in the lift. What had I even been thinking?

"There's no point wasting more time," Neil said. "I'll keep this short and sweet. Yes, the future of Luxmore is at risk. Is that the confirmation you were after?"

A collective sinking feeling was palpable. No one called out. No one dared say anything.

Neil continued. "For the company to stand a chance at

survival, changes are going to have to be made, and not everyone will like them. Anyone who doesn't wish to comply can walk away and leave the company at any time. Voluntary resignations will make my task of organising a restructure that much easier."

Restructure. The word seared itself into my brain like a hot iron brand. It was true. People were going to lose their jobs—and I could be one of them.

The audience bristled. A few individuals were brave enough to raise their hands, but Neil ignored them. "Please, do not speak to the press. Anyone who does so will ensure their position is terminated. That is all I have to say on the matter at this point. I won't be taking any questions."

With that, he strode off stage and exited the conference theatre.

Brooke furrowed her brow. "What's with that guy? What an arsehole."

"We might lose our jobs," I whimpered. That was all I could think about.

Chapter Three

"This is SO unfair!" Brooke wailed.

She had the same email up on her screen that everybody else did; a message from Neil Kingston outlining all the big changes that were coming to Luxmore Appliances.

"I know," I said. "It's only his first official day as CEO, and he dumps all this on us. What a prick."

The list of changes included staff redundancies, an end to the staff trip to Fiji, the removal of the subsidy on cafeteria food, free car parking for senior staff scrapped, and a salary freeze on all management and executive positions.

Tension ran high in the office. My coworkers grumbled and groaned at their desks.

"The staff trip... Fiji..." Brooke's eyes shone with uncried tears.

I swallowed my sip of coffee. "Wait. Jobs are on the line, and you're most concerned about the staff trip?"

"Of course. It was my turn to go this year. I bought a new swimsuit and everything."

To encourage staff retention, starting in their third year working at the company, employees were eligible to go on the trip that year and every third year after that. Or they were, until now.

A notification sound pinged around the room. One new message in the work chat. A light tittering started up before turning into a full-blown giggle fest. Even Brooke cracked a smile.

Wondering what all the fuss was about, I opened the chat. When I saw the picture, I had to hold a hand over my mouth not to laugh out loud and spray coffee everywhere. I snorted instead, causing some of the hot liquid to shoot up the back of my nose with an unpleasant stinging sensation.

Someone called Sunny from the IT department had posted an unflattering photo of Neil Kingston with a grumpy look on his face, edited to include a pair of devil horns, pitchfork, and a pointed tail. A repeating pattern of looping fire texture animated GIFs formed the background, reminiscent of nineties web design.

"Oh my gosh. What is this?" I asked when I had swallowed my coffee and recovered from laughter convulsions.

"Looks like someone had some spare time on their hands," Brooke said, smirking at the picture on her screen.

In the days that followed, the picture became an office meme, spawning multiple humorous variations, including Neil in a tutu surrounded by sparkles, and Neil with his hair and nose removed to make him look like Lord Voldemort—that one was my favourite.

I was enjoying the latest rendition when the landline phone on my desk rang. At first, I didn't realise it was mine. No one ever called me on it—everyone sent messages in the work chat. I wasn't client facing, so it was unlikely to be an external call.

Wrong number?

I tentatively picked up. "Hello?"

"Is this Amelia Cross?" a man asked.

It was for me after all, and the use of my full name made it seem important. "Yes, that's me."

"Are you free to attend a quick meeting in ten minutes?"

I hesitated, caught off guard by the sudden request. What meeting and who with? "Uh... Yes, that should be okay—"

"Excellent. Please report to the twentieth floor at four fifteen. Thank you."

The line went dead before I could ask what it was about, leaving me staring at the receiver, my palms clammy.

The twentieth floor.

No one had ever asked me to go there before. What business could I have on the twentieth floor?

Unless…

My mind rushed to a terrifying conclusion. Could it be a redundancy meeting? Had the restructure already begun? Neil Kingston had only just stepped into the role of CEO. If it was as I suspected, then I hated him even more. How could he start firing people so quickly?

Heartless monster.

"Who was that?" Brooke asked.

"I don't know. Someone asked me to go to the twentieth floor."

"Whoa. That sounds scary."

"I'm a little worried. My heart's pounding."

She waved her hand. "I'm sure it's nothing."

"That's not what you just said!"

"I overreacted. Probably."

"You're doing very little to reassure me right now."

She patted my back. "You'll be fine, and if not, I'll be here to commiserate with you when you get back."

"Gee, thanks."

Elbows on my desk, I rested my head in my hands and groaned. I didn't want to commiserate. I wanted all of this to be nothing more than a bad dream. No new boss, no restructure, no changes at all. I was content with the way things were.

The minutes dragged by until it was time to leave.

"Are you going to the mystery meeting now?" Brooke asked.

I nodded.

"Good luck." She held up crossed fingers on both hands.

With a knot of dread in my stomach, I marched towards my

fate. The knot tightened as the lift climbed—sixteen, seventeen, eighteen, nineteen...

The ding of the doors opening made me jump in fright. After a deep breath to calm myself, I stepped out and absorbed my surroundings. I had arrived in a luxurious reception area with a curved desk and a grey stone floor that was so shiny I could see my reflection in it. The yellow hue of the downlights and a bright bouquet of alstroemerias in a glass vase on the desk warmed the otherwise monochromatic colour scheme. White fibre-optic lights displayed the company's logo on the wall—a stylised snowy mountain peak.

I approached the receptionist, a tall young man with floppy brown hair. His name tag said James Campbell. "Hi, James. I'm Amelia Cross. I was told to come here—"

"Yes. You may take a seat." His voice was the same as I had heard on the phone—somehow energetic, yet bored at the same time. He seemed high-strung.

I dithered for a second, unsure whether I wanted to ask questions or just do as he said. When he fixed me an odd stare in response to my hesitation, I blurted my query. "Uh, could you please tell me what this is about? Who am I supposed to be meeting?"

"Didn't I tell you? I'm sorry. Neil Kingston is going to see you."

Neil Kingston.

The name I had feared. My heart sped up and my muscles tensed. Neil Kingston, the new CEO, wanted to see *me*. In all my time working at Luxmore, I had never met with the CEO before. He was far too big and important.

At least he has the guts to fire his employees face to face. No, I bet he gets a kick out of it.

"Please, take a seat. I'm sure he'll be with you soon," James said.

"But what does he want to see me about?" I asked.

James frowned. "I don't know much except that he's been talking to a lot of employees over the last couple of days. Sorry."

"Oh. That's all right. Thanks."

I slunk to the couch, defeated. A glass pitcher of water with lemon slices and half-melted ice cubes sat on the coffee table. I poured myself a small cup.

So far, all signs pointed towards redundancy. Why else would the CEO be meeting a bunch of employees one by one in his office?

The top on inside-out incident replayed in my head. Why, oh why, did that have to happen? Mr. Kingston's first impression of me was as someone who couldn't even dress herself properly, and if he realised I had been trying to flirt with him, even worse.

I'm so doomed.

Gulping the icy, lemony water did little to deter my rapidly rising body temperature. My legs were beginning to adhere to the leather upholstery. Left for much longer, I might permanently fuse with it.

A woman emerged from beyond the reception area and strode towards the lifts. Had she just come from meeting Mr. Kingston too? Did that mean it was my turn now? I watched her with laser eyes, analysing her behaviour for clues. She didn't look upset, but she seemed contemplative with her furrowed brow and the way she chewed her lip.

Hmm.

Someone else appeared a moment later. I noticed the baby bump first, then I took in the rest of her. She was an elegant woman, dressed in black, wide-legged trousers and a blue-grey silk blouse. No makeup, apart from a subtle shade of lipstick. Her black hair was pulled back with a chic claw clip. "Amelia Crook," she called.

Peeling myself from the couch felt like ripping off Velcro. Sounded like it too. I cringed, hoping she didn't hear. Once I had extricated myself, I introduced myself properly. "Actually, it's Amelia *Cross*. There's an Amelia Crook in the marketing department. Our names are so similar, we get mixed up all the time. Most people just call me by my nickname, Milly."

"That *is* confusing. Milly Cross. I'll remember that. My name's Christine Liu. I'm Neil's secretary."

"Nice to meet you, Christine."

"Come on through. Let me take you to see Neil."

Christine seemed warm and friendly, but her cheeriness felt at odds with the situation at hand.

"So... what's this meeting about?" I asked.

"Don't worry. Neil is going to talk to every head office employee over the next few days. It's not just you. Nothing has been decided yet."

Whew. He wasn't going to fire me after all. Not now, at least. He was talking to everyone, and he couldn't fire all of us—as much as I was sure he'd like to.

"That's a relief," I said, my shoulders loosening up a tad.

She ushered me inside a modern office with large windows overlooking the busy central business district. A series of black-and-white framed photographs displayed a timeline of the company's history on taupe walls, and two wooden desks stood at opposite sides of the room. Between them, an open door led to another area.

"This is my office," Christine said. "Neil's office is through that door."

I eyed the open doorway with trepidation, but from my current angle, I couldn't see inside.

"Would you like a tea or coffee? Water?" Christine asked.

"No, thank you."

"Then let's go in. Neil's waiting."

I followed her through the door into Neil's office. The room was spacious and decorated in a tasteful, modern fashion. Floor-to-ceiling windows lined the left wall, roller blinds pulled partway down to impede the stream of sunlight. A seating area occupied the front of the room, with two long black leather couches on opposite sides of an oval glass coffee table. Neil's desk stood at the end of the room in front of a wall of shelves stuffed with books and files. He sat on his black executive chair, head down, eyes on the paperwork in front of him. He hunched his shoulders. His jaw was tight, and a vein popped out on his forehead. I wasn't sure whether he was in a bad mood or if he always looked like that. I was leaning towards the latter theory. Either way, my guard was up.

We approached his desk.

"Neil, this is Milly Cross from the comms department," Christine said.

Neil lifted his head and zeroed in on me with an unnerving stare. The flash of recognition in his eyes told me he hadn't forgotten our recent encounter. I tried not to shrink from his gaze, lest he take it as a sign of weakness.

Please don't bring up the inside-out-top incident.

Christine left my side and retreated from the room. Neil stood up. He wore a clean white shirt, a navy tie, and grey trousers. He smelled faintly of dark floral cologne. Though he wasn't tall, he possessed a commanding, take-no-prisoners presence. He extended a hand that was unadorned apart from the luxury watch on his wrist.

I reached out to shake his hand, but the moment we connected, a jolt of electricity coursed through me, and I pulled away. "Ouch! Did you feel that?" I asked.

"Static," he said.

He didn't attempt to shake my hand again. He sat back down and gestured to the chair opposite him. I lowered myself onto the seat.

"Amelia Cross…"

His voice was low and silky, with a nice little rumble to it. If that voice came from another man's mouth, I'd find it sexy. Too bad it had to belong to *him*.

"Mr. Kingston," I said.

"In this country, we use first names in the workplace, do we not? It's Neil."

"Yes, *Neil*." His name felt strange on my tongue.

He continued to scrutinise me in a way which made me want to squirm in my seat. I tried to stay still and breathe calmly, though my thoughts threatened to deteriorate into a scrambled mess.

Hold yourself together.

"Thank you for coming at such late notice," Neil said after an agonising pause. "I didn't intend to start on the communications department today, but I'm running ahead of schedule."

"I would have appreciated some detail in advance," I said, arms folded tight across my chest.

He lifted a dark eyebrow. "Would you? I think this information is best heard face to face."

I felt my blood drain. "Christine said that no decisions have been made yet."

"Not so. There are a few things I have already decided."

He was toying with me; a cat playing with its prey. I couldn't just sit back and take it. I had to know.

"Do you mean that I'm going to lose my job?" I asked.

Neil smirked. "That is a strong possibility. I would like to cut the communications department by half. At least."

Half!

The faces of my colleagues paraded through my mind. Many of them would be let go, and there was a decent chance I'd be one of them.

What am I going to do?

Neil read the paper at the top of the neat pile on his desk. I glimpsed my name and realised it must be some kind of employee profile.

"Your job title is communications assistant. Is that correct?"

"Yes."

"You've been in the role for three months."

"That's right."

"You don't have a degree, and you have no prior experience related to your current role. You've worked as a part-time cleaner, an office temp, and in the call centre. That's interesting." The glint in his eyes told me he aimed to intimidate me and throw me off guard.

It wouldn't work.

I lifted my chin and met him eye to eye. "I'm self-taught. While I worked in the call centre, I used my lunch breaks to shadow staff in the communications department, and I spent my evenings learning all the skills and software necessary to get a junior role on their team. I didn't want to stay in the call centre forever, so I bugged Brendon until he gave me a job. I think he realised I wouldn't leave him alone until he did."

Neil's lips quirked up at the corners, forming more of a sneer than a smile. "That's quite impressive."

Genuine compliment or snide derision? I couldn't tell. "Thank you," I said, daring to take the compliment.

"You're hardworking, intelligent..."

Is he mocking me?

"Tell me, what's this gap in your employment history between leaving school and temping?" he asked.

I gritted my teeth.

Trust him to point that out.

It seemed like there was no alternative but to tell him the truth, though I doubted he was capable of sympathy. I kept my explanation brief.

"After high school, I went to university to study medicine, but a family emergency forced me to drop out."

He didn't need to know I spent a year wallowing, unemployed, after that.

A tad of his cockiness evaporated. Or was it my imagination?

"I see."

"When are we going to find out who's getting made redundant?" I asked, changing the subject.

"Soon. Within two weeks at most."

"Something to look forward to."

He ignored my sarcastic remark. "I will inform you by email. If you are made redundant, you will be invited to an exit interview, and you may bring a support person if you wish."

"What about redundancy pay?"

"I will honour the terms of your contract. I suggest you read yours and check the notice period and potential payout."

"I will."

"That covers everything I need to tell you. You may leave." He nodded in the door's direction.

That's it?

I rose and wondered whether I should try to shake his hand again, but his attention had already returned to the papers on his desk. I muttered, "Thank you," and exited the room, the prospect of unemployment weighing on my shoulders.

Chapter Four

"What are you looking at?" Brendon asked from behind my shoulder.

Shit.

I hadn't realised he was watching me. The perils of an open-plan office where anyone could sneak up behind you and catch you looking at something you shouldn't. "N-nothing," I said, exing out of the tab on my screen. "Not porn," I felt the need to add.

Not porn? Well done, Milly. Well done.

Brendon laughed. "Of course not! Was it a job site?"

I cringed. Caught red-handed.

Since my meeting with Neil Kingston, I had been browsing job sites and submitting applications both off and on the clock, around the clock. If what Neil had said was true, fifty percent of my team was going to lose their jobs, and with just three months' experience under my belt, I didn't like my odds of surviving the cut. I needed to secure another job offer, stat. Even if it was just as a backup for peace of mind.

Brendon loomed over my shoulder, awaiting an answer. Lying at this point was futile, so I confessed my transgression and brought the tab back up. The job search page listed all the communications roles in Auckland, sorted from newest to oldest listing. "Sorry. I've just been so anxious about the restructure. It's hard to stay focused. I feel the need to keep checking for new job listings."

Brendon sighed. "I don't blame you. I've had the odd peek as well."

"You're worried about losing your job too?"

"Of course. Neil made it abundantly clear that *no one* was safe."

"Damn. If you're not confident you'll make it through, what chance do I have? I have the least experience out of everyone on this floor."

"For what it's worth, I've put in a good word for you. I can't promise it will have much impact, though."

"Thanks, Brendon. That means a lot to me."

"Right then, I'll leave you to it," he said with a wink.

* * *

A few days later, Mike casually dropped a bombshell on us.

"You did WHAT?" Specks of coffee went flying from Brooke's mouth.

"Are you that surprised?" Mike asked.

"He *did* mention it before," I chimed in.

The three of us sat around a table in the staff cafeteria on the ground floor, beverages of choice in front of us—a cappuccino for me, an iced latte for Brooke, and a flat white for Mike. The coffee break was a much-needed reprieve from the ongoing agony of the pending restructure results, which could arrive any day now.

"So, let me get this straight," Brooke said. "You weren't joking when you said you might quit and become a full-time gamer living in your parents' basement?"

"I don't joke, B. I've already started my channel and got my first few subscribers."

Wild as it was, I was glad one of us could turn the situation into something positive and follow our dreams.

"Good for you, Mike," I said. "Sounds like you know what you're doing. I'll definitely follow your channel."

"Thanks, Milly. I knew you'd support me."

"I'll follow your stupid channel too," Brooke said.

"Uh, thanks."

With Mike confirmed to be leaving the company, that left me and Brooke. Was I going to make it? The question had plagued me for weeks now. The only positive to come out of the situation was that I had stopped dwelling on the former CEO's demise. But was that really a positive? The worry about losing my job was just as consuming.

Mike gulped his coffee. "I don't envy you two right now. The uncertainty would be killing me."

Brooke tucked a thick strand of her brown hair behind her ear. "I'm pretty confident I'll make it through unscathed."

Her assuredness made sense, given her uncle would do everything in his power to ensure her role was safe. I didn't resent her for it. I'd use my connections too, if I had any.

"What about you, Milly?" Mike asked.

"I'm preparing for the worst. Then it won't be a nasty shock if I lose my job, and it will be a pleasant surprise if I don't."

"Mr. Kingston would be making a huge mistake to let you go."

"I'm sure he doesn't see it that way."

"Then another company would be lucky to have you."

"If they'll take me. I've been job hunting, but it's so disheartening."

"No bites then?"

"Not even a nibble."

"Man, that sucks."

"I don't know what I'll do if I lose this job without another one lined up. I'll only be able to go a few weeks before my money runs out, and the unemployment benefit won't even be enough to cover my rent."

"If worse comes to worst, could you move back in with your parents while you job hunt?" Brooke asked.

Her words were a punch to my gut.

My parents.

Two people I could no longer rely on. Two people I would never see again in this life.

Tears sprang to my eyes.

Brooke cringed. "Shit. I'm so sorry."

I wiped my eyes with the back of my hand and forced myself to perk up. She hadn't meant to hurt me. I didn't want her to feel bad. "It's okay," I said.

"I'm such an idiot."

"Don't beat yourself up about it."

"I'm sorry."

"What's wrong?" Mike asked, glancing back and forth between us.

"My parents are dead," I explained.

"Oh…" He frowned. "That's rough."

A heavy cloud of awkwardness settled over our table. For a minute, no one spoke. I struggled to keep my tears at bay while I finished my coffee.

At last, I set my empty cup down. "I'm going to go outside and get some fresh air," I said.

"I'll get back to work," Mike said.

"Me too," Brooke said.

As Brooke and Mike hurried off towards the lifts, I left through the most secluded exit of the building. Parked cars lined the street. The sound of a passing helicopter rained down overhead. I leaned against a wall covered in graffiti and wiped my eyes again, sniffing back tears.

The reality of losing my job and having nowhere to go if I ran out of money was beginning to hit home. People like Brooke and Mike didn't realise how lucky they were, having family they could fall back on at the first hint of a crisis.

My mother died when I was three; a brain aneurism. She just dropped dead one day. I can hardly remember her.

My father died when I was twenty-one. He took his own life. I barely knew him, either. Not really. He became a husk of his former self after my mum passed away. I did my best to make him happy, make him proud, but it wasn't enough. I was never enough.

I dropped out of med school after it happened and lived on the unemployment benefit, renting a large rundown house with several other tenants who were also down on their luck. That was the hardest time in my life.

After several months in that situation, the discovery that one of my flatmates was hoarding rubbish in their bedroom was what snapped me to my senses. I knew I had to leave. I worked, saved for a rental deposit, then moved into my own apartment so I would never have to deal with flatmates again.

But here I was, on the precipice of being dragged back to square one. No job. No money. Massive student loan debt from the degree I never finished hanging like a weight around my neck.

To think, just a few months ago, my primary concern was getting a boyfriend. How times had changed.

I huffed out a long sigh, slouching as I ruminated. Various scenarios played out in my head until the sound of the door opening yanked me from my funk. None other than Neil Kingston stepped out of the building.

Oh great. Just the person I wanted to see.

I didn't want to look at him, but it was too late. His presence was magnetic. He wore a sharp, tailored suit, and the shirt underneath hugged his slim yet muscular frame. His expression was terse as usual, his forehead creased, and his lips set in a slight scowl.

We made eye contact.

I straightened up and tried to compose myself, hoping he hadn't noticed my vulnerable state. I expected him to walk right past me, go on his way, but when he stopped beside the door, I realised he wasn't going anywhere. He was outside taking a breather, just like I was.

He watched me, wearing that same inscrutable expression as

the first time we met. It looked like he was working up to say something, but I didn't let him. I couldn't stand it. He was the root cause of my anxiety. I had to leave. "Excuse me," I said.

Our bodies brushed as I passed him to go through the door. The brush must have lasted a split second, but it felt as though it dragged on for a minute. The texture of his suit lingered on me like an imprint. I was relieved when I made it to safety on the other side of the door.

Back at my desk, Brooke apologised yet again. "Hey, sorry about before. I should think before I speak next time."

I shook my head. "You're not the first person who's said something like that to me. I'm used to it."

"It shouldn't have to be that way. People shouldn't assume anything."

"It's human nature to make assumptions."

"But still… I'm sorry."

"Anyway, forget about it. All the stress has made me emotional. I'll feel better once everything's sorted." I plastered a weary smile on my face.

Brooke returned the smile.

I dived into my work, editing a document. It kept me occupied until an anguished whimper broke out beside me.

Chapter Five

I snapped my head towards Brooke. "What's wrong?"

She didn't say anything, but her bottom lip trembled.

The office buzzed with murmurs to full-on exclamations, and I quickly caught on to what was happening.

The restructure results had been announced.

I frantically opened my email inbox, scanning the list of messages for any sign of the announcement. Nothing stood out.

"Come on, come on," I muttered as I mashed the refresh button.

Finally, a new message appeared at the top of the list. My heart pounded as I read the subject line: "Outcome of Proposed Restructure."

My hand quivered on the mouse as I opened the email. I read it through scrunched eyes like I was watching a scary scene in a horror movie. The message contained a vague preamble and an instruction to open the PDF attachment.

My nerves ratcheted up a level when the PDF loaded—a document in the company's official letterhead with "PRIVATE AND CONFIDENTIAL" printed across the top.

My heart hammered a drumbeat in my ears as I read the letter.

Dear Amelia Cross,
We refer to your meeting with the CEO on 9 March and the
follow-up letter in which we notified you of the company's
proposal to disestablish and merge several existing positions
within the organisation.
This correspondence is to advise you of the decision we have
reached.
To summarise the process followed by the company...

Paragraph after paragraph of background information ensued until I reached the part that mattered most. I held my breath.

We are pleased to announce that you will remain in your position
in its current form.

I reread the sentence several times to make sure I had my facts straight, then another few times until it sank in.

My position would remain.

I was safe.

I let out my breath and threw my head back in relief, thanking the heavens.

But poor Brooke...

She snuffled beside me, her shoulders shaking.

"Bad news?" I asked.

She nodded.

I placed a hand on her arm. "I'm so sorry."

She brushed me off. "What about you? Are you keeping your job?"

It felt cruel to tell her, but what else could I say? "Yes. My job is staying."

"He made the right decision."

"Don't say that."

"Everyone knows you're the hardest working person in this department, and the smartest too. You've been here three months and you've already surpassed what I can do."

"Even if that were true—which it's not—how would Neil Kingston know? He only just got here. It could have gone either way. It was luck of the draw. That's all."

"I'm not so sure, but thanks anyway." She pulled her bag off the floor and stood up. "I'm off."

"Where are you going?"

"Home. Where else?"

The work day was far from over, but it was clear that Brooke had already reached her "fuck it" phase.

"Wait. Is there anything I can do? Do you want to hang out and chat for a bit? Go for another coffee or a glass of wine or something? I'll buy you a drink—"

"Thanks for the offer, but I'll be fine." She pulled her shoulders back and puffed out her chest. "The shock is wearing off already. I don't need this job, anyway."

I admired her tenacity. If I had lost my job, I'd be freaking out right now. Brooke left with her head held high.

Slumped in my chair, I reflected that I didn't feel as relieved as I thought I would. Sympathy tainted the triumph. How could I be one hundred percent happy when so many other workers were suffering? Looking around the room, it was obvious who had lost their job and who hadn't just from their body language. Brendon appeared to be safe. So did Ellen. But Dylan and Olivia and Caroline… I tallied up the final number in my head, a pang of guilt for each unfortunate coworker.

Then the guilt turned to a strange sense of unease. Something was off. There were fewer redundancies than I thought there were going to be. What had Neil said?

"I would like to cut the communications department by half. At least."

If my calculations were correct, he had cut less than half. One person less. He must have changed his mind, or else I had miscounted. I shrugged it off and thought nothing more of it.

* * *

Four weeks had passed since the restructure results came out. Now, a palpable sense of emptiness filled the office. Everyone who had lost their job had left. The room was quiet, nothing but the sound of mouse clicks, keyboard taps, and the odd phone ring to fill the void. Empty desks lined the floor. I left my old desk and moved to a secluded corner spot, with a wall behind my back, where I could work in peace and privacy.

Trying to re-establish a sense of normalcy, I began my usual morning routine. I set up my desk, placing my diary, pens, phone, and notepad in their designated positions, and turned my computer on. With that done, I strolled to the break room to make a strong cup of coffee. These days I was okay with going into the break room, as long as I avoided looking at the window.

Only two other staff members occupied the room, one playing a game on his phone while waiting for tea to brew, and the other stashing her Tupperware-stored lunch in the fridge. I used the coffee machine.

When I returned to my desk, hot coffee mug in hand, I tried to open my emails, but a pop-up sign-in form blocked me from further action.

I frowned at the screen, wondering why it didn't log me in automatically like it usually did. Something to do with the restructure? Maybe the system had been reset. I typed in my email address and password, thinking that would be the end of it. But it wasn't. An error sound played, and a message appeared under the email address field. "Email ID not found."

I tried again. Same error message.

No big deal. I'll just flick a note to IT.

I opened the work chat, certain there would be a quick and easy fix to my dilemma. But there it was again—a bloody sign-in form. I had a funny feeling I wouldn't be able to log in to this one either, and I was correct.

Now what do I do?

I scanned the room, hoping to see someone else who was having the same issue as me, but everyone seemed fine.

I asked around the office. "Is anyone else having trouble logging in to their accounts?"

No response except for a few people shaking their heads.

"No? I guess it's only me then."

A trip to the IT department was in order.

I took the stairs one floor down. Emerging through the glass fire-exit door, I arrived in the corridor between IT and HR and took the left passage.

In the office, rows of white cubicles stood on blue carpet with identical black, ergonomic chairs at each one. A large proportion of seats were empty. Most of the remaining workers wore headphones, and no one gave me so much as a glance.

A sign directed me to the help desk—a long counter at the side of the room, where a surly-looking man stared at the computer in front of him. I approached. "Hello," I said, trying to get his attention.

He ignored me and continued whatever he was doing on the computer.

"Uh, excuse me." I looked for a name tag, but he wasn't wearing one.

He looked up. "How can I help you?" His bored voice was evidence that he had no actual interest in assisting me.

"I'm having trouble logging into my accounts."

"Which accounts?"

"Email and chat. Probably others too, but that's all I've checked."

"We switched off the accounts of everyone who got made redundant last night."

I gaped. "But I didn't get made redundant."

"Obviously. Or else you wouldn't be here, would you? We must have shut yours down by mistake. What's your name?"

"Amelia Cross."

"Let's see…" He typed away. "Everything looks fine on my end. Let's try resetting your password."

He typed some more, then wrote something down on a square

of blue paper he pulled from the top of a memo cube. He passed it to me. "Here. This should work."

The note read "Turkey_Lozenge_Dynamite_23."

"Is that the new password?"

"Obviously."

That seemed to be his favourite word.

"Well, thanks."

I had already lost his attention.

Back at my desk, I couldn't wait to show that vexing sign-in form who was boss. I threaded my fingers together and cracked my knuckles before typing the new password in. I pressed enter, and…

The same error message.

No. This isn't happening.

I tried the chat. Same thing again.

I stood up, ready to march straight back to the IT department, when a thought struck me. The guy at the help desk never asked for my email address, just my name. That wouldn't normally be an issue—the email addresses followed a strict naming convention: first name dot last initial at Luxmore dot com. But there was more than one Amelia C in the company, and the other Amelia had that email address, not me. With this in mind, I tried the password with the Amelia dot C email address.

Bingo.

The other Amelia's emails filled up my inbox.

I realised with a sinking feeling that this did nothing to remedy the situation. All I had accomplished was locking Amelia Crook out of her emails by changing her password. I wanted to bang my head against the wall in frustration.

I would have to go back to the help desk to sort it out, but first, I decided to call Amelia Crook and explain what was going on. She worked in the marketing department. I didn't have her direct line, but I had a laminated list of the main numbers for each department taped in the corner of my desk. I made the call. After a few rings, a man picked up. "Hello, Luxmore marketing department, Harry speaking."

"Hi, Harry. Can I speak to Amelia Crook please?"

"Sorry. Amelia doesn't work here anymore. Would you like me to put you through to someone else who can help you?"

She doesn't work here anymore...

"No. That's okay. Did Amelia get made redundant in the restructure?" I asked.

"Yes, I'm afraid she did."

"I see. Well, thanks for letting me know. Bye."

I hung up.

So, Amelia Crook had lost her job. That meant IT must have made a mistake. *Yeah.* They got our names mixed up and closed my account instead of hers.

Or...

With a creeping sense of dread, I realised there was a second possible explanation.

Chapter Six

An ominous message in the work chat greeted me on Monday morning.

Hi, Amelia! Could you please pop in to HR today?

Despite the message's cheery tone, my blood ran cold. Had HR caught on to the Amelia mix-up? Did they even know they were chatting with me and not Amelia Crook?

I replied that I could come now. This couldn't wait. I had to face this head-on, or I'd never be able to focus on work.

I descended the stairs to the fourth floor and took the right-hand passage to the HR department, where I arrived in a small reception area. A plaque on the wall behind the vacant desk read "Human Resources." White fluorescent tube lights beamed overhead. I shuffled my weight between my feet, waiting for someone to come to the desk. What was I going to do if they brought the Amelia Crook thing up? Play dumb, or confess that I knew something was afoot? And then what? Would they fire me? An image of stern, unrelenting Neil Kingston appeared in my mind, and I knew that if he got involved, he wouldn't hesitate to fire me on the spot.

A pretty young blonde woman approached, snapping me from my thoughts. "Can I help you?" she asked.

"Err, yes. I got a message asking me to come to HR."

"Amelia?"

"That's right."

"I'm Lauren. Come on through."

She led me to a back office. The room was furnished with all black furniture, white walls, and silver accents. A bouquet of white flowers scented the air. The woman behind the desk wore a tailored suit and silver jewellery. Even though I hadn't met her face to face before, I recognised her straight away. She was a prominent figure to employees in the business, the head of the HR department, Clara Evans.

My pulse sped up. If the head of HR was involved, it had to be something serious.

"Amelia is here," Lauren said.

Clara smiled at me. "Take a seat."

Lauren left the room as I shakily lowered myself onto the chair. I didn't say anything. I waited for Clara to make the first move while I fidgeted with my hands in my lap.

"There's no need to be so nervous," Clara said.

I forced my hands still. "It's not every day you get called to a meeting with the head of HR."

Clara chuckled, her freckled nose crinkling. "This meeting is just to check up on you, to see how you're doing."

A sense of unease lingered at the back of my mind. "Oh. Why's that?"

"I have it on file that you were a witness when Alex Patterson died. Is that correct? It must have been a traumatic experience for you."

"Oh! That's right. I *did* see Alex fall off the building." I didn't mean to say it so cheerfully, but I couldn't help it. I was so relieved that this wasn't about Amelia Crook.

Clara eyed me with a funny look. "It must have affected you quite badly."

I tried to reel back my enthusiasm. "Yes, it did. I had flashbacks for weeks, and I still can't look out the window where I saw what happened."

"I'm sorry to hear that. Did you see the counsellor?"

"I did. She helped a lot."

"Wonderful. Anyway, I just wanted to reach out and ask if there's anything else we can do to support you. It's been a stressful time, both with the death of Alex and the restructure going on in the business."

"It has been stressful, but I think I'm managing."

"That's good." She leaned in, sighing. "Between you and me, the new CEO has my own stress level going through the roof. This whole restructure has been an absolute nightmare. No one's happy with the situation, and it's my department that has to deal with all the staff complaints."

"I know what you mean. The communications department also has its hands full with both the internal and external comms, and we're just drip-fed information from management."

"I think all the departments are struggling. It's not easy when staff have been cut, but the workload remains the same. Anyway, enough of my grumbling. Any other issues you'd like to raise while you're here?"

I felt my temperature skyrocket and hoped it didn't show on my face. If I were going to come forward about the suspected employment mix-up, now was my chance.

"Anything at all?" Clara asked.

"No," I said. "All good."

"Are you sure? There's no need to be afraid to speak up. I want to make sure you're comfortable and supported here."

"I appreciate that, but I'm fine."

"Very well, then. If that's all, you can go, but just know that I'll back you up if you ever need anything."

"Thanks, Clara." I stood up to leave.

"Nice meeting you, Ms. Crook. Enjoy the rest of your day."

I felt the colour drain from my face.

Crook.

"Thanks. You too," I squeaked.

I hurried away, hoping she didn't catch my startled reaction.

As I made my way back to my desk, I wondered whether I should have told Clara the truth. How long would I leave things as they were, hoping it would all blow over?

I reminded myself that this wasn't my fault, and it wasn't my mess to sort out. Besides, I needed to keep this job, no matter what.

Since the login mix-up, I had taken over Amelia Crook's accounts as my own. It only made sense that the email address with the proper naming convention should belong to me now that Amelia Crook had left.

My inbox, as usual, overflowed with emails intended for Amelia Crook instead of me. I labelled them, then forwarded them, one by one, to the marketing department. I had just about cleared my inbox when a new email came in. Yet another message for Amelia Crook. This time, a red exclamation mark stood at attention by the subject line. I read the email.

Hi Amelia,
Can you please urgently send through the final report for the
March dishwasher campaign?
Kind regards,
David

I was about to file and forward this message too when I realised the report he was asking for was the same one I had just received in an earlier email from the media agency.

The red exclamation mark flashed in my vision.

I have the report. I'll just send it through. What harm could it do?

Before I could talk myself out of it, I typed a brief reply, attached the report, and pressed send.

A disastrous mistake.

Chapter Seven

This might be the craziest thing I've done in my entire life.

I hadn't intended to impersonate Amelia Crook, but that's what happened, and now I was in too deep.

Responding to that email had triggered a chain of events that ended with me here, standing in the corridor outside the boardroom on the twentieth floor, clutching a stack of printed reports, about to present a media report to the COO and an unknown number of other staff members.

I'm so dead.

Through the transparent glass wall into the boardroom, I saw two people sitting at the long, rectangular table—David Green and a brunette woman beside him. He caught my eyes and gestured for me to come inside. I couldn't turn back. I couldn't run away. I had to face my fate, surrender to the inevitability that at least one person would recognise me for the imposter I was.

I sucked in a deep gulp of air before stepping into the boardroom. The table dominated the space, with a whiteboard at one end of the room and a large-screen TV at the other. On the external wall, large windows overlooked the city centre.

David and the woman stood when I entered. I avoided their eyes, certain they'd be looking at me with suspicion.

"Amelia Crook?" David asked.

He sounded polite. After all this build-up, he still thought I was her. He must not have met the real Amelia Crook before. I dared align my gaze with his.

"It's Amelia Cross, actually," I said.

Outright stealing her name was a step too far. At no point had I lied about my identity, and I wasn't about to start now.

He wrinkled his brow. "Cross? Why did I think it was Crook?"

"There was someone else called Amelia Crook who used to work here. That would be why."

"Ah. My mistake. I'm David Green, and this is my assistant, Aroha Williams. We're taking over from Greg due to the reshuffle."

I had no idea who Greg was, but I nodded along.

They took turns to shake my hand.

"Please, set yourself up." David gestured to the screen. "The others won't be long."

Others. I swallowed a lump in my throat. "How many are we expecting to join us?"

"Just two. Neil can't make it."

I prickled. "Neil Kingston?"

"That's the one. He has another commitment."

I hadn't even considered that he might attend. Thank goodness he wasn't going to.

"Oh, here they are now," Aroha said.

A man with salt-and-pepper hair and a blonde woman, both dressed in corporate attire, entered the room.

"Amelia, this is Cindy and Howard from operations management. They'll be overseeing the whiteware portfolio from now on," David said.

I shook their hands and introduced myself as Amelia Cross, with emphasis on the "Cross."

We exchanged vague pleasantries, neither of them questioning me beyond how my day was going.

The group of four sat down. I took it upon myself to pour

each attendee a glass of water from the chilled glass jug in the centre of the table. Next, I distributed the printouts I had brought with me.

While David and the others engaged in light chitchat, I set up the presentation on the provided laptop and connected it to the TV. I brought up the first page of the document, and everyone turned their attention towards me.

This is it.

I was either going to fool them and have to continue my charade, or fall flat on my face in a spectacular fashion. I wasn't sure which outcome was worse.

Over the last few days, I had spent countless hours preparing for this presentation, learning the ins and outs of each line of every table, the meaning behind each chart, and the definitions of all the terminology. With four pairs of eager eyes watching me, I mustered a sense of pseudo-confidence, cleared my throat, and began. "As you're aware, the dishwasher advertising campaign ran—"

Clunk.

The boardroom door opened.

Everyone's focus shifted from me to the late arrival.

In stepped Neil Kingston, clean-shaven, razor-jawed, dressed in a three-piece suit. His stare hit me like an icy blade. His impenetrable black eyes narrowed, and I felt like a deer in headlights. I could tell he was thinking, calculating.

My heart dropped into the pit of my stomach.

Did he remember who I was? I recalled the meeting in his office, where we had talked about my position in the company. However, he had met so many other employees over the course of a few short days, it would be understandable if he, too, had muddled me and Amelia Crook.

"Ah, Neil. So glad you could join us after all," David said.

"Sorry to interrupt." Neil didn't lift his searing gaze from me.

"This is Amelia Cross."

"We've met."

I tried to wrangle my sense of panic before it could reveal itself through my body language.

He knows. He definitely knows. Is he going to say something?

"Take a seat," David said.

Neil stalked to the back of the room and sat down, resting an elbow on the table and his chin on his knuckles.

I waited for him to speak up and expose me, but he didn't say a word. He wasn't going to bring it up. No, he was going to watch me squirm like a fly caught in a spider's web and derive some weird sense of pleasure from it.

"Please, continue," Neil said.

My mind had gone blank.

Where am I up to?

My heart rate escalated. A cold sweat broke out on my hairline.

I can't do this. I have to confess.

The expectant eyes watching me turned a shade sceptical. Or was I just imagining it?

I tried to shake myself out of my funk.

Get a grip! I've come this far. Even if I break down and admit everything afterwards, I should at least present the report and show them how capable I am.

Mind made up, I refocused on the task at hand.

I'll just start from the beginning.

With a deep breath, I reeled off the words I had drilled into myself. I didn't leave any gaps for questions, hoping that would deter anyone from asking.

I somehow made it through the entire presentation without slipping up. But now came the hard part. If someone was going to ask a question, now would be the time.

I didn't ask, "Any questions?" but I couldn't just stop and leave. I waited for someone to speak.

"Thank you, Amelia," David said. "That was very comprehensive."

Is it over? Did I survive?

I made a beeline towards the laptop to close the presentation, but Neil spoke up in a manner which conveyed, "Not so fast."

"I have a question," he said, eyes glinting.

Of course you do.

"Yes?"

"Page four."

I scrolled to the aforementioned page.

"There, in that table," he said. "Could you explain something to me? I would like to know why we invested more on programmatic banner ads than social media, even though social media performed with a much higher conversion rate."

Oh crap.

His question stunned me for a second.

This is a test. He knows the answer. He just wants to trip me up.

"Good question." I stalled for time.

Come on. I should be able to answer this. Don't let him win.

I cleared my throat, buying myself another second to think. "There could be several factors," I said.

Thinking back to what I had studied to prepare for this presentation, I fished up an idea and ran with it.

"I think the main thing to remember is that banner ads function as an awareness medium. People don't see a banner ad, then immediately go out and buy a dishwasher, but it might make them more aware of our brand and product."

Murmurs of agreement arose from everyone except Neil.

"That doesn't mean it's a waste of money," I continued. "Without brand awareness, people are less likely to engage with social media ads in the first place."

"So, one can't work without the other," Cindy said.

"Exactly. It's a synergetic relationship."

David, Aroha, Cindy, and Howard all looked pleased with my explanation and my use of the buzzword "synergy." Neil, on the other hand, scowled, the angry vein on his forehead throbbing.

"Did that answer your question?" I asked.

"Yes," Neil said. "It did."

"Then, if that's everything, shall we end here?" David asked. "I'm sure we all have busy schedules to attend to."

Everyone apart from Neil got up, thanking me as they did so. I turned off the TV and closed the laptop as they left the room. Neil continued to sit, arms folded, watching me.

I quickly made towards the door, trailing behind the others.

"Amelia," Neil said.

Uh-oh.

I stopped in my tracks. "Yes?" I squeaked.

"You stay here. I want to have a little word with you."

Chapter Eight

I felt like a naughty schoolgirl summoned to the principal's office to get punished.

"Shut the door," Neil said from his position at the head of the table.

I followed his command while apprehension simmered in every fibre of my being.

"Sit," was his next instruction.

I approached the table, slid out a chair two spaces from him, and dropped into it. I stared at my hands in my lap, unable to take the ferocity of his unflinching gaze.

An age seemed to pass before he spoke. "Tell me, Amelia, is it usual practice in this company for a junior worker to present a report to senior staff?" His voice was even, deliberate, and had the texture of velvet, making me shiver.

"No," I said, biting my lip.

"I didn't think so."

"I can explain—"

"I'm sure you can. You must have a brilliant explanation as to why and how you went about impersonating another staff member with a similar name."

He was patronising me, looking down at me with an unsettling fixation.

I lifted my chin. "I didn't do it on purpose! It just sorta... happened."

He fixed me a sardonic sneer. "Why are you here, and where is the real Amelia Crook? No, don't tell me. Let me guess. She got made redundant, and you did not."

"That's right!"

"Yet, I distinctly remember making you redundant and keeping her on. Isn't that strange?"

My heart dropped. "What?"

His tone turned a shade harsher. "Don't play dumb with me, Amelia. You must have known there had been a mistake. Why else would you be here?"

"I thought I was being helpful... I didn't know..."

"It didn't cross your mind that perhaps the letter intended for Amelia Crook went to you, and she received yours?"

He had me in a metaphorical chokehold, and his grip was tightening around my throat, inch by inch.

"Of course it did! But I hoped it wasn't true."

"That's not good enough, Amelia."

"In my defence, someone had to present the report. David said it was important, and no one in the marketing department would hear me out—they're too busy with the launch of the new product line. I felt like I had to go along with it, just this once."

"I'm not interested in your flimsy rationale."

"I never lied. Not once."

"But you didn't bother to tell anyone. How is that not dishonest?"

"I have an official letter saying my role remains. Of course, that's what I'd believe."

Neither of us spoke for a minute. He observed me while I avoided eye contact. Then he loosened his navy tie and massaged his neck. "Look, Amelia, a mistake was made, and I apologise for that, but like most mistakes, it can be fixed, and that's what I intend to do."

"What's going to happen?"

"I'm going to call Ms. Crook, apologise profusely, and ask if she wants her job back."

"What's going to happen to *me*?"

The corners of Neil's mean lips twitched, and he made a noise which was half exasperated sigh, half evil laugh. I knew I wouldn't like what was coming next.

"You're fired," he said.

The words echoed in my head like he had shouted them into a cavern.

"Sorry?"

"You heard me. Pack your things and leave. Right now. Unless you want to keep working over your notice period. It's up to you. You'll get paid whatever you're owed, regardless."

I stood up, hands fisted at my sides, flooded with outrage. "You can't do this. I need this job!"

"More than Ms. Crook needs hers?"

I looked away. "I don't know."

"No, you don't. Now leave. This meeting is over."

"But—"

"Go quietly, and I'll cover up your transgressions. Kick up a fuss, and I'll have no choice but to make sure everyone knows what you did."

He was dead serious. I was fired. Terminated. Just like that.

An avalanche of hot tears threatened to burst through the banks of my eyelids. I didn't want him to see me cry, so I hurried out the door before I could break down in front of him.

That cruel man. How could he fire me over a mistake that wasn't even my fault? No lenience. No grace period. Nothing. And now I had to go and humiliate myself, pack up my things, and leave in front of my colleagues who knew nothing about what was going on. How would I explain myself?

My stomach twisted and turned while uncontrollable tears

leaked from my eyes, leaving wet streaks down my face. I couldn't go back to my desk like this. I marched to the women's bathroom instead.

The twentieth floor had a much fancier bathroom than the rest of the building, but it hardly registered in the whirlwind of my emotions. I traipsed to the nearest cubicle, slammed the door shut, twisted the lock, and collapsed onto the closed toilet lid with my head in my hands.

I only had time to heave one shaky sob before I heard a noise from another cubicle. A long, pained groan.

Oh great. I come here for a private sob, and someone's having tummy trouble next to me.

I wiped my wet cheeks with a piece of toilet paper and stood up, planning to go elsewhere. As I opened the cubicle door, another groan rang out, this time laced with palpable agony. I was wrong. This person was suffering from much more than a run-of-the-mill upset tummy. Worried now, I tapped on the closed door of the occupied cubicle. "Excuse me. Are you okay? Are you sick?"

A lengthy pause ensued before the muffled reply, "I think my baby's coming."

Chapter Nine

I recognised that voice. All of my self-pity vanished in an instant, replaced by an overwhelming concern for the woman behind the door. "Christine, is that you?"

"… Who's there?"

"Milly Cross. Can you open the door? I have some medical training, and I'm going to help you."

A moment of hesitation passed before the lock clicked from occupied to vacant, and the door swung open.

The put-together woman I last saw had been transformed. Her face was flushed, hair wild, eyes shining. She clutched her stomach and said, voice wavering, "I'm only thirty weeks pregnant."

A surge of adrenaline jolted through me, but I tried to stay calm. "Okay, Christine, I need you to tell me what symptoms you're experiencing."

Six years had passed since I left medical school, but from the symptoms she described between visible spasms of pain, I knew straight away that I had to get her to hospital—and fast.

"Christine, I'm going to take you to the hospital. We just need a driver. Otherwise, I'll call an ambulance."

"Winston," she rasped.

"Who's Winston? What about Neil? Should I go get him?"

"Yes, get Neil."

"First, let's get you out of here. Lean on me." I offered her my shoulder.

Bearing some of her weight, I steered her out of the stall, then from the bathroom. I didn't want to leave her alone while I fetched Neil, so I planned to drop her with James, the receptionist.

A hitch in my strategy emerged when we reached the empty reception desk. No one else was around, either.

"I'm going to leave you here for a second while I run and get Neil. I'll be right back. Promise."

She nodded, leaning up against the desk and cradling her belly.

No time to lose, I raced down the corridor and through Christine's office where the desks at each end of the room were empty and the door through to Neil's office was closed.

Is he here?

I rapped on the door loud enough to signal that this was a matter of urgency. No response. I couldn't stand around waiting, so I flung the door open and charged inside.

There he was, standing in the centre of the room, framed by the two leather couches, half of him bathed in sunlight, the other half in shadow. He had his phone pressed to his ear. His suit jacket had been discarded over the back of the chair behind his desk. Those dark, unnerving eyes met mine, flashing with something unrecognisable. His jaw tightened like a bowstring about to shoot an arrow.

"Neil!"

He analysed me for a second, then spoke to the person on the end of the phone. "I'm going to need to call you back." He lowered the phone from his ear and gave me his full attention. "What do you want?"

"Christine needs to go to the hospital. Right now."

His eyes widened. "Where is she?"

Did I detect a hint of panic in that smooth voice of his?

"This floor. Reception."

Without a moment's hesitation, he jumped into action, striding to the exit behind me. "Did you call an ambulance?"

"No. I think it will take too long to wait for one. Can you drive us?"

"I'll call Winston."

That name again.

He tapped on his phone and lifted it to his ear as we walked briskly, side by side, down the corridor. "Bring the car around the front," he said. "It's an emergency."

At reception, a very anxious-looking James had returned and was attending to Christine. I could imagine what he was thinking: *Please don't have the baby here.* He slumped with obvious relief when he saw us approaching.

Neil lent his arm to Christine. "We're going to get you to the hospital," he said calmly. "You're going to be okay, and so will the baby."

Christine gave a weak nod.

I dashed ahead to push the down button on the control panel between the lifts. The lift came quickly, and I held the button down to keep the door open as Neil guided Christine inside.

The whole time my brain ticked over, planning what to do next. I decided the most logical next step was to call the hospital's maternity unit to report Christine's symptoms and let them know we're on our way.

While the lift descended to the ground floor, I Googled the phone number and made the call. An automated message greeted me and told me to hold the line. Gentle music played.

"I'm calling the maternity unit," I explained to Neil and Christine.

Neil acknowledged this with a sharp nod.

I continued to hold the line as the lift door clunked open onto the ground floor. Neil and I flanked Christine and brought her to the main entrance, where a black Audi sedan awaited us outside, its engine running.

I didn't ask if I could come. In my mind, there was no question whether or not I should. If something happened on the journey to the hospital, I might be able to provide at least some help. Plus, I was still waiting for someone to pick up the phone.

Neil bundled Christine into one side of the back seat, and I opened the door to the other side, about to get in next to her.

"The front," Neil said to me in a tone of voice I didn't dare argue with.

Whatever. I could still be of use from the front.

Clutching my phone to my ear, I got into the front passenger seat. The driver, whom I assumed was Winston, was a bald man with leathery brown skin, maybe around sixty years old. He wore black sunglasses and a suave navy suit.

Neil took the seat next to Christine. "Winston," he said, "to the hospital. As fast as you can."

"Got it," Winston said in a gruff yet proper accent. He pulled the car out from the curb.

Meanwhile, the hold music stopped, and someone picked up my call. "Hello, Steph speaking. How can I help you?"

"Hi. I'm with a woman called Christine Liu. She's thirty weeks pregnant and experiencing strong contractions, pressure on her back and lower abdomen, and heavy discharge. We're on our way to the hospital now."

"Understood."

Steph asked for some information to identify Christine in their system. I lowered my phone and turned to the back seat. Neil was letting Christine squeeze his hand for support. The gesture surprised me. I didn't think him capable of providing comfort to another person, even if she was a close colleague.

"I need to give the maternity unit her details," I explained. "An address or date of birth or something."

"December first, nineteen-eighty," Neil said without faltering.

I parroted the date to Steph, and she gave me the information needed for our arrival.

"They'll be expecting us at the labour-and-birthing unit on the ninth floor," I reported after ending the call. "We can get to the drop-off zone via the Park Road entrance."

"Roger that," Winston said, as he wove in and out of traffic.

I peeked at the back seat again. Neil was still holding Christine's hand. Her face was pallid and moist with sweat. It looked like she was about to pass out. Knowing full well just how risky the situation was, considering her age and the length of her pregnancy, I prayed she and the baby would be okay.

Now it was Neil's turn to make a call. He took out his phone and spoke to whom I assumed was Christine's partner. He asked them to come to the birthing unit at the hospital, and to bring everything that Christine would require.

A few minutes later, the barrier arm lifted for us at the entrance gate. The hospital was a campus of several white, multi-story buildings surrounded by concrete roads, carparks, and grassy areas dotted with trees.

Winston stopped the car outside the automatic sliding door into the building, then hopped out and assisted Neil with moving Christine from the back seat. "You're going to be just fine, my dear," Winston said to Christine, a hand on her shoulder. "I'll be thinking of you."

Christine offered him a weary smile, then Neil and I escorted her inside while Winston got back in the car and drove off to find a proper park.

A strong antiseptic smell invaded my nostrils upon entry. Everything was a bright, cold white. Our shoes squeaked on the linoleum floor as we made our way to the lifts, then followed the signage to the labour-and-birthing unit. Neil looked after Christine while I reported our arrival at the desk.

"A doctor will see her shortly," the receptionist said. "If her condition deteriorates, let me know straight away, and I'll do what I can to have her seen sooner."

I nodded. "Thank you."

She passed me a clipboard of paperwork and a blue ballpoint pen. "Could you please fill out as much of this as possible?"

"Uh, sure."

Knowing as little as I did about Christine, I wouldn't be able to complete the form. I didn't think Christine would be up to it either, but Neil might.

I presented the clipboard to him. "She gave me this."

He took it from me without a word, ran his eyes over the attached form, then began to fill it out. Meanwhile, Christine writhed in the chair between us.

"Not much longer," I said. "Someone's going to come and sort you out. Everything will be okay. Deep breaths."

I tried to sound soothing, but inside, I was frazzled.

How much longer are we gonna have to wait?

Finally, a blonde-haired woman wearing a blue uniform with a white lab coat over the top approached us. "Christine Liu?" she asked.

"Yes," Neil and I said at the same time.

"I'll take that." She swiped the clipboard from Neil. "Right this way, please."

She guided us down a corridor with several doors on each side and a window at the end, sunlight streaming through. We stopped outside a room.

"How are you holding up?" she asked Christine.

"The pain is easing, but maybe I'm just numb."

"I'll check you out right away." She looked at Neil. "Are you her partner?"

"No. We work together. Her husband is on his way, though."

She turned to me. "And what relation are you?"

"I also work with her."

"In that case, both of you, please take a seat in the waiting area if you wish to stay." She gestured to an adjoining corridor before returning her attention to Christine. "Come on through." She ushered her into the room and closed the door behind them.

I followed Neil to the waiting area, not knowing what else to do. A few others occupied the space, either playing on their phones, flipping through old magazines, or staring ahead at the plain, white wall. Even with plenty of empty chairs, Neil stood. Though he didn't look it, I assumed he was too anxious to sit down. So was I. We stood, side by side, in awkward silence, with what felt like an electric field crackling between us.

Only a couple of hours had passed since he had fired me. Now, I had possibly helped save his secretary's baby's life. That had to count for something, right? Didn't he have anything to say on the matter? Apparently not, since he seemed to ignore my very existence, his arms folded across his chest and a grim look on his face.

Why won't he say something? Anything?

I couldn't take it any longer. "Would you like me to get you a drink?" I asked, eyeing the tea and water station in the corner of the room.

"No, thank you."

"I might make myself a tea." I took one step away.

"You can go now."

I stopped. "Excuse me?"

"You're not needed. You can go."

I tensed. How could he dismiss me so easily after everything I had done and without so much as a word of thanks? "I guess I'll go then," I retorted in an even grumpier tone than I intended.

I started towards the exit without looking back at him, but something stopped me. A hand clamped on my shoulder. His hand.

"Amelia."

"What?" I twirled around to meet him eye to eye.

He swallowed, his Adam's apple bobbing. "Thank you."

Finally.

"For your help today," he continued.

I shrugged him off, including his grip. "Anyone would have done the same."

"You showed initiative."

I felt a flutter of surprise at how sincere he sounded. He had dropped his guard. I had to say something while I had this slither of opportunity. I lifted my chin, and with every ounce of confidence I could muster, I asked the question which had worked its way to the tip of my tongue. "Can I please have my job back?"

My question hung in the air between us.

Please say yes. I need my job. I need the money. I can't go back to the way things were before.

Neil did that thing again—that unsettling gaze which felt like he was analysing me, making silent calculations.

Then he smirked.

Suddenly, I didn't like my chances.

Chapter Ten

I held my breath, waiting for Neil's answer.

He shook his head. "I'm afraid that's not possible."

"Why not?" I shot back. "After all this, can't you make an exception just this once?"

"It's like you said. Anyone would have done the same."

You bastard. Using my own words against me.

My blood boiled, and I teetered between wanting to yell and wanting to cry. The only thing stopping me was the other people in the room. All of them seemed to be watching us or pretending not to. I didn't want to cause even more of a scene. "Okay. I'm leaving." I was about to storm off, but at the last second I added, "At least let me know how Christine gets on," which somewhat ruined the impact.

Neil answered with a terse nod.

I stepped away from him.

"Wait," he said.

"What?" I asked without turning back.

"I'll get Winston to give you a ride."

I shook my head. "Don't bother. I can walk home from here."

"Correct me if I'm wrong, but all your belongings are still at work, are they not?"

Shit. He had me there. My keys, wallet, HOP card—all of them were in my bag, which I had left under my desk at work. I couldn't go home without them.

Neil took his phone out of his pocket and called someone. "Winston, bring the car to the door. Amelia needs a ride back to work and then her home."

He ended the call as I stood there dumbly.

"Go," he said.

I had no comeback. All I could do was obey.

Damn that smug bastard.

I walked off with my hands clenched into fists, following the exit signs until I wound up outside the building, gasping the fresh air free from the pervasive chemical tang.

Winston rolled up to the curb. He got out and opened the back door for me.

"Thanks. Actually, could I sit in the front, please?"

I didn't want to treat him like a taxi driver, even if, in a way, that's what he was.

"Of course." He closed the back door and walked around to open the front passenger door.

I settled on the seat and pulled the belt on. The AC blew a light current of cool air in my direction. I breathed a heavy sigh.

"Back to the office?" Winston asked, pulling out.

"Yes, thank you. I have to get the stuff I left there."

We exited the carpark and entered the stream of city-bound traffic. Troubled thoughts plagued my mind as we drove. I had lost my job. What was I going to do if I ran out of money before I could line up another one? Where would I go? How could I avoid a second visit to rock bottom?

I felt Winston side-eying me with concern.

"You did a great thing helping Christine today," he said.

"Thanks, but it was nothing, really."

"Nonsense. You're a hero."

I couldn't help but scoff a little.

"Did you know that Mrs. Liu and Mr. Kingston have worked

together for ten years?" Winston asked. "She came with him from Singapore. She brought her husband here too. Same thing happened during Mr. Kingston's stint in Germany. She packed up her life to follow him. Those two are inseparable."

"No. I didn't know that."

"They have a close relationship. More like friends than colleagues."

I flashed back to Neil holding Christine's hand in the back of the car, and I could believe what Winston was telling me, even though it didn't compute with the version of Neil I knew.

"I hope Christine's going to be okay," I said.

"Me too. He might not have told you, but I'm sure Mr. Kingston is very grateful for what you did."

I touched my shoulder where Neil had grabbed me. His "thank you" may have been sincere, but so were his reprimands.

"Did he tell you he fired me today?" I asked.

Winston's mouth dropped. "No. What reason could he have to do that?"

I hesitated. "It's a long story."

"Hmm. I'll have to have a word to him about it."

I shook my head. "That's okay. You don't have to say anything."

The thought of Winston learning what I had done was too much. I'd rather just leave it be.

"You know, Mr. Kingston's not a bad guy," Winston said. "I've seen his kindness."

"Kindness? Really?"

"Yep. I was in a desperate situation when he gave me this job. It was a lifeline. I'll be forever grateful to him."

I wanted to ask him to tell me more, but I sensed it was a personal subject, so I left it alone. Besides, what did it matter? I was never going to see Neil again, anyway.

Chapter Eleven

James Campbell texted me—Christine's symptoms were a false alarm. That was the last I heard from anyone at Luxmore.

Three weeks later, I sat in a restaurant booth, scrolling social media while I waited for my friends to arrive.

A photo of Brooke popped up on my feed. She beamed from beneath a wide-brimmed hat and oversized sunglasses, her little black bikini showing off her perfect figure. In the background, clear water spread out below a hill covered in whitewashed buildings with blue window frames.

"Who needs Fiji when you can have Mykonos?" the caption read.

My chest tightened. *Lucky for some.* While Brooke was living it up overseas, I was struggling to make ends meet. I tossed my phone into my bag with a huff, glancing up just as Hannah and Nicole approached the table.

The first thing I noticed was the contrast of their outfits—Hannah in a jumpsuit with a loud, colourful print, and Nicole in a simple black dress. Hannah swept towards me, strands of her unruly dark hair escaping her loose ponytail. "Milly!" She threw her arms around me. "It's so good to see you. How have you been?"

I hesitated. This dinner was supposed to be her going away party. I didn't want to dampen the mood. "Oh, you know, just keeping busy. How about you? All packed for your big OE?"

"Yep. Sure am!"

"You must be getting pretty excited now."

"I'm equally thrilled and terrified. It still doesn't feel real, ya know?"

"London is going to be an absolute blast. You're going to have the time of your life."

As happy as I was for Hannah, my heart still clenched at how much I wished I were in her shoes. Travelling around Europe was a long-held dream of mine. A dream which felt further out of reach than ever.

Hannah looked at Nicole with a frown. "Too bad I won't be able to make it to your wedding."

Nicole waved her hand. "Don't worry. It's just the way the timing worked out. Lots of my other overseas friends can't come either, and I wouldn't expect them to. New Zealand is too far away."

"Milly, you'll have to say a little speech on my behalf."

I couldn't tell if she was joking or serious, but I played along. "If you write it, I'll read it."

"It's a deal!"

The chitchat continued while we looked over the menu. I tried to work out what would be the cheapest and most filling option. Every dollar counted. "Hey, is it okay if we all pay separately?" I asked.

It felt awkward, but I knew I had to say something or risk getting stung.

"Fine by me," Hannah said.

"As long as one of you does the sums," Nicole said. "I'm not good with numbers."

The waiter arrived, notepad in hand, and asked if we were ready to order drinks. Nicole and Hannah jumped in with their cocktail orders. Then it was my turn. "Just water for me, please."

Nicole lifted a sculpted eyebrow. "Water? At least get a glass of wine or something."

I squirmed. "Well, the thing is... I'm trying to save money."

"So that's why you're hung up on paying separately."

Hung up? That was a bit harsh. I hadn't planned on talking about my unemployment, but now I felt a need to explain myself. "I actually got made redundant a few weeks ago."

Hannah gasped. "Redundant? Oh no!"

"Bring her a glass of the house red," Nicole told the waiter. "My treat."

I shook my head. "You don't have to—"

"Consider it a 'sorry you got shafted at work' drink on me."

"And I'll buy your next drink!" Hannah said.

They were so enthusiastic, all I could do was sheepishly accept. "Thanks, guys. I appreciate it."

The waiter confirmed our order, then disappeared behind the bar.

Hannah leaned in. "So what happened? Why did you get let go?"

I fiddled with my napkin.

How should I explain this?

"Did you hear about what happened to the CEO of Luxmore?" I asked.

Nicole perked to attention. "He jumped off a roof, right? It was all over the news."

Hannah's hand flew to her mouth. "Oh my gosh. You mean he killed himself?"

I nodded. "That's what started this whole mess. So, the CEO died, then a new boss came and started making all sorts of changes, including a big restructure. I was one of the unlucky ones."

I wasn't about to go into the whole Amelia Crook saga. This was all they needed to know.

"Oh man. That sucks."

We fell silent for a minute. Then our drinks arrived.

Hannah swirled her straw, making ice clink against the glass. "You know, Milly, maybe losing your job is a blessing in disguise. It's the perfect time for you to finally do your big overseas trip."

"Good idea, but I don't have enough money. Not to mention my student loan. I'll have to start paying interest if I move overseas."

Nicole frowned. "Ugh, don't even get me started on student loans. What a rort."

"Well, you never know what the future might hold," Hannah said. "Maybe something will change, and you'll be able to make it happen sooner than you think."

Her optimism heartened me, even if I didn't share it. "I hope so. Anyway, don't worry about me. Tonight's your night, Hannah. Let's make the most of it."

As the conversation shifted to wedding and travel plans, I did my best to stay engaged and positive. But inside, I felt like I was getting left behind while my friends moved forward with their lives.

Once Hannah left for her overseas experience, Nicole would be the only friend I had left in Auckland. All my other friends had moved to other parts of the country, or to Australia or the UK. And now Nicole was about to get married, cementing her place in that coveted next stage of adulthood. While my friends were building their careers, getting engaged, and jetting off to exotic locales, I was struggling just to stay afloat.

I took a deep, steadying sip of my wine, trying to push down the sense of dread and inadequacy. What if I couldn't find a new job soon? Would I end up falling even further behind, watching helplessly as my friends continued on to bigger and better things?

The thought made my gut twist up in knots. I'd worked so

hard to get to where I was, to build the life I wanted. And now, in the blink of an eye, it felt like it was all crumbling around me.

As Nicole launched into a detailed description of her wedding dress, I mustered up what I hoped was an interested smile. Now wasn't the time to wallow.

Chapter Twelve

The rejection email stared back at me from my laptop screen, the words blurring as I blinked back tears. Two months of this—endless applications, tedious interviews, nothing but dead ends. Just when I thought I was close to landing something, another door slammed in my face.

I closed the laptop and slid off the edge of my bed, needing to move, needing to do something with my hands to stave off negative thoughts.

Cleaning always helped soothe my anxiety. I looked around my tidy studio apartment—not a speck of dust in sight, the beige curtains perfectly aligned, every surface gleaming. My sight landed on the vacuum cleaner propped up in the corner. There was no such thing as too clean, right?

Without a second thought, I grabbed the vacuum by the handle and began running it over the floor, the rhythmic hum drowning out the chatter in my mind. Up and down the length of the floor, around the perimeter, back and forth across the centre. The repetitive motion lulled me into a familiar trance. When I finished, I moved on to the kitchen, scrubbing the countertops and appliances until they shone.

As I worked, an idea began to form. Cleaning—that was something I knew how to do, and do well. During my teenage years, I had a part-time job cleaning at a local motel, and after my last stint of unemployment, I cleaned at a mall until I had regular work as an office temp.

Even though the prospect of returning to manual labour stung my pride, I couldn't deny that it was reliable work. Something I could do in the meantime while I continued searching for my next proper job.

The thought filled me with a glimmer of hope. Abandoning the sponge, I hurried back to my laptop and began researching.

* * *

I ended up making a profile on a cleaning app as a vetted independent contractor. A few days later, I scored my first cleaning client—someone who went by the username "Cat Dad." The fact he was a proud cat owner was enough to make me like him without knowing anything else about him.

On cleaning day, I lugged a backpack full of supplies onto the train, then off at Britomart station. Cat Dad lived in an apartment in the Viaduct—an area quite close to my old office. As I strode along the waterfront, I hoped to avoid awkward run-ins with former colleagues.

The Viaduct was made up of trendy restaurants, fancy office premises, and five-star hotels, but the side streets were leafy and quiet, with residential buildings rising from the commercial street front.

So, this is where Cat Dad lives.

I looked up at the building in front of me. Glass-encased balconies jutted from the medium-rise structure in a zigzag configuration, looking like something from the pages of an architecture magazine. I reached out and tugged the entrance door handle, but it didn't budge. A suited-up doorman unlocked it for me and let me in.

The vaulted ceiling and chandelier lighting cemented my impression that this was a high-end apartment building. Cat Dad had to be wealthy to live in a place like this.

"Good afternoon, madam. Are you a visitor?" the doorman asked.

"I'm the new cleaner for apartment 8C."

"Your name, please?"

"Jean."

It was my middle name, and the name I was going by on the cleaning app. I didn't want to use my real identity since I was still job hunting and prospective employers might see my profile.

"Right this way, please."

He led me to the lifts and swiped a card to grant me access to level eight—the top floor. Up I went. When the doors opened, I stepped into a wide corridor, then continued around a bend to a door marked 8C.

Cat Dad wasn't meeting me here, so I had to let myself in. I punched in the door code he had sent me, pushed open the door, then stared wide-eyed into the most luxurious apartment I'd ever seen in my life.

Sunlight poured through floor-to-ceiling windows, showing off a spacious open-plan room with a kitchen, dining room, and two lounge areas. A staircase promised more rooms on the floor above, and a sliding door led to a rooftop patio and garden with a view of the Viaduct harbour beyond.

After a minute frozen in awe, I closed my gaping mouth and set my mind to the first order of business—locating the cats. He had two, according to his profile. I wanted to introduce myself to them.

After scouring the lower level to no avail, I ascended the stairs to a landing with two doors. Through the door on the left, I entered a home office furnished with a large desk and a bookshelf stuffed with paperbacks. No cats. I checked the other room—the bedroom, with a king-sized bed as the centrepiece and an armchair in the corner with a few pieces of clothing slung over it.

Bullseye.

Two cats lay cuddled up on top of the chair. Two tabbies. One dark brown, one grey. I advanced with my hand out to welcome sniffs of curiosity. The grey cat stretched and blinked at me, tail swishing. The other one was asleep, its fluffy white tummy rising and falling, whiskers twitching.

Sooo cute!

Neither of them seemed to mind my presence. After a couple of gentle strokes, I had to tear myself away not to lose any more time. Following the instructions Cat Dad had set out for me, I located the supplies in the entranceway cupboard and got to work, dusting and polishing every surface, then vacuuming the floors.

It took me longer than I expected because I kept stopping to look around, picking up on more details about the man who lived here. He had a walk-in closet full of suits, but also plenty of casual, comfy-looking clothing like hoodies, sweatpants, and sneakers. The bathtub in the ensuite was spotless, apart from a thin layer of dust, so I assumed he only used the shower. I could tell he didn't live with a woman because there was nothing feminine anywhere, just men's cologne, bars of soap, and shaving supplies. At a glance, there was no women's clothing in the closets either.

Shelving units throughout the apartment heaved with books, and video game cases and controllers cluttered the space around the television. Reading and gaming seemed like major hobbies for him. Meanwhile, the kitchen appliances looked brand-new, showing that he wasn't much of a cook.

Something on the kitchen bench caught my eye. A plain white envelope with *Jean* written on it.

I picked it up, ran a finger through the seal, and peeked inside. Two crisp twenty-dollar notes. I gasped. Didn't this guy realise payments were supposed to be made through the app, not in cash? Or was this a tip? The amount was wrong, which supported the tip theory, but it was very high for a tip. Not to mention that tipping wasn't the norm in New Zealand. But it had my name on it, and Cat Dad was obviously rich, so…

I slipped the envelope into my bag, and that was the end of that.

I had one thing left to do in the house—feed the cats. I opened the pantry to retrieve the cat food. The state of the pantry confirmed my earlier suspicion. The cupboard was bare apart from a packet of penne pasta, two tins of tomatoes, a container of muesli, two bottles of wine, and a small bottle of whiskey—all unopened. Two large sacks of cat biscuits took up the most space. I grabbed the one that was already open and poured two scoops into separate bowls. The grey cat padded over at the tinkling sound of the biscuits hitting the china bowl.

I watched the small cat crunch through the contents. After the kitty had had its fill, I reached out a hand to offer a pat. "Good kitty."

The cat shied away at first, but with a little more coaxing, I gave a couple of long strokes down its silky back. The cat rubbed its damp nose on my hand, purring. I played with it for a while before it got bored and slunk out the cat flap leading onto the patio.

Thinking of the other cat now, I shook the bag of biscuits, trying to get its attention. No response.

Probably still asleep somewhere.

The apartment was clean, the plants watered, and the cats fed —well, one cat, at least. Time to pack up and go home.

* * *

Later that evening, as I cooked a pot of tomato soup on the stove, I received a notification on the cleaning app. Cat Dad wanted to book me for every second Tuesday on an ongoing basis.

I accepted the booking without a second thought.

Cat Dad…

His username alone brought a smile to my face. Before I knew what I was doing, I thumbed through the app, trying to catch any more details about him I might have missed at first glance. His real name, for example. But there was nothing. I supposed he had his reasons for preferring anonymity—much like I did.

The app had a built-in chat function. I thought I might query him about the money he had left me, but I decided against it. Cash payments were against the terms and conditions of the app, and the chat might be monitored. I didn't want to risk getting either of us banned. I typed a different message.

Your cats are so cute! What are their names?

I hit send and kept my eyes glued to my phone in one hand while I stirred the pot with my other hand. A few seconds later, a reply popped up inside a white speech bubble.

Chichi (grey) and Bowey (brown).

I cracked a wide smile.

Love those names.

I named Bowey after the bowtie-shaped patch in his fur.

Adorable. What about Chichi? Where did that name come from?

It's a character from Dragon Ball. Suits her personality, don't you think? Chichi is the headstrong princess, and Bowey is slightly dim-witted but loveable.

I could see that from meeting them today.

I chuckled. This guy was funny. And cute. And quite possibly single, judging by the state of his apartment…

Ha! What am I thinking?

I was about to slip my phone into my pocket when it pinged again. Our conversation wasn't over.

Feel free to play with the cats. They don't bite or scratch, and they love the attention.

Then I will shower them with affection. I love cats.

Do you have cats of your own?

No, unfortunately not. One day, maybe.

I'm sure Bowey and Chichi will love playing with you.

I grinned at my screen like a madwoman as the soup bubbled away. Who knew having a chat with an anonymous cleaning client could be so enjoyable? Way better than the quality of conversations on dating apps.

A little while later, my phone started to vibrate. I scrambled to grab it as I ate my dinner and nearly dropped it in my bowl of soup. But it wasn't another message from Cat Dad. It was a call from an unknown number. Another job interview request? But it was late in the day for that…

I cleared my throat, summoned a professional demeanour, then answered the call. "Amelia Cross speaking."

A moment passed before the caller said anything.

"Hi. Do you have a minute to talk?"

That voice.

Smooth, deep, luxurious. Its seductive qualities seemed amplified over the phone compared to real life.

No. It can't be him! What the hell?

"Neil?"

Why on Earth is he calling me?

"How are you placed tomorrow? Can you meet with me?"

I tried to reply, but I was tongue-tied.

"Are you there, Amelia?"

"Yes."

"Can you come to my office? When are you free?"

"Why do you want to see me?"

"I have a proposal to discuss with you."

Chapter Thirteen

I had walked through these doors hundreds of times in my life without a second thought, but this time was different. I was an ex-employee now, and I felt shifty and out of place in the high-ceilinged lobby full of gleaming chrome, black tile, and faux marble. I prayed I wouldn't run in to anyone I used to work with. The situation was too embarrassing.

Why did Neil want to speak to me? I still hadn't figured it out. A change of heart seemed unlikely at this late stage, but what else could it be about? Unless he had thought up some genius new way to humiliate me… I shuddered.

James Campbell manned reception on the twentieth floor. He wore a suit that was too large on his wiry frame, giving the appearance he was playing dress-up. His youthful face added to the effect. I suspected he was one of those people who was older than they looked—the same as me.

"Hi, James." I said, approaching.

His eyebrows shot up at the sight of me. "Amelia! What brings you here?"

Despite his surprised look, he had a cheery tone that made me feel like an old friend.

"Neil called me in. He should be expecting me. I'm a few minutes early, though."

"I don't think he's in his office right now. I saw him step out a while ago."

"No problem. I'll wait. By the way, thanks for giving me that update about Christine. I was so relieved to hear she's okay."

"We all were. But why'd you have to go and leave her at my desk like that?! It was the scariest moment of my life! I'm still not over it."

I grimaced. "Sorry. I didn't know what else to do."

"Well, I'm just glad it wasn't for long and that she's okay now. Did you hear she's had her baby?"

My mouth dropped open. "What? No. I didn't."

"A little girl."

"That's wonderful. When was that?"

"About a week ago, I think. I only just found out today."

"And everything's okay?"

"From what I know, she's doing fine."

"What a relief. I'm so happy for her."

"Me too. She's such a nice lady."

I heard the metallic clang of the lift opening behind me. The atmosphere shifted in the room. I sensed it was Neil without having to look.

"Oh—there he is. Mr. Kingston, Amelia is here to see you."

I turned around. He wore a three-piece charcoal suit with a white shirt underneath and a scarlet tie like a gash of blood at his throat. His expression was terse, his forehead veins pronounced. He swallowed, taking me in.

Why do I always feel naked in front of him?

"Good afternoon," I said.

He said nothing in return, just tilted his head back in a sharp, angled gesture that instructed me to come with him.

I followed him down the corridor. In Christine's office, her desk sat empty. A woman I didn't recognise occupied the other desk at the opposite end of the room. She had long, mousy hair and a thin, mousy face to match. She gave me a meek smile of acknowledgement as I passed.

Neil took me through to his office and closed the door behind us. He gestured to a couch and waited for me to take a seat before he claimed the opposite couch. He sat pin-straight, hands at his sides, and didn't speak. I wondered if he took pleasure in my discomfort. It was unbearable. I had to say something, anything, to break the silence. "James told me that Christine had her baby."

Neil nodded. "Her name's Rosie. I have a photo, if you're interested."

"Oh? Yes, please."

He slid his phone from his jacket pocket, brought up the photo, then passed it across to me. The picture showed Christine, teary-eyed, with her newborn baby cradled in her arms. Rosie's face was pink and chubby. She had a button nose and rosebud lips and one faint tuft of black hair on her head.

"Adorable," I said.

"Yes." He had a soft fondness in his voice that caught me off guard.

Once I had recovered from my shock, I passed his phone back to him. Our hands touched, and I felt a current pass between us. Not static this time—something else. But it was gone as soon as we broke away.

"Is Christine doing well?" I asked.

"About as well as one can expect. She's supposed to be resting, but she's not the type to sit still for long. Her sister is here from Singapore to help out. Her husband's off work as well. A nanny looks after Rosie at night so Christine can sleep."

"Wow. It sounds like she's in good hands."

"Yes. It's important she gets the support she needs so she can make a full recovery."

"Absolutely."

At least we have something we can agree on.

I gestured to the door. "Is that woman out there Christine's replacement while she's on maternity leave?"

"No. She's from the admin department, providing temporary cover."

"I see."

"And Christine's not on maternity leave. She has left the role permanently."

"Oh. Is she going to go back to Singapore or stay in New Zealand?"

"Her husband's got a job as a maths teacher here, so they're staying."

"It's a nice country to raise a child."

"Yes, that's a big reason they moved here."

"Makes sense."

I twiddled my fingers in my lap, feeling the crushing weight of silence as it descended again.

Okay. Enough chitchat.

"So, why did you call me here?" I asked. "Is there something you want to discuss?"

"Why do you think I did?"

There he is. The Mr. Snarkypants I know and hate.

"Is that a trick question?"

His lip curled. "I assure you it is not."

"Then why would you ask me that?"

"I thought you might have an inkling."

"I don't."

He opened his mouth, but someone knocked on the door, cutting him short. The mousy woman entered, carrying a stapled A4 document in her hand. She passed it to Neil. He accepted it without comment, and she left the room. He ran his eyes over each piece of paper and appeared satisfied. Then, to my bemusement, he held out the document to me.

Huh? Is it for me?

Brow furrowed, I took the document. "What is this?"

"I should think that's self-evident."

I looked down and read the title on the front page.

Secretary to the CEO, permanent, full-time, salary negotiable.

"A job ad?" I asked.

"Obviously, I will need a new secretary."

My mouth dropped open. Did this mean what I thought it meant?

It can't be. I must have the wrong end of the stick…

"Have a read," he said. "If the job interests you, I'd like to make you an offer."

He wants me to… take Christine's place?

I thought he didn't like me. Why would he want to hire me as his secretary? It took physical effort to close my gaping mouth and retract my wide-eyed stare.

"Well?" he prompted, arms folded. "Any thoughts?"

"Why me?" I stammered.

A smirk spread across his lips. "You're devious, Amelia."

I boggled. *Devious?!*

Never in my entire life had anyone called me devious. Hard-working, diligent—I had heard those plenty of times before. Conscientious had been a teacher favourite. Devious! It would have appalled me if he hadn't said it in a way that made it sound like it was a good thing.

"Excuse me?" I spluttered.

"It's as I said."

My eyes darted around the room. "I think you must have me confused."

He leaned in, making me even more aware of his presence, his scent, the heat radiating from his body. "Tell me, how long did you intend to keep up your little charade, hmm?"

Is he really bringing this up again?

My face grew hot. "I was going to confess to everything after that presentation."

"Were you? You stood up there, acting like everything was just fine, and gave a perfectly good presentation which fooled everyone—except me. Do you have prior marketing experience?"

"No."

The sound which left his mouth was half laugh, half sneer. "Impressive."

Was that a compliment? I couldn't be sure. Nothing he was saying made much sense.

I tried to put him straight. "Like I said, it wasn't my intention—"

"And not just that. The way you wormed your way into a comms role with no degree, no experience, just sheer determination and perseverance."

Wormed my way?!

"Yes. I'm impressed," he said.

"Wait a minute. If you think that's so impressive, why did you fire me?"

"Need I remind you that you were supposed to be laid off to begin with? And even if that weren't so, I must uphold Luxmore's zero-tolerance policy for dishonesty."

"But you would rehire me in a role with even greater responsibility?"

He shook his head. "Luxmore isn't hiring you. I am."

He could do that?

"You don't care if I'm dishonest?" I asked.

"As long as you are not dishonest with me."

I crossed my arms. There was still something I didn't understand. "Why did you want to make me redundant in the first place?" I asked.

"I had to let many people go, Amelia."

"So, it was an arbitrary decision?"

"Not quite."

"How so?"

"My impression of you was that you would be able to find another job."

I had to hold in a scoff. "Do you have any idea how high the unemployment rate is right now?"

"I do."

"And I've hardly got any experience."

"Your determination could overcome the limitations of your experience."

"You think I could just strut out and pick up another job just like that?"

"Yes."

I laughed. He was in a bubble, sitting in his cushy office all day with his CEO paycheck. He had no idea.

"Read it." He gestured to the paper still clutched in my hands. "If you're not interested, I'll find someone else. It's no bother."

A big part of me wanted to tell him, "No, I'm not interested." Me, working for him, after how he had treated me? He could forget it. But the remaining shred of me was more sensible. I should at least read it, weigh up the pros and cons, and make an informed decision. I could be tossing a major opportunity away if I didn't.

I lowered my head to read the pages in front of me. Neil watched on as I did so. The job description was thorough and included everything from event planning to calendar management, taking meeting notes, organising gifts for clients, making travel arrangements, filtering emails and phone calls, and keeping everything in his office neat and organised. A lot of these things I didn't have any experience in doing, however, pretty much all of it sounded manageable and even piqued my interest.

Would it really be so bad working for Neil? Christine was okay with it, and she seemed very respectable. Winston liked Neil too… Then again, there were other companies I was still waiting to hear from, and I'd rather take any of those jobs over working for Neil. Even being a cleaner was preferable if I could get more clients.

"What do you think?" Neil asked when I had turned over the last leaf.

"I think I could do this."

"Naturally. I wouldn't have offered it to you otherwise."

"But there are other jobs I've applied for, so I'm not one hundred per cent sure."

"I need you to be sure, Amelia. Someone else can fill the role." He reached for the document.

"Wait—" I tightened my grip and pulled the papers to my chest. "I just need a little more information. It says salary negotiable. How much were you thinking?"

He scratched his chin. "For you, I'd like to offer a starting package of eighty-five, plus benefits including health insurance, phone contract—"

I was still stuck on the eighty-five, so I didn't absorb the rest.

"Eighty-five *thousand*?"

"Is that not satisfactory?"

It was more than satisfactory. I had never contemplated making so much money at my age and with my level of experience. *Eighty-five thousand dollars.* That was a good chunk more than I had ever made before.

"No, no. That sounds good," I said.

"So, do you accept?"

This was too much pressure. The money was tempting… But I'd have to work for Neil, be at his beck and call. Could I handle that?

"Can I please have some time to decide?" I asked.

Neil appeared to consider my request, then he nodded his head. "Twenty-four hours. No more than that. Then I expect a firm yes or no."

"Thank you, Neil. I'll let you know."

Twenty-four hours. The countdown was on.

Chapter Fourteen

"Thanks for your time. Bye."

The words tasted like ash in my mouth as I ended the call.

Another rejection.

That was my last chance. I had followed up on every single one of my outstanding job applications to no avail.

With a sigh, I tossed the phone onto the coffee table and stared up at the ceiling, willing myself not to cry. What was the point? Tears wouldn't change anything.

I had no more job leads and no more cleaning clients. Neil's offer was all I had left. The thought of working for him still made my stomach turn, but what other choice did I have? I'd be a fool to turn down a salary like that, especially when my savings were dwindling faster than I cared to admit.

Maybe it wouldn't be so bad. If I could just tough it out until I paid off my debts and saved up enough money to move overseas, I could finally join Hannah and the others and leave all this behind.

The more I thought about it, the more appealing the idea became. A few months of hard work, a bit of sacrifice, and then… freedom.

I ran some calculations in my head. With the secretary salary, I should be able to save a decent amount, and if Cat Dad would let me work evenings, I could keep him on as a cleaning client and save up even faster.

I glanced at the time. The twenty-four hours were almost up. I snatched my phone from the table and scrolled through my contacts until I found Neil's number. My thumb hovered over the call button, a flutter in my chest.

Here goes nothing.

I pressed the button and held my phone to my ear. Neil answered after a few rings. "Yes?" His brusque tone set my hairs on end.

"Hi. It's me, Amelia Cross. I'm calling about the job offer."

"I trust you have made a decision."

I swallowed the lump in my throat. "Yes, I have."

Chapter Fifteen

I examined my reflection in the full-length mirror, double-checking each item of clothing I wore wasn't inside out or back to front. A repeat of what happened on my first run-in with Neil was something I intended to avoid at all costs.

No visible tags, no unsightly seams, nothing on the front that should have been on the back. I wore all of my clothing correctly, but I still narrowed my eyes, scrutinising my appearance. Christine was so elegant. In contrast, I looked sloppy in an ill-fitting polyester shirt, wrinkled black pants, and a ratty cardigan. Unfortunately, this was all I had, and I couldn't afford to go out and buy a whole new work wardrobe. Not right away, at least.

Eighty-five thousand.

Maybe I could treat myself to a mini shopping spree once my first paycheck hit my bank account. A long time had passed since I last bought myself any new clothes.

I checked the time. It was eight o'clock already, so I had no more time to obsess over my outfit or put on makeup. I had to get going. I threw on a coat, pulled my bag over my shoulder, and strode out of my apartment, locking the door behind me.

This was it. My first day as Neil Kingston's secretary. I was too nervous to read my book, so I spent the train ride calming myself with positive affirmations.

You can do it. Think of the paycheck. You'll be able to pay down your student loan in no time, then you can move to London and travel like you've always wanted.

Working for Neil won't be so bad. He said I impressed him. He said I'm devious—whatever that's supposed to mean. Out of all the people he could have chosen, he picked me. Who cares why? Eighty-five freaking thousand!

When I entered the lift, I pressed five by accident, realised my mistake, then hit twenty. The door opened on the top floor. I gave a nod to James at the reception desk. "Morning, James," I said.

He beamed at me. "Hi, Amelia."

"Call me Milly, if you like. Most people do."

"Okay, then. Milly it is. I hear you've joined the little team up here."

"Yes. I don't quite know how or why it happened, but here I am."

"Good luck."

"Thanks. Well, see you around."

"Sure. I'm here if you need anything."

I walked the path to Neil's office, which was familiar by now, and entered the room where I'd be working at the desk that used to be Christine's. At the opposite end of the room, the woman I saw last time occupied the other desk. She wore a simple pant suit and her long hair tied in a low, thin ponytail.

"Hi," I said. "I'm Milly, Neil's new secretary."

"Petra," she said. "I'm from admin, but I'm helping out here for now."

"Have you been filling in for a while?"

"A couple of weeks. Christine's original replacement quit! Just walked right out. I think it was too much for her."

So, there was someone else before me…

I cringed. "That doesn't bode well. Do you know what happened?"

"Not really."

"Damn. What was she like?"

She shrugged. "Never met her."

The butterflies in my stomach thrashed their wings. Neil had already made one person quit. How was I going to fare?

"So, uh, I guess I should let Neil know I've arrived. Is he in?"

"Yes. He's here."

I approached the door to Neil's office. It was ajar, but I still gave a little knock to announce myself. He sat at his desk down at the end of the room, elbows on the table. His fingertips massaged his temples as he examined a stack of papers in front of him. Upon my entry, he dropped his hands and lifted his gaze to me. His dark eyes slid down my body, then back up again, a look of displeasure on his face. He pinched the bridge of his nose in apparent exasperation.

I suddenly felt self-conscious, and I crossed my arms like I could cover myself from his scrutiny. He said nothing, so I walked closer and greeted him, not knowing what else to do. "Good morning," I said, then blushed, remembering our first encounter and the way I had used those words to flirt with him. I could only hope he had been oblivious to my motive.

He didn't bother to return my greeting. "The office manual is on your desk," he said. "I expect you to familiarise yourself with it."

I nodded, biting my tongue.

"Petra is here for a few days until you've settled in. She has assisted Christine on occasion in the past, so she knows what to do. If you need anything, ask her."

"I will."

"If she's unable to help you, you may ask me if my door's open. If it's closed, I expect no interruptions."

"Understood."

He glanced at his watch. "I have a meeting to get to." He rose and pulled his suit jacket off the back of his chair and put it on over his white shirt and dark grey vest.

"Should I come with you?" I asked.

He eyed me as if my question offended him. "No."

With that, he marched out. I took a seat at my new desk as he disappeared down the corridor, heavy footsteps fading into the distance.

Why even hire me if he's going to be so rude?

"What's up his arse?" I grumbled as soon as I judged him to be out of earshot.

A faint smile crossed Petra's lightly freckled face. "He's always like that."

I rubbed my forehead. "What have I got myself into?"

"He's not *that* bad. He's grumpy, but he's not mean."

"Not mean," I repeated. "That's a pretty low bar. Do you know if Christine usually went to meetings with him? Shouldn't a secretary go and take notes or something?"

She shrugged. "Sometimes, I guess. Depends on the meeting."

I slumped in my fancy office chair. Everything was fancier in this office. The computer had one of those extra wide, curved monitors which replaced the need to have two separate screens. The wireless mechanical keyboard and wireless mouse had special ergonomic designs. A headset rested on a stand on the left of the desk, a landline phone on the right, and a soundbar speaker sat below the raised monitor. The desk itself seemed to be made from solid wood. A thick, spiral-bound document took pride of place on its surface, office manual printed on the cover page beneath a transparent plastic flyleaf. Next to the manual was a mobile phone—the flagship Samsung model.

"Is this mine?" I asked, picking up the phone.

Petra giggled. "Of course. Neil sent me out to buy it for you. It's your work phone."

"Oh."

"I've already set it up with contacts, emails, and calendars."

"Thanks."

"Work pays for the plan. Unlimited everything."

I admired the smooth, glass-encased device. I played with it for a minute, unfamiliar with its interface, since I was used to my old, low-spec phone. After that, I took a moment to set up the desk the way I liked before diving into the thick manual. It covered everything, including login information, daily tasks, contacts, file management method, details about Neil's preferences and his daily schedule, and much more. Christine had scattered Post-It notes throughout, with extra commentary rendered in her beautiful handwriting.

Even if I dedicated all day to reading the manual, I didn't think I'd make it through to the end. So I flicked through, bookmarking anything which jumped out as being useful in the short term.

I spent the most time studying Neil's daily schedule, admiring his structured routine. Up at five in the morning, at the gym by six, then at work by half-past seven. He stayed at work until the evening and sometimes continued to work until late at night. The rest of his evenings and weekends were free time. I counted up the hours to discover he worked at least eighty hours a week. He was a workaholic through and through.

The list of Neil's preferences was also interesting. I learned he was a vegetarian and a non-drinker, which surprised me for some reason.

As I turned to another page, the landline phone on my desk issued a loud ring. I looked at Petra with a hint of panic. "What should I do? I don't know what to say."

"They will probably ask to speak with Neil. Say he's in a meeting and ask if you can take a message."

I heeded Petra's advice and picked up the call.

"Neil Kingston's office, Amelia speaking."

"Milly," a warm, familiar female voice said. "It's Christine. How are you getting on?"

"Christine? Why are you calling? You've just had a baby!"

Christine chuckled. "Don't worry! I'm coping very well. My sister is here. She's had four kids, so she's a seasoned pro at this.

And the nanny Neil hired for me has been an absolute godsend. It almost feels like cheating."

Neil hired the nanny for Christine? I guessed it was no skin off his nose. He was rich, and they had worked together for a long time. It was the least he could do.

"That's good. I'm glad to hear you're doing well."

"Thanks again for helping me that time. It was a big wake-up call. Neil forbade me from stepping foot back into the office afterwards, even though it left him in quite the bind. We weren't expecting me to leave for a few more weeks."

"Did you want to speak with him?"

"No, I called to talk to *you*. So, you've taken my place as his secretary. I'm thrilled he agreed to it."

"Neil agreed to it? What do you mean? Wait—was this your idea?"

"Oops. I guess the cat's out of the bag. Yes, I may have had something to do with it."

"So, he offered me the job because you asked him to."

"Not at all. He wouldn't hire just anybody at someone's suggestion. I bet he was thinking the same thing before I even mentioned it. He must have seen something in you."

"You think so?"

"I know so."

"You're devious, Amelia."

I had replayed those words in my head a lot since Neil spoke them. Maybe that's what he saw in me. Still, I hadn't been his first choice.

"He hired someone else before me," I said.

"Yes, and what a mistake that was."

"Do you know what happened?"

"No. Neil won't talk to me. He doesn't want to put anything on me while I'm recovering. Anyway, what matters is that you're there now."

I wondered if Christine knew about the whole Amelia Crook thing, but I didn't want to bring it up to find out.

"Anyway, I just called to give a few pointers, as it's your first day and all," she said.

"That would be helpful. I don't know what I'm doing right now."

"I've worked with Neil for a long time. So trust me, I know a thing or two. First tip, bring him a coffee every morning as soon as you arrive. Large, black, no sugar."

I opened my notebook and grabbed a pen to jot the tip down. "From a cafe or from the coffee machine here?"

"The coffee machine is fine. He consumes it for the caffeine fix, not the taste."

"I see. What next?"

"Remind him of his upcoming appointments for the day and let him know if there's anything urgent he needs to respond to. After that, he might assign you some tasks, which can vary from day to day. If not, then you'll spend most of the time managing his inbox, phone calls, and visitors, responding to what you can, taking as much off his plate as possible. Aside from that, you will need to keep the task management system up-to-date at all times, which is a big job in itself."

"What kind of tasks will Neil give me?"

"Anything. Proofreading a document, compiling a presentation from his notes, buying a gift for a client, booking travel or restaurants… Things like that. Once you've been at it for a while, you'll pick up what needs to be done on intuition. He won't even need to ask."

"Okay. Anything else?"

"When his door's closed, don't interrupt him unless it's something urgent. When he's stressed out, give him space."

"Trust me, I'll be giving him plenty of space."

Christine chuckled. "You'll get used to him. I promise. Think of this job as doing everything you can to make his life easier and reduce his stress. If you can do that, he'll come to treasure you."

"I think I get it."

A noise startled me out of the phone conversation, and I

realised Neil had just re-entered the room. He came to the front of my desk and loomed over me, his eyes shooting daggers.

I lost track of what Christine was saying. All my attention was on Neil.

"Is that Christine?" he asked.

I nodded.

He yanked the phone right out of my hand.

"Rest," he barked into the phone, before slamming it down into its cradle. He proceeded to glare at me as if I had committed a deadly sin.

"I didn't call her. She called me!" I said in self-defence.

"It's true," Petra said from the other end of the room.

"Oh, I believe you," Neil said. "But that doesn't excuse what you've done. Do not, under any circumstances, talk to Christine. Not for however long it takes for her to recover. Do I make myself clear? She's just given birth, for God's sake. She's done here."

I was dumbstruck. All I could do was nod my head.

Having made his point, Neil stormed into his office and shut the door behind him.

"Whoa," Petra said. "I haven't seen him get that angry before."

Whoa was right. The pure fury emanating from him was spectacular. It would have upset anyone on the receiving end of it. And yet, I was in awe. The power he commanded without so much as raising his voice… He had rendered me breathless. I had goosebumps.

"I don't think it was your fault," Petra said. "She called you on her own accord, so she must have been up to it."

I shook my head. "No. He was right. I should have put my foot down and insisted she didn't need to help me. It's not like she told me anything I couldn't have worked out on my own."

Why I was coming to Neil's defence, I didn't know. Maybe it was the honourable intention buried somewhere underneath all that chilling rage.

"Okay. But he still shouldn't have treated you like that. It's no wonder the other woman up and left."

I took a breath. "It's okay. I can handle it."

It was more a pep talk to myself than a response to Petra's concern.

Once I had recovered from Neil's outburst, I turned my focus to the email inbox on my computer, studying how Christine had sorted and tagged messages in the past, and already thinking up some improvements to her system.

The rest of the morning flew by. I took my lunch break at one o'clock, eating the fruit, crackers, and hummus I had brought with me from home. Petra had gone out for lunch, and Neil had disappeared to another meeting, so I was alone in the office.

From my chair, I could see straight out the window behind Petra's desk. I watched the sky grow dark and dreary, writing off plans to go for a walk outside after lunch. By the time I finished eating, it began to rain, fat droplets pelting the glass.

My eyes went to the window latches. Unable to resist the magnetic pull of the rain, I crossed the floor and unlatched the window, pushing it open as far as it could go before the safety lock kicked in. The rhythmic sound of the rain filled the room. I spent several minutes just listening, enraptured. If cleaning were my top form of stress relief, the sound of rain came in a close second. I closed my eyes, leaning close to the cool glass.

"What are you doing?" Neil snapped behind me.

I shut the window and swung around, hands clasped together behind me. "Nothing. Just letting some air in."

He regarded me with narrowed eyes and pursed lips, veins popping.

I tried not to squirm or look away. What was so bad about opening a window? *Jeez.*

"I need you to do something for me," he said at last. "Read this and summarise the key points." He passed me the manila folder he clutched in his grip.

"When do you need it done by?"

"Have it on my desk before you leave today."

His mobile phone rang. He fished it from his suit jacket pocket and answered en route to his office.

I set the chunky file on my desk and opened it.

A few hours later, I had typed up a document of notes, printed it out, and stapled the neat stack together. At the same moment I stood to deliver it to him, Neil came out of his office. I presented it to him.

"Done already?" He furrowed his brow as he flicked through the document. "What is this?"

"Um, the summary you asked me to write."

He frowned. "Summary? This isn't a summary. I wanted a one-pager, not an essay."

"Actually, you didn't specify—"

He flicked to the back page and snickered. "You even included references."

"I thought—"

He slammed the paper down on the desk, making me flinch. "This is the business world, Amelia, not school. You might be able to impress a teacher with this, but not me. My associates are busy people. I can't expect them to sit and read a two thousand word essay. They need bullet points. They need information in a way that's concise and easily digestible. Can you do that?"

"Yes. I think so."

"Good." He tossed the document in the bin. "Now redo it."

I cringed. I had spent so long writing that summary. It was perfect in my eyes.

But not his.

After getting what he came out for, Neil returned to his office. I slumped into my chair in defeat. Now to start all over again. *Ugh.*

I had never been told off at work before. I was only used to praise. And now, Neil had scolded me twice in one day. It was confronting, but also strangely exhilarating. My heart was pounding.

I opened a blank document and started over. Concise bullet

points were more difficult than they seemed. In a way, it was easier writing the "two thousand word essay" as Neil had called it —never mind the fact that it was only seventeen hundred words.

Ugh. This is going to take forever.

Petra got up, put on her jacket, and lifted her bag.

"Where are you going?" I asked.

"Home. Work's over."

I looked at the time. It was already ten minutes past five. "So it is. I lost track of the time."

"You should get going soon too."

"I will as soon as I finish this."

"Don't take it personally—what Neil said. He's done that to me before, as well. Okay. Maybe not as bad as that, but still…"

"Don't worry. I'm not upset."

Neil had ruffled my feathers, for sure, but I was far from at breaking point.

"Good. Well, see ya tomorrow."

"See you. Thanks for your help. I couldn't have survived the day without you."

"Nonsense. You did fine."

We exchanged one last goodbye before she left the office. I returned my attention to the bullet point summary and realised there was no way I'd finish it anytime soon.

"Have it on my desk before you leave today."

I sighed. Back in my old role, I was used to working a little late, but this would be *a lot* late. And if working late was going to be a regular occurrence, how on earth was I going to fit the cleaning job into my schedule as well? Cat Dad had agreed to evenings, but not past seven thirty. Perhaps my plan wouldn't work out after all.

Oh well. I had nothing else to do tonight, and as much as I disliked Neil, I still wanted to make a good impression. It was my first day, and I wanted to prove he had made the right decision to hire me. So I continued to write the summary, without taking another look at the time.

Lost in the task at hand, the sound of Neil's door opening gave me a start. Neil looked at me with surprise. "You're still here."

"You need this done today, right? I still haven't finished. There's a lot of information to process."

"It can wait until tomorrow. Go home."

He took me off guard. I thought he would make me stay and finish up. But I wasn't going to argue with him. "All right. Thanks."

I turned off my computer and stood up.

"Oh, and Amelia—"

"Yes?"

His eyes flicked over my outfit, his harsh features twisting into a familiar look of distaste. "We have a stricter dress code up here than you're used to."

My third scolding of the day—just to round things out. And this one struck a nerve.

Not all of us can afford designer suits, you know.

I fought my desire to snap back at him and answered politely. "Sorry. I don't have anything more professional than this. I'll have to buy some new outfits."

There goes my first paycheck.

"You can expense them," Neil said, as if reading my mind. "Actually, put it on a company card."

He pulled out a sleek leather wallet from the internal pocket of his suit jacket, and selected one of the many bank cards he possessed.

"Here." He passed me a platinum Visa card. Then he leaned over to the pad of sticky notes on my desk, jotted down the pin number, and stuck it on the card. "Don't lose it."

"I might not have time to go shopping until the weekend."

"That's fine. I don't need that card back right away. Just go shopping when you can."

"Okay. Thank you. Wait—how much am I allowed to spend?"

"Hmmm. Two grand should cover a couple of nice outfits, shouldn't it?"

I wondered if I'd misheard. *Two… grand?*

"Y-yes. That should be more than enough. Are you sure that's okay?"

"Look, as my secretary, you represent me and the business. You should be well dressed."

"Yes. You're right."

"Make sure you get receipts."

"I will." I pulled on my coat. "Good night."

He didn't respond. He went back to his office.

Two grand to spend on office attire. Two grand. I didn't even know where to begin. I had never had so much money to spend on clothes before. Where would I even shop?

Chapter Sixteen

"That comes to two thousand and eighty-nine dollars," the shop assistant said after scanning the last item of clothing.

I stood there gawping like an idiot. How could those few pieces of clothing add up to so much? Sure, I hadn't paid attention to the price tags as I shopped, but that's because I thought there was no way I'd blow my budget.

Stupid me.

I felt self-conscious enough in the store as it was, surrounded by the chic and professional apparel on display while I slouched around in worn jeans, a basic sweatshirt, and well-loved Chucks. Now I had to confess that I couldn't afford to pay.

The shop assistant looked at me expectantly, but I could see a hint of understanding in her eyes. "Is there a problem?" she asked.

I bit my lip, realising I had to come clean. "Sorry. I'm going to need to put something back. My budget is two thousand."

The assistant reacted with a kind smile. "Tell you what. Let's see what I can do for you. I might be able to get you a better discount, knock a bit more off."

This was an outcome I hadn't considered. A sense of relief washed over me. "That would be great. Thank you."

She typed away on the computer. "Right. I should be able to do that for you. I just need to get my supervisor to approve the discount. Back with you in a minute."

She walked away to confer with another staff member, then both of them returned. The other staff member took control of the computer. An elongated round of typing and furrowed brows ensued. I wasn't sure if it was going to work out. I started trying to decide which piece of clothing I'd have to let go of. The silk blouse? The pencil skirt? Whatever I removed would limit my outfit options. Maybe I could swap a piece for something cheaper?

"The new total is one thousand, nine hundred and ninety-eight dollars," the first assistant said, snapping me from my thoughts.

Though I still felt a twinge of discomfort at the final total, it was within the budget. "Perfect. Thanks."

I scanned Neil's credit card on the card reader and used the pin number he had given to me. The assistant packaged my items by folding them, wrapping them in fragranced tissue paper, and stowing them in two large paper shopping bags emblazoned with the store's logo. I put the receipt in my purse for safekeeping. Neil would need it for tax deduction purposes.

Well, that was a successful outing.

I had bought several beautiful new pieces to wear to work, and I didn't have to spend a cent of my own money. I felt like kissing Neil's Visa card.

Armed with my two full shopping bags, I stepped out of the store and into the bustling mall. That's when I came face to face with Nicole. She was with a friend I didn't recognise. They had their arms linked and held Starbucks drinks.

"Nicole," I said, raising my hand to wave to her, though it was weighed down by the bag on my wrist.

"Oh, hey you," Nicole said with a vague smile. Her eyes went straight to the shopping bags I carried, and she raised her brows. "Valentina's? Nice."

I giggled nervously. "I don't normally shop there. I just got a new job, and I had to buy a new work wardrobe."

"Good for you! What's the new job?"

"Secretary to the CEO."

"Wow. Weren't you working in a call centre before?"

"I used to, but more recently, I was working in comms."

"Well, congrats. Oh, this is my friend Gemma." Nicole gestured to the woman beside her.

The friend smiled at me. She had dyed-blonde hair and wore loads of eyeliner and jewellery.

"Hi, Gemma. I'm Milly."

"Hi. Nice to meet you."

"Are you two here to do some shopping?"

"Uh-huh," Nicole said. "Retail therapy. I've been so stressed out recently."

"Oh? Why's that?"

"Wedding preparations. My parents and in-laws have been fighting non-stop lately. They can't agree on anything."

"Oof. That's rough. I'm sorry you're going through all that."

"Nothing a bit of shopping can't alleviate."

"We're going to buy new outfits for the hen's," Gemma explained.

I had been expecting Nicole to have a bachelorette party before her wedding, but this was the first time I had heard anything about it.

"*Your* hen party?" I asked Nicole. "When is it?"

She frowned, and Gemma stared blankly at me. I wondered if I had said something wrong.

"Didn't you get the invite?" Nicole asked.

"No, I didn't."

She winced. "I'm so sorry. There must have been a mix-up. I'll resend it to you. It's next month, on the fourteenth. So still a while a way. You have to come, okay?"

"Of course. I'll definitely come."

"Yay! Then I'll see you there."

She started to tug Gemma away with her.

"Good luck with shopping," I said.

"Thanks!"

The two friends strode off together.

As I lugged my shopping bags to the exit, I couldn't shake the feeling that something was off. Was it my imagination, or was that entire exchange rather awkward? Nicole had seemed distant and not so excited to see me. And what was the mix-up with the hen's invite? Was there something going on that I didn't know about? I sighed, stepping out towards the pedestrian crossing. Whatever it was, I somehow knew this would have played out differently if Hannah were still around.

Chapter Seventeen

ood enough for you, Jerky McJerkface?

G I stared at my reflection, admiring the stylish ensemble on my petite frame. Slim black wool pants, a structured blazer, a silk blouse, and patent leather loafers. I looked good. Classy. Professional. I was even wearing undies that matched my bra for once. Not that Neil would ever need to know that. Perish the thought.

As well as the pieces I currently wore, I had purchased a pencil skirt, another blazer, and two more tops, all optimised for maximum mix-and-match ability. Too bad my outfit lacked one crucial element: a good bag. As I reached for my peeling, faux-leather handbag, I wondered if Neil would let me expense a new one or whether that would be pushing it. I decided I'd save up for one. My salary was more than enough to cover a new bag while I saved for my OE.

Feeling invigorated, I left twenty minutes early, ready to tackle whatever hurdles Neil Kingston threw my way.

He was picking some printing off the printer when I entered the office. He wore his signature three-piece suit and his signature scowl. Petra's desk was empty. Friday had been her last day. From now on, it was just me and Neil. Could I handle it? If I were going to make it to the end of the year, I'd have to.

"Good morning," I said cheerily, but the two words made me blush. Somehow, I always forgot their significance until they came out of my mouth.

"Good—" Neil's eyes landed on me. He looked me up and down. "You went shopping."

"Yes, I did."

"You look…" He cleared his throat.

This is it. He's going to compliment me. My first compliment from Neil since I've started working for him.

"…Acceptable."

My heart sank. I had expected too much from him. Why was I so hung up on receiving his praise, anyway? I didn't need him to like me. I didn't care what he thought about me, as long as I could keep this job.

Neil's eyes lingered on me. I stared back at him, defiant. Then something unexpected happened. He smiled at me. A wisp of a smile, but it caught me off-guard, and I broke my gaze from him, blushing.

What the heck was that?

I stood there dumbly while Neil turned his attention to stapling his document, all traces of the smile long gone, as if it had never happened. Maybe I had imagined it.

Why am I being so ridiculous this morning? Focus, Milly.

I remembered I needed to give Neil back his credit card. I rummaged in my bag, retrieved the card, and presented it to him. "Here's your card."

"Keep it. Use it for any office expenses that come up—with my approval, of course."

"Right then. I will."

"Scan and send any receipts to Denise."

"Okay."

"Oh, and Amelia, now that you have the proper attire, would you accompany me to this morning's meeting?"

I took a second to respond, stunned by this sudden request. I've never cared for meetings, yet I couldn't help but feel excited. It was like he was inviting me into his secretive world for the first time. After a week of nothing but pointed looks and snarky comments, it felt like a breakthrough.

"Of course!" I said, a little too enthusiastically. I tried to calm down. "Is there anything you need me to prepare?"

"No. All you need to do is listen and observe. I will introduce you. We'll leave in an hour."

"Right. Can I get you a coffee in the meantime?"

"Yes, please. Make it a large one."

"Coming right up."

I scurried to the kitchen, pleased to get away from Neil for a few minutes. On my way there, I saw James. He was humming an upbeat tune to himself, a vacant look in his eyes. My approach burst his bubble. He stopped humming but didn't seem to care I'd overheard him.

"Hi, James," I said as we both entered the kitchen.

"Hey, Milly. How are you settling in?"

All I could do was sigh in response. Sure, Neil had just invited me to a meeting with him, but it didn't make up for everything else he had put me through.

James grimaced. "That bad?"

"I don't know. I've never experienced a new job like this. Neil doesn't do a lot of hand-holding. He just lets me fail, then criticises me for it."

"That must be why Bridget left."

"You mean the woman before me?"

James nodded. "She didn't last long." He reached for a box of berry-flavoured tea bags from the overhead cupboard.

"How does Neil treat *you*?"

James shrugged. "I suppose we get along okay, but I keep my communication with him to a minimum. He's not my direct report. Charlotte Dalton is—the head of admin."

"I see." I pressed the button on the coffee machine, and it groaned to life.

"Most of the other execs on this floor like to keep their distance from him too. It's like they're scared of him or something."

I recalled how the COO had cowered in Neil's presence that time he unexpectedly took the stage.

"I wonder why that is."

"Beats me. I'm just the receptionist. All that stuff is way above my pay grade." James stirred his tea, then dumped the used spoon in the sink with a clang. "Well, all I can say is good luck, and I hope you outlast Bridget," he said on his way out of the kitchen.

At least there was someone around here I could talk to about my troubles. James was a good guy, even if it seemed like he was away with the fairies half the time.

I tidied up after myself, as well as washing the spoon James had left in the sink. Neil's coffee mug was full to the brim. I carefully walked it to his office.

Neil sat in front of his computer with a heavy frown on his face. A familiar scene. I placed the coffee cup down in front of him, but with a little too much force. The hot liquid splashed over the edge of the cup and fell right in the vicinity of Neil's lap, making him wince.

I gasped. "Oh my gosh! I'm so sorry."

"Be more careful," he bit back.

"I'll get some cloths and clean it up."

Neil stood, revealing the wet patch on his crotch. I never thought I'd have a reason to look at his crotch, but there it was. Were his trousers always that snug? I looked away, feeling even more hot and flustered. One thing was clear; a dab with a cloth wasn't going to fix this mess. We would have to go to the meeting soon, and he couldn't go with pants looking like that.

"Oh no. What can I do to help? Where can I get you another pair of trousers?"

Neil brushed me off. "It's fine. Stop fretting. Do you think I wouldn't keep a spare suit for cases just like this? In fact, I have several." He walked across the room to a closet and opened it. Three suits, in immaculate condition, hanging up side by side.

"Thank goodness. I'll go grab those cloths to clean your desk and chair."

When I returned to Neil's office bearing cloths and tea towels, he had gone. I cleaned up the mess in his absence. How could one small splash wreak so much havoc?

Neil returned shortly in a clean pair of trousers. He held the stained pair in his arms and thrust them towards me. "Take these to the dry cleaner."

"Now?"

My response surprised me. It wasn't like me to argue about the urgency of stain removal.

"Yes. Now."

"But what about the meeting?"

"Forget about the meeting. You don't need to come."

"Oh. All right then."

I tried not to look so dejected. Why should I be upset? It's just a stupid meeting. I'd rather not go, anyway.

* * *

By the time I returned from the dry cleaner, Neil had already left. Two hours later, plodding footsteps drifted from the corridor. Not Neil. Neil didn't *plod*. I watched the open doorway as the sound grew louder, then James poked his head in. "Knock, knock," he said.

"Come in."

He entered carrying a giant dog plush toy.

"What in the world?" I asked, staring at the oversized toy.

"Delivery for Neil."

"*That's* for Neil?"

"Yep."

I scratched my head. "Who would send him that?"

"No idea. But the card is clearly addressed to Neil Kingston." He flashed me the gift tag attached to a blue ribbon around the dog's neck.

"Oookay. Well, I'll put it in his office, then."

I took the soft toy from James's hands; a German shepherd with shiny black eyes and a pink felt tongue. "It's pretty cute," I said, stroking its brown fur.

James grinned. "Yeah. I love stuffed toys."

"More than Neil, I'm sure. What was the person who sent him this thinking?"

"Who knows?"

"Well, thanks for bringing it here."

"No problem. By the way, feel free to get stuff delivered to work. I know all the courier drivers. They leave the packages for this floor at my desk, and I'm usually around to sign for them."

"That could be a good idea. Sometimes there are package thieves at my apartment building."

"Package thieves? That's the worst! Definitely get your deliveries here—and I promise I won't rag on you for ordering loads of stuff. I do it too."

I chuckled. "Okay. Sold."

That solved the package-thief problem.

I waved James goodbye with the paw of the stuffed dog. As soon as he left, I took a closer look at the tag around the dog's neck. Neil's name and work address were printed on one side. On the other side, there was a message.

Dear Neil,
Thank you so much for your continued support.
Margaret (AAS)

Neither the name nor the acronym stood out to me, even though I had studied our list of contacts in the office manual back to front. I shrugged it off.

The door to Neil's office was closed but unlocked. I pushed it open. The room was dark, quiet, and still. Dust particles floated in a beam of dull light through a half-open blind. The room seemed even larger in Neil's absence. Large and empty. The smell of the coffee I spilt lingered in the air, mixing with the comfortable scent of leather and old paper.

It crossed my mind that maybe I shouldn't be here, but wouldn't he have locked the door if that were the case? I was just going to put the dog down, then I'd leave.

Stacks of paper topped Neil's desk in an orderly fashion. It wasn't tidy enough for my liking, but it appeared he had some kind of system going. The surface was free from personal effects—no photographs, no knickknacks. Hardly surprising. Neil didn't seem like the sentimental type.

I placed the dog on Neil's chair. As I moved away, I realised it looked like the dog was sitting at the desk. I chuckled to myself. Neil probably wouldn't find it half as amusing, but at least he couldn't miss it.

My focus drew to the shelves behind the desk. Something had caught my eye. All the books and folders stood flush in neat rows —except for one file. It stuck out as if Neil had recently accessed it. It bugged me so much that I couldn't leave it like that. I walked to the shelf and pressed my fingertips to the spine. I hesitated. What was it that Neil had been looking at? I pulled the file out further, just enough to read the label. My eyes widened.

The label said Alex Patterson.

Why had Neil been looking at information about the deceased former CEO? Curiosity overwhelmed me. Neil wasn't back yet, and if I listened carefully, I'd hear him if he was coming. Could I risk a peek?

Yes, I decided.

I pulled out the file and flicked through the documents inside. Details about Alex and his family. A personal profile. A picture of the crime scene on the office roof. A graphic photograph of the body on the ground. I gasped, slamming the file shut in disgust.

What the… ? Why does Neil have this?

A connection I hadn't made before flashed through my mind. Neil was here on the morning of Alex's death, and there was a rumour that someone had tampered with the railing on the roof. Did Neil know something? Was he involved somehow? If he wasn't set to become CEO yet, why was he even here on that day?

Footsteps approached. Footsteps that matched Neil's urgent, even stride. I tried to shove the file back into place, but in my rush, I fumbled and dropped it. The pages fell out and scattered on the floor. I got on my hands and knees and tried to gather them in time, but my effort was futile.

"Do you make a habit of entering my office and snooping around while I'm out?"

I felt Neil's deep, silken voice in my bones. He stood over me, assessing me through narrowed eyes. He had an uneasy look on his face. A look I hadn't seen from him before. "Stand up," he said.

I did so, my cheeks burning.

"Explain yourself."

"I brought in a delivery for you, then I saw this file sticking out—"

This piece of information seemed to disarm him. "It was sticking out?"

I nodded.

"I was careless."

He bent down to pick up the papers. I followed suit. In the scramble, I didn't notice much more information than I had already seen. When one page was left, we both reached to grab it. Our hands brushed. His touch startled me so much that I couldn't move. Neil pulled away first. I picked up the last piece of paper and handed it to him. Rather than returning the file to the shelf, he unlocked a filing cabinet and stored it in there instead.

I wanted to ask him why he had all that personal information about Alex—not to mention crime scene photographs—but I feared the consequences of prying. While I was still deciding whether to bring it up, Neil spoke. "I take it that dog is for me?"

"Someone called Margaret from AAS sent it to you."

"I should thank her."

"Do you want me to email her a thank-you note?"

"No. It's a personal matter. I shall do so myself. Did you sort the dry cleaning?"

"Yes. It'll be ready by tomorrow afternoon."

"Good."

"Did your meeting go well? Anything you need me to action?"

"You didn't miss anything by not being there. Tomorrow morning's meeting with operations, however, that I would like you to attend. Eight-thirty sharp."

"I'll be there."

As I left his office, I ruminated on the notion that Neil was hiding something. I couldn't trust him, he seemed dangerous, and yet… he intrigued me.

Chapter Eighteen

S unlight stung my bleary eyes. I yawned, stretched, then realised something was wrong.

Why is it sunny?

At this time of year, the sky was dark when I got up for work. It wouldn't be sunny unless…

I fumbled for my phone on the bedside table and peered at the time.

No. It can't be.

I rubbed my eyes, hoping it was just my blurry eyesight playing tricks on me. But it wasn't. The time was twenty minutes past eight. My stomach bottomed out. The meeting would begin in ten minutes, and I was still in bed. Even if I made it to work as fast as humanly possible, missing a large chunk of the meeting was inevitable.

I didn't have time to contemplate why or how my alarm didn't go off. All I could focus on was getting out of bed and off to work ASAP. My bare feet found the carpet as I shed the duvet. No time for breakfast. I threw on the same outfit I wore the day before, unable to dedicate a smidgeon of brainpower to thinking about what clothes to wear. I didn't brush my teeth or wash my face. Dragging a brush through my hair was the extent of my grooming. I put on a pair of boots and threw on my wool coat and a scarf. My bag was still fully packed from yesterday. I pulled it over my shoulder and walked out the door in record time.

I ran from my building to the train station. Just as I arrived on the platform where the city-bound train awaited, a whistle blew, and the train doors shut with a thump.

No! Just my luck.

I glanced at the departures board and saw that the next train would depart in ten minutes. Defeated, I collapsed onto an empty bench and checked my work phone. One missed call from Neil. I half-heartedly called him back, knowing he'd be unlikely to pick up because he'd already be in the meeting by now. As I suspected, the call went through to voice mail. I texted him instead.

> My alarm didn't go off, and I'm running late.
> Sorry. I'll be there as soon as I can.

Ten minutes passed with no sign of another train. Fifteen minutes…

There it is. Finally!

The train screeched to a halt at the platform.

Safely on board, all I could think about was how Neil would react when I slunk in late. I had already screwed up so many times in my short period of employment, and now this. As a perpetual perfectionist, it bruised my ego. This had never happened before. I wondered if Neil regretted his decision to hire me. Maybe I'd become the next Bridget. People would say, "She didn't last long," whenever someone referred to me. The thought made me recoil.

As soon as the train stopped at Britomart station, I legged it to the Luxmore building. The lobby was quiet. Everyone had already arrived and gone to work. The meeting was on the seventh floor. I checked my phone on the way up. Neil hadn't responded to my text. I wondered if he had even seen it. I had already missed forty minutes of the meeting. Maybe it would be better to skip the whole meeting than to turn up this late. Then I remembered Neil's words—how he expected my attendance.

Better late than never?

The seventh floor was vast, and I didn't know where to go. I had to ask a random staff member where the meeting was, and she pointed me towards some closed rooms. A sign on one of the doors read "meeting in progress." I took a deep breath, then pushed open the door.

There were more people around the table than I expected. The conversation stopped, and all eyes looked at me. But Neil Kingston wasn't anywhere to be seen. That's when it dawned on me…

I grimaced. "Sorry. Wrong room."

None of the other doors had the same notice up, but I could hear voices coming from one of them. Once again, I took a breath and entered. I spotted Neil straight away. Everyone glanced towards me, except for him. He seemed determined to ignore me.

"Excuse me." I said. "Sorry."

There was only one spare seat at the table—next to Neil. I sheepishly settled down beside him. He looked unamused, seething with palpable disappointment. It felt worse than if he were to say something aloud. I took out my notepad and pen, but I had little idea what anyone was talking about due to missing so much context.

When it was over, Neil said nothing on our way back to the twentieth floor. It was up to me to break the awkward tension. "I'm sorry for being late this morning. My alarm didn't go off, and I accidentally slept in. I know you wanted me to attend this meeting. I let you down."

"You demonstrated a serious lack of professionalism."

"It won't happen again."

"If you're ever running late for an important meeting, take a taxi and expense it."

"A taxi wouldn't have been fast enough. Could I have

expensed a helicopter?" I regretted the snark the instant the words left my mouth.

Neil scowled in response.

Note to self: Don't use sarcasm on Neil. Or any kind of joke.

Time for a different approach. I returned Neil's silent treatment with my own. It worked for a while, then my stomach betrayed me. It let out a loud gurgle. I clutched the offending body part, my eyes wide. Neil stared at me.

"I didn't have breakfast," I explained.

"Get yourself something from the cafeteria."

"Now?"

"Yes. Go. Put it on my account."

"O-okay."

I backtracked to the lift. Neil's behaviour confused me. One minute he was cold fury, the next he was, dare I say, a little bit understanding. A *tiny* bit. I couldn't make sense of this, let alone whatever secrets he was hiding.

I bought myself an egg-and-cheese bagel, returned to my desk, and wolfed it down as I worked. Neil left me undisturbed until the afternoon, when he approached me with a request. "Amelia, I need to ask you a favour."

"Of course. Whatever you need."

"I have a huge load of paperwork to get through by tomorrow morning. I'm going to need to stay late tonight. I won't ask this of you often, but can you stay a while this evening and help?"

His request made sense. I was late to work this morning; it was only fair that I stayed late to make up for it. I was about to agree, then I remembered I had other plans. *Cleaning.* I couldn't cancel the appointment at this late stage. I'd lose the client—my only client. As much as it pained me, I had to deny Neil's request. "I can't. I already have plans. But I can get here extra early tomorrow, if that would help."

"That won't be necessary."

Neil walked off.

Ugh. Why do I feel so bad about this?

Chapter Nineteen

I arrived at Cat Dad's apartment just in time to admire the harbour view from his living room as the sun melted beyond the horizon, splashing the sky pink, orange, and purple.

When the last remnants of sunshine faded, I flicked on the light. The cats lay on the worn-out rug in front of the fireplace. Bowey was curled up, snoozing, while Chichi licked her grey fur clean. I approached them, offering my hand for them to sniff with their wet little noses. Bowey lifted his head. I noticed the poor thing had a little scratch by his nose. He sniffed once, then resumed his nap. Chichi rubbed her face against my hand, purring and tickling me with her whiskers.

Just like last time, the house was tidy, with only a few errant paperbacks, a half-finished glass of water, an empty video game case, and a newspaper marring the otherwise uncluttered surfaces. The air smelled clean, apart from a trace of stuffiness.

In my rush to leave this morning, I had forgotten to bring any cleaning supplies, but Cat Dad's stock was adequate to get the job done. I dusted, then polished, then vacuumed. The cats scarpered onto the patio when the vacuum cleaner roared to life. I daydreamed while I took care of the monotonous task. Who was the man who lived here? Why did I feel such a strong connection to him? Was it just because I liked his apartment? What kind of man was he? What did he do?

Smash.

I hurtled back to reality at the ominous sound.

What was that?

I scanned the floor around my feet and saw a black rectangular object lying at the foot of the bookshelf. I must have knocked it off while I was vacuuming. I picked it up.

A photo frame?

Why hadn't I noticed it before? I had looked all around for a clue that might point to the identity of Cat Dad, but I hadn't seen this. I turned the heavy frame in my hands, heart thumping. A small crack cut through the thick layer of glass. Underneath, a woman and a boy smiled out at me from a park bench. Mother and son? The grainy quality of the photograph suggested it had been taken with a film camera, so it was unlikely to be a recent picture. Could the boy in the photograph be Cat Dad? He had wavy chestnut-brown hair, dark eyes, and pudgy cheeks. Even if it were him, he'd look a lot different now.

I put the photo frame back on the shelf and returned to cleaning. Hopefully, the frame wasn't valuable.

Cat Dad had left me an envelope on the kitchen counter again. When I finished up, I checked inside. Another forty-dollar tip. My heart sank, knowing I couldn't rightfully accept the money. I left it to cover the cost of the broken photo frame.

At least there was one good thing to come out of my clumsiness: an opportunity to chat with Cat Dad again. I sent him a message through the app.

I broke a photo frame. Sorry!

On my way down to the lobby, my phone buzzed. I grinned in anticipation, certain he'd be nice about the broken frame. I swiped the screen, revealing one new message. But it wasn't from Cat Dad.

It was from Leon.

I stared at my phone in disbelief. I thought I had blocked him, but evidently not.

> Hey. Want to meet up again soon?

Was he delusional? Why on earth would I agree to see him again? Did he think I hadn't seen his last message—or had he forgotten he even sent it to me? This time, I made sure I blocked him for real, then I went one step further and deleted the dating app off my phone. I hadn't used it since that disastrous date, and I didn't intend to again. In fact, I hadn't thought about the prospect of romance at all since then. Everything else going on in my life had occupied my mind. Besides, there was little point in starting a relationship when I planned to move away in the near future. Romance would have to wait.

Outside, the air was brisk and biting. I buttoned my coat all the way down and pulled my scarf tighter around my neck. Bright stars twinkled above the placid harbour, where the colourful city lights reflected in the water. Acoustic guitar music drifted from a restaurant. The outdoor seating was deserted, but the interior looked inviting, teeming with groups of diners, their plates laden with hearty meals.

As I walked to the train station, I passed multiple office buildings, noticing the lights still on in some windows and the occasional silhouette of a worker. It made me think about Neil. Was he still at the office taking care of that paperwork? It wasn't unusual for him to work this late, but I couldn't help feeling guilty—especially after disappointing him this morning.

An idea struck me. What if I went back and checked up on him? Maybe he would still need my help, maybe he wouldn't. Maybe he had already left. But if he was there, it could help me score some points with him and make up for some of my mistakes. We had to work together, and I didn't want to remain in his bad books forever.

Mind made up, I headed back to Hobson Street. I looked up at the Luxmore building from the footpath and took in the patchwork of lit and unlit windows, but I couldn't see up to Neil's office from this angle. My all-hours access card granted me entry through a side door. The lobby was vacant except for a security guard and a cleaner making the rounds.

When I got to the twentieth floor, I had to use my card again to access the corridor. The light spilling from Neil's office proved his presence. My nerves ratcheted up. Had I made the right decision to come here? I could be at home reading a book and drinking hot tea...

No. I was here now.

Let's do this.

I walked up to Neil's half-open door. Through the gap, I could see him hunched over his paperwork with a pen in hand. He had ditched his tie and unbuttoned the top two buttons of his shirt, exposing the expanse of his throat, the swell of his Adam's apple, and a dash of collarbone. I knocked on the door to get his attention as I entered. He looked up at me with a surprised expression. "What are you doing here?"

His voice was huskier than usual. The texture of it made me shiver.

"I'm not busy anymore, so I thought I'd come back and see if there's anything I can still help you with."

"You needn't have."

"Are you almost finished?"

"No."

"Then what can I do? I'm here now, so I might as well help."

Neil sighed. "All right. You can sort these documents. Approved, declined, and pending."

"Got it."

I sat in the chair opposite his desk and pulled it up close. Working in such close proximity to him felt strangely intimate. I could smell the spicy undertone of his fragrance, see how his forehead wrinkled as he concentrated...

I shook myself out of it. Why was I getting so distracted by him? I turned my attention to the task at hand.

When I next looked up, it was Neil's gaze that was transfixed on me. My eye contact broke him out of his trance. "Could you stop that?" he said.

"Stop what?"

"Your…" He gestured near his lips.

What on earth?

"My…?"

Then it clicked. I had been poking my tongue out in concentration—an old habit I thought I had grown out of, but apparently not. "Ah. Sorry." I sealed my mouth into a tight line.

After sorting the documents, I scanned and saved them to the drive, then Neil gave me a fresh batch of instructions. Most of the time, we sat in silence. I heard only his breathing and the scratch of the nib of his ballpoint pen against paper.

The work was taking longer than expected and with no end in sight. A twinge of sharp pain stabbed my stomach. Hunger. I hoped my stomach wasn't going to growl in front of him again.

"Are you okay?" Neil asked. He must have noticed my discomfort.

"I'm just a bit hungry. I haven't had dinner. Have you?"

"No." He looked at the time on his phone and seemed surprised. "Perhaps it would be a good idea to eat."

"Why don't I go out and buy something?"

Neil shook his head. "I need you here if we're going to get through all of this tonight. Let's get some food delivered."

"What would you like?"

"It's your choice."

"How about Japanese?"

"Okay. You've still got the credit card?"

"Yep."

I organised the delivery. I had forgotten that Neil was a vegetarian, but he reminded me when I showed him the menu. The food arrived in forty minutes. I collected it from the lobby. By the time I brought it up to Neil's office, I was ravenous. I used a fork instead of chopsticks so I could eat faster. Neil was a dainty eater compared to me. After I filled up on rice, I slowed down to match his unhurried pace.

"How's your tofu?" I asked.

"Good. And your chicken?"

"It's delicious."

I took a sip of miso soup and revelled in its savoury warmth with a sigh of contentment.

Neil stared at me.

"Do I have something in my teeth?" I asked.

"No." He returned his attention to his meal. "Once you've eaten, you can finish up. I should be able to handle the rest of the work."

I shook my head. "I'm re-energised now. I can keep going. Let's get this done."

"If you're sure."

I cleaned up after our meal and returned for the next round of work.

"Do you often stay this late?" I asked, signing a document as a witness.

"Not if I can avoid it."

"Do you have family waiting at home?"

"I live alone."

"Do you have family back in Singapore, then? The UK? You're British, right?"

"I grew up in the UK. It's just me these days. I have no wife or children. My mother passed away a few years ago. I'm not in contact with my father."

So, he was alone then. Just like me. I felt my heart squeeze.

"What about you? Do you have family here?" Neil asked.

"No. We're similar in that way. I'm single, and I live alone. My parents are dead, and I don't have any siblings."

"I'm sorry to hear that about your parents. You are young to have lost them."

I bowed my head, feeling the weight of his pity. "Yeah. Well, I lost my mother when I was still a toddler, so I don't really remember her, and my dad... in hindsight, he wasn't exactly a great father."

The sound of a phone ringing interrupted the solemn atmosphere. Neil's phone was lit up on the desk. I glimpsed the name on the screen—Ruby. No surname. Just Ruby.

"I need to take this," Neil said, grabbing the phone. "Yes?" he answered on his way out of the door with the phone pressed to his ear.

Ruby. I had overheard Neil speak that name before. More than once. It wasn't anyone work-related that I knew of. I wondered who she was. He didn't have a wife, but could she be a girlfriend? I didn't know why the thought bothered me so much. I pictured her all glamorous and mysterious for some reason. The opposite of me.

I strained my ears to hear what he was talking about with her, but I couldn't make out his murmuring. I checked my own phone. Still no reply from Cat Dad. I shrank in my seat.

Neil returned to his desk a few minutes later. "You've done enough," he said. "You should go home."

I was about to protest, but a yawn escaped my mouth, sealing the deal. "Okay."

"How will you get home?"

"I'll take the train."

"Are you okay walking to and from the station this late at night?"

"Of course. I'll be fine."

Neil looked like he wasn't so sure, but he didn't stop me. "Thanks for your help tonight," he said. "I'll compensate you for the extra hours you've put in."

"It was no trouble."

"See you tomorrow."

"See you." I threw on my coat and headed out.

As I descended to the ground floor, I realised I had meant

what I said. It really was no trouble. It was actually kind of pleasant. Maybe Neil would stop mistreating me from now on, and we
could work in harmony. Wishful thinking?

I pushed open the exit door, about to step outside, when I
heard hurried footsteps coming straight towards me. I swung
around. It was Neil, holding something in his hands—my scarf.
"You forgot this," he said, passing it to me.

He had caught me off guard. All I could do was mumble,
"Thanks."

Neil didn't have to come running after me. I could have got it
back the next day, no big deal.

"It's cold outside," he said, as if that explained his gesture.

I wound the scarf around my neck, smiling to show my appreciation. It felt warmer than usual—Neil's body heat?

"Good night," Neil said.

"Good night."

I left the building feeling bemused. Was that him being nice
to me?

* * *

Cat Dad replied to my message the next morning.

> Don't worry about it. Thanks for telling me.

I sprang upright in bed.
I knew it!

He wasn't mad at me at all. So far, he was still living up to the
man I imagined him to be. I typed my reply, fully awake now.

> I'm not normally that clumsy, I promise! How are
> the kitties? I noticed Bowey had a wee scratch
> on his face.

> He's always getting hurt. I don't know how he
> does it.

Poor lil fella.

Maybe he annoyed Chichi too much. She's been known to take a swipe at him now and again.

Haha! I can imagine her doing that.

We continued to text back and forth as I got ready for work. The next message was a photograph of his cats cuddled up together on the couch. Bowey's head was tucked under Chichi's chin, and Chichi's front legs were wrapped around him like a hug. Something else in the picture caught my attention. Cat Dad was partially visible—but just his knee, sadly.

So cute!

It's the one-year anniversary since I adopted them today.

Happy anniversary!

He sent another picture. This time of two scrawny, scraggly looking kittens staring at the camera with wide, frightened eyes.

This is what they looked like when I adopted them.

Wow! They look so much happier and healthier now. You must be looking after them well.

They had a rough start in life, but they're doing much better now.

Thanks for giving them a better life. That was so kind of you to adopt them.

I wish I could adopt more, but sadly I'm too busy
to look after more animals at the moment, and
an apartment isn't the best place for them.
Maybe in the future.

I'd like to adopt animals too one day. I never had
pets growing up.

Cat Dad didn't reply. I set my phone down with a wistful sigh.

Who was Cat Dad? I wondered what he looked like, what his voice sounded like, and what he did for a living. Part of me wished I could meet him face to face, but I shook my head, banishing the thought. What was the point? It seemed inevitable that he wouldn't live up to the fantasy man in my head. Not to mention I'd be leaving the country at some point. No. I was his cleaner, nothing more, and that's how it would stay.

Chapter Twenty

I noticed something strange about Neil's appearance as I set his morning coffee on his desk.

He was unshaven.

I couldn't figure out why this rattled me so much until I realised it was the first time I had ever seen him even slightly ungroomed. It was out of character for him. Had the late night taken its toll? My eyes lingered, absorbing his new look. He had flecks of grey in his stubble, which was oddly appealing…

Neil looked at me, and I averted my eyes, pushing his coffee towards him.

"Thanks," he said.

"Did you manage to get everything done last night?"

"I did, thanks to you."

"I'm glad it's sorted. What was all that paperwork about, anyway?"

"I'm pushing through a lot of changes before the union's dead-line. They have demands I'm striving to meet."

"I didn't know you were so involved with the union."

"You didn't notice the lack of strikes since I started?"

"No, but now that you mention it…"

"Our factories have been neglected for years under Patterson. Fixing them is my top priority."

Neil's conviction surprised me. I'd never known anyone in the head office to care for the factory workers. The usual reaction to their constant strikes was a lot of eye rolling and grumbling. But Neil was taking action.

"The next time I visit the factories, I'll take you with me," he said. "It's important you understand that side of the business and their working conditions."

"Sounds like a good idea. What about this morning's meeting?"

"Yes. Come with me. I want to introduce you to our biggest national client. It's a casual meeting. Nothing to prepare. David and Aroha are supposed to be joining us, but last I heard, they might not be coming. They're busy with their own lot of paperwork, so it might just be us. Be ready at ten."

The meeting was at a cafe in Ponsonby. Neil loomed over my desk when it was time to leave. I followed him down to the main entrance where Winston awaited in the black Audi. Winston opened the back door for Neil. I hopped into the other side. The interior was flawless, as usual. Winston seemed to take great pains in keeping the car in immaculate condition, as if it were his pride and joy.

We were about to pull out when there was a sharp knock on the window. David and Aroha were outside. Neil rolled his window down.

"Room for two more?" David asked.

"I thought you weren't able to come," Neil said.

"There's been a change of plans. No time to organise another car. Can we go with you?"

"All right. Get in."

I cringed inwardly. David and Aroha's presence never failed to resurface the awkwardness of the Amelia Crook incident. I didn't know how much they knew or what Neil had told them, but so far, they'd never brought it up, and I hoped it stayed that way.

David took the front passenger seat next to Winston. Aroha asked me to scoot over into the middle seat. Now I was crammed in between her and Neil. I paid little attention to Aroha, but I was painfully aware of just how much of me was touching Neil. Boy, was he tense. So was I. We were pressed far too close for comfort. I could feel him all down my side, his warmth radiating out. I had to dip my hand in between us to buckle my seatbelt. I groped around, trying to find the buckle without success. Neil glowered. He reached down and fished it out for me, the contact of his hand against my outer thigh sending a fluttery feeling all through my body.

"Thanks." I clicked my seatbelt on.

The drive to Ponsonby was quick. Winston dropped us off right in front of the cafe. David held the door open for us as we filed in.

Neil scanned the room. "They're not here yet."

The cafe was large, with tables in long vertical columns. An abstract art print decorated the otherwise blank white walls. The clientele looked like professionals. A few people were working on laptops.

"What drinks do you want?" Neil asked, slipping his wallet out of the inner pocket of his suit jacket.

"Flat white for me, ta," David said.

"I'll have a mocha," Aroha said.

"Amelia?" Neil asked.

I had been busy eyeing the colourful display of macarons in the cabinet looking like precious jewels. "Oh, uh, a cappuccino, please."

Aroha and I followed David to a free table while Neil stayed in the queue at the counter.

"Neil says you're getting on twell with the new job," David said.

I was just about to sit down and nearly missed the chair entirely. "He does?"

David laughed. "You sound surprised."

I composed myself. "Because he has very high expectations."

"And you're living up to them, apparently."

I didn't know how to respond. Did Neil really say that, or was David just trying to encourage me? I couldn't picture Neil singing my praises. "Fine" or "adequate" were normally the best I could get out of him.

Neil joined us, taking the chair opposite me.

"I was just telling Amelia what an asset she is," David said.

Neil blanched. "Yes. Quite the asset." He cleared his throat. From there he veered the small talk to another topic.

The drinks arrived, and we finished them before the client even turned up.

"What's taking them so long?" David asked. "Any word?"

Neil checked his phone, frowned, then made a call. "Neil Kingston here. Are you on your way?"

The rest of us were silent as we listened in.

"I see," Neil said. "Then we'll reschedule."

David mimed a dramatic sigh.

"They're not coming," Neil said as he put his phone down. "Something else has taken precedence."

"Unbelievable," David said. "What a waste of time."

"It's a bit rude of them not to tell us until now," Aroha said.

"That may be so," Neil said, "but they're big and important enough to get away with it. Amelia, make a note to reschedule the meeting."

I added it to the task list on my work phone.

"We need to get back to the office," David said. "Things to do. This has already taken up too much time."

"You two go ahead," Neil said. "I'll call Winston to bring the car over."

"We're not going back with them?" I asked.

"I thought we could stay and have a talk."

A talk?

"Oh. Okay."

What was this about, and why did I feel so nervous about it?

Neil called Winston, and David and Aroha left the cafe.

"I'm going to get another coffee," Neil said. "You want one?"

"Sure. Thanks."

He returned after making the order.

"What did you want to talk about?" I asked.

Neil swallowed, taking his time to pick his words. "How are you doing? In the job, I mean. I know it hasn't been long, but are you getting on okay?"

The sincerity of his concern caught me off guard. "Well, uh, okay, I guess. I feel like I'm doing a pretty good job, but I know you have high standards."

"As I should."

"Of course. I also have high standards. Well, I thought I did, but compared to you…"

A server placed a small white plate with a delicate little stack of macarons in the centre of the table.

"Did you order this?" I asked Neil.

He nodded. "Go ahead."

I stifled the little spark of joy that threatened to work its way onto my face. "Thanks. They look amazing."

Now that he had bought them, it would be rude not to try one. I took a bite and let it melt on my tongue like a sweet, crispy cloud.

Neil rested his chin on his fist, watching me with apparent interest as I ate. It was slightly unnerving.

"Aren't you having one?" I asked.

"They're for you. I don't like sweet things."

I wondered if he had noticed me looking at them before. He must have. He was observant. "They're good. Thank you. What were we talking about? Oh yeah. Do you think I'm doing okay with the job? I know I've made mistakes."

"Very few, considering no one was here to train you. After Bridget, I have no complaints."

"She was bad?"

"Useless. Don't get me wrong, I'm sure she'd fare well in any other job, but she wasn't good enough for me."

"And I am?"

"So far, yes."

This was high praise indeed. Coming from Neil, at least. Perhaps I wasn't struggling as much as I thought I was.

Neil leaned back in his chair. "You know, I had my doubts about this arrangement, but I think it's going to work out nicely."

I smiled politely while the knowledge I planned to leave the job as soon as possible niggled at the back of my mind.

Chapter Twenty-One

In the few weeks since I became Neil's secretary, I had avoided my old colleagues from the comms department, but I knew I couldn't avoid them forever.

"Milly!" came a voice from across the cafeteria.

I looked up from my table and saw Ellen squeezing through the lunch crowd. Her blonde curls bounced as she bounded towards me. "Oh, hey." I forced a smile, though my insides knotted.

How much does she know?

Neil claimed to have swept the Amelia Crook situation under the rug, but my sudden termination, followed by my elevated new position, must have raised a few eyebrows.

"Can I sit here?" Ellen asked.

"Of course."

She plopped into the chair opposite me and planted her number on the table. "Where have you been hiding all this time? We've been waiting for you to drop by the fifth floor and give us the goss."

I aimed for a casual tone. "It's just been hectic, settling into my new job and everything."

"One minute you're with our team, the next minute you're laid off, then somehow you're the CEO's secretary. What's up with that? We're all curious."

I sat up straighter. "No one told you anything?"

"Brendon said there was a mix-up during the restructure. Something about Mr. Kingston having to let you go because you were supposed to get laid off but got the wrong notice in error. We all thought that was totally unfair. Why should you get punished for a mistake that HR made? But then, Mr. Kingston rehired you as his secretary…"

"Yep. That's pretty much what happened." I wasn't about to illuminate the other aspects of the story.

Ellen knitted her brow. "But why did he rehire you? He already laid off so many capable staff and didn't offer the role to any of them—as far as I know. Not saying you don't deserve it or anything. I'm just confused."

"That's understandable. I was confused too. Then I found out that his former secretary encouraged him to do it."

I recounted how I had helped Christine during her pregnancy ordeal.

"Wow. That's quite the story," Ellen said. "It sounds like everything worked out for you in the end. I'm happy for you," she exhaled a sigh, "but I really wish we still had you in our team. It's been so stressful."

I winced. "It's that bad, huh?"

She nodded. "And not just our department. The entire head office is suffering. To cut staff and expect the rest of us to pick up the slack… It's a shambles."

"It must be tough."

"Everyone's fed up. Someone started a petition—" She bit her tongue and clapped her hand over her mouth.

"What petition?" I asked, my brain whirring.

Ellen frowned. "I shouldn't have said anything."

"Why? Is it a secret?"

"No, it's just… you work for him, don't you? If he loses his job, you'd lose your job as well."

"Lose his job? What's this about?"

Ellen clamped her mouth shut, but I could tell she was struggling. She couldn't resist the allure of spreading gossip.

"Ellen," I pressed.

She sighed. "You didn't hear this from me, okay?"

"Just tell me."

"There's a petition by the head office staff to have Neil Kingston removed as CEO."

The revelation sank to the pit of my gut. The staff wanted Neil gone. They were trying to oust him. "They can do that?"

"No guarantees, but if the petition gets enough signatures, and we can get it in front of the media—and even to the big boss in Singapore—we might be able to get him to resign."

I looked at my lap, not knowing what to think. A few weeks ago, I would have given my full support to such a petition. Now, I wasn't sure. Where did my loyalties lie? With Neil? My old coworkers? Or just me?

"You could be collateral damage," Ellen said. "Sorry. It's nothing personal."

I groaned. "At least you've given me a warning."

"Are you going to tell him?"

"I'll have to."

"I suppose he would have found out sooner or later." She took a bite from her grilled panini sandwich.

I had been so wrapped up in the conversation, I hadn't noticed her food arrive, nor had I remembered to eat mine. My soup and sandwich were almost cold, but I forced myself to finish them, lest hunger pangs distract me later.

After swallowing the last spoonful, I excused myself. "I better get back to work."

"Hope I haven't upset you."

I shook my head. "It's fine. I'm glad I know now."

"Don't be a stranger, okay? Just because you're Mr. Kingston's lackey now, it doesn't mean you're not still one of us."

I laughed half-heartedly.

One of them? It didn't feel like that to me. Not anymore.

When I got to my office, Neil's door was closed, but I didn't think twice about knocking. No response. I pushed the door open anyway. Neil looked up at me from behind his desk as I approached. "What?" he barked.

"I have news."

"This better be important."

I sensed his threshold for importance was higher than mine, but I continued regardless. "Do you know about the petition?"

He leaned back and folded his arms, giving me his full attention. "Enlighten me."

"I've just heard that there's a petition going around the head office. A petition to have you removed as CEO."

I didn't know what I expected, but some kind of reaction, at least. Instead, I got nothing.

"Is that all?" Neil asked.

"Well, yes. Is it not a concern for you?"

"Let me explain something, Amelia." He motioned for me to sit in the chair opposite his desk. "Putting it bluntly, your colleagues downstairs are fortunate that Luxmore as they know it even continues to exist."

"What do you mean?"

Neil got up and crossed to the front of his desk, then reclined against it, facing me. From this new angle, he loomed above me, radiating his signature brand of quiet dominance. I held my breath.

"Zelthia's master plan was a merger, not a mere restructure," he said at last. "Flerotech was going to take over the company."

"Flerotech... The Chinese appliance company?"

"Correct."

I digested this new piece of information. "So Luxmore would have moved to China, and the New Zealand staff would have lost their jobs?"

"More or less."

I shot to my feet. "But that's ludicrous! Luxmore's entire brand identity is based on being a New Zealand company. That's why people buy our products. Why would we become part of Flerotech?"

"In the end, what matters most is that people want cheap goods."

He had me there. "So what happened? Why didn't the merger go ahead?"

"Because I decided to take Luxmore on as a pet project."

I blinked. "A *pet project*? That's what Luxmore is to you?"

"It would have been a shame for Flerotech to take over. Don't you agree?"

"You're telling me that the only reason Luxmore is still going is because it's your pet project?"

"Yes."

No wonder he was so nonplussed about a pathetic little petition. How was anyone going to oust the man who was the sole reason the business was still operating? The sheer ignorance. Still, there was one thing I couldn't wrap my head around. "Where does Alex Patterson fit into this? I thought you became CEO because he died."

Something shifted in Neil's demeanour, a fleeting unease. "Patterson's death had little bearing. Everything was in the works long before he passed. I came here over a year ago to oversee the audit, exert some pressure on Patterson to resign, then take over. That was my directive."

"But why did he..."

"Kill himself?" A pallor washed over Neil's face. He rubbed his temples. "That I do not know. The audit was damning, but I never anticipated this outcome."

My eyes flicked to the locked filing cabinet where he had stashed his Alex Patterson file. Did he really not know?

I felt Neil follow my gaze and quickly looked away. Time for a change of tack. "Okay, so you're not worried about a petition, but what about staff morale?"

Neil ran his tongue over the back of his teeth. "It's true they haven't bounced back from the restructure as quickly as I thought they would."

"So, what can we do about it?"

"There's a simple fix."

"Oh?"

"Increase pay."

"You don't beat around the bush."

"Of course not. What did you expect me to say? Free pizza lunch on Fridays?"

"A lot of bosses think like that."

"Yes, and I'm not one of them."

He had me lost for words for a second.

"You seem surprised," he said.

"Pleasantly surprised. A boss who thinks increasing pay is a good idea… That's a new one."

"I'm glad I'm keeping you on your toes."

"You certainly are."

A faint smile crossed Neil's lips, and I found myself fixated on it, like it was a treat I wanted to savour…

I cleared my throat, willing myself to snap out of whatever had just come over me. "So, this hypothetical pay rise—where will the money come from?"

Neil turned serious again. "Ah. Now that's the tricky part." He straightened his posture and began to pace the floor alongside his desk, hands grasped behind his back. "The restructure freed up funds, but not enough. I have prioritised the factory staff getting an increase, and I stand by that decision. Meanwhile, head office salaries are already in line with market rates. I can't offer anything more at this stage."

"But you just said you would—"

"I said it was the simplest fix. But nothing's simple."

"Then what else can we do?"

"I can promise pay rises in the next financial year and offer something non-monetary for now. Flexible hours and work-from-home options. That should suffice."

"I think we should publicise that you saved the company from a merger—"

His reaction was swift. "No."

"Why not?"

"Because the merger could still go ahead if I can't turn the business around in a timely fashion."

"But shouldn't the staff know about this?"

"I don't want them to operate in an environment of fear. This is my burden to shoulder."

He had a point, even if it seemed like a wasted opportunity.

He retreated behind his desk and sat down. "The information I just shared with you is confidential, understood?"

"Yes. Of course."

"Good. Now leave. You've stalled me long enough." He shooed me from his office with a wave of his hand.

I had learned by now not to take offence at his brusqueness. Instead, I felt satisfied that we had just engaged in a productive discussion.

Progress.

I shut Neil's door. Rather than returning to my desk, I visited the kitchen to make a cup of tea. My thoughts lingered on the conversation with Neil as the tea brewed. He had saved the company from a merger... He was trying to turn the business around...

"Hey, Milly." James entered the room, carrying a coffee mug.

"Hey."

He strode to the microwave and put the mug on the turntable with a thunk.

"Forgot to drink your coffee?" I asked.

"You got it."

He pressed some buttons, and the microwave whirred to life. "Any plans for the weekend?" he asked.

I was about to answer "no" automatically, then I recalled I did, in fact, have plans. "I have a hen party tomorrow night."

"Oooh. Fun! What are you going to do? Men of Steel?"

I laughed. "No. I think it's going to be pretty low-key. We're having drinks and nibbles at a bar, then going clubbing."

"Perfect. I'm jelly."

"Yeah. I'm looking forward to it."

"And the wedding? When will that be?"

"Late next month, at a vineyard on Waiheke Island."

"Nice! I love weddings. Need a plus-one? Fake boyfriend?"

I grinned. "Don't think so, but thanks for the offer."

"Shame."

The microwave beeped, and James collected his reheated drink. "Have fun at the hen's," he said on his way out.

"Thanks."

I couldn't think about the hen party. My thoughts were stuck on Neil.

"I don't want them to operate in an environment of fear. This is my burden to shoulder."

I stirred my tea as Neil's voice echoed in my head.

Something was becoming clear. Neil wasn't the man I thought he was.

Chapter Twenty-Two

Until now, my experience of bachelorette parties came from TV and movies. That's why I half-expected to see Nicole dressed in a tacky outfit with a sash, veil, and tiara when I walked through the wrought-iron gate to the courtyard outside the bar. But no, she wore a tasteful little black dress like most of the other women surrounding the large table. I seemed to be the only one wearing any colour. Had I missed a memo about a black-and-white theme? I felt under-dressed compared to everyone else, wearing a denim jacket over a short-sleeved top and a skirt with tights and boots.

At least I'll be warm.

Moonlight and gothic-style lanterns lit the courtyard. Ivy climbed the red brick walls. Every table was occupied. Conversations in raised voices competed with the hip hop music pumping through the speakers.

I approached Nicole's table, but she was too engrossed in chatting with her friends to notice my arrival. I tapped her shoulder. Even then, she didn't acknowledge me until she had finished speaking with the friend opposite her. At last, she looked over her shoulder and smiled. "Oh! You're here! Thanks for coming."

I counted ten people around the table, including Nicole. I must have been one of the last to arrive, which was strange since I was only a few minutes late. "Am I late? Sorry."

"Don't worry. Some of us had dinner at my place first, then we headed here early. Have you met my friends?"

I looked from face to face, searching my memory. "Some of them…"

"I better introduce you." She turned her attention back to the group of ladies around the table. "Everyone, this is…" Her voice dropped away and blankness spread over her face.

Why isn't she saying my name?

"This is…" She grimaced.

All the little conversations dried up until awkward silence reigned, nine pairs of curious eyes staring at her expectantly. Nicole laughed nervously, combing a hand through her long blonde hair. I felt the colour drain from my face.

She's forgotten my name. Eight years of friendship, and she's forgotten my name.

Nicole laughed again, her eyes and nose crinkling. "Oh my gosh! I must be drunk already. This is *Milly*. That's right. My old friend from uni."

I exhaled. She got there eventually. I could forgive the lapse since she had been drinking, and I knew how wedding preparations and family drama were stressing her out. It was enough to mess with anyone's brain.

Yeah. That must be it.

"Milly, this is Alicia, Stacy, Eden, Jodie, Gemma, Felicity, Jacquie, and of course, Gwen and Lisa, who I'm sure you already know."

The names passed in a blur, but I tried to remember as many as I could. The women all greeted me before returning to their private conversations in pairs or threes. No one made space for me at the table.

I looked around, trying to spot a spare chair, but couldn't see one.

"Hey," the brunette woman on my left said. "I'll grab you a chair."

"Would you? Thanks. That would be great."

I watched her disappear inside the bar, then emerge with a stool. She dragged it across the pavers to our table. Everyone had to shuffle their chairs along to make a gap for it to fit.

"Thank you so much. Stacy, isn't it?"

She nodded. "And you're *Milly*. How awkward was that?"

Heat spiked up my neck and flared on my cheeks. "Yeah. We've only been friends for eight years."

"Wow. You've probably known her the longest, apart from Gwen and Lisa."

"I think so."

"Well, now you can bring it up whenever you feel like giving her shit. 'Remember that time you forgot my name in front of all your friends?'"

"Good point. I hadn't thought of that."

A heaviness settled in my chest. Nicole and I didn't have the kind of relationship where we could give each other shit anymore. Those days were long gone.

A waiter came by. He placed three large bowls of fries on the table. "Can I get you anything else?" he asked Nicole.

"Who wants another drink?" Nicole asked the group.

"Let's get espresso martinis," someone said.

"Oooh. Espresso martinis all round?"

"Yes, please!" was the resounding answer.

I recoiled at the notion of the sickly coffee and alcohol concoction. "Actually," I cut in, "I'll have a glass of red wine, please. A Pinot noir."

Maybe I imagined it, but I thought I saw Nicole roll her eyes. "Ten espresso martinis, please," she told the waiter. "And *one* glass of Pinot noir."

He nodded and retreated inside.

My wine came out first, followed later by the noxious brown cocktails.

"Cheers," Nicole said, raising her glass.

Gwen followed suit. "To the bride-to-be."

"Cheers," everyone rang out, clinking glasses.

Nicole took a sip, but a thought seemed to strike her mid-swallow. She downed her mouthful. "I almost forgot! I made goodie bags for all of you, but one item didn't get delivered, so they weren't ready for tonight. I'll have to give them to you another time."

"What's inside?" Alicia asked.

Nicole had a glint in her blue eyes. "It's a secret. You'll have to wait and see."

"I haven't had a goodie bag at a party since I was a little kid," Eden said.

"Let's just say these aren't your little kid party favours."

Giggles erupted all around. Once the laughter died down, chatter started up again. Everyone seemed to know each other well—except for me. The only person I really knew and wanted to speak to was Nicole, but she was way down at the other end of the table, and fully engaged with two friends sitting opposite her. I took a long sip of wine.

"How's your drink?" Stacy asked.

Relief swept over me at the sound of her voice. Someone to talk to. "It's nice. How's your…" I eyed her cocktail. "*That.*"

She laughed. "Well, it's a bit too sweet for my liking."

"That's not surprising."

She sighed. "I know, I know. But I better enjoy it. Tonight's the last night I get to drink for a long time."

"Why's that?"

"My husband and I are going to start trying for a baby soon."

I plastered on a grin to cover my shock. "Wow. Congratulations!"

This was my first encounter with someone around my age who was married and trying to get pregnant. Marriage and babies were so far out of my comfort zone, I didn't know how to react.

"It's my goal to have three babies before I turn thirty," Stacy explained, glowing with pride. "So, I've got to start now if I have any chance of making it happen—unless I'm lucky enough to have twins or triplets. I'm hoping the first one's going to be a girl. That's my dream. At least one girl."

I downed my glass of wine much faster than I intended. I hadn't expected to have to talk about babies. To me, having three kids while under the age of thirty sounded more like a nightmare than something aspirational, but I tried to seem excited for her.

Stacy went on and on about her plans. She seemed so happy. I didn't want to spoil it by attempting to change the subject.

When a twelfth guest arrived at the table, it was a welcome interruption.

"Marley! You made it!" Nicole hugged the tall, dark-haired woman and planted a kiss on each cheek with a *mwah*. "Let's find you a seat."

Nicole secured an extra chair. She pulled it up beside her, somehow creating a space along the packed table. But Marley didn't sit down. She wandered around, greeting everyone with hugs and gushing remarks.

"Hello, I'm Marley. I don't think we've met," she said when she got to me.

"No, I don't think we have. I'm Milly."

"How do you know Nicole?"

My first instinct was to call her my best friend, but I snuffed out the words before they could leave my mouth. Best friend no longer seemed apt these days. "We went to uni together."

"Are you a doctor too?"

"No. I dropped out long before getting qualified."

"Oh no. Why did you drop out?"

"My father died, and I couldn't focus on studying after that."

"That's terrible. I'm so sorry."

"How do you know Nicole?"

"My partner and Paul have been friends since primary school."

"That's cool. I lost touch with primary school friends years ago."

Our exchange ended there because she moved on to Stacy. The pair embraced.

"I haven't seen you in such a long time!" Stacy said.

"We saw each other at Eden's place two weekends ago," Marley reminded her.

"Oh yeah! That's right. Why does it feel like ages ago?"

The two women entered a passionate discussion about all things babies and pregnancy while I listened on the periphery with nothing to contribute. All the other conversations going on around me were much the same: wedding talk, house hunting, husbands and partners. Why did I feel like some kind of alien?

I slipped off to the bar and ordered another glass of wine. When I went back out, rain began to pitter-patter on the awning over the courtyard. Our table was sheltered, but others weren't, and several people abandoned the courtyard to head indoors. The temperature had plummeted. It would be freezing if it weren't for the heaters mounted to the brick walls blasting warmth through glowing orange grates. I huddled into my denim jacket and tried to position myself for maximum heater exposure.

Once I had finished my second glass of wine, talking came easier. I joined in several discussions and felt like I was getting along with everyone much better, even if I had little in common with them and didn't always find the subject engaging.

Soon, the rain intensified, and not even the heaters could compete with the strong chill in the air.

"Let's go inside," Nicole said, hugging her shivering body. "The DJ should be starting soon."

"Dancing will warm us up," Marley said.

The interior of the bar had a raw yet sophisticated industrial theme, all black iron, grey concrete, and exposed brick. The DJ was setting up at her station by the dancefloor.

"I'm getting another drink," Nicole said. "Who else?"

"Me!" Eden said.

Others echoed her sentiment. We bought our drinks and consumed them in a booth of modular couches around a low table.

The DJ began her set, dance music booming from the speakers. Marley was the first of us to descend on the dancefloor, but everyone else quickly joined in. Except for me. I ordered another drink because I didn't feel like dancing. The bartender poured gin and tonic over ice. I took the cold glass in hand and wandered over to the sidelines of the dancefloor. I sipped my drink and bobbed in time to the beat while I observed everyone else dance. At some point, I noticed a man watching me from the opposite end of the dancefloor. He seemed around my age, and he wasn't bad looking, but I sensed something off about him and looked away.

"Come on, Milly. Let's dance!" Stacy grabbed my hand.

I gulped the rest of my drink, put my glass down on a nearby table, then let her drag me to the dancefloor.

The mass of moving bodies absorbed me. Lights flashed. Vibrations pulsed through my body. The room spun. It hit me just how drunk I was. I hadn't intended to drink so much—It just happened. Everything was a blur. I couldn't tell who I was dancing with. When did it get so crowded?

Then I felt someone grab my butt.

Indignation rose within me, but I swallowed it down, writing the gesture off as an accidental brush.

Then it happened again. Not a brush. Definitely a grope.

I swung around to face my assailant, but they had disappeared within the twisting mass.

A hand came down on my shoulder. "Are you okay, hun?"

I couldn't tell who the voice belonged to. Then I connected the outstretched arm to Marley. She looked at me with a crease of concern between her eyebrows.

"I think I need to sit down for a moment," I said.

"Sounds like a good idea."

I pushed a path out of the dancefloor and made for the empty booth.

Whew.

I collapsed onto the couch, resting my head in my hands. After a few deep breaths to calm myself, I pulled my phone out of my bag and pretended to occupy myself with it. That way, no one would interrupt my solitude.

Or so I thought.

Out of the corner of my eye, I detected someone moving towards me. I lifted my head and saw him. The man who had been staring at me earlier. Was he the one who grabbed me? Before I could register what I was doing, I was on my feet, dashing to the restrooms. I wouldn't put it past that weirdo to follow me, so I shut myself inside and locked the door. I sat down on the closed toilet lid, head spinning.

How did I end up here, hiding in a bathroom while everyone else was out having fun? I always knew socialising with Nicole's friends was going to be awkward, but I never imagined it would be *this* awkward.

I spent a long time in the bathroom before I emerged. Part of me expected to see the creep waiting for me as soon as I opened the door, but he was nowhere to be seen. Thank God.

I marched up to the bar in desperate need of something to dilute the alcohol inside me. "Can I get a glass of water, please?"

"Sure thing." The bartender bent down and retrieved a glass.

I looked around, trying to spot Nicole and her friends, but I couldn't see them anywhere. I figured they were somewhere within the crowd on the dancefloor.

Once I had downed the water, I dove back into the throng, trying to find them.

What the hell? Where is everyone?

I went back out to the courtyard. It was empty. Deep puddles covered the ground. It must have poured with rain while we were inside.

Could they have left without me? Surely not.

I looked around the bar again, but I still couldn't find them. Not knowing what else to do, I approached the bartender. "Excuse me. The group of women I came with—did they leave? I was in the bathroom, and I've lost them."

He grimaced. "I'm afraid I saw them leave."

"How long ago was that?"

"Just a few minutes ago."

I frowned. "Right. Thank you."

The night was still young. They must have gone to another bar or club. *Without me.*

I raced outside, hoping I'd be able to see them somewhere down the street. But no, no sign of them. They could have gone to any of the numerous bars or clubs nearby. There were too many to search. I went back inside with my head hung low.

How could they leave me behind? It was a large group, but still. All eleven of them forgot about me. Even Stacy, who had seemed so friendly, and Marley, who spoke to me not that long before I hid in the bathroom. I tried to convince myself it was an honest mistake, but in the back of my mind, I wondered if Nicole just didn't care. She had barely said a word to me all evening. Maybe she wanted to lose me on purpose.

I shook the idea out of my head.

That wasn't the Nicole I knew. Any moment now, she'd realise what she'd done and be mortified. In the meantime, there was still one thing I could do.

I returned to the bathroom to escape the blaring music. With quiet restored, I pulled out my phone to make a call. Nicole might not answer, but it was worth a shot. Standing in front of the mirror, I pressed my phone to my ear. She picked up much quicker than I expected.

But the voice that answered wasn't Nicole's.

Chapter Twenty-Three

"Amelia?"

A man's voice. Deep, silky, British.

My heart jumped into my throat. "N-Neil!"

How had I called him instead of Nicole? Were they next to each other in my contacts?

I must be very drunk indeed.

"Is everything okay?" he asked, a slight hitch in his voice.

"I've called you by mistake. I'm trying to reach my friend, Nicole. Ugh. Everything's gone wrong. Nicole's gone. Someone groped me. That creepy guy's still out there. Sorry for disturbing you. Were you asleep?"

"Someone… *Christ.*"

"He's out there, and I'm all alone. Nicole went somewhere without me."

I knew I wasn't making much sense, but it was difficult just to string a coherent sentence together.

"Are you drunk? You sound drunk. Is that music? Where are you?"

"I *am* drunk. *So* drunk."

"Where are you?"

"A bar."

"Which bar?"

Wow. He was being awfully insistent. "Why do you want to know that?"

"I'm going to pick you up and take you home. Which bar are you at?"

Take me… home?

I couldn't quite wrap my head around his offer, but he sounded concerned, so I relented. "The Society Bar."

"I'm going to come and get you, okay? Just hold tight. Don't leave the bar. Do you understand? Amelia?"

"I understand."

"And stay away from that man."

"Okay."

"Good. Wait for me there."

He hung up.

Oh my gosh. Of everyone I could have accidentally called, why did it have to be him? Now, my boss was going to pick me up, drunk, from a bar. I'd never be able to live this down.

After fixing myself up in the mirror, I stumbled out of the bathroom. That's when I ran straight into *him*.

The creep, loitering outside the bathrooms.

He reeked of cigarettes and alcohol, and he stared at me, unblinking, with bloodshot eyes. "Are you here alone?" he asked.

My skin crawled.

Do not engage.

I ignored him and walked straight to the exit. He followed. I approached the security guard standing by the door—a tall, beefy man dressed all in black. "Excuse me, that man is bothering me." I pointed to the creep.

The security guard shot him a significant look, and he backed down, pretending to look innocent.

I need to get out of this place.

The music was giving me a headache. I was hot and bothered and needed fresh air. Neil had told me not to leave the bar, but I was just going outside. Besides, if I waited outside, I'd be able to spot him as soon as he arrived.

The street was dark and frigid. Puddles rippled under the moonlight. A group of young people mooched about, smoking and talking between themselves.

Neil better get here soon.

While I waited, I tried calling Nicole again. I wanted to tell her I was going home, so she wouldn't come looking for me if she realised I was missing. This time, I concentrated extra hard through my brain fog to make sure I called her and not Neil or anyone else. Several rings went by. She didn't pick up. *Figures.* I composed a text message instead. After many attempts to write something legible, I pressed send.

> I'm going home now. Thanks for everything.

It had a sense of finality to it. She would realise what had happened and feel regretful. Mission accomplished.

"Milly?" came a voice.

I shuddered in reaction before I could make the mental connection of who the voice belonged to. I looked up from my phone and faced the speaker.

Leon.

He wore black skinny jeans and a brown cord jacket over a faded band t-shirt. Another man, dressed in a similar ensemble plus a slouchy beanie on his head, accompanied him, watching on with vague interest.

"What are you doing here? Who are you with?" Leon asked in a tone I couldn't place as either friendly or accusatory.

I was paralysed, too shocked by the confrontation to know what else to do except tell him the truth. "I was at a hen's. Just waiting for my ride home."

"Going home already? It's still early."

I shrugged.

"Why don't you come with me? We can go somewhere."

"No, thanks."

"Come on."

"I'm getting picked up. My ride will be here any minute."

"Don't be such a bore. Just come with me."

"No."

"Uptight bitch."

The other man snickered.

This seemed to spur Leon on, and he continued. "You think you're better than me, don't you? I know you blocked me. That's why you haven't responded to any of my messages."

I said nothing. I looked over to where the security guard stood in the entrance, but he wasn't there. Before I could make a move to go back inside, Leon grabbed my arm and yanked me towards him and his friend.

"Leave me alone!" I shrieked.

"Shut your mouth."

A third voice entered the fray, calm and measured, but laced with an undertone of fury. "Get your hands off her."

Leon froze, eyes wide. He released his grip. "Whoa. Okay, dude. Chill out. I wasn't gonna do anything."

"Neil!" I gasped.

I had never been so relieved to see him. He came to my side and placed a possessive hand on my shoulder.

Leon gaped. "You're *with* that guy?"

I nodded. I wasn't about to clarify the specifics of my relationship with Neil.

Leon's friend nudged him. "Let's go."

Leon gritted his teeth, his nostrils flaring as he examined Neil from head to toe. One more nudge, and he backed off and skulked away with his friend.

I turned to Neil as a whimper of relief escaped my lungs. I could have hugged him. *Hugged* my damn boss. He dropped his hand from my shoulder. "Let's get you home," he said, all the scary intensity drained from his voice and replaced by a softness that made me turn to mush.

Facing him now, I realised this was the first time I had seen him outside of work. He was wearing casual clothing—jeans and a sweater. He looked much younger without the suit. Maybe I had been wrong about his age? He could be in his late thirties, not early forties. His hair was a bit mussed, and his salt-and-pepper stubble made a comeback appearance. It could have been the alcohol blurring my perception, but I thought he looked kinda good. *Attractive* even.

No. It definitely had to be the alcohol.

What am I thinking?

"My car's parked further down," Neil said.

"You didn't have to do this," I mumbled.

"Yes, I did. I shudder to think what could have happened if I hadn't intervened."

I looked down at the pavement, feeling my cheeks burn. "Thank you. For saving me."

"Was that the creepy guy?"

"No. It was someone else."

He winced. "Two predators in one night? Ugh. I'm not naïve enough to say I'm surprised. I'm just glad I got here in time."

It began to spit with rain as we walked along the footpath, passing shops and restaurants and bars. Occasionally, our arms bumped. Even through the haze of drunkenness, I felt hyper-aware of him beside me. To anyone who saw us, we probably looked like a couple rather than boss and employee. That was a strange thought.

The headlights of an approaching bus cut through the fine drizzle. In a swift and precise movement, Neil grabbed me and pulled me back from the side of the road. I landed against his chest, hard and warm. I was stunned, frozen in his embrace. What just happened? Why was he holding me? I couldn't comprehend what was going on.

Then I heard the crash of water and felt it slap against my side. A mini tidal wave descended upon the footpath, spraying everything in its wake as the bus roared through a flooded section of road.

Neil eased his hold on me before fully letting me go. I stepped back from him, head reeling.

"Are you okay?" he asked.

I touched the damp patch on my jacket. "I got a little wet, but you saved me from the worst of it. Good thing you noticed that was about to happen."

"Stay back from the road. It could happen again if you're not careful."

I took his advice to heart, even as I struggled to walk in a straight line. My chest pounded, and my legs felt like jelly. Neil had swept me off my feet. I kept replaying the moment in my head, mesmerised. It was like a scene from a movie.

"Here we are," Neil said.

His car was a white Tesla. He opened the front passenger door for me. I slid into the leather interior. The heater was already on, but despite the warmth of the car, I couldn't get comfortable. I felt the cold, dirty water seep through my jacket to the lower layer. My teeth chattered. Deciding it would be preferable to take off the jacket rather than marinate in its dampness, I removed it, revealing the delicate white top I wore underneath. Goosebumps spread over my exposed arms.

Neil watched me from the driver's seat. "You're freezing."

"I'm fine," I lied, my voice jittery.

Neil's seatbelt clicked as he ejected it. He reached down to the hem of his sweater and pulled it off over his head, flashing a small band of taut skin below his shirt as he did so. Startled by the peek of flesh, I averted my gaze.

"Here." He held out his sweater.

I stared at it as if he were offering me something sacred and off-limits.

"Take it," he urged.

I accepted the sweater and pulled it on. The fabric was soft, warm, and lightweight, and it smelled just like him—dark florals and a hint of black pepper. Neil wasn't a big man by any means, but it was still baggy on my small frame. The sleeves extended to my fingertips. I rolled them up to my wrists. "Thanks," I said.

Neil stared at me as if he had forgotten everything else in the world. I looked back at him.

"It suits you," he murmured.

As soon as the words emerged from his mouth, he tore his gaze from me. Redness crept up his neck and tinged the tips of his ears. He cleared his throat and returned his attention to the task at hand: driving me home. He put his seatbelt back on and started the car.

What was that all about? Did he just flirt with me? No. I must be mistaken. There's no way he'd do something like that. Would he?

I put the thought out of my mind. I was drunk. My thoughts were scrambled and unreliable.

"What's your address?" Neil asked.

I told him my street name and number. He typed it into the dashboard, then off we went.

"Who was that guy?" Neil asked as he drove. "Did you know him?"

"His name's Leon. I went on a date with him once. He turned out to be a major arsehole."

Neil clenched his jaw. "Stay away from men like him."

"Don't worry. I will."

"Good."

"I don't usually spend my Saturday nights like this. It was my friend Nicole's hen party. Somehow, we got separated—"

"I don't care how you spend your Saturday nights, as long as you turn up and do your work on Monday."

"And as long as I stay away from men like Leon."

"Exactly."

We spent the rest of the drive in silence. Neil pulled over outside my building.

"Thank you so much," I said.

I moved to grasp the car door handle, but there wasn't one.

Neil noticed me struggle and leaned across to open the door. Our bodies were close. I could feel the heat emitting from him. My heart raced. I was so focused on his position, how close he was, that I didn't see how he opened the door, but I felt the cold breeze from outside rush into the car.

"It's not a handle, it's a button," he said, pulling back to his seat.

"I'll know for next time."

I cringed as soon as I said it. Why would there be a next time?

I got out of the car, but I landed on my feet funny and stumbled, feeling woozy.

Neil got out and came to my side. He put his hand on my side to steady me. "Are you okay? You're not going to throw up, are you?"

I shook my head. "Don't worry. I have a stomach of steel."

"Let me walk you to your apartment. I want to make sure you get inside."

"I'm not *that* incapacitated. I can make it to my apartment."

Neil didn't push the matter, but I could tell he was concerned and wanted to help me. I decided it wouldn't hurt to let him walk me up. He wasn't going to take advantage of me. If he were that kind of guy, he would have done so already with the ample opportunities he had at work. Also, I trusted him. "Okay. Walk me up."

By the slackening of his stance, Neil seemed pleased and relieved.

We walked up to the building door. While I fumbled trying to find my access card in my bag, Neil pushed the door open. "It's unlocked," he said with a frown. "That's poor security."

"Yeah. There's a problem with the door. If someone doesn't close it properly, it doesn't lock."

"That needs to get fixed."

"Plenty of residents have complained, but the body corp still hasn't done anything about it."

Neil glanced around as if measuring up the other security features of the building entrance. He looked displeased.

"Packages get stolen pretty often, and sometimes, homeless people get into the building at night," I said.

"Christ," Neil muttered.

He concluded his survey and accompanied me inside. On the two occasions we encountered male residents on the way up, he stood close by my side, aiming a withering glare in their direction. I felt like he was my personal bodyguard.

"This is my place," I said when we arrived outside my door.

I tried to insert the key in the lock, but couldn't get it to go in.

"Allow me," Neil said. He removed the key from my grasp and took over. But it didn't work for him either. "This isn't the right key," he said, frowning.

That's when I realised my mistake. This wasn't my apartment, it was my neighbour's.

"Oops." I walked over to the next door. "This is my place."

Neil sighed. "And you said you could make it to your apartment."

"I know, I know."

This time, the key slid in without resistance.

"Good night, Amelia," Neil said, stepping back and making his lack of nefarious intentions clear.

"Thank you, Neil. For everything. I feel bad for ruining your evening."

"You didn't."

"You're actually a very sweet man, you know that?"

"Enough," he grumbled.

I didn't know what came over me. It was like I was possessed. Before I could stop myself, I closed the gap between us and flung my arms around him.

Chapter Twenty-Four

I woke up the next morning with a dull headache and a fuzzy memory of a strange dream. In the dream, Neil had walked me up to my apartment, and when we reached my door, I had hugged him.

I had *hugged* my boss.

No. I buried my face in my pillow. *No, no, no. I must be confused. Why would I have a romantic dream about Neil? That's crazy. Maybe I'm still drunk.*

I turned onto my cheek with a sigh. My half-open eyes fell upon a sweater sprawled in the middle of the floor. A man's sweater.

Neil's sweater.

It wasn't a dream. I did see Neil last night. He rescued me from Leon and pulled me out of the way of getting splashed. He lent me his sweater, drove me home, and walked me to my apartment.

And I hugged him.

I threw my arms around him like a madwoman and clung to him. Neil's reaction was to peel me off, tell me to get some rest, then hurry away before I could do any further damage. The correct response.

I groaned. What did Neil think of me now? Getting drunk, calling him from a bar, hugging him, telling him he's *sweet*… I wouldn't blame him if he fired me for inappropriate behaviour.

My head throbbed, and my throat was dry. I needed a glass of water. I dragged myself out of bed, pulled on a dressing gown, shoved my feet into a pair of slippers, and shuffled to the kitchen. The water rushed from the tap into my glass. I gulped it down. More details from the previous night came back to me. Nicole forgetting my name, ignoring me all night, and abandoning me at the bar. I wondered if she had replied to the text message I sent her. Maybe she had realised her mistake and apologised. I grabbed my phone off the bedside table and checked my messages. One new text. Not from Nicole—from Gwen, Nicole's sister.

> Hope you all had a wonderful night. Total each person owes: $243.

I bristled. That amount had to include activities or food and drinks consumed without me. *Whatever.* I didn't have the energy to cause a fuss.

Meanwhile, no word from Nicole. Not even a missed call. My heart sank.

Our friendship is over.

It was over a long time ago. She only kept in touch with me because of Hannah. She had invited me to her wedding out of pity, not friendship. And the hen party… God! I was such an idiot. She felt obligated to invite me after Gemma ran her mouth. That was obvious to me now.

I punched my pillow, not knowing whether to feel angry, sad, or both. I took a deep breath and tried to calm myself down.

I'll get over this.

My eyes fell upon Neil's sweater again. I had been careless, tossing it on the floor like it was nothing. I'd never treat my clothes that way, and it was probably more expensive than anything I owned. I got up and pulled the sweater off the floor. The fabric was light and soft. Without thinking about what I was doing, I lifted the sweater to my face, buried my nose in it, and inhaled. It smelled like a mixture of Neil's dark scent, my perfume, and a faint mustiness. I realised it must have got damp from when I wore it last night. It needed to be washed. Returning it to Neil clean and fresh was the least I could do.

I marched to the washing machine and turned the settings dial. A cold wash on the delicate cycle had never failed me before. I put a little detergent in the compartment and placed the sweater in the steel drum, closed the door, and turned it on.

* * *

As soon as I took Neil's sweater out of the washing machine, I knew I had made a huge mistake.

So much for returning his sweater in perfect condition. Instead, I'd be bringing it back shrunk and strewn out of shape.

Crap.

What had gone wrong? I inspected the settings on the washing machine. The answer became clear. It wasn't set to delicate; it was one notch over on heavy duty. I winced.

I knew little about menswear, but the brand name on the label was Italian and sounded expensive. I should never have even attempted to wash the sweater. Now I had ruined it. Argh!

* * *

The thought of facing Neil on Monday filled me with trepidation. Having to confess to ruining his expensive sweater was daunting enough, but the fear he might mention the hug made me even more nervous.

The hug.

I cringed. What on earth was I thinking? Being drunk was no excuse for throwing myself at him like that. I could only imagine what Neil must think of me now. I had visions of him calling me to his office and giving me a stern talking to. Could he fire me over a hug? Was it sexual harassment? If it was the other way around, it certainly would be.

On my commute to work, I played with the idea of pretending I had no memory of the hug. It would be the perfect solution—if I pulled it off. But something told me I wouldn't be able to fool Neil. He was too perceptive. He'd see right through my act. *No.* I'd just have to hope he wouldn't bring it up.

I clung to this hope as I arrived at work and made my way up to the twentieth floor. I clutched a plastic bag containing the sweater in my clammy hand as I approached Neil's office. The door was open a crack, and I took that as a green light to enter without knocking.

What I saw made me freeze in shock.

Neil stood by his desk, shirtless, his back to me. I couldn't help but stare at his physique. He was lean, and he had wide, pronounced shoulder blades. My gaze followed the trail of his spine down to where it disappeared below his belt. I swallowed hard.

He must have heard me. He turned around as he pulled on a shirt. Now I could see his front between the undone buttons. His long, toned torso, a scattering of dark hair on his chest and stomach.

Holy moly.

I had always been vaguely aware that Neil was in good shape, but I never imagined just how gorgeous he was.

He quickly pulled his gaping shirt closed. "Amelia," he snapped.

I jolted from my trance with a wince. "Sorry! I only just came in." I gestured behind me. "The door was open."

"I thought I closed it. There was a stain on my shirt," he angled himself away from me, hastily doing up his buttons, "so I had to change. Do you need something?"

"I'll just—"

Come back later.

Before I could finish what I was saying, Neil had fully dressed and turned to face me. His eyes flicked to the plastic bag in my hands, and I remembered why I had gone into his office in the first place. "Neil, I..." *Okay. Here goes.* I pulled out the sweater, grimacing. "I ruined it. I'm sorry."

His eyes narrowed. "You washed it?"

"Yeah."

He gave a small, exasperated sigh, his shoulders drooping. "I appreciate what you tried to do, but it was unnecessary. And now it's ruined."

"I can replace it."

"No. You can't. It would cost you far too much."

"Then what should I do?"

He shrugged. "I don't know. Keep it. Looks like it would be small enough to fit you now."

I flashed back to his words the other night in his car. The way he looked at me.

"It suits you."

My cheeks burst into a fierce blaze. Meanwhile, Neil was suddenly unable to meet my eyes. An awkward silence weighed down on us.

I didn't intend to bring up Saturday night, but it was the only way I could think to change the subject. "About the other night— I'm sorry for getting you involved in my personal issues outside of work."

Neil shook his head. "I'm glad you called me."

"I don't normally get drunk like that."

"It happens."

"Even to you?"

He scoffed. "No. I don't drink."

"Oh, that's right. Respectable."

Just like everything else about you.

He started putting on his tie. "I hope you didn't feel too unwell yesterday."

"Just a little. I'm okay now, though."

"Good." He lifted his chin and knotted the tie.

I noticed his other shirt hanging over the back of his chair.

"Do you want me to take your shirt to the dry cleaner?" I asked.

He shook his head. "I'll get someone else to do it. You're coming with me to the nine o'clock meeting."

"I am? I wasn't on the invite."

"I want you involved because the meeting will cover how I aim to raise staff morale. Your perspective will be valuable to management."

"I'd love to help."

"And from now on, I want you to attend every meeting with me unless it falls outside your normal hours or I specify otherwise."

His request caught me off guard. I had expected him to make me keep my distance after what I did. Instead, he was inviting me to work closer with him—closer than ever before. It didn't make sense.

Or did it?

"Okay. Every meeting. Got it."

Chapter Twenty-Five

The cats seemed to have learned by now that I was the bringer of food. As soon as I stepped into the apartment, they padded towards me, meowing eagerly. I filled their bowls with biscuits and replenished their water. They devoured their dinner like it was a race. Bowey was first to the finish line. He licked his bowl clean, then claimed his chosen prize—Chichi's food. He nudged his way to his reward. Chichi snarled in response, but he persisted. Chichi raised her paw and unsheathed her claws, preparing to take a swipe.

"Hey! Quit it, you two." I pried the two cats apart.

I scooped some extra biscuits into Bowey's bowl and shook it to get his attention. He lifted his head and stared at the bowl, whiskers twitching.

"Come on." I shook it again.

He pounced on the bowl and dug in with gusto.

"Good boy. Eat up."

As Bowey enjoyed his extra biscuits, Chichi kept a watchful eye on him, her ears flattened against her head. I knelt down and stroked her back, reassuring her. She eventually relaxed and resumed eating her dinner at her own steady pace.

I glanced around the apartment, assessing what needed to be done. It was relatively clean as per usual, just some cat hair that needed to be vacuumed up and a few crumbs on the kitchen counter. I waited for Bowey and Chichi to finish their dinner before I turned the vacuum cleaner on, sending them scurrying.

As I vacuumed, my thoughts drifted to Cat Dad. Our interactions had been minimal as of late. The last message he sent was to tell me the new door code. He seemed to change it frequently—a sign of his caution and attention to security. I supposed he had to be careful since he was sharing it with me. Even though I had to go through a background check to list myself on the app, letting a stranger in your house still had risks.

Once I had finished cleaning the living areas and kitchen, I moved on to the bedroom. The room was tidy apart from the crumpled duvet on the bed. I smoothed it out.

This is where Cat Dad sleeps…

I caught myself wondering what he looked like again. Then I had a flash of another thought: Neil's toned back and chest. I tried to shake it out of my head, annoyed with myself.

Neil was invading my thoughts more often than I cared to admit. It had to stop. He was my boss, for goodness' sake. He wasn't my type, and his coarse personality still rubbed me the wrong way more than half the time. I had no business thinking about his intense eyes, the grey whiskers in his stubble, the way he ran his tongue over the back of his teeth, his seductive voice…

Stop!

I banished thoughts of Neil for the rest of the cleaning session, then I gathered my belongings and prepared to leave. Just as I was about to open the door, I felt something soft and furry brush past my legs. It was Bowey. He rubbed his face on me, purring.

I stopped what I was doing to give him some attention. "Aren't you adorable?"

He leaned into my touch and emitted a low rumble of pleasure as I scratched behind his ears.

"Okay, okay. I'll stay a little longer."

I sat on the couch, and he jumped on my lap and settled there, curled into a ball. I lay my head back and relaxed.

At some point I must have dozed off, because I suddenly snapped to attention, feeling disorientated without a sense of how much time had passed. Bowey was still on my lap. I grabbed my phone and checked the time. It was forty minutes past seven. I had overstayed my time slot. Cat Dad could be back any minute. I pushed the vibrating mound of fluff off my lap. He gave a sharp yowl in response, then landed on all fours. He scarpered off, paws tapping on the floor. The cat flap slammed behind him as he escaped onto the patio.

I sprang from the couch, flung my bag over my shoulder, flicked off the light switch, then exited the apartment.

When the lift door opened, I stepped forwards without looking and almost collided with an emerging occupant. As I lifted my head to apologise, my eyes landed on a good-looking man, maybe four or five years older than me. He had a head of ruffled blonde hair and a square-jawed face. Blue eyes. He wore a shirt and suit jacket with blue jeans.

"Sorry," I said.

"It's all right," he replied with a grin, before moving on.

I scrunched my face in thought.

Wait… could it be?

The mystery man turned the corner. I didn't enter the lift. I tiptoed back down the corridor, stopping short of the corner, then peeked my head around to spy on him. He approached Cat Dad's door. My heart raced.

It's him! It's Cat Dad! It must be.

Just then, the door behind me opened, causing me to lose sight of him in a moment of panic. A woman emerged. She shot me a disapproving look, as if to say, "What are you doing here?"

I quit spying and tried to act natural, joining her by the lift. She pressed the button.

The gravity of what had just occurred hit me on the way down. I had made the ultimate discovery. Cat Dad was young and good-looking. Cat Dad lived up to my fantasies and then some. He was cute in his messages and cute in real life. I was smitten.

But what happens next?

I exited the building. Part of me wanted to stop and text Cat Dad, ask him, "Was it you I just bumped into by the lift?" But I controlled my urge. Now wasn't the time. I needed to think about whether I wanted to reveal myself to him or not. One wrong move, and I could ruin my lucrative side hustle.

A cold breeze swept off the harbour, making me shiver. I passed the familiar row of busy restaurants, envying all the happy families, groups of friends, and couples I saw through the windows.

Once I move overseas, that's when I'll sort my life out. I'll reunite with old friends and make new friends. I'll find a partner…

Someone in the restaurant caught my eye. I stopped in my tracks and did a double take.

It was Neil.

He was dining with a woman. At first glimpse, I thought it might be Christine, but when I focused, I realised the woman was younger and more glamorous. She had long brown hair, dimples, and a sweet smile. Red lipstick accentuated her lips, and her dangly earrings sparkled in the light. They leaned in towards each other across the table with effortless intimacy.

Was she his girlfriend?

Ruby?

My insides knotted, a lump rising in my throat.

Neil started to turn his head my way. I tore my eyes from him and strode onwards without looking back.

So what if Neil has a girlfriend? It's fine. It doesn't bother me. I don't even like him, anyway.

* * *

Back at home, travel blogs and articles about Europe served as a welcome distraction from thoughts of Cat Dad, Neil, and the mystery woman. I sat in pyjamas, laptop perched on my lap, as I scrolled through images of cobblestone streets, quaint cafes, and historical landmarks, transporting me far from the confines of my tiny apartment.

I needed this. How could I keep going with the way things were while everyone I cared about was living their dreams on the other side of the world? I had to leave and spread my wings.

One thing led to another, and I found myself on an airline website. Why wait? Thanks to my new job, I could afford to book my ticket now, and prices would only increase the longer I left it. The thought of having everything locked in, of knowing that my dream was attainable, was too tempting to resist.

I entered a travel date and destination. A list of flights populated the search results. I scanned the options, hunting for one which struck a balance between price, timing, and number of stopovers. A one-way ticket via Dubai ticked all the boxes.

As I hesitated over the "book now" button, my stomach tightened. Did I really want to do this? Why did I suddenly feel so anxious about pulling the trigger?

I pulled myself together. There was no reason to put it off. I clicked through and filled in the booking form, checking each field twice before moving on to the payment screen. My heart raced as I entered my credit card details. All I had left to do was click "confirm payment," then it would be official.

I took a deep breath, my cursor hovering over the button.

Okay. Let's do this.

My hand trembled on the mouse. The ticket was non-refundable. Once I pressed the button, there was no going back.

I held my breath and clicked.

The cursor turned into a spinning wheel as the confirmation page loaded.

The success screen congratulated me on my booking and told me to check my emails to download my ticket.

My flight was booked. I was going to London in January—five

months from now. From there, the rest of Europe would be within reach.

I leaned back against the couch, interlacing my fingers behind my head. Good things were around the corner. I just had to stick it out as Neil's secretary for the rest of the year, then I'd be on my way to a new life. Nothing could stop me now.

Chapter Twenty-Six

Oh my God. What have I done?

I tumbled out of bed the next morning, recalling the impulsive decision I'd made the night before. Why did I let FOMO get the better of me? I should never have booked that flight to London on a whim. I hadn't done enough research. I hadn't even sorted out a working visa, and I'd just thrown a huge chunk of my savings at a non-refundable ticket.

Argh!

Oh well. The damage was done. The ticket was booked, and there was no turning back. I had to make it work, somehow.

I went through my usual morning routine on autopilot. Shower, coffee, toast, makeup. The whole time, my mind buzzed with anxieties. Would I be able to pay off my student loan in time? Could I get a job in London? What about a flat? Would Hannah let me flat with her? How would I divide my time between work and travel?

Stop it. You'll figure it out.

I stepped outside the building, letting the door swing shut behind me. It made a satisfying clunk as it closed.

Wait a second.

That sound was unfamiliar. I turned back and pulled the handle. The door wouldn't budge. It was locked.

Has it been fixed?

I opened the door with my key card and tried it once more, in case it was a fluke. The door swung shut on its own and locked securely.

There was no other explanation. The door had been repaired. Hooray! No more worrying about packages getting stolen or strangers wandering into the building.

But when had it happened? It wasn't like this yesterday, and I hadn't noticed any work being done.

I shrugged. No time to dwell on the mysteries of apartment maintenance. I had a job to get to.

* * *

As I prepared Neil's morning coffee, I wondered whether it would be awkward to mention that I had seen him last night. Just casually. Maybe he'd tell me who that woman was. I was curious about her. That's all.

The smell of the black coffee wafted from the mug, waking my senses as I walked to Neil's office. Neil didn't seem to register my approach. He sat at his desk, working on his computer, the cuffs of his shirt falling back to reveal a glimpse of his strong forearms. Lines of concentration creased his forehead.

The coffee cup made a thunk as I set it in front of him. I cleared my throat.

I'm going to do it. I'm going to say something about last night.

Neil stopped typing and looked at me. The words that were on the tip of my tongue dried up.

"What?" Neil asked.

I couldn't do it. I was too embarrassed to admit I had seen him.

Neil scrutinised me, unblinking. I had to say *something.* "The door of my apartment building has been fixed," I blurted.

"Yes."

"*Yes?*"

"I know."

It took me a second to process what his odd reaction meant. "Are you telling me you're behind it? You got someone to fix it?"

"I don't like you living in a place with such a lax definition of security."

"Why are you so concerned about my security?"

"Because you're associated with me."

"And being associated with you puts me at risk, does it?"

Neil ground his teeth, the throbbing vein on his forehead a telltale sign I was annoying him. "Just do your job and stop asking questions."

"But—"

He glowered at me.

Wow. He was in a foul mood today.

"Right," I mumbled.

I returned to my desk, seething.

Why do I even care who that woman was? I don't like Neil. She can have him. It's fine by me. Once I leave the country, Neil will be a distant memory.

Despite what I told myself, bitterness gnawed at me like a persistent ache. I turned my attention to work to take my mind off it.

We didn't have any meetings that morning, but after a couple of hours in my chair, I needed to get up and stretch, so I walked to reception to chat with James.

"Ah. Just the person I needed to see," James said.

"What's up?"

He placed a nondescript white package on the desk. "Were you expecting a package? This got delivered here, but I can't read the label. It looks like it ends with an S, don't ya think? It could be the end of Cross."

I studied the label, trying to decipher it. Some kind of inky smudge had blotted out most of the name. But James was right. The last letter was partially visible, and it resembled an S.

"I wasn't expecting anything. Does anyone else's name end in S on this floor?"

"Nope. Only you."

"Hmm. Maybe if no one else claims it today, I'll take it."

"Good plan."

I racked my brain, trying to recall whether anyone might send me something at work, but I couldn't think of anything. Maybe it wasn't an S. Maybe it was for someone else.

It didn't strike me until a couple of hours later what the package contained, and by then, I prayed it wasn't too late.

Chapter Twenty-Seven

I called James in the middle of my lunch break in a panic. This couldn't wait until I got back to the office. Claiming the package before anyone else did was my top priority.

I chewed a nail as I waited for James to pick up.

After what felt like an eternity, he answered. "Hello?"

"James, it's me, Milly. Do you still have that package?"

"I do indeed."

I slumped in relief. "Thank God. I'm pretty sure that it's actually for me, so make sure no one else takes it, okay?"

"You got it."

"Great. Thank you. I'm on my way back now, so I'll see you soon."

"Okay. See you."

I ended the call.

Whew. That takes care of that.

Setting up an automatic redirect to have my deliveries sent to work instead of home had seemed like a good idea at the time. But no more. If my suspicion was correct, then this was something I didn't want to end up in the wrong hands.

Even with James's reassurance, I still felt the need to race back to the office—just in case. I battled the crowds of office workers, cruise ship tourists, and university students, making my way from downtown to Hobson Street.

The lobby was busy with employees coming and going from the building. As soon as the lift door opened onto the twentieth floor, I marched to James's desk.

It was vacant.

James was nowhere to be seen, and neither was the package.

I tried to calm myself down. The package was safe, according to James. He had probably just gone to the bathroom or something. He'd be back in a minute. I waited for him.

Sure enough, a few minutes later, I heard footsteps, then I saw James's friendly face as he emerged from around the corner. "There you are!"

"Looking for your package? I took it to your office."

I let out a little yelp and hightailed it to my office. When I entered, I looked around in a flurry. Where did he put it? It wasn't on my desk or the spare desk. It wasn't on the table by the printer, or on top of the cabinet. I couldn't see it anywhere.

Then I took a cursory glance towards Neil's office.

No. Please, no.

His door was open. I peeked inside, and I saw the worst possible scenario unfolding before me.

Neil stood there, holding what looked suspiciously like my package in his hands.

It was already half opened... no, three quarters opened. He was pulling out the gift bag contained within the outer packaging.

"Neil," I stammered, rushing forward with my hand outreached. "Don't open it. That's mine!"

But it was too late. He had already opened it.

What happened next played out in slow motion.

Startled by my sudden entrance, Neil fumbled and dropped the gift bag. Its contents scattered on the floor.

Oh dear lord.

It was buzzing. *Vibrating.* Loud and intense.

A bright pink bullet vibrator, surrounded by other naughty items, had turned itself on with the impact of the fall.

"Oh my gosh." I dove to pick it up.

Neil started to bend over to help clear the floor as well, but then he appeared to think better of it and snapped upright, averting his gaze.

"It's a bachelorette gift," I explained, frantically trying to figure out how to turn the buzzing sex toy off. "It wasn't supposed to get delivered to work!"

Neil cleared his throat. "My apologies. There was no name on the parcel, and I'm expecting a delivery today. I shouldn't have opened it."

"Ugh! How do I turn this off?"

I finally found the off button, and I mashed it until the buzzing stopped. I shoved the vibrator back in the gift bag, then the rest of the items along with it—a scented candle, body oil, and some rudely shaped candy.

As I got back on my feet, I wiped my brow with the back of my hand. My face was red. I could feel it.

Neil chewed his lip, watching me with an expression which was half bewildered, half intrigued.

I backed away. "I'll just… get back to work."

"Yes," Neil said. "You do that."

* * *

I couldn't look Neil in the eyes for the rest of the day.

When I got home, I shoved all the goodie bag gifts into the top drawer of my bedside table and slammed it shut, too mortified to even look at them.

Why oh why did Nicole send this to me with no advance notice? I was shocked she even sent me anything after what happened at her party. One thing was for sure. I was never getting personal mail sent to work again—especially now that the apartment building door had been repaired.

I sent a thank-you message to Nicole. Then I lay on my bed, buried my face in my pillow, and let out a muffled groan of frustration.

How am I ever going to live this down?

I couldn't stop replaying the scene in my head. Neil opening the package, the vibrator shimmying on the floor, the look of utter discombobulation on Neil's face...

Agggh!

I released another wail into my pillow, followed by a round of punches until I ran out of energy, and the exasperation faded into reluctant acceptance. I turned onto my back, my lumpy old mattress squeaking beneath me.

It's no big deal. I'm an adult woman with sexual needs. Who cares if Neil saw the vibrator? Every woman has one.

Well, not *every* woman. I had never owned one until now.

I glanced at the top drawer of my bedside table, suddenly curious. My heart started to beat faster. Before I knew what I was doing, I opened the drawer. The pink vibrator lay among the compartments where I stored my jewellery and accessories. I picked up the device and felt it in my hands. It was lightweight, with a matte rubber surface. I turned it on. It buzzed powerfully against my palm. A wave of excitement came over me.

I wanted to use it. I had to use it. *Now.*

I scrambled to get out of my pants and flung myself back onto the bed. My heart pounded as I moved the vibrator up my inner thigh towards the throbbing ache between my legs...

A shrill sound rang out from elsewhere in the room, almost giving me a heart attack. *My work phone.* I rarely received calls outside of my office hours, so I figured it must be important.

The phone continued to ring as I struggled to turn off the obnoxiously loud vibrator. The off button did nothing. I pressed it harder and repeatedly with no result.

Ugh. Piece of junk.

The phone had rung so many times by now I was sure it was about to stop. I tossed the vibrator under my duvet to muffle the sound and took my phone as far away from the bed as my confined space allowed.

The caller displayed on the screen was Neil Kingston.

"Yes?" I answered, breathless.

"Sorry for calling you after hours."

His voice was smooth and deep. A treat to my ears, even at a time like this.

"It's no problem," I panted.

"Are you okay?"

"I was just… in the middle of something."

"Oh? You sound… Hmm. Never mind."

Could he tell? Did he know what I was just doing? *Oh my God.* Could he *hear* it?

I knew I was being irrational, but the slim possibility he might know weighed on my mind.

"What were you calling me about?" I asked, eager to change the subject.

"The meeting tomorrow at three—it has been moved to nine in the morning. I want you there, so don't be late. We need to leave at quarter to nine at the latest."

"Okay. I'll be there."

"All right. That's all I needed to say. I'll leave you to… *whatever* you were *doing*. Have a good evening."

It sounded like he had emphasised certain words just then, but it might have been my imagination.

"You too," I squeaked.

I couldn't end the call fast enough. I dove onto my bed, found the still-buzzing device under the covers, shoved it firmly between my thighs, and rode out the rest of my frustration with Neil's voice still ringing in my head.

Chapter Twenty-Eight

Number of days since last awkward interaction with Neil: Twelve.

It was a new record as far as I was concerned. Ever since the, *ahem*, package incident, we had somehow managed to coexist in a state of relative normalcy. We'd had meetings, discussions, even the occasional shared lift ride, all without a single blush-inducing moment. It was a miracle!

But as I watched Neil emerge from his office, preparing to head to a one-on-one meeting with the mayor of Auckland, I knew my streak was about to come to a crashing halt.

There, right in the centre of his usually impeccable suit, was a *gaping* wardrobe malfunction.

Oh no.

He was just steps away from the door, exuding his aura of confident authority.

My internal alarm bells chimed. I couldn't let Neil walk into his meeting like *that*. I had to say something. "Neil!"

He paused, one hand on the doorknob, and raised an eyebrow at me. "Yes?"

"Your..." I gestured towards his midsection, hoping he'd get the hint.

He frowned. "What?"

"It's... um..." Heat rose in my face.

His eyebrow inched higher. "Spit it out, Amelia. I have a meeting to get to."

I took a deep breath and blurted it out. "Your fly is undone!"

The words hung in the air between us. Neil's eyes widened for a split second before his face settled into a stoic mask. He glanced down, confirming my observation, then turned away from me and zipped himself up.

"Thank you," he said curtly. "I appreciate your... attentiveness." He winced slightly.

With that, he turned and strode out of the office, leaving me standing there with my heart pounding and my face burning.

"You're welcome," I mumbled to the empty room.

Number of days since last awkward interaction with Neil: Zero.

* * *

By lunch time, the embarrassment of the fly incident still hadn't worn off. I hoped getting outside might help to clear my mind, so I walked to Saint Patrick's Square to eat my lunch in the pretty surroundings of the cathedral.

The weather was crisp and clear. A water fountain trickled down the levels of a tiered garden. I settled on a bench along the perimeter of the manicured lawn. I had just taken one bite of my sandwich when my phone began to ring. I scrambled to retrieve it from my bag, wondering who it could be. I nearly choked on my mouthful when I saw the caller ID. Barry Douglas—my landlord. The last person I wanted to speak to on my lunch break. It was never good news when he called.

I braced myself. "Hello, Amelia speaking."

"Hi, it's Barry here." His gruff voice sounded even more brash than I remembered. "I'm calling about my property—the apartment in Newmarket."

"Yes?"

"The thing is, I have a relative I'd like to move in there as soon as possible."

My head spun. "Move in… to my apartment?"

"That's right."

Reality sank in and settled at the pit of my stomach. "Are you giving me my notice?"

"Two months. That's what I'm obligated to give you."

"You're kicking me out…"

"It's well within my rights as the owner. You've been a good tenant, and I'd be happy to offer you a reference."

I didn't know what to say. I was stuck on the fact he was kicking me out.

"To tell you the truth, it would be ideal if you could leave sooner," he said.

"You see, the thing is, I'll be leaving the country in a few months. It will be inconvenient to have to find another place —"

"Not my problem."

I huffed. "Fine. I'll have to see what I can arrange. Could you send me the notice in writing?"

"Will do."

"Thanks."

"Okay. Ta."

He hung up.

Oof.

I had two months to find somewhere else to live. That would cover me until the end of October. But then what? Could I get a rental without signing a one-year contract? Or would I have to get something short-term on a month-by-month basis?

My mind raced on my way back to work. I almost collided with Neil when I entered my office. He stood in the middle of the room with his back to me—but something was off about him. He turned to me. That's when I realised he wasn't Neil after all…

He was a stranger.

He cut a strikingly similar figure in his suit, but that's where the similarities ended. The eyes that stared at me were small, black, and twinkling. He had sallow, textured skin and slicked-back hair. His tongue darted over thin, parched lips. He looked older than Neil, but not by much.

"Excuse me. Can I help you?" I asked.

He grinned at me, revealing stained yellow teeth. "Well, well, well. You must be Amelia Cross."

How does he know who I am?

I forced myself to be polite, despite the creepy-crawly sensation under my skin. "Yes, I am. May I ask who you are?"

He offered his hand. "Daniel Ling."

I knew that name.

My mind emptied of everything else upon realising that the man who stood before me was none other than Neil's boss, the president of Zelthia Group. One of the richest and most powerful men in Asia.

Chapter Twenty-Nine

I shook Daniel's hand. With his snake-like features, I half expected his skin to feel scaly, but it was smooth. "Mr. Ling. It's an honour to meet you."

His beady eyes glinted. "And you. Neil's new right-hand woman—a very privileged position indeed."

His words seemed laced with hidden meaning, but all I could do was take them at face value. "Um, thank you."

I wondered why he was here. He was a long way from Singapore, and Neil's schedule said nothing about a visit from his boss. "Are you here to see Neil?" I asked.

"I am. Do you know when he'll be back?"

I was about to respond when I heard someone burst into the room from behind me.

"Speak of the devil," Daniel said, his thin lips quirking up.

Neil had entered the room. He was puffing, his face chalk white. His eyes darted from Daniel to me and back to Daniel again, a look of vexation and displeasure washing over him. "When did you get here?" Neil asked.

"That's how you greet me? It has been a few months. It's good to see you again." Daniel extended his hand to Neil.

Neil accepted it. They exchanged a firm handshake.

"To what do I owe the pleasure of this surprise visit?" Neil asked.

"I had business in Sydney, and I decided to make an extended stopover in Auckland on my way back."

"A last-minute decision?"

"You could say that."

"I would have appreciated some notice."

"You always make time to see me though, don't you? We have much to discuss."

Neil turned to me. "Cancel everything on my schedule for the rest of the day."

I nodded, feeling overwhelmed by the exchange playing out between the two powerful men. The tension in the room was palpable.

"Green tea?" Neil asked Daniel.

"You know me well."

"One green tea coming right up," I said. "Anything for you, Neil?"

"My usual. And for the tea—use the box in the top of the cupboard."

With that, Neil directed Daniel into his office and shut the door behind them, leaving me to ponder what had just occurred as I walked to the kitchen.

My impression was that Neil disliked Daniel, but Daniel seemed to take Neil's ire in good humour. There was no boss-and-employee dynamic as far as I could tell. To me, they resembled siblings who knew each other well, who had good times and bad times in their long history and who often got on each other's nerves.

In the kitchen, I looked for the box Neil told me about. Top of the cupboard—but which cupboard? There were several. I rummaged until I found an unopened box with Chinese writing on it at the back of the top cupboard. I pulled it out and examined the beautiful packaging. There was no English on it, but the leafy green imagery was enough to clue me in.

This must be what Neil meant.

I opened the box, then the packet within, and sure enough, the pungent, grassy aroma of green tea wafted out. *A special tea that Daniel Ling likes... Maybe Neil keeps a supply in stock for situations just like this.*

As the tea brewed, I went through Neil's appointments on my work phone, cancelling them one by one. Apologies and explanations could wait until I was back at my desk.

I placed the hot drinks, plus a jug of chilled water and two glasses, on a tray and carried them to Neil's office.

Neil and Daniel sat opposite each other on the couches. I caught a snatch of their conversation as I entered the room, my ears pricking at the word "Patterson" from Neil's mouth. They stopped talking in my presence. Feeling like an intruder, I placed the drinks on the coffee table between them, then retreated, shutting the door behind me.

They must have been talking about Alex Patterson. His name triggered the memory of the fall and the picture of the crime scene in Neil's file. I shivered.

Why are they talking about him?

I had an uneasy feeling, but I brushed it off.

At my desk, I sent apologetic notes to everyone affected by the cancelled appointments and rescheduled as much as I could. After that, with a lack of much else to do, I looked up information on Daniel Ling. The search results turned up a trove of pictures of him at extravagant events, as well as posed shots in business attire. A short biography said he was the son of the chairman of Zelthia and the heir to the business—one of the largest companies in the Asia-Pacific region. When his father passed away, he would take over as the new chairman, and since his father was terminally ill, that could be in a matter of weeks or months.

Next, I typed both Daniel Ling and Neil Kingston in. Only a few results popped up. A picture of Daniel and Neil looking suave at a glitzy party, and a news article from 2012 stating that Daniel was the head of finance at Zelthia, and Neil was second-in-command. Their ages were listed as thirty-four and thirty-one, respectively. That meant Neil would be forty or forty-one by now. I couldn't help but ponder our thirteen-year age difference.

I wonder if Neil would ever date someone as young as me?

I thought of the woman I saw him with. She looked a little younger than him, but definitely age-appropriate. *Hmm.*

Five o'clock passed, and the meeting in Neil's office was still going. I prepared to leave, not knowing how much longer they were going to take. With the news of having to vacate my apartment in two months, there was a lot to arrange, and I wanted to get onto it as soon as possible.

Just as I was about to walk out the door, Neil and Daniel emerged from Neil's office, chatting like two old buddies. I hung back to see Daniel off.

"Lovely to meet you, Amelia," Daniel said, taking my hand in both of his.

Neil watched on with a rigid posture and pursed lips.

"Nice to meet you too," I said.

"I hope our paths cross again soon. Maybe in Singapore."

Not knowing how to respond, I just nodded my head.

Neil practically tore Daniel away from me and ushered him towards the door. "I'll walk you down."

Daniel shook his head. "No need. I can see myself out."

"In that case, have a good evening and a comfortable flight home."

"I'm sure I will. The private jet usually offers a modicum of comfort."

"I'll see you at the annual meeting."

"Looking forward to it." Daniel took one step through the door, then paused. "Oh, and Neil, give my regards to my sister, won't you?"

Neil's eyes narrowed for a flicker of a second, then he composed himself. "As you wish."

Daniel's perpetual smug look intensified as he walked out. Neil kept a watchful eye on him until he disappeared down the corridor.

I wonder what that was all about?

I resumed getting ready to leave.

"Before you go, can I have a word?" Neil asked.

"Sure, go ahead," I replied.

He took a cursory glance down the empty corridor, then closed the door for good measure. I suddenly felt apprehensive. Whatever he had to say seemed serious. He leaned back against my desk with folded arms, then spoke in a lowered voice. "How long were you alone with Daniel?"

"Just for a minute. Why?"

"He didn't do anything… *untoward*, I hope."

"What? N-no. Of course not."

Neil clenched his jaw, his expression stony. "Good. If it happens again, call me straight away. I don't trust him around you."

"Why not?"

"He has self-control issues around attractive young women."

Attractive?! "I-I see."

"He's also just a nasty piece of work in general."

It seems I had underestimated Neil's animosity towards Zelthia's president. "But he's your boss…"

Neil looked me dead in the eyes. "Take it from me, Amelia, you don't become as rich and powerful as he is by playing nice. You have to get your hands dirty—and I know where his hands have been."

"Then are your hands dirty too?" I asked, a quaver in my voice.

He didn't miss a beat. "Yes. They are."

I wasn't expecting that. And by the tone of his voice, he wasn't messing around. I felt chilled to my core. I should never have let my guard down with him. He wasn't as sweet as I thought.

"One more thing," he said. "It would be in your best interest to forget anything you might have overheard us talking about."

Something told me it would be a bad idea to push back or ask questions. "Yes, Neil."

"Good. You may go now."

I left the office without a goodbye, shaken.

Chapter Thirty

A startling scene awaited me at work the next morning. The door to Neil's office was wide open, and it looked like a tornado had struck the room. Every piece of furniture had been moved and upturned. The light fittings had been taken down. The covers stripped from the couch cushions, the light shades off the lamps, and plants ripped from their pots. Even the dog stuffed animal had been torn open and the stuffing ripped out.

I looked around, bewildered. "What in the name of—"

Neil rose from behind his desk. His eyes drilled into me as he straightened, a scathing look on his face.

"What happened here?" I sidestepped scattered objects on the floor as I approached him. "Did your office get burgled or something?"

"No."

"Then what—"

"I was looking for something."

"Looking? You tore up your whole office!"

"I did what was required."

I scoffed. "How could this be required? If you lost something, why would it be inside a couch cushion or a light fitting?"

The vein on Neil's forehead throbbed. "I didn't *lose* something. Someone *hid* something in my office."

"Why would anyone do that?"

"I got thinking last night. Daniel said something yesterday that he couldn't have known unless he had insight into my private conversations. I began to suspect he may have had my office bugged."

I shook my head. "Bugged? That sounds like something out of a movie. Normal people don't just go around planting bugs and spying on each other."

"If you think that's abnormal, you know nothing of what Daniel Ling and his associates are capable of."

"All I know is what you told me about him." I crossed my arms. "So, did you find a bug, then?"

"I did."

Words escaped me. This was surreal.

Neil strode to the door.

"What are you going to do?" I asked, following him.

"I'll take care of it."

"I can help you clean up—"

"That won't be necessary."

Neil shut us out of his office and locked the door. He dropped the key into the inner pocket of his suit jacket.

Why did I get the feeling he was mad at me? He couldn't think I had something to do with this… could he?

He was just about to leave the room.

"Neil," I said.

He bristled as he turned to face me.

"Who do you think did this to you?" I asked.

He swallowed hard, eyes on me. He didn't even need to say it. The condemnatory look he gave me told me everything I needed to know.

"You think it was me, don't you?" I stammered.

"Well, was it?"

I was too aghast to respond.

"Did you do it, Amelia?" Neil pressed. "Are you working for Daniel Ling?"

"Are you serious right now? I hadn't even met the man until yesterday afternoon. How could I be working for him?"

"You're smart, and you're capable of deceit. Who else has such easy access to my office? I've caught you in there before, when you shouldn't have been."

"That was…"

"Hmm?"

"Completely unrelated."

"If you say so."

"I can't believe this! You have no grounds to accuse me of anything."

Neil rolled his eyes. My blood boiled.

"Cancel all of my appointments for the rest of the day," he said.

"Where are you going?"

"No more questions."

With that, he stalked away, leaving me to stew in my indignation.

* * *

Neil didn't return all day, nor did he respond to any of my emails, calls, or text messages. I asked James where he went, but he was just as clueless as I was.

My irritation had yet to fade by the time I left the office after work. Our confrontation looped in my head all the way to Cat Dad's apartment.

That jerk! How could he think I'd do that to him, after all the progress we've made?

Standing in Cat Dad's bathroom, I stripped out of my work clothes and my bra, and changed into the jeans and t-shirt I had brought with me. I put my headphones on and cranked some music up to drown out my thoughts. Vacuum cleaner in my grip, I channelled my fury into cleaning the floor. The cats scurried as far away as they could.

By the time I had vacuumed every inch of the apartment, my rage had subsided. Now, I just felt hurt. How could Neil think I would betray him like that? I thought we were on the same page. I thought…

I don't know what I thought.

To lift my spirits, I put some upbeat music on and sang my heart out as I mopped the kitchen floor. The music was so loud, and I was so lost in it, that I didn't hear the door open. I didn't hear a person enter the room. I was singing, shaking my butt, mopping. Then, out of the corner of my eye, I saw him.

I shrieked.

Chapter Thirty-One

Cheeks burning, I yanked my headphones off and took in the man before me.

Dark hair, shrewd eyes, stern lips. Immaculate from head to toe in a tailored suit and black leather shoes. A Rolex on his wrist.

I couldn't believe my eyes.

What is he doing here? Did he follow me? How did he get in?

Meanwhile, Neil stared at me as if I were the most fascinating creature he had ever laid eyes on.

I dropped the mop into the bucket with a clatter. "Neil! What are you doing here?"

He snapped out of his trance and approached me. "I live here."

"Wait—what?"

"This is my apartment. I own it. I live here."

My brain was short-circuiting. This didn't make any sense. "But... No, it can't be. Who was that other guy?"

"Other guy?"

"I saw him walk up to the door the last time I was here."

Neil scratched his chin. "I think my neighbour slipped a letter under the door a while back. It could have been him."

"Well, what about… the alcohol in the cupboard? You said you don't drink!"

"Ah, those. They're bottles I received as gifts. I kept them for guests. Not that I ever have anyone over…"

"Then how about all the books? I've never seen you read."

"Of course I read."

"B-but…"

Neil folded his arms, eyebrow raised. "But what?"

"But Cat Dad's cute!"

The corner of Neil's lips twitched. "You think I'm… *cute*?"

"Not *you!*" I buried my face in my hands. "Ugh. This can't be happening."

Neil clucked his tongue. "I should be the one questioning you." He stepped closer, backing me into a corner between his kitchen cabinets. "What are you doing here? Why are you cleaning my house?"

"I was just trying to make some extra money. I didn't know it was your house."

"Are you a spy? Do you work for Daniel Ling?"

"Not this again!" I let out an exasperated sigh.

And then I laughed.

I wanted to be angry, but I couldn't help it. The concept of me being a spy was just so ludicrous. My laugh seemed to break the tension because Neil eased up too, uncrossing his arms and relaxing his shoulders. "Jean?" he asked.

"It's my middle name."

"So it is. Amelia Jean Cross. Why didn't I think of that?"

"Then… *you're* Cat Dad?"

"Is that so hard to believe?"

"I thought… I thought Cat Dad was a nice man."

Neil threw his head back and laughed. "You don't think I'm nice? That is amusing."

"Why are you home, anyway? I haven't finished cleaning. You're not supposed to be back yet."

"It's been a hectic day. I just wanted to come home and relax. I forgot my cleaner might still be here."

It was sinking in. Neil was the man I had been chatting with all along… and he had just caught me with my messy hair, braless, singing, dancing, mopping his goddamn kitchen floor. I wanted to lock myself away in shame.

"I never expected she would be you." Neil's inquisitive eyes roamed over me before settling on my face, his brow furrowed.

"Are you still thinking I might be a spy?"

"If you are, then I must congratulate you for successfully infiltrating my home and my office. Credit where credit is due."

I shook my head. "You're crazy, you know that? Now, if you don't mind, I think I'll finish up." I glanced across the room to the living space. "Where did I put my bag?"

I brushed past Neil as I moved to grab my belongings, but his hand came down on my shoulder, stopping me.

"Milly—wait." His voice had a guttural quality as he said my name.

I froze, heart in my throat.

What's this? Did he just call me Milly? He's never called me that before.

I shot him a questioning look.

He caught himself and lowered his hand. "*Amelia.* I don't think you're a spy."

"Then why would you accuse me of being one?"

"Let's sit down and talk about this." He gestured to the couch. "Please."

I hesitated. Part of me wanted to run away and hide, but another part of me wanted answers.

What should I do?

"Please," Neil repeated.

I breathed a sharp intake of air. Why did I find it so difficult to deny this man? All I could do was give in. "Okay. Let's talk."

I settled onto the couch with crossed arms and legs.

"Would you like something to drink?" Neil asked. "Some water?"

His offer made me aware of how dry my mouth was. "Yes, please."

I stared at the harbour through the window while Neil tinkered in the kitchen behind me. Multi-coloured lights shimmered on the rippled surface of the sea, and a lone yacht drifted in the distance. It was almost romantic.

Neil placed the glass of water on a coaster on the coffee table, then he shrugged off his suit jacket and tossed it over the armrest of the couch. He had already ditched his tie. I sipped from my water as Neil sat down, angling himself towards me. Our knees almost touched.

A strained silence descended between us. I watched Neil chew his lip as his eyes wandered over me. He seemed to be grappling with his thoughts. I was equally at a loss for words. He opened his mouth, then he abruptly closed it again. Just as the tension was becoming too much to bear, a furry visitor joined us. Chichi scaled the top length of the couch, brushing past both our heads before climbing down to curl up on Neil's suit jacket.

Neil let out an exaggerated groan through a half-smile. "You little rascal. You're gonna get fur all over that."

I found his reaction so endearing that I couldn't help but giggle. "Too late. It's hers now."

Neil's smile broadened. "That's right." He reached a hand out to the adorable offender. "Chichi." He stroked her fur. "Are you fed? Did Milly give you your dinner?"

"I did."

Chichi purred, nuzzling Neil's hand. I watched on, feeling my heart stir, almost like Neil's affection was directed at me rather than his pet. I could bask in its warmth.

He continued to pet Chichi with one lazily outreached hand as he returned his focus to me. "I'm sorry if I scared you before. Daniel Ling's visit rattled me."

"There's something going on between you two, isn't there?"

"It's complicated."

"Does it have anything to do with Alex Patterson?" My assertiveness surprised me, and I felt an urge to punctuate my question by covering my mouth with my hand.

Neil stopped petting Chichi. I tensed up, wondering if I was about to regret what I had asked.

"Hmm." Neil rubbed his temples. "I don't know how much to tell you."

"You still don't think you can trust me?"

"I'm choosing to trust you, Amelia. Maybe it's unwise, but that's the decision I've come to. I spent all day going through the security logs and camera footage, and there was nothing to suggest you had anything to do with planting the bug."

"Of course—because I didn't do it. But did you find out who did?"

"Daniel entered my office during the brief period he was alone there. He could have placed it then, yet that doesn't explain how he knew…"

"About Alex?"

Neil shook his head.

"If you've decided to trust me, then why won't you tell me what's going on?" I asked.

"Because the more I tell you, the more I get you involved in something I'd rather you weren't involved in," he snapped.

My heart lurched. Neil seemed pained and conflicted over this. Maybe it really was in my best interest to be kept in the dark.

Neil sighed, lowering his hands to rest by his lap. "Then again, it's too late to shield you completely. And I wouldn't have picked you for this job if I didn't think you could handle some part of the truth."

I remembered how he had called me devious once. Was that the quality he had been searching for in a new secretary? Someone with cunning…. Someone who could handle getting caught up in whatever this was…

"What about Christine?" I asked. "Does she know?"

"Christine was with me almost since the beginning. Of course she would know a few things. You're… *different*."

"Different? How so? Because we haven't worked together as long?"

"It's not that." Neil sighed. "I don't know why I'm struggling so much with this." He undid an extra button of his shirt and tugged at his collar as if to let some hot air out, before composing himself. "Okay. I think I'm ready. Are you?"

I straightened up and gave him my full attention. "Yes. I'm listening."

He locked eyes with me, breathed deeply, then began. "First of all, I meant what I said about Daniel Ling. He's a dangerous man. You might see me act like his buddy, but know that's purely for self-preservation."

"Okay. Daniel Ling equals bad man. What else?"

"Alex Patterson…"

My interest piqued. I leaned closer, as if Neil were about to whisper a secret.

"Your concerns are not unfounded," he said. "I have my own suspicions. Daniel may have been involved, but I can't be certain."

I gasped. "Is that why you have the file? You're trying to look into Alex's death… Is that what you were worried Daniel knew about? Why he bugged your office?"

"No."

"Then what is it?"

Neil said nothing. He just swallowed, his Adam's apple bobbing in his throat.

"This is what you don't want to tell me…" I said, trying to work it all out in my head.

"Let's leave it at that for now. I've said enough for one day."

I masked my dejection, not wanting to push it. "Okay."

"Needless to say, what I've told you this evening stays between us."

"Of course. Your secrets are safe with me."

On top of Neil's suit jacket, Chichi stood up on all fours and stretched. I had forgotten she was there. She walked across Neil's lap, then settled on mine. Her presence put me at ease. I scratched behind her ears. She purred in response, whiskers bristling.

"She likes you," Neil said.

I grinned. "Probably because I feed her."

Neil leaned closer, one arm resting over the back of the couch. "No. It's not food she's after. But it's strange. She doesn't tend to warm up to other people so easily."

"A bit like you," I said without thinking.

Neil swallowed. "Yes."

Our knees bumped.

My pulse throbbed in my neck. I dared look at Neil's face and saw him biting his lip, his dark eyes fixated on me. I felt weak and helpless, like if he so much as touched me, I would die.

It was so obvious to me now. This was a crush. A *huge* crush. *No.* More than a crush. I yearned for him, ached for him, pined for him.

But it could never be.

He was my boss, and besides, what about that other woman? My mind went rushing back to that scene through the restaurant window. The beautiful woman sitting across from Neil at the table, the palpable intimacy between them.

Who was she?

Suddenly, a light bulb switched on in my brain.

Daniel's parting words…

The flicker of confusion on Neil's face…

"Give my regards to my sister, won't you?"

It echoed in my head, the significance sinking in.

"Is everything okay?" Neil asked.

I snapped to my senses, noticing Neil had pulled away from me. He squinted his eyes, head tilted.

"Sorry," I said. "I zoned out for a moment there. You were saying?"

"It's getting late. Do you want a ride home?"

The prospect of him taking me home was tempting, but I already felt overwhelmed and overstimulated from so much close, one-on-one time with him. Any more and I might explode from the tension. The walk to the train station would calm me down and help me process my thoughts. "That's okay. I'll take the train."

I gently pushed Chichi off my lap. She padded back over to Neil's suit jacket.

Neil walked me to the door. "Have you got everything?"

"I think so."

"Oh—don't forget this." He swiped the envelope containing my tip off the kitchen island and passed it to me.

"Thanks." I slipped it into my bag, blushing with renewed embarrassment that I was his cleaner.

Neil opened the door for me, and I stepped into the corridor. "See you at work tomorrow," he said from the doorway.

I nodded. "Good night."

We lingered there for a second before Neil finally closed the door. I didn't catch my breath until I heard it lock. My head was reeling.

While I waited for the lift, I typed a string of words into the search bar on my phone. "Zelthia Singapore Daniel Ling sister."

Chapter Thirty-Two

I psyched myself up to confront Neil at work the next morning. I knew he'd be mad at me for digging, but there was something I had to ask him. Something I had to know.

My heart thudded as I approached Neil's office, but when I reached his door, I realised it was locked shut. That was strange in itself, but even stranger was the blue Post-It note attached to the surface. In Neil's spidery scrawl, it read:

Meet me on the roof.
N.

Dread blossomed in the pit of my stomach.

The roof?

I thought the roof had been locked and out of bounds since Alex died. Why would Neil go there? And why did he want me to join him?

It crossed my mind that it could be some kind of test, or maybe even a trap, but my concern for Neil overrode those thoughts. What if the police had missed something in their investigation, and danger lurked? The rumoured rickety railing, or an uneven surface which could cause him to stumble towards the edge...

The memory of Alex falling to his death replayed in my head. The human-shaped downward blur. The all-consuming sense of terror as I realised what I had witnessed.

I took a deep breath. What mattered most was checking on Neil. I couldn't bear it if something happened to him.

The fire exit door was next to the lifts. I pushed it open and entered the cold concrete stairwell. The stairs did one zigzag up before reaching a windowless landing, lit by a faint, flickering bulb. This was the end of the road. A large, heavy-looking steel door awaited me—the door that had been locked to staff since Alex died.

I turned the handle and forced the stubborn door open. It squeaked on its hinges, and a vortex of howling wind leaked through the widening gap and into the stairwell. I squinted my eyes against the gust and the brightness of the overcast sky.

The roof was a wide concrete surface, flat apart from the air-conditioning units, vents, and satellite dishes jutting out. A safety barrier bordered the perimeter. Neil stood at the edge, looking out at the cityscape. The blustery wind ruffled his hair and whipped at his tie.

Before I could close the door, the wind slammed it shut for me. The banging sound alerted Neil to my presence. He turned and locked eyes with me. I cautiously approached, stopping a few steps short of the edge, unwilling to go any closer.

Neil leaned back on the barrier, hands in his pockets. "You came."

"Of course. You asked me to."

"I thought you might think twice."

"I was worried about you."

Neil smirked. "Why? Did you think I might fall?"

"I don't know. Yes. It seems dangerous. My heart is pounding just seeing you lean on the wall like that. Can you please stop?"

He acquiesced. "There. Is that better?"

"Much better."

He stepped closer to me. "You're brave to come here. Or foolish. Let me ask you something. Did it ever cross your mind that *I* might have killed Alex?"

I stared at him in shock.

"Well?" he asked.

"Of course it crossed my mind!"

"Yet you were willing to go alone to meet me on the roof?"

"Because I trust you now."

"Trust no one, Amelia."

"Well, I trust myself, and I don't believe you're a villain."

"Life is not black and white. There are no heroes and villains."

I crossed my arms, starting to get tired of his bullshit. "Okay. I get it. Cut it out and tell me why you came here."

A pensive look replaced his smirk. "Talking to you last night… it got me thinking." He focused on the ground and made a precise step towards the barrier. "There used to be a chalk mark right here. This is the approximate position Alex fell from."

"Oh God." I backed away, shuddering.

"It's common knowledge that Alex used to come up to the roof several times a day to smoke, so it's not surprising he was up here." Neil measured the height of the barrier with his hand, placing it somewhere between his waist and his chest. "The wall is not particularly high. One could easily climb over it if they intended to jump. Or they could be pushed. An accidental fall seems unlikely, even in winds such as this, but who knows? If one leaned too far over and lost their footing… Perhaps it's possible. I'm unwilling to put it to the test."

"Maybe he liked to sit on top of the wall while he smoked."

"Maybe."

"What do *you* think happened?"

"The police were certain no one else was on the roof, but even if I take that as fact, I'm still of two minds. Daniel could have threatened Alex, provoking him to jump. 'Kill yourself or I'll have your children killed.'"

"That's awful!"

"That's how he operates. Though maybe not in such plain words. He'll threaten whoever you care about the most in order to manipulate you. On the other hand, maybe no such threats were required. It could be as the police concluded. Alex's mental health struggles were well-documented, and he would have been worried about his mishandling of the company's finances coming to light."

"Could there be another explanation? There was a rumour someone tampered with the railing, but I see now that it's a solid wall. What about his cigarettes?"

Neil tensed. "What do you mean?"

"As you said, he came up here several times a day to smoke, and lots of people knew that. Could someone have tampered with his cigarettes? Laced them with something that could mess with his head? Ugh. Forget it. I just realised how stupid that sounds."

Neil shook his head. "It's not stupid at all, but that method would lack certainty."

"It was just a thought."

"Of course. This is all speculation. I have no evidence Daniel was involved, just a gut feeling. His dislike of Alex was part of the reason he sent me here in the first place, but maybe it's just a coincidence."

The wind died down as we reached a natural lull in our conversation. Neil looked out over the barrier wall, holding his hands behind his back, his expression contemplative.

I remembered I had something important to ask him. This was my opportunity.

"Neil." I stepped closer to him and the wall separating us from the sheer drop to certain death.

He turned and gave me his full attention, his arms crossed and his head cocked to one side.

I forced the words to the tip of my tongue as a rush of nerves threatened to engulf me. "I think I know what it is… What you're scared Daniel knew about."

Neil clenched his jaw. "Go on."

This was the moment of truth. I braced myself. "Are you in a relationship with Daniel's sister, Veronica Ling a.k.a Ruby?"

My question hung heavy in the wind-whipped air.

Neil looked down his nose at me, dissecting me through his narrowed eyes. "It seems, yet again, I've underestimated you."

Does that mean I'm right? Neil and Veronica…

"How on earth did you know her alias?" Neil asked.

"I've seen that name pop up on your phone a few times, and I wondered who she was. It was just a hunch."

A muscle ticked in Neil's jaw. "You're very perceptive."

"So, it's true then? Is she your girlfriend?"

"No."

"…Huh?"

"But you're on the right track. I'm not in a relationship with Daniel's sister, but I have been in contact with her."

"You're not… *together*? But you looked so close…"

Neil's eyebrows shot up. "What are you talking about?"

"I saw you with her. I was on my way home from cleaning your place a couple of weeks ago when I saw you at a restaurant."

"Ronnie is an old friend. Okay, she's my ex. She was visiting from Singapore."

"Your ex?" The words felt tinged with bitterness in my mouth.

"She was my fiancée for a while, but we split up a long time ago."

I dropped my gaze to the ground. "Oh. I see."

I still couldn't quite believe it. Were exes usually so at ease with each other? What if they wanted each other back? It certainly looked that way.

He even has a nickname for her…

"If you've done your research, which I suspect you have, then I suppose you know why I would want to keep my recent contact with her a secret," Neil said.

"It seems like there's bad blood between Veronica and Daniel. They're estranged."

"Yes. Relations in the Ling family are very tense. Donald Ling, the chairman of Zelthia, is on the verge of death. The future of his assets is at stake."

"Daniel is his only heir…"

"Right. The company and assets are to pass down the male line only, leaving nothing for Ronnie."

"But Veronica already has a fortune. She's a self-made businesswoman with her own successful company."

"It pales in comparison to the chairman's fortune. But this isn't about money. I, and many others, strongly believe she would take the company in a more ethical direction if she were in charge instead of Daniel."

"But what can you do?"

"Change the chairman's mind. Ronnie and I have been trying to achieve this for some time now—behind Daniel's back. So, it's a problem he somehow knows I've met up with her. Unless he was bluffing—I couldn't be sure."

"Just meeting her doesn't have to mean anything. You used to be engaged, after all."

"True, but if Daniel catches even a whiff of what's really going on, he has the power to make my life a living hell."

An involuntary tremor coursed through me, goosebumps erupting on my skin. "You really believe Daniel was behind Alex's death, don't you?"

"I do."

"Then what you're doing is incredibly dangerous."

"Yes."

The conviction in his voice gave me chills. "You're willing to risk your life for Veronica's sake?"

Neil shook his head. "I'm not doing this for her sake. I'm doing it because I truly believe the world would be better off with her at the helm of Zelthia rather than her brother."

I could accept his stance. From all I had read about Veronica Ling, she was a virtuous person—a known humanitarian and philanthropist. "You could have told me all this yesterday. I would have understood."

"I suppose I was delaying the inevitable. You're in the middle of this now. You know what's going on. The future of a two-hundred-and-fifty billion dollar conglomerate is at stake."

Before I could process the scope of Neil's words, the wind suddenly picked up in an immense gust, which nearly knocked me off my feet. I grabbed hold of the barrier ledge to support myself, but the view I had been avoiding entered my field of vision.

The drop.

A dizzying spectacle. Twenty flights down to the hard, unforgiving pavement. A yawning abyss of concrete and steel that threatened to swallow me whole.

A vision of my father plummeting to his death flashed in my mind, accompanied by the sickening sensation of falling. My knees buckled, and my stomach lurched. I felt lightheaded and unstable. The world was spinning around me. Neil said something, but his voice was distant and muffled. It felt like I was underwater. My vision was blurry. My legs... My legs... *Ah.*

"MILLY!"

Chapter Thirty-Three

The earth slipped from beneath my feet. Everything went dark as I collapsed into a void.

"Milly."

…Neil?

His voice cut through the fog in my brain. The next thing I knew, his strong arms were around me, pulling me up, holding me to his chest. I felt his body behind me, his reassuring presence anchoring me to reality as the wind swirled around us. "I've got you," he said. "I won't let anything happen to you."

His voice was so raw and earnest, I believed him in the depth of my soul.

"I'm okay," I said.

He clung to me like he was scared of letting me go. I didn't resist, savouring the feeling of him against me. I let my head fall back against his shoulder and closed my eyes to stop the world from spinning.

The moment Neil loosened his grip, my legs gave out. He caught me again. "Let's get you back downstairs. It was a mistake to ask you to come here. I'm sorry."

I shook my head, still in a state of shock.

"I'm going to carry you," he said. "Wrap your arms around my shoulders,"

I did as he instructed, feeling his solid warmth under my hands. In one fluid movement, he scooped me off the ground, cradling me in his arms. I nestled my face in the crook of his neck like it was a security blanket, relishing his familiar scent. His pulse quickened beneath my cheek.

He shuffled me as he opened the door to the stairwell, then I felt him descend the steps. He lowered me when we reached the landing by the door to the twentieth floor, my body sliding down his until my feet touched the ground.

"Can you walk?" he asked, keeping me steady with one hand on my waist.

"Yes. I think so."

He stayed close to my side on our way to my office. As soon as we were inside, he closed the door, then guided me to the couch with a firm hand. "Sit down," he said. "Take a breather."

I obliged, still a little shaken and disorientated.

Neil made his way to the water cooler stationed in the far corner of the room. I heard the rustle of a cup being taken from the stack and placed under the dispenser. The tank gurgled as a steady stream of water gushed out.

When Neil returned, he sat beside me and passed me the cup. "Drink."

I gulped it down, the cold water soothing my parched throat. "What happened?" I asked when I had finished.

Neil studied me with concern etched on his harsh features. "You fainted."

"I... I..." My voice trailed off, the words catching in my throat.

"You don't need to say anything."

"I saw Alex fall."

Neil looked stricken. "What?"

"On the day he died. I saw him through the window."

Neil ran a hand down his face. "I should never have asked you to come to the roof. Forgive me."

"It's not your fault. You didn't know."

"I should have known! Why didn't I know?"

He had a pleading look in his eyes. I was lost in them as I grasped for words. "I would have told you… I thought I was over it, but I guess I'm more traumatised by his death than I thought I was. When I looked down… I saw Alex. *No*—I saw my—" A pain shot through my temple. "Agh!"

Neil placed his hand on my back as I keeled over with my palm pressed to the ache. We sat in silence until my ears pricked to a gentle tip-tapping. The pain subsided as I listened. "It's raining," I said.

"Hmm?" Neil tilted his head. "So it is."

The sound intensified to a steady drumbeat. Neil got up and walked to the window. He opened it, letting the sound of the rain fill the room—the same thing I always did when it was raining. He must have caught on to my habit. I closed my eyes and let the sound wash over me, a sense of calm spreading through my body.

The couch dipped as Neil returned to my side. "How are you feeling now?"

"Better."

"I think you should go home. I'll ask Winston to give you a ride."

I shook my head. "I'm fine now. I swear."

"Are you sure?"

"Yes."

"If you say so. But take it easy. I'll be in my office if you need me. If you change your mind and decide to go home, please go."

He lingered for a second, as if expecting me to reconsider, but I said nothing. Going home wouldn't solve anything. Working would help occupy my mind, and besides, I wanted to stay close to Neil—for my own selfish reasons.

Neil stood up and unlocked his office door with a sharp twist of his key. As he opened the door, the state of his office came into view. Little had changed since he tore it apart.

I leapt from the couch as if the incident on the roof had never happened. "Let me help you tidy up."

Neil shook his head. "What did I just tell you? Take it easy today."

"But tidying is like therapy for me. I enjoy it. It's relaxing."

Neil narrowed his eyes. "Is that why you're a cleaner?"

"Yes."

He walked me back to the couch and made me sit down. "I don't want you to over-exert yourself. And I'm not sure if I made this clear last night, but you understand, don't you? You can't be my cleaner anymore."

"What? Why not?"

"Because it's inappropriate. My secretary at work shouldn't be my personal cleaner at home."

"I don't mind. I want to keep doing it."

"No. That's final."

He was serious. An income stream gone. Just like that.

"But I need the money!"

"Do I not pay you enough in this role?"

"You do. That's not the reason—"

"Then what is? Go on, tell me."

I went silent. The weight of my situation bore down on me. My student loan. Having two months to move out of my apartment. The one-way ticket to London.

"Tell me, and I'll be able to help you with whatever it is," Neil said.

If I lied to him now, I'd be digging myself into an even deeper hole, and that was something I wasn't prepared to do. I took a deep breath to loosen the knot in my stomach, then I let it all out. "I want to pay my student loan down as much as possible before the end of the year, and I need to find a short-term rental because I'm being kicked out of my current place."

"Easily managed. But why short-term?"

I avoided his questioning gaze. This was it. The crux of the matter. My heart rate soared.

"Because—" I braced myself, "—I'm going to move overseas."

Neil said nothing for a second.

I squirmed.

"When?" he asked at last, a hitch in his voice. "And for how long?"

"January. For at least a year. Longer, if I can make it work."

"And when were you going to tell me this?"

"I don't know. Soon, I guess."

"Was it always your plan to leave?"

"Yes."

"Why didn't you say something back when I offered you the job?"

"Would you have hired me if you knew I was going to quit within a year?"

"No."

"There's your answer."

Neil sighed, the weight of his disappointment palpable. "Perhaps it's for the best."

I lifted my chin. "Really?"

"I'm not sure this is working out."

His words stung like a slap.

"In what way?"

He didn't answer me.

My mind raced. Why didn't he think it was working out? I thought we had been getting on tremendously, everything considered. Didn't he think I was doing a good job? Didn't he like me?

"Never mind," Neil said. "I'd be a hypocrite to blame you for acting in self-interest. Don't worry. I'll take care of everything. I'll raise your salary to cover the lost income from cleaning, and I'll make a contribution to your student loan upon the end of your employment."

I struggled to process all he was saying. "That's... that's very generous."

"As for your housing situation, I can help with that too. I know a place where you can stay."

I gasped. "You do?"

"But I'm afraid there's a catch."

"I'm not in a position to be picky. What's the catch?"

"I'll be your landlord, and you'll live in the same building as me."

* * *

My stomach did somersaults as I stood in front of Neil's apartment building, admiring its jutting form against the dark sky. It was my first time here without the context of cleaning Cat Dad's apartment, and if everything went well, it wouldn't be the last time.

The doorman greeted me as I stepped inside. I texted Neil to say I had arrived, then I sat on the bench by the lifts to wait for him to come down.

I jiggled my knee. Viewing the apartment was an intriguing prospect in itself, getting to spend more time with Neil outside our work bubble even more so.

I recalled our conversation on the roof, how he had denied that Veronica was his girlfriend. Not that it meant anything could happen between *us*. A relationship with my boss would be wildly inappropriate. Not to mention him disliking me—especially since I pulled the rug from under him regarding my move to London. Yet, I couldn't help fantasising…

Neil would show me to the bedroom in the apartment. He would kiss me and throw me down on the bed. Just the thought of how his lips would feel on mine sent shivers coursing through my body.

The lift door opened, jettisoning me from my fantasy. Neil walked out, giving major dad vibes in dark-wash jeans and a half-zip sweater. My heart fluttered at the rare glimpse of him in casual mode. I got to my feet as he approached. His eyes flicked over me in a way that made me feel self-conscious, even though he wore the same inscrutable expression he always did. "Thanks for coming by so late," he said. "I had to finish up a few things at work."

I tucked a loose strand of hair behind my ear. "It's no trouble at all. Thanks for letting me view the apartment."

I wasn't sure how this potential arrangement would work out. An apartment in such a high-end building was going to be way out of my budget. Did Neil have something up his sleeve? I tried to keep my expectations tempered.

He showed me to an apartment on the fourth floor. He typed the code into the digital lock, and the door clicked open. I stared with wide eyes as the interior came into view. The open-plan living area was spacious and modern, furnished with pieces that looked like they came straight from the pages of a glossy catalogue. The kitchen was small but fully equipped with stainless-steel appliances. White marble countertops complemented the light oak cabinetry, and the kitchen island doubled as a dining table, with leather-upholstered bar stools tucked underneath.

The view of the harbour called to me. I rushed over to look out the window. The view was less magnificent than the one from Neil's apartment, but it surpassed the blank concrete wall visible from my current residence. I watched the sea gently churn, dappled with reflected light sparkling on its choppy surface.

I felt Neil come up behind me, then his smooth, deep voice over my shoulder, so alluring that I shuddered. "What do you think?"

I turned to him, hands clasped together in excitement. "It's perfect!"

He lifted an eyebrow. "That's strong praise when you've yet to see everything."

"R-right."

I was so overwhelmed, I had forgotten there were more rooms to explore.

Neil gestured to the open door which led to the bedroom, and my recent fantasy flooded back to me in vivid detail. His hands gripping my hips. My back on the mattress. Those dark eyes burning with desire…

Neil flicked the light switch on. The sudden brightness chased my illicit thoughts away and revealed the comfy bedroom in front of me. A king-sized bed was the centrepiece, framed by two bedside tables and wall lamps. An armchair and a bookcase in the corner formed a little reading nook. I could imagine myself curling up with a book there before bed each night.

Neil kept his distance as I looked around. He observed me from the doorway, leaning against the frame with his arms folded and a faint smile on his lips. I dared to test the firmness of the bed in front of him, sitting on the edge, then lying back with a sigh of contentment as the mattress yielded to me. When I snapped back onto my feet a few seconds later, I saw Neil averting his eyes, a hint of redness inching up his neck. I savoured the endearing little crack in his confident facade before it quickly disappeared without a trace.

Returning to the task at hand, I opened a door off the bedroom and discovered a large closet. The second door led to a small but luxurious bathroom with grey and white tiles on the walls and floors, a glass-encased shower, and a vanity made of shiny white porcelain. From the bathroom, another door led back to the living room.

The final room was a laundry and utility space, functional yet beautiful. The big washer and dryer had me excited for the prospect of laundry, and the shelves had tons of space to store my collection of cleaning supplies.

Will I actually get to live here?

I regrouped with Neil in the living room, buzzing with hope, yet nervous that it was too good to be true.

"Well?" he asked. "If it's unsuitable, I might be able to find another option—"

"I stand by my original opinion."

"I figured you'd want something furnished so you can sell your current furniture before you leave, and this is the best furnished apartment I have available for your size requirements, but I'm sure I could rustle up an alternative if need be—"

"I already told you, it's perfect. How many apartments in this building do you own, anyway?"

"All of them."

I just about choked on my breath. "Excuse me?"

"I own all of them. I own this building."

I gawped at him. "The entire building? But this place must be worth tens of millions of dollars!"

"One hundred million, give or take."

I knew Neil was rich, but I didn't know just how rich. The income he earned from the rent alone must be insane. I was speechless.

"Most of the apartments are already tenanted," Neil said. "I think this is the best one I can offer you. It's yours if you want it for short-term accommodation until you leave, but I understand if you don't. It might be uncomfortable living in the same building as me, and having me as your landlord as well as your boss. I know it's far from ideal."

I shook my head. "It *is* ideal. The thing is… how much are you expecting for rent? I don't think I'll be able to afford it."

"How much are you paying now?"

"Four hundred a week. Utilities extra."

"You can have this place for the same."

I gaped. "Seriously?"

"Yes."

"But you could make so much more by renting it to someone else."

"Your stability and security are of far greater value to me."

My heart stirred. I just about wanted to cry.

Concern washed over Neil's face. "What's wrong?"

"N-nothing. It's just… this is so generous. It's almost too much. I feel so bad for letting you down, for not telling you about my plan to go overseas."

Neil looked into my eyes, his softness intensifying to such a degree that I felt weak at the knees. "I'm not mad at you for that. It took me off guard, but you were just looking out for yourself, and that's something I fully understand."

"Neil—"

"Yes?"

"If you didn't want me to go, I think I'd be willing to keep working for you."

My spontaneous confession surprised me. I wanted to retract my words and ponder them, but it was too late. They were out in the open. My real feelings laid bare.

Neil studied me through narrowed eyes, his jaw flexing. He took his time to pick his words. The wait was agonising. "That is a tempting offer," he said at last, "but I think you should go. You are young. The world is full of opportunities. I wouldn't want to stand in your way."

I appreciated his support, but it somehow felt like a blow. A part of me must have been hoping he'd ask me to stay by his side.

"Besides, I don't know how long I will be needed at Luxmore, and with the situation in Singapore... You should go. It's for the best."

It's for the best. He had said those words before. Something else occurred to me, and I spoke up once again. "Neil, what did you mean the other day when you said 'this isn't working out'?"

His eyes widened, and his voice seemed caught in his throat. "Ah. Forgive me."

"If my performance is—"

"Your performance is not the issue."

"Then what is?"

Neil turned serious, his demeanour stiffening and straightening. "It's my problem, not yours. Will you take the apartment?" he asked, changing the subject.

I brightened at the reminder I'd get to call this place home. "Of course I will!"

"I have a property manager in charge, but for you, it would be simpler if we engaged directly."

"That makes sense."

"And I'll have to inform HR we'll be living in the same building, or people might get the wrong idea…"

"Ah. Good thinking. So, when can I move in?"

"As soon as you're ready. I imagine you'll need to discuss a leaving date with your current landlord. Just one thing. You'll be busy during the fourth week of September."

I racked my brain. What was happening then? The annual Zelthia shareholder meeting was the only thing I could think of—but that wasn't something I thought I'd be involved in. "What's happening then?" I asked.

"We'll be in Singapore."

Chapter Thirty-Four

Neil's announcement took me by surprise. Not the trip to Singapore itself, but that he wanted me to go with him.

"I had a call from Daniel this afternoon," Neil explained. He stood by the window which overlooked the harbour, his hands clasped behind him in a businesslike manner. "The shareholder meeting is later this month, and he wants me to present a financial update on Luxmore."

"And you want me to come with you?" I asked, still processing the news, trying to get my facts straight.

"Yes."

I thought of Daniel, his sallow skin, his beady little eyes. A creepy-crawly sensation took over my body, Neil's warnings ringing in my head.

He has self-control issues around attractive young women... He's dangerous...

"I thought you wanted me to stay away from Daniel and all this business going on in Singapore."

Neil clenched his jaw. "Believe me, I do want you to stay away from him, but not taking you would look suspicious. Christine always joined me on business trips, and that has set a precedent. Daniel will expect you to come. If you don't, he'll think I'm shielding you from him, and that will only increase his interest in you."

I struggled to wrap my head around the ensuing mind games, but I trusted Neil's analysis of the situation.

He let go of his hands and faced me front on. "I also don't like the thought of leaving you alone while I'm gone."

My heart twinged. I tried to keep my cool. "I'm sure I could manage."

"I'd prefer to keep an eye on you. Not because I don't think you could manage. It's other people I don't trust."

My crush-addled brain struggled to interpret his protectiveness as anything but affectionate. "Will anyone else from Luxmore come?" I asked.

"Not this time. Just you and me. Is your passport up to date?"

"Yes, it is."

"Good."

It was starting to sink in. A business trip to Singapore with Neil. Just us two. What would it be like? "I've never been to Singapore," I said. "The only countries I've been to outside New Zealand are Australia and Fiji."

"I'm afraid there won't be much time for sightseeing."

I huffed. "I know that."

"Book the flights and accommodation on Monday. I want to get this locked in."

I whipped my phone out to enter the task into my to-do list. "Got it."

"That's enough work chat for tonight. Shall we finish up here? Do you want to see the gym?"

"There's a gym? In this building?"

"Of course. Don't worry, I use a different gym, so we won't run in to each other working out."

Pity.

Just like that, my attention swung back to the apartment building and the prospect that soon, Neil and I would be living under the same roof.

* * *

At work on Monday, I had the plane tickets for Singapore up on my screen, all ready to be booked in, when I suddenly felt like I was forgetting something. It niggled at the back of my brain until I checked my diary, flicking to the pages of the week in question. There it was, spelled out in capital letters and underlined:

Nicole's Wedding.

I winced. It had completely slipped my mind. I double-checked the dates, hoping I was mistaken, but no. The wedding was on the twenty-first of September, when I was supposed to be in Singapore. I slammed the diary closed with a huff of frustration.

My first thought was that I'd rather go on the business trip. My second thought was that it would be rude to pull out of the wedding at such late notice. I leaned back in my chair with my hands behind my head and groaned.

What should I do?

The wedding had been booked in for a long time. Bowing out now would seal the end of my friendship with Nicole once and for all. Did I really want that? Part of me still clung to a shred of hope that we could revive our friendship. Was that foolish? I thought of her party and how she had snubbed me and not cared or noticed when she left me behind. Did she even want me at her wedding? Maybe she'd breathe a sigh of relief if I told her I couldn't come.

I knew what would happen if I brought it up with Neil. He'd tell me to go to the wedding. No question. But if I was honest with myself, I would prefer to go on the business trip. My work life was more important than Nicole. Neil was more important.

That settles it.

Before I could talk myself out of it, I grabbed my phone and composed a text message.

> Hi, Nicole. I don't think I'm going to be able to make it to your wedding anymore. An important business trip has come up, and I can't really get out of it. Sorry for the late notice. Wishing you all the best for your big day.

I hesitated over the send button for a second, then, with a deep breath, I sent the message.

Just like that, the deed was done.

A weight lifted off my shoulders. Deep down, I must have been dreading the wedding the whole time. Now that I didn't have to go, I felt a sense of relief. Nicole would be fine without me. I'd be fine without her. It was time to let go and move on.

With that sorted, I returned my attention to the plane ticket booking page. It had timed out, so I had to go through all the steps again. I used Neil's credit card to pay the ludicrous fare for two business class seats departing on the twentieth of September and returning on the twenty-fourth.

Accommodation was the next thing I had to arrange. Neil had a membership with a particular hotel chain, which made things simple. I pulled up the reservation screen for the location closest to Zelthia headquarters and started to fill in the details. Partway through, the form froze. An error message appeared.

We are currently experiencing a problem with our booking system. Please call us to make a reservation.

Grumbling, I picked up the landline phone and punched in the number. As I listened to the dial tone, my mobile phone started ringing at the same time. Nicole's name flashed up on the screen. A surge of panic coursed through me. I hadn't expected her to call me back. Flustered, I hung up the landline and answered Nicole's call. "Hello?"

"I got your message," Nicole said.

Her subdued tone struck me as out of character, and I felt a wave of guilt. "I'm sorry, Nicole. It's just this work thing… It's very important for me to go. You know, for my career."

Nicole didn't say anything. I wondered if she was upset with me and started to regret pulling out of her wedding. I should have sucked it up and just accepted that I had to go for the sake of what little remained of our friendship.

"Nicole?"

When she spoke up again, her voice was even more sombre. "Actually, the thing is, we have postponed the wedding."

Postponed?

I wondered what could have happened. "Is everything okay?" I asked.

"Totally," she said with sudden cheeriness that sounded forced. "It's just, you know, family stuff. I was planning to send an update to everyone soon."

"So, when's the new date?"

"We haven't decided yet."

"Oh. Okay. Well, let me know, and I might be able to attend the new date."

"Sure. I'll let you know. Well, that's all I had to tell you."

"Okay."

"Bye."

She hung up before I could say bye back to her.

That was odd. I had never heard Nicole sound so down in the dumps before. I wondered what was going on with her. Well, whatever it was, I couldn't let it bother me too much. I had other things to focus on.

* * *

Neil and I worked closer together than ever in the lead-up to the Singapore trip. Literally. Our shoulders almost touched as I leaned in to focus on his computer screen, my chair pulled up beside him in his office. "I wonder if we should move this slide back. What do you think?" I asked.

"To the previous section? Hmmm. That could work," Neil said.

We had dedicated ourselves to working on the presentation for the past two weeks. The finance department had provided us with all the data. Neil's job was to compile the information into a coherent story, and my job was to help organise his speaking notes and to make it look visually appealing. The stakes were high. We had to make a good impression at the meeting or a merger with Flerotech could go back on the table. The pressure was palpable, though Neil remained stoic.

On top of all that, I had my upcoming move to Neil's apartment building playing on the back of my mind. My moving date was set for the Saturday after my return from Singapore. I was more than ready to leave my tiny studio behind.

Neil clicked through to the next slide. A spelling error jumped out at me straight away. "Oh, I see a typo."

"Where?"

Both of us reached for the mouse, our hands colliding. My heart skipped a beat at the skin contact. I froze. After what felt like a protracted state of connection, Neil withdrew his hand, clearing his throat at the same time. A trace of his touch lingered on my skin, warm and sensitive.

"Go ahead," Neil said, reminding me of the task at hand.

"Right."

Where was I? Oh! The typo.

My hair fell into my eyes as I leaned in to fix the mistake. I tucked the stray strands behind my ears. My hair was getting long. I'd need to book a haircut soon if I wanted to maintain the bobbed style I preferred.

After correcting the error, I searched my pockets for a spare hair tie while Neil ran through his notes again, rehearsing his spiel. I found one and swept my hair into a ponytail. Neil's voice trailed off, his eyes drifting from the screen to my exposed neck. He seemed captivated by something there. Wondering what it was, I touched the spot he was fixated on, but felt nothing but smooth skin. He continued to stare. My cheeks burned as self-consciousness set in. "Neil?"

"Hmm?" He lifted his gaze from my neck to my eyes, breaking free of whatever spell he was under. "Sorry. I lost my train of thought." He glanced at the clock on the wall and frowned. "It's late."

I checked the time too and saw what he meant. It was almost half-past six in the evening. I had worked a full hour and a half overtime without realising it.

"You should go home," Neil said. "You've done enough."

"Are you sure?"

He nodded. "I can finish it this weekend."

I would have gladly stayed up all night helping him, but telling him that would sound overeager. "Okay, thanks." I stood up, getting ready to leave.

"Are you all sorted for Monday? Have you packed yet?"

"Not yet. Maybe I'll do it tonight."

"It will be hot and wet in Singapore. Keep that in mind."

Hot and wet?

It took me a second to register his meaning. "I-I will."

"Get a good sleep on Sunday night and don't come in to work on Monday morning. Winston will pick you up from your building."

"Got it."

"Good night, Milly."

The sound of my name from his lips reverberated through me. I still felt a little thrill of pleasure whenever he said it.

"Good night. See you on Monday."

Chapter Thirty-Five

Even the luxury of first class wasn't enough to help me sleep on the flight, and I disembarked from the plane at Changi Airport exhausted. The arrival process passed in a blur. The next thing I knew, I was in the back of a cab next to Neil, leaving the airport behind. I gazed out the window, absorbing the unfamiliar sights, but my eyelids grew heavier with each passing moment, and soon I was struggling to stay awake. The gentle hum of the car's engine and the warmth of Neil's presence beside me lulled me into a drowsy haze, and I felt myself drifting off despite my best efforts to stay alert.

"Amelia," Neil said.

His grip came down on my upper arm.

I jolted awake, and for a second I didn't know where I was. My face was squished up against something warm, solid, and slightly rough. As soon as I inhaled my next breath, I recognised Neil's scent. Someone's pulse was thrumming. His or mine? Both?

I pulled away from Neil's shoulder with a muttered apology. How long had I been like that? So embarrassing.

Neil's face was pinched in a look of mild annoyance as he smoothed the wrinkles out of his suit from where I had unwittingly rested my head. "We'll be at the hotel soon," he said. "Then you'll be able to have a good sleep."

I tried to stay awake for the rest of the journey, keeping myself occupied with the cityscape unfolding outside the car window; modern high-rises mingled with lush tropical greenery, bathed in vibrant hues of artificial light under the starry sky.

Neil sat stiffly throughout the ride, his brow growing heavier and his forehead lines deepening by the minute. He was worried about something, but I didn't know what. I followed his line of sight to the rearview mirror, where the driver's reflection loomed. Neil's eyes were shooting daggers. I got the sense that something was wrong. Very wrong.

As the car wound through busy streets, the tension in the air grew thicker until Neil snapped, "This isn't the way to the hotel."

The driver didn't respond.

"What's going on?" I asked Neil.

He lowered his voice. "This isn't the transfer you booked. Daniel must have sent this driver to intercept. I suspect we're on our way to meet him now."

I was too tired to analyse what this meant. One answer was all I needed.

"Will we be okay?" I whispered.

"Don't worry," Neil whispered back.

The driver pulled up outside a towering building of metal, glass, and sharp angles.

"Could you at least take Amelia to the hotel?" Neil asked.

"I was instructed to bring you—both of you—here," the driver said. He got out and opened the door for Neil, then for me. I stumbled out of the car into the warm and humid night, shaky on my feet, but alert now from a burst of adrenaline pumping through me.

"Zelthia headquarters?" I asked, staring up at the building.

"Yes," Neil said. "We're supposed to come here tomorrow, so why now? I wonder what Daniel's playing at."

"He must have his reasons."

"You would think so."

The driver handed us off to a pair of big men in suits, both of whom looked like they could snap someone in half with their bare hands if they so desired. Neil and I had no choice but to go with them.

"Stay close," Neil said, voice low and steady. His calm demeanour was the only thing keeping my panic at bay.

The men escorted us through the revolving door into the building. The lobby was expansive, with high ceilings, a tiled floor, and lighting that resembled an art installation. The air was cool and sterile from what felt like industrial-strength air-conditioning. Despite the late hour, we passed a handful of lingering employees. Our escorts led us to a lift. They flanked us as we went up to the highest I've ever been up in a building. The winding corridors that followed only added to the disorienting effect. At last, we arrived in a luxurious office room, furnished with a large table surrounded by black leather armchairs. Floor-to-ceiling windows with a view of the city skyline lined the far wall. Daniel Ling sat at an imposing desk in front of them. He rose to his feet as we approached, and I heard the door close behind us with a snick. Daniel's grin was unnaturally wide and his greasy hair was slicked back, revealing a sharp widow's peak. His eyes bulged as he took in the sight of us. He oozed oily charm. "Neil, Amelia, so glad you made it." He spoke as though he hadn't just forced our presence.

"We were scheduled to visit tomorrow morning," Neil said. "Tell me, what's so urgent that you needed to see us now?"

"My, my. Lovely to see you too."

"Pardon me. It's been a long flight. Amelia is tired. She is not used to travelling."

"But of course. Sit down. Relax. Would you like a beverage?"

"No, thank you."

"And you, Amelia?"

I didn't trust the man not to poison me, so I declined. "I'm all right, thank you."

"Very well. Sit down. Make yourselves comfortable."

We took up seats around the table. I sat next to Neil, heeding his advice to stay close. Daniel sat opposite us. The two big men stood on either side of the door, like guards. I wondered if we were locked in. A troubling thought.

"I trust you had a pleasant flight?" Daniel asked.

"Yes, thank you. A bit bumpy, but nothing out of the ordinary," Neil said.

"And both of you are well?"

"There is always a certain amount of stress involved in the work I do, but apart from that, I am well. Amelia has settled into her role too."

I steeled my nerves and spoke up. "Yes, I have. It's going great."

"Good, good," Daniel said. "Glad to hear it."

"And you?" Neil asked. "How are you managing while the chairman has taken a back seat?"

"As you're well aware, I was born to lead this company."

"Then I trust all is well."

"Of course."

"And the chairman? How is his condition?"

Daniel's smile faded into a solemn line, though it came across as fake. "He's still got his wits about him—for now. His physical decline is more pronounced. He's in the hands of the best health-care professionals in the country. What more can be done?"

"I would like to visit him while I'm here."

"So you should. He still considers you as a second son even now."

"I will go so long as my schedule allows it."

"I'm afraid you're going to be quite busy. Your expertise has been sorely missed."

Their back-and-forth continued in a similar vein for quite some time. Both of them had their guards up, and Daniel's motive for the meeting was still unclear—unless it was just to mess with us.

I was beginning to zone out, my tiredness catching up with me, when Daniel shifted from his seat, half rising. "Anyway, enough chitchat," he said. "Come. A group of my associates are waiting for us at Chang's. Let's have a drink with them."

My heart sank at the thought of prolonging the evening, the promise of a comfortable hotel bed drifting further from my grasp.

"Very well," Neil said. "But I ask that Amelia be excused from joining."

I perked up, heartened by him coming to my defence.

Daniel's expression soured. "Now, that's no fun, is it?"

"I'm serious, Daniel. I wouldn't have let Christine drink with your associates, so why would I let Amelia? She has no business with them, and they have no business with her. I won't allow it."

Daniel let out a condescending chuckle. "You've always been funny like that. How you treat your subordinates is very amusing to me."

"Are we going or not?"

"Fine. Let's go. Eric can drop Amelia off at the hotel on the way."

Daniel rose fully from his seat. Neil and I followed suit and made our way across the room. I mouthed "thank you" to Neil when Daniel wasn't looking.

Leaving the enclosure of the office brought me relief from the feeling of being trapped in and at Daniel's mercy. The effect was fleeting, however, as Daniel ushered us into the confines of the same car we had arrived in, him and Neil in the back, me in the front next to the driver.

"Stop off at the Laurent Hotel, Eric," Daniel told the driver. "It's past the young lady's bedtime."

I was too tired to let his patronising comment get under my skin.

A few minutes later, we pulled up outside the hotel entrance.

"Rest well, Amelia. We have a big day ahead of us tomorrow," Neil said.

"I will. Want me to take your luggage in as well? I can leave it at reception."

"Yes. Thank you. Let's reconvene tomorrow morning."

Daniel leered at me. "Nighty-night," he said with a smirk.

I forced a polite reply through gritted teeth. "Good night, Mr. Ling."

Eric opened the door for me, and I hopped out of the car. A porter was already at my side, ready to whisk me and the luggage through the revolving door and into the hotel lobby. I heard the car drive off as I crossed the threshold, and I spared a thought for Neil, whose night was far from over.

The hotel lobby had a stylish and sophisticated design with black, cream, and gold decor. Two attendants manned the reception desk. I checked in without any issues, then made my way up to my room. I unlocked the door and slipped inside. A comfortable-looking bed awaited me with the cover invitingly turned back. I wanted to dive straight in, but I made myself unpack first so I wouldn't feel rushed in the morning. I set aside my outfit for the next day in a neatly folded pile, placed my books on the bedside table, my laptop on the desk, and my toiletries in the bathroom.

After a quick shower and a minimal skincare routine, I finally sank into the bed. The time on the digital clock said eleven PM, which was three o'clock in the morning in New Zealand time. No wonder I was so tired. Cocooned by the soft mattress, smooth sheets, and fluffy pillows, I quickly succumbed to a deep sleep, uninterrupted, at least for a while…

At an unknown hour, the door creaked open, jolting me awake.

Chapter Thirty-Six

An intruder entered my room and flicked on the lights. I let out a startled shriek, blinded and disorientated.

"A-Amelia?" The voice was Neil's, thick with shock and confusion, giving way to a trace of fascination. "What are you doing here? Why are you in my room? My—" He swallowed. "—*Bed?*"

The bitter smell of alcohol and cigarette smoke hit my nostrils before my vision adjusted. Neil stood at the foot of the bed, his jaw agape at the sight of me. He had dark circles under his bloodshot eyes, and his hair was in disarray. His clothes were dishevelled—shirt wrinkled and half untucked, collar open, sleeves rolled up. He swayed slightly on his feet. A confronting sight when I was used to him being the picture of composure and control. I didn't know what to make of it. All I knew was that Daniel must have put him up to this behaviour because it was so out of character.

I sat up straight against the headboard, shaking off my grogginess and blinking clarity into my blurry vision. "This is *my* room. Why do you have the key?"

Neil peeled his eyes off my body and averted them. That's

when I remembered I was wearing nothing but a thin white tank top and boy shorts. I hastily pulled the blankets up to cover myself.

"I checked in, and this is the room they gave me," Neil explained. "Did you book only one room?"

"Of course not! I don't know what happened."

Neil paced, rubbing his temples. "Okay, okay. I'll sort this out. Just give me one minute. Ugh." He clutched his stomach.

"Are you all right?"

A pallor came over him. "Excuse me."

He slipped into the bathroom and shut the door behind him. The muffled sound of retching seeped through the wall. I steeled myself against second-hand queasiness, feeling sorry for him at the same time.

After several minutes, I heard the toilet flush, then the tap run. Neil emerged, sheepishly running a hand through his hair. "Sorry. You shouldn't have to see me like this. You, of all people… I'm a mess." Self-loathing laced his voice.

I shook my head, trying to downplay the situation. "It's no big deal. You've also seen me drunk. We can call it even."

He scanned my face like he didn't know what to fixate on, then his shoulders slumped in defeat. "You're… sweet."

"Sweet?" I blushed, remembering how I had also called him sweet when I was drunk. If he hugged me now, we'd both be as bad as each other.

Neil winced. "I mean, er, I'll just go downstairs and sort out —" Another stomach clutch. He looked like he might be sick again.

I practically launched myself out of bed. "You're not going anywhere. I'll do it."

"Would you? I'm so sorry." He averted his gaze again, looking everywhere around the room except directly at me.

I went digging through my clothes to find a pair of leggings and a t-shirt to cover up in. Meanwhile, Neil wilted into a sitting position on the edge of the bed with his head in his hands.

I dressed in the bathroom, then grabbed both our key cards. "I'll be back in a minute," I said on my way out the door.

Neil grunted in response.

I wove through the quiet, empty halls, then took the lift down to reception. A lone woman with jet-black hair and a bored expression manned the desk. She didn't notice me arrive because she was too busy looking down at her phone.

"Um, excuse me."

She glanced up at me with a raised eyebrow. "How can I help you?"

"My, uh… my *friend* just checked in before. There's been a mistake. We've got two key cards for the same room, but we're supposed to have separate rooms. The booking's under my name, Amelia Cross."

"What's your room number?"

"Four one nine."

She typed on the computer. "I see what the problem is."

"Oh?"

"You're booked into the same room."

"I know that. Can we get separate rooms, please? We can't sleep in the same room."

"Sorry, but we're fully booked."

Her words slapped me further awake. Fully booked? This didn't bode well. "Can you double-check that? Is there not a single room left? Any room?"

Half-sighing, she typed away on the computer. *Clack-clack-clack.* "There are no rooms left. I can check with one of our sister hotels nearby…"

"I'm not sure. What about tomorrow? Are there any rooms available for tomorrow night?"

"Yes, there are."

That solved part of the problem, but wouldn't help with tonight's situation.

"Hmm. I better update my friend on the situation."

My gut feeling told me that neither of us was in a state to pack up and go to another hotel, but I had to inform Neil, regardless. Maybe he'd have another idea.

I ran through our options in my head on my way back to the room, but when I opened the door and saw Neil, everything changed.

Chapter Thirty-Seven

I took in the scene before me. Neil was sprawled on the bed, eyes closed, his back rising and falling with his breath.

I studied his sleeping form with a mixture of appreciation and uncertainty. He looked far too peaceful to wake—but he was on my bed, taking up all the space, leaving me with nowhere to sleep. He had all his clothes on still—even his shoes. His arms and legs were splayed, his head tilted to the side, a placid look on his face…

Ugh. This was going to be unpleasant for him, but what else could I do? I reached out, braced myself for impact, then gripped him by the shoulder and gave a tentative shake. "Neil?"

He snored softly.

I repeated his name, louder this time.

No response.

I shook him harder. "Wake up!"

Still no response.

It was no use. That was all the force I was willing to use, and he was still completely out to it. Neil had the bed. It was his now.

I dropped onto the edge with a sigh.

What do I do now? Go to another hotel on my own?

I didn't want to. I had already unpacked, and I was sooo tired.

By the time I repacked and moved to another hotel, it would nearly be time to get up. What was the point? No. There was no way I was going to do that. But there was nowhere in the room to sleep except a sliver of floor space, or upright in the desk chair, or the bed—the soft, cloud-like bed…

I looked at Neil, admiring his resting body as the weight of my tiredness threatened to crush me.

At least you're *comfortable.*

Before I knew what I was doing, I unlaced his shoes and pulled them off, then I lifted his head and wedged a pillow underneath him. I didn't realise how intimate my actions would feel until I was midway through doing them, and by then I couldn't stop myself. I lingered with his head in my hand, his skin rough with stubble against my palm, my fingers entwined in his dark hair.

"Melia," Neil mumbled as I gently released him.

I froze. "Neil?"

He didn't say anything else. His eyes were still closed, his breathing even.

Was that my name? Was he having a dream about me? The notion piqued my interest, but I shrugged it off. So what if he was? It wouldn't be unexpected. I was the last person he saw before he fell asleep, after all. It didn't mean anything.

I glanced at the time. It was nearly three in the morning. If I closed my eyes now, if I lay my head down…

Screw it.

With the last remaining shred of strength I had, I got up and turned off the lights, then returned to the bed, where I carefully slipped under the covers and moulded myself into a position that left as much distance between us as possible. The softness of the mattress embraced my tired body, and I let out a sigh of relief. I could feel Neil's presence beside me, hear his breathing. He was the last thing to occupy my thoughts before I fell asleep.

* * *

I awoke to an unfamiliar ceiling above me, its flat white surface bathed in early-morning sunlight. The next thing I noticed was the arm draped over my waist, skin to skin since my t-shirt and tank top had ridden up, exposing my stomach. The toned forearm was lightly tanned, with veins running through it and a dusting of fine, dark hair. Realisation who it belonged to sank in as the events of the previous few hours came rushing back to me. I tilted my head to the side and saw Neil lying beside me, fast asleep, oblivious to the compromising position we were in. At some point, he must have got under the covers, consciously or unconsciously, and the space between us had evaporated. He was so close I could feel his breath.

I lay in a stupefied state, paralysed by the conflicting desires to eject myself from the bed at once and to burrow so flush to the contours of his body that I could feel every inch of him pressed to me. I let out a shaky breath and tried to collect myself. I had a sliver of opportunity here. If I got out of bed now, before Neil woke, I could pretend I had never slept beside him and save us both a whole load of embarrassment. If he did somehow remember me in bed with him, I could tell him it must have been a dream.

Yes. That's what I'll do.

With a newfound sense of resolve, I flung the covers half off of me and tried to roll out from under Neil's arm without disturbing him. This proved impossible. Neil was clinging to me, and the weight of his arm had me pinned to the mattress. Heart pounding, I grasped his wrist to lift his arm off me. Neil grunted and stirred. I froze, my hand still wrapped around his wrist. I sucked in a breath before resuming the task of carefully lifting his limb and moving it off me.

Almost... there...

My alarm sounded, blasting its familiar melody at a volume which should be illegal. Startled, I dropped Neil's arm right back into its original position. Neil groaned with a sound that was almost lewd.

My phone was on the table on Neil's side, and I couldn't reach it to turn off the alarm. Neil twisted towards me and cracked open his eyes. I winced, feeling like a deer in headlights. He blinked several times, as if he didn't believe his eyes. Maybe he thought he was dreaming. Next, his gaze darted to his arm outstretched over me, and he let out a startled noise. "Ah!"

He snapped away from me like a magnet being repelled, taking up residence at the furthest reaches of the bed.

The alarm finally stopped blaring, but my heartbeat was still drumming in my ears.

Neil shyly returned his gaze to me. "What happened?" he asked, his voice husky.

I grimaced, unsure where to begin. "How much do you remember?"

Neil swallowed. "We didn't… we didn't… did we?"

Oh my gosh.

My cheeks felt like you could fry eggs on them. "Of course not!"

Neil heaved himself into a sitting position, his shirt a crumpled mess, while I adjusted my top, covering myself up.

Neil scratched his head. "I remember arriving in this hotel room, but I don't remember getting into bed with you."

"Because you didn't." I couldn't let Neil believe he was the one who had instigated this scenario. I respected him far too much for that. "You fell asleep on the bed while I went down to reception. I couldn't get another room because the hotel was fully booked, and I couldn't wake you up when I returned… I was just so tired. I didn't know what else to do. I'm sorry."

Some of the stiffness melted from Neil's shoulders. "Hmm. I should have tried harder to stay awake and not put you in such an unreasonable position."

"It's not your fault."

"Neither is it yours."

An awkward lull passed between us. I was more aware than ever that we were in bed together. Neil and I. Me and my boss.

"I'm going to have a shower," I said quickly.

"Go ahead."

I jumped out of bed and scurried to the bathroom, unable to take a breath until the door was closed and locked behind me. My heart was still beating a million miles a minute. Neil had been understanding of the situation, so why was I an emotional wreck?

The hot shower soothed my frayed nerves, but I still felt skittish afterwards. I had to get changed back into my leggings and t-shirt because I had forgotten to bring other clothes into the bathroom with me. When I emerged, Neil was sitting at the foot of the bed, cradling his head in his hands with a pained expression on his face.

"Are you okay?" I asked, coming to his side.

"My head is killing me."

I had an urge to lay a sympathetic hand on his shoulder but stopped myself. "I have paracetamol. Do you want some?"

"Yes, please."

I poured a glass of water in the bathroom, then located a foil blister pack of pills in my toiletries bag. Neil was massaging his temples upon my return. He accepted the water and paracetamol and gulped them down.

"I'm not surprised you have a headache after the state you were in last night," I said. "But I am curious. I thought you said you didn't drink."

"There are two sides of me."

I quirked a brow. "What does that mean?"

"I have to be a different person in Daniel's presence."

I kind of caught his drift, but I also wondered if he was still slightly drunk.

"I'm sorry you saw me like that," he said.

I shrugged his comment off. "You were remarkably put together for someone so inebriated."

The corner of Neil's lips twitched up. "Was I?"

"Apart from the throwing up, I mean."

Neil winced.

"Don't worry. I'm not judging you."

He glanced at his phone. "We better get ready. We should leave soon."

"Will you be okay?"

"I have to be. The shareholder's meeting won't get cancelled over my hangover. Everyone's expecting me to speak."

"I'm sure you'll feel better once the paracetamol kicks in."

"Yes. I'm sure you're right."

The hint of doubt in his voice didn't escape me.

Chapter Thirty-Eight

I was the only woman in the room at the shareholders' meeting and definitely the youngest. Grey hair, spectacles, and business suits were the prevailing features of the attendees, with Neil and Daniel sticking out as youthful by comparison.

During a long round of introductory pleasantries, Neil steered me towards a tall man with silver hair, a neat beard, and glasses with thick black rims.

"Good morning, Alan," Neil said.

The man grinned. "Ah! The protégé has returned!"

I noted he had an English accent much like Neil's. What did he mean by protégé?

"Alan, I'd like you to meet my new secretary, Amelia Cross. Amelia, this is Alan Dixon, CEO of Avenex Holdings, an investment firm based in London and one of Zelthia's largest shareholders."

"Nice to meet you, Mr. Dixon," I said.

"Pleasure, Ms. Cross."

He had a kind of dark and twinkling charisma, which made me think he might swoop down and kiss my hand. He did not, however. Thank goodness.

Dixon's attention returned to Neil. "I must say, you're looking rather peaky. Are you quite all right?"

"Late night last night and one too many drinks, I'm afraid."

"That will do it."

The pair of them chatted for a spell before Neil whisked me away to talk with other people.

Following the period of pre-meeting socialising, everyone settled into their designated places at desks arranged in a layout of two concentric square-cornered U shapes. The open ends of the formation faced a central desk, the placard on which read "Daniel Ling, President, Zelthia Group." A lectern stood on a raised platform behind the desk, with a large screen dominating the back wall bordered by a pair of black curtains draping from ceiling to floor. A flag bearing the company's logo hung limp in the corner.

Looking around, most of the shareholders had come unaccompanied by an assistant or business partner, so in addition to being young and female, this also made me feel conspicuous. I sat up straight and squared my shoulders, trying to conceal my self-consciousness. Meanwhile, Neil shifted in his seat beside me, his posture slouched as he rested a hand on his stomach. I instinctively reached for the complimentary bottle of mineral water on our desk and poured him a glass. "Stay hydrated," I said.

Neil accepted the glass. "Thank you."

Daniel Ling took up residence at the main desk, his beady eyes scanning the room. When his gaze fell upon Neil, the corners of his mouth twitched up in a deranged sort of smirk. He tapped the microphone in front of him.

"Now that we're all settled, let's get on with today's agenda. First up, we have the proposed alliance with Magnium Oil. We need a majority vote to go ahead with the partnership—"

A man stationed at the desk opposite Neil's and mine suddenly stood to his feet. He fidgeted with his phone in his hands, forehead wrinkled and lips quivering.

"Yes, Mr. Lee?" Daniel asked with thinly veiled irritation.

"Chairman Donald Ling will be here soon."

The room erupted into murmurs.

"How can that be?" someone asked. "He's confined to a hospital bed."

"Chairman Ling is coming to the shareholder meeting," Mr. Lee reiterated. "Right now."

The words had barely left his mouth before the double doors at the back of the room flung open. A hush fell as everyone's heads turned to witness the late arrival. An elderly man in a wheelchair entered the room, surrounded by an entourage of black-suited men with straight-faced expressions.

So, this is the chairman.

I was in the presence of one of the richest and most powerful men in the world. I took in his dour expression and bushy white eyebrows. Part of his face looked slack, as if he had lost control of its function, and his arms and legs were withered. Despite his frail appearance, he maintained an aura of power. I sensed he was a man you wouldn't want to mess with, even in his current condition.

With my focus on the chairman, it took me a second to notice that everyone in the room had stood up. I followed suit.

"Chairman," Daniel said. "What brings you here?"

"Why do I need a reason to be here?" the chairman barked in a gruff voice with a slight speech impediment. "I'm the primary shareholder and the chairman of the board. Of course I should be here. Where's my table?"

"Chairman Ling," Neil said, gesturing to the empty desk next to us at the left tip of the inner U.

A member of the chairman's entourage wheeled him over. Neil moved the seat out of the way to make room for the wheelchair.

Once the chairman was in position, everyone sat back down. The chairman gave Neil a once-over. For a fleeting moment, I thought I saw fondness in his stare, but his expression quickly turned stony. "Neil, my boy, are you ill?" he asked.

"I admit I'm feeling a tad under the weather today."

"Hmph. That's unlike you."

"Yes, well, it's unfortunate." Neil examined him. "At least you look well."

The chairman made no comment. Instead, his gaze wandered over to me. It looked like he was about to say something, but Daniel cleared his throat, drawing everyone's attention back to him.

"We were about to vote on the Magnium partnership," Daniel said. "All in favour?"

I watched Neil raise his hand without a hint of hesitation, along with the vast majority of others in the room, including the chairman. That Neil would so readily agree to a partnership with an oil company surprised me. His vegetarian diet and electric car had me under the impression he was conscious about the environment. Maybe not. Or maybe he had his reasons.

Daniel struck his gavel, passing the motion. From there, he moved through the rest of the agenda, but I was too preoccupied by Neil's deteriorating condition to pay much attention to the business decisions being discussed. Neil's presentation drew closer, and he was doubled over in his chair, face drained of all colour, hands clutching his gut. How was he going to present in this state?

"Now, I'd like to invite Neil Kingston, CEO of Luxmore Appliances in New Zealand, to give an update on the company's finances," Daniel said. "As you will remember, Neil put a stop to the Flerotech merger and took over as CEO, promising an uplift in the company's performance. Let's see how he has fared. Neil?"

Daniel directed a sly grin at Neil, and all of a sudden, it fell into place. The reason Daniel had insisted on taking Neil out last night and plied him with alcohol and who knows what else. He had planned on sabotaging this presentation by making him look incompetent in front of the chairman and the shareholders. Why he would do such a thing, I did not know, but it seemed in line with his character based on what Neil had told me. It could be a power move to assert his dominance and remind Neil who's boss.

I watched Neil shakily stand up, looking like he could pass out at any second. Was he aware that he was about to walk straight into a trap?

I got to my feet before I knew what I was doing. "Wait."

Neil halted.

"I can't let you do this. You're unwell. I'll give the presentation. I'll do it. Sit back down. Please."

Neil studied me, his jaw muscle straining.

"What's going on?" Daniel asked.

"Neil is feeling sick," I announced. "I will present in his place."

Even as I said the words, I had yet to process my spur-of-the-moment decision.

Daniel gnashed his teeth. For a second, it looked like he might push back against my proposal, but ultimately, he conceded. "Very well," he said, the twinkle returning to his black eyes. "Please come forward."

I didn't give Neil the chance to stop me, hastening to take the stand, but as I turned to face the audience, the reality of what I was about to undertake hit me. Here I was, in a room full of some of the wealthiest people in Asia, about to give a presentation that could make or break the future of Luxmore Appliances and the jobs of thousands of employees. My throat turned dry. I gulped.

On instinct, I looked to Neil. His jaw worked as he watched me, a mixture of concern and intrigue displayed on his pallid face. I told myself that if he truly thought me incapable, he would have stopped me, no matter what. I kept this in mind as I brought up the presentation on the provided laptop.

With the first slide up on the wall and my notes on the laptop in front of me, I checked the microphone, then took a deep breath, ready to begin.

Here goes.

I emptied my mind of everything except the contents of each slide and the underlying goal of showing that Luxmore was on the brink of an uplift in financial performance. The thorough speaking notes saved my life as I bluffed my way through the presentation just like I had when I presented in Amelia Crook's place all those months ago.

I didn't stop for questions, keeping the momentum going as I moved from slide to slide. At last, I reached the end, and for the first time since I had begun, I allowed myself to look directly at the audience members and gauge their reactions. Some faces showed mild interest, but the prevailing mood resembled boredom. Boredom was fine. I could work with boredom. At least it wasn't outrage or disapproval.

Satisfied with my performance, and glad it was over, I made a move to step down, but before I could leave the platform, Daniel spoke. "Does anyone have any questions for Miss Cross?" he asked with a malicious undertone.

My whole body clenched as I anticipated probing questions designed to trip me up.

A man in the audience leaned forward and bellowed into his microphone. "I would be interested in knowing how those results compare to the original projected outlook of a merger with Flerotech."

The question was just as thorny as I expected, and my mind was blank. I couldn't see Daniel's face from my position, but I could imagine his glee. Finally, something that would out Neil's foolishness.

But Neil wasn't having any of it.

Though his face was scrunched in pain, he bent towards his microphone. "There is no such comparison to be made. The Flerotech merger would have effectively dissolved the company. Any more questions can be directed to me. You all have my contact details. I'll get back to you over the coming days. All will be answered, I assure you."

The rigidity of my body melted away in relief. I hurried back down to my seat before anything else could go wrong.

"You have your secretary well-trained," the chairman said to Neil in a way that made it sound like I was a domestic animal.

Neil just nodded in response.

Neil and I left as soon as the meeting concluded. Once we had some distance from the meeting room, Neil guided me to a vacant area on the same floor and asked me to stay put while he sorted himself out. Seated on a bench between two tall and leafy potted plants, I pulled out a book to read and awaited his return.

While I was absorbed in my reading, I didn't notice someone come up to me.

"Miss Cross."

My skin crawled in reaction to the voice. I looked up from my book and saw Daniel Ling glaring down at me.

I tried to appear calm, though I felt anything but. I had to be on my guard. "Mr. Ling," I said politely, getting to my feet.

Daniel regarded me with interest. "That was quite the performance you pulled back there."

"I know it wasn't ideal, but I couldn't let Mr. Kingston present while sick."

"How considerate."

I plastered on a smile. "Just doing my job."

"It worked out to be very convenient that he brought you along, didn't it?"

"You're right. I'm glad that Neil trusted me enough to accompany him and to let me present in his place."

"I wonder—"

I didn't get to hear Daniel finish with his train of thought because a third party interrupted our conversation. Neil had returned. I relaxed straight away, just knowing he was with me.

"Daniel, what business do you have with Amelia?"

Daniel rearranged his face into an affable look. "I was just complimenting her on the informative presentation."

"She did well."

Daniel looked him up and down. "You seem to have a spring back in your step."

"I'm feeling much better now, thank you."

"Had I known you had become such a lightweight, I wouldn't have insisted on taking you out last night."

"New Zealand does not have much of a workplace drinking culture compared to Singapore. I'm out of practice."

Daniel let out a noise that was half scoff, half chuckle.

Neil pointedly checked his watch. "I have a busy schedule ahead of me."

"And Miss Cross?"

"She has Luxmore business to attend to."

"I'm sure I could rustle up a desk for her."

"There's no need. She can work at the hotel, and I'm sure it will be more comfortable for her."

"Very well. Then I'll see both of you tomorrow."

"Yes. Have a good day, Daniel."

Daniel gave a sharp nod in response before striding off.

"It appears I can't leave you by yourself for a few minutes in this building," Neil said.

"Do you think Daniel purposefully went looking for me?"

"I do. What did he say to you?"

"Nothing much. He made some comments about the presentation, and how it was convenient you brought me with you. I wonder what he wants?"

"I can think of a few ideas. Like I said, it would be best if you returned to the hotel. The rest of my meetings today are one on one."

I scrutinised Neil's appearance, looking for lingering signs of ill health. Some of the colour had returned to his face, and his eyes looked clearer and brighter than before.

"Will you be okay?" I asked. "How do you feel now?"

"Much better."

"That's good."

I considered mentioning my belief about Daniel drugging Neil on purpose, but thought better of it. Daniel's home turf wasn't a good place to bring it up.

"There's a taxi stand across the road from the main entrance of the building," Neil said. "On second thought, I have some time. I'll escort you to a cab."

I followed Neil to the ground floor, then outside to the taxi stand. The contrast between the air-conditioned building and the blistering heat outside was stark. A warm clamminess bloomed on my forehead and underarms.

Neil leaned close to me before I got in the cab. "Be alert if you decide to leave the hotel. I don't mean to alarm you, but it's possible someone could be watching you."

His words spooked me. I didn't know how to react except to nod. I climbed into the cab, and Neil closed the door.

His warning echoed in my head as the car started to move.

"Miss?"

I realised the driver was trying to get my attention. "Yes? Ah, sorry. The Laurent Hotel, please."

Did Neil really think I was of such interest to Daniel that he would have me monitored? I supposed it would explain how Daniel found me so easily after the meeting. But to have his eye on me outside the confines of Zelthia headquarters as well…

I shook my head. Neil just wanted me to be cautious. That's all. He had to play it safe in case Daniel was suspicious of his actions—and my actions were an extension of his.

When I got to the hotel, paranoia made me check my surroundings as I walked to my room. No suspicious individuals in the lobby, no one getting into the lift with me or following me down the corridor. My room was just how I'd left it, except for the fresh bed linen, towels, and vacuum cleaner tracks in the carpet. Neil's belongings were all gone—he had already moved into another room.

I set my laptop on the desk and pulled out the chair to sit down. That's when I noticed one thing Neil had forgotten. His shirt from the previous night was draped over the chair. I picked up the crumpled garment. Even though it was dirty from the long hours of wear and the humidity, I admired it because it belonged to him. My thoughts returned to being in bed with him, and my cheeks broke out in a flush of heat. How did I even make it through the day in his presence when *that* had happened? Sighing, I placed the shirt on my bed and made a mental note to return it to Neil when he came back to the hotel—whatever time that might be. At last, I settled at the desk to check my emails and catch up on work.

Hunger pangs interrupted my working session late in the afternoon. It made sense since my body was still operating on NZ time, and I hadn't eaten lunch apart from the snacks provided at the shareholder meeting. I thought about checking out the nearby eateries, but Neil's warning replayed in my mind. It was enough to put me off going exploring on my own. The hotel restaurant wasn't open yet, so I ordered room service instead. I returned to my work while I waited for my meal.

Even though I expected the knock at the door, it still made me jump. I gathered myself and rose to answer it. The promise of hot noodle soup to satiate my hunger had me grasping the handle without checking the peephole, and I flung open the door. I gasped as I came face to face with the person on the other side.

Chapter Thirty-Nine

At first, I didn't recognise the woman standing in front of me. She looked so different compared to the last time I had seen her, with her face bare and hair loose, wearing black sneakers and a simple long shirt dress which skimmed over a baby bump I hadn't noticed last time. Her identity didn't reveal itself to me until she smiled, dimples forming in her cheeks. The same dimples I had seen in pictures online. The longer I stared at her, the more certain I became. She was Ruby—Veronica Ling—and she was even more beautiful like this than she had been on the night I saw her with Neil. I was in awe.

"You must be Amelia Cross," she said. Her voice was warm and serene.

I nodded, still dumbfounded by her surprise appearance.

"I'm a friend of Neil's." Her eyes flicked to the room behind me. "Is he here?"

So, she was here to see Neil. A risky move given Neil thought Daniel might be having us watched. Even her talking to me was dangerous enough. I took a cursory glance both ways down the corridor. "Sorry," I said, after confirming we were alone. "He's still working. I'm not sure when he'll be back, and this is my room, not his."

Veronica's radiant smile did not dull. "I see. Then sorry to bother you."

"I can let him know you came by."

"Thank you. I'll just—agh!" She brought a hand to her belly, her face twisted in discomfort.

A surge of panic coursed through me as I relived the moment I found Christine in the bathroom stall, keeled over in pain. "Are you okay?"

"I'm—" She sucked in a gasp of air. "I think I need to sit down for a minute."

Without hesitation, I cast aside my lingering worries to offer my aid. "Please, come in and take a seat. I'll get you a glass of water."

"So kind. Thank you."

I ushered Veronica into my room and to the desk chair. As she settled, I poured her a glass of water, my mind racing with concern both for Veronica and the potential consequences of her unexpected visit. But in that moment, all that mattered was tending to her needs. I handed her the glass of water, and she took a sip. I perched on the edge of the bed, watching her closely, ready to offer my support at any moment.

"Thank you, Amelia," she said, her voice filled with genuine appreciation. "I didn't expect to run into you, but I'm glad I did."

"I wasn't expecting you, either."

She studied me. "You know who I am, don't you?"

"Yes. Neil told me... well, only because I worked it out on my own."

I noticed her eyes flit to Neil's shirt lying on my bed, and I blushed, knowing what she was thinking.

"You must be getting along well with him," she said, a smile returning to her lips.

"That's, uh, it's not like that, I swear. It's a long story."

"Don't worry. I believe you. Neil is a good man. Whatever happens, I just want him to be happy."

The fact that Veronica and Neil used to be engaged sprang to the forefront of my mind, and I felt a twinge of jealousy. I could never measure up to Veronica's level of success, wealth, and beauty. If those were the standards required to attract Neil's attention, I felt foolish for my silly little crush on him. But despite my insecurities, I felt no animosity towards Veronica. She was too lovely.

"He told me you used to be a couple," I said, testing the waters, wondering how much information I could glean about their relationship.

"Yes." She had a wistful look in her eyes. "That was ages ago."

"If you don't mind me asking, why did you break up? Sorry, I know that's a personal question. You don't have to answer."

"My brother didn't like the idea of us getting married, for one thing, but that's not the main reason. We weren't compatible. It's as simple as that."

I looked at her baby bump, then at her hand, which was bereft of a wedding or engagement ring. "Did you meet someone else?"

She smiled, patting her stomach. "Yes. But that's not public knowledge. Nor is my pregnancy. I'm very private about all that."

"I understand. It must be tough for a woman in your position."

She nodded. "I keep business and my personal life separate, and that's the way I intend to keep it."

She finished her last sip of water. I retrieved the empty glass from her. "Are you feeling better now?"

"Yes. I don't know what that pain was, but it's gone now. Thank you so much for allowing me into your room."

"You're welcome. Sorry you didn't get to see Neil."

"I should have known he would be busy. Never mind."

"You could come back later, but I'm not sure if he'll be up to much when he gets back. He was very sick this morning."

"Oh dear. Promise you'll look after him for me."

Her playful remark renewed the sting of embarrassment on my cheeks. "I will."

Veronica struggled to get out of the seat. I came to her aid, lending her my arm.

"Thank you," she said.

I showed her the way to the door.

"Goodbye, Amelia. I'm glad I got to meet you."

"Me too."

She offered one last angelic smile as we parted. I found it hard to believe she was related to a snake like Daniel Ling.

Our meeting had been so engaging that I had forgotten all about my food order until the next knock on the door. This time, I didn't neglect to check the peephole.

* * *

With Neil's folded shirt in my hands, I mustered the courage to walk to his hotel room. The shirt was a pretext. My true intention was to check in on him and see how he was doing now he had returned.

Standing outside Neil's door, I hesitated for a moment, wondering if it was okay for me to drop by unannounced like this. My brain taunted me with memories of sharing a bed with him, whipping up a frenzy of butterflies in my stomach and giving me second thoughts. With a deep breath, I dismissed my doubts and readied my fist to knock, but before my knuckles reached the door, it swung open to reveal Neil standing before me, looking half surprised, half amused. "Amelia, what are you doing here?"

He was still dressed in business attire, but without the jacket, and with his collar undone and his sleeves rolled up. I was so captivated by his presence that I forgot to answer his question.

"Is that my shirt?"

I snapped to my senses and held the shirt out to him. "Yes. You left it in my room."

"Ah. Thank you." He took it from me, his fingers brushing against mine, making my skin prickle.

I gathered myself, focusing on the purpose of my visit. "How are you feeling?"

"Yes, much better, though I think an early night is in order."

"I'm sure that's for the best. Were you about to go somewhere?"

"Just to grab something to eat." Neil scrutinised me, his arms folded. "Is there something you want to discuss?"

His prompt reminded me of the other reason I came. I had to tell him about Veronica. "Yes. There is. It's about—" I stopped myself. I looked up and down the corridor, making sure we were alone. "I had a visitor this afternoon. Did you know?"

Neil jolted in response, then his demeanour turned serious. "Let's talk inside."

His room was just like mine but with a slightly different layout, and he was less tidy with his belongings than I was, his work spread out on his desk, and his suitcase lying open on his bed. He closed the door, put the shirt aside, and without inviting me to sit down, he got straight to the point. "Who came to your room? Don't tell me Daniel sent someone after you."

I shook my head. "Nothing like that. Actually, it was Ruby."

Neil's face twisted into an expression which betrayed an even deeper shock. "What?"

"She was looking for you."

"That's strange. I haven't heard anything from her. Are you sure it was her?"

"Yes. Though she looked a bit different to the last time I saw her. She was pregnant. I recognised her dimples—they're quite distinctive."

"What did she say?"

"She asked if you were at the hotel. I told her you were still working, then she suddenly got a stomach cramp. She looked uncomfortable, so I invited her inside to sit for a minute. I was worried about her."

Neil digested all of this. "Hmm… Did she say anything else while she was with you?"

"We just got talking. Chitchat. Nothing deep."

"Can you be more specific? What exactly did you talk about?"

I shuffled my feet. "Well, uh… *you*, mainly." My voice faltered. "She saw your shirt in my room, and I think she got the wrong idea."

If my face wasn't red before, it was now.

Neil let out a long, audible sigh and said nothing.

"She recovered from her pain, and she left. Do you think it wasn't her?"

"No, it sounds like her, and it will be easy enough for me to verify. I wonder what she's playing at." Neil rubbed his temples.

"Is it strange she came to see you without any notice?"

"Yes, but I don't believe that's what happened. I think she came to see *you*."

I gaped. "You mean she tricked me?"

"Yes. That's exactly what I think."

I flashed back to Veronica clutching her stomach and the strain on her face. Had that been an act? Did she just want me to invite her inside so she could speak with me? Surely not…

"But why would she want to see me? That doesn't make any sense."

"She must have wanted to check you out for some reason. I will be questioning her about this, mark my words. I told her I didn't want you dragged into this any more than you already have been, and she turns up here in broad daylight, without an ounce of consideration for your safety. What was she thinking?" Neil clenched his fists, a deep scowl marring his already stern face.

I tried to placate him. "I'm sure she had her reasons."

He grunted in response, a sound I felt deep in my bones.

I changed the subject, feeling like the thick tension in the room might break me if I didn't. "I better leave you to get your dinner. It's getting late."

Neil glanced at his watch. "So it is. What about you? Have you eaten?"

"Yes. I had an early dinner."

"What did you have?"

"Noodles from room service. I didn't want to leave the hotel after what you said."

Neil grimaced. "Perhaps my warning was excessive. I didn't mean to scare you."

"Better safe than sorry, I guess."

Silence descended between us. It looked like Neil was trying to gather words to say something, but in the meantime, my heart was thrumming so hard I was certain he could hear it. I needed to leave before it gave me away. "I'll just… get going then."

"Milly."

There it was again—my nickname. He used it more frequently these days, but I still noticed whenever he did.

I faced him front on. "Yes?"

"I didn't get to thank you properly. For today. For your input at the meeting. You were…" He swallowed. "Very classy."

Classy? He thinks I'm classy?

I couldn't hold back the smile bursting onto my face. "That means a lot coming from you."

Neil's composure wavered, his eyes flitting away before meeting mine once more. "I'll see you tomorrow morning." His formality did little to mask something boiling under the surface.

I nodded. "Good night, Neil."

"Good night."

I left him with one final, lingering gaze, trying to analyse if he felt the same things I felt, but I couldn't get a read on him.

Chapter Forty

"Stay by my side today," Neil said as we prepared to embark on our second day of business at Zelthia headquarters.

I knew the reason for his request was to protect me from Daniel Ling, but in any case, I was all too happy to oblige. Any excuse to bask in the proximity of Neil's presence.

We attended back-to-back meetings throughout the day, executing our plan to stick together without a hiccup. Complacency was beginning to set in when the boardroom door swung open, and a young man barged in with a grave expression etched on his face. The atmosphere grew tense, all heads turned towards the intruder.

"Excuse me, Mr. Kingston." The man's voice quivered. "You're needed in an urgent meeting. A critical situation has come up."

Neil maintained his outward calmness. "What's the situation?"

"I don't know the details, just that it's an urgent matter, demanding your immediate attention."

"Hmm." Neil didn't seem convinced, but he got to his feet, regardless. "Very well. Amelia?"

"She can't come," the messenger interjected. "It's a top-level staff meeting only. I hope you understand. It's very sensitive information being discussed."

Neil glanced at me with a flicker of concern. I could tell he was torn about leaving me behind. The sentiment was touching, but I didn't want him to disobey his orders for my sake. Murmurs had broken out in the room, and from what my ears picked up, Neil's hesitancy was already inviting suspicion. He couldn't afford to delay his response another second.

"It's okay," I said. "You go ahead and handle this. We'll catch up later."

Neil searched my face with a tinge of worry in his eyes. I put on a self-assured front so he wouldn't feel guilty. At last, he gave a reluctant nod, then followed the messenger out the door in a hurry.

Not long after Neil left, the rest of the gathering dispersed. I headed back to my assigned office room on a quiet floor of the building with a plan to work on Luxmore business until Neil returned. As I approached the room, one glance through the internal window told me everything remained as Neil and I had left it. Satisfied that I'd be able to get on with my work in peace, I reached for the doorknob, fingers grazing the cool metal. I turned my wrist, but met with resistance. The door was locked. I racked my brain. Had Neil locked the door when we left? I couldn't recall him doing so, but maybe he had. We had left valuable belongings in the room, after all. I jiggled the doorknob a few times, to no avail. It was definitely locked.

Now what do I do?

I had no idea how long Neil was going to take, and I didn't know who to approach about unlocking the door. Calling Neil during his important meeting seemed like a bad idea as well. I could find somewhere else in the building to work, but my laptop was locked inside the room, and I wouldn't be able to get much done without it. Besides, Neil wouldn't like me wandering around the building on my own in case I bumped into someone he didn't want me to.

I was still floundering about what to do when footsteps drew near. I perked up, hoping whoever it was could help me. A man turned the corner. He was tall and beefy, wearing all black apart from the gold glint of a security badge. He looked familiar, but I couldn't place him. Had he been on duty in the lobby when I arrived? Regardless, he looked like someone who could assist me, so I didn't hesitate to grab his attention. "Excuse me."

The security guard came up to me. "How can I help you?"

"I'm locked out of my office. Is there someone who can unlock it for me?"

"Certainly. I can sort that out if you follow me."

He had a friendly and sympathetic demeanour, and I just about went along with him without thinking. Then my senses kicked in. "Can I just wait here?"

He pointed to the visitor card on the lanyard hanging around my neck. "I'm going to need to scan that and verify your identity."

"Here." I removed the lanyard and tried to hand it over to him, but he wouldn't take it.

"You should keep that on. You need it to go anywhere in the building."

"I'll wait right here."

He shook his head. "I can't promise I'll be able to come back straight away if I get caught up with other business. It's best you come with me, or I won't be able to help you."

I hesitated.

"It's up to you," he said.

I took another glance through the internal window. It occurred to me that my laptop wasn't the only significant item I had left in the room. My hotel key card was stashed in the pocket of my laptop bag. I winced, feeling my resistance slip away. "Okay. I'll go."

It didn't take long for me to realise I had made a terrible decision.

When the lift door closed on us, and we lurched upwards, I

realised I had seen this view before. I peered up at the man beside me, and recognition finally triggered. He was one of Daniel Ling's henchmen who had escorted me and Neil up in the lift to Daniel's office on the night we arrived.

My breath caught in my chest, the walls of the lift closing in on me. We weren't on our way to get a key. He was delivering me to Daniel Ling, just like last time. Escape was futile. The man would easily overpower me if I dared try.

"Where are we going?" I asked as he led me through winding corridors.

His stony silence was confirmation of what I already knew to be true.

We stopped outside the entrance to Daniel's office. The man pushed open the door, granting me passage into the lion's den. Daniel sat behind his desk at the end of the long room, watching me with calculating eyes, his fingers interlaced. Daniel's henchman closed the door behind us, and this time, I heard the unmistakable sound of a lock clicking. I girded my loins.

"Miss Cross, we meet again." Daniel rose from his desk, beckoning me closer.

I reluctantly approached, my insides churning. "Good afternoon, Mr. Ling. Sorry, but I'm a bit confused. Why have I been brought here?"

Daniel smirked. "You are, are you? I thought you were an intelligent woman."

He was mocking me. Clearly, the wide-eyed and innocent act wasn't going to work on him.

"What can I do for you?" I asked, serious now.

"Why don't we sit down? Please." Daniel motioned to the seating around the table.

I shakily lowered myself into a chair. Daniel sat opposite me. My heart galloped.

"You gave a remarkable performance at the shareholder meeting yesterday." An undercurrent of malice mingled with the appreciation in his voice. "I must admit, I underestimated you."

"The situation called for me to step up."

"Oh, indeed. Neil must have been pleased."

I had a sense that Daniel was about to spring something on me, but I didn't know what.

"You and Neil..." He traced an invisible pattern onto the table's surface with his finger. "You have a *special* relationship. Am I wrong?"

My confusion was genuine this time. "Special? What do you mean?"

Daniel gave a hollow laugh. "Come now. Neil Kingston is a wealthy man, a powerful man, exceedingly intelligent, influential. He can open doors for you in ways you can't even fathom. Women have fallen into his arms for far less."

I gawked at him. "You think we're—we're—"

"Fucking? There's no need to be coy, dear. You're young, attractive, and inexperienced. Why else would Neil hire you?" He leered at me. "You're his type too."

I crossed my arms, partly in defiance, partly to shield myself from Daniel's repulsive gaze. "We're not—"

"So you're going to deny it, then? Suit yourself."

I could protest all I wanted, but I knew he wouldn't believe me.

Daniel leaned in across the table, close enough I could smell his stale breath. "Let me tell you something, Amelia Cross. Neil is *nothing* compared to me. I can offer you so much more. Join forces with me, and anything you desire could be yours."

I shuddered. What exactly was he proposing? And what consequences would I face if I turned him down?

"Well?" he prompted.

"I don't know you," I spluttered. "I don't want anything from you."

He narrowed his eyes. "How can you be so sure? You haven't even heard me out yet."

The last thing I wanted to do was anger him. I'd have to play along for now. "What do you want me to do?"

Daniel sat back in his chair. "A simple arrangement. Keep an eye on Neil for me, report what he's up to, including his liaisons with you and with anyone else. In return, I'll pay you handsomely. Just name your price. What do you say?"

Suddenly, Neil's former assertion that I could be a spy for Daniel was no longer outlandish. I let his offer sink in, mining it for all its ramifications. Based on what Neil had told me about Daniel, as well as my own misgivings, my answer was never going to be yes, but I hoped that stalling for time could defuse the situation somehow.

"I don't have all day," Daniel said, his laid-back facade turning prickly and tense.

I swallowed my fear and met his eyes. "There's something I just don't understand. Why do you want to know all that about Neil?"

Annoyance flickered across Daniel's face. "Sorry, but you don't get to ask questions. So what will it be? Are you in?"

Nothing I said now could lead to a positive outcome, no matter how carefully I picked my words. All I could think to do was to rebuff him as gently as possible. "Your offer is tempting, but to be honest, I don't see how I can be much use to you." I kept my voice steady despite the fear bubbling beneath the surface. "I'm just Neil's employee. I don't know much about what he gets up to privately."

Daniel scoffed. "He must have you wrapped around his little finger. Well, guess what, dear. If you think he cares about you, you're sorely mistaken. I know the man far better than you ever will, and he won't hesitate to throw you to the wolves when the time comes. If you know what's good for you—"

A sudden loud bang at the door shattered the oppressive atmosphere and injected a surge of hope in my chest. Another bang. Urgent, frantic. Someone desperate to get in.

Daniel sighed through gritted teeth, rolling his eyes. "Let him in."

His henchman opened the door. Neil burst in with raw fury

burning in his eyes. He marched straight up to Daniel like he was about to throttle him. He was a sight to behold. "What do you think you're playing at?" he spat.

"Oh dear me." Daniel re-adopted a mocking tone. "Are you upset to find me alone with your woman? It's unlike you to lose control of your emotions."

"Whatever problem you have with me, leave her out of it. She has nothing to do with anything."

Daniel sneered. "So you say."

"You are not to lay so much as a finger on her. Do I make myself clear?"

Daniel held up his hands in surrender. "She's all yours, my friend. I know you don't like to share."

"No, I don't," Neil said without a trace of irony. He turned to me. "Let's go."

I was still partly in shock from what was going on, but I managed to nod my head, then clamber to my feet. Neil grabbed hold of my sleeve and forcefully steered me to safety. His face was as hard as stone as we rode the lift down in silence. I wondered if he was mad at me for my reckless actions putting me in danger's path. Had I undone all the progress we had made in our relationship through my sheer stupidity? I avoided his cold eyes, biting my lip in anxious anticipation of whatever punishment he had in store for me.

Once we stepped out, Neil pulled me into a deserted storage room and closed the door. In the confined space filled with boxes and shelves, his mask slipped away, revealing vulnerability. He grasped my shoulders. "Are you okay?"

I mustered a nod. "Yes. I'm okay."

In an instant, he flung his arms around me and drew me to his chest.

Chapter Forty-One

I blinked in surprise as Neil wrapped me in a tight embrace. Before I could return the hug, or even fully register the sensation of his sudden display of affection, he released me, averting his eyes and clearing his throat. "Sorry. I was worried about you. What happened? What did he do to you?" His eyes searched mine, pleading for answers.

I attempted to gather my scattered thoughts, my eyes scanning the stacks of boxes and shelves that cast elongated shadows in the dimly lit space. "He questioned me about our relationship. He accused us of, uh, *sleeping* together."

Neil seemed unfazed. "He's projecting. Is that all he said?"

I shook my head. "No. He wanted to pay me to gather intel on you, specifically about your personal relationships."

"Did you refuse?"

"Of course. But I let him down as gently as I could manage. I told him I couldn't help him because I don't know much about your private life."

"How did he take it?"

"Well, he wasn't exactly pleased. He tried to warn me that you don't have my best interests at heart—But don't worry, I'd rather believe you than him."

Neil let out a trembling sigh, fingertips pressed to his forehead.

"Did I do something wrong?" I asked.

"No. You did nothing wrong. Nothing wrong at all. *I* did wrong by believing the meeting I was summoned to was something serious. I should have known better."

"Then the whole situation was a setup?"

"Yes."

Silence descended between us while I tried to get my facts straight, wondering if I could have done something differently. "Do you think I should have agreed to Daniel's offer?" I asked as the thought occurred to me. "Maybe I could have been a double agent to help you."

Neil's response was swift, his voice filled with conviction. "I would never agree to something so dangerous. No. You handled it well. I'm proud of you."

His words heartened me. "I didn't know what to do or say, but I did my best. Hopefully, it was enough to get him to leave me alone."

Neil's jaw tightened, his expression serious. "He'll leave you alone. I'll make sure of it."

The energy radiating from him charged the atmosphere. I struggled to look at him because it was so intense. Just how far was he willing to go to protect me?

"What should we do now?" I asked, a tremor in my voice.

"First things first. I'm going to escort you back to the hotel."

"What about the rest of the day's schedule?"

"I'll handle everything on my own from here on out. You've been a great help to me, but you've taken on enough for one day."

"Okay. That's probably for the best. Oh—my room key and laptop are locked in the office—"

"I'll sort it out. We should go."

Both of us reached for the door handle, our hands touching. Startled by the sensation, I looked up to find Neil's eyes locked onto mine. My breath hitched. I searched his stare, trying to read what he was thinking, but the moment passed as quickly as it occurred. Our connection severed, Neil stood back, allowing me to open the door.

* * *

Back at the hotel, my heart rate still hadn't quite settled from the encounter with Daniel. We paused outside my hotel room door, the air filled with awkward tension. Neil gave me a look as if trying to decipher the whirlwind of emotions I was sure must be written across my face. "Are you all right?" he asked.

I mustered a smile. "Yeah, I'm fine. Just a little rattled, I guess." A beat of silence hung between us, then I added, "And maybe a bit disappointed. It's our last night in Singapore, and I haven't had the chance to do anything except work."

"That was to be expected."

"True. But still…" I fumbled with my key card, tracing the plastic edges with my thumb.

Neil cleared his throat. "Well, I should get going. I have more work to do."

"Right. See you tomorrow morning."

Neil gave a nod, taking a half a step back. Just as he turned to leave, his phone pinged. He glanced at the screen, squinting. "My evening meeting has just been cancelled."

"That's good. You can finally relax."

Neil's eyes met mine. He seemed to have forgotten his intention to leave. "Milly…"

I lifted my chin. "Yes?"

Neil shifted his weight from one foot to the other, and it seemed like he didn't quite know what to do with his hands. "Would you, perhaps, er, fancy grabbing dinner with me? I could show you a little bit of the real Singapore before we leave."

My heart did a flip. Was he serious? I knew he was only offering out of a sense of sympathy, and maybe wanting to keep an eye on me after what had happened with Daniel, but that didn't stop the ripple of excitement coursing through me.

"I'd love to," I blurted, unable to contain my enthusiasm.

Neil puffed up a little. "Excellent. Get ready, and I'll come back at half past seven."

"Got it. See you then."

Giddy anticipation bubbled inside me as I watched him walk away. I closed the door and leaned against it, biting my lip. Dinner with Neil. Maybe this business trip wouldn't be a total bust after all.

Chapter Forty-Two

It's not a date. It's a friendly dinner between colleagues, that's all. There's no point getting worked up over it.

Despite my attempt at self-reassurance, I couldn't help but wonder if there was something more brewing beneath the surface. Neil's fierce protectiveness when he found me with Daniel, how he hugged me in the storeroom, the intense way he always looked at me... Did he really just see me as his secretary? I shook my head, willing myself to accept the evening as no more than a chance to enjoy his company and deepen our professional relationship. Yet, the tiny spark of hope was difficult to ignore.

I shed my work attire and changed into a wrap skirt and a tank top. A pair of strappy sandals completed the look. I touched up my makeup, then checked the time. Neil would be back any minute.

He knocked on my door at seven thirty on the dot. I grabbed my purse and took one last glance in the bathroom mirror.

Not a date, I reminded myself.

I opened the door.

Neil stood before me. He had changed out of his suit and into a blue linen shirt and pair of white shorts which came up above his knees, revealing toned legs scattered with fine dark hair. I was so enamoured by how cute he looked that I stood there dumb-struck for a moment, unsure if he had said anything.

"Are you ready?"

His voice broke through my dazed state. "Yes. Ready!"

His eyes raked over me with an appreciative gleam and a hint of mischievousness which threw me off-guard. "Really? Because your top is inside out."

"What?" Feeling a blush rise in my cheeks, I quickly checked my top. "No, it's not."

Neil cracked a smirk. "I couldn't resist."

Wait a minute.

I gaped. "Did you just make a *joke*?"

"Did you think I was incapable of making jokes?"

He set off towards the lift. I closed the door, then followed him, the memory of our first encounter playing in my head. Looking back on it now, he intrigued me even then.

"I can't believe you'd bring that up! I thought you had forgotten."

"I have an excellent memory." He pressed the button for the ground floor, and we descended.

I fixed him an exasperated glare. He chuckled, his face lighting up in a way that made me melt. I'd happily be the butt of his jokes just to hear him laugh like that.

"I could also make a joke about the time your fly was undone, you know."

"And how exactly did you notice that again?"

My embarrassment metre spiked, threatening to burst. "I don't know! Probably because you always look perfect, so it jumped out at me."

"Perfect? Thank you."

"You know what I mean."

The door opened into the lobby.

Well, that had certainly broken the ice. Was that Neil's plan all along? I side-eyed him with interest. He had revealed yet a new facet of himself to me, and I wondered what else I might discover about him.

"So, where are we going?" I asked.

"There's a hawker centre nearby. I used to go there often when I worked here. I'm sure you'll be able to find something to eat that suits your tastes."

"Hawkers? That sounds fun!"

"Well, like you said, it's our last night here. You should at least get to experience some local cuisine."

"I'm sure it will be amazing."

We exited the hotel. As we took our first steps side by side along the pavement, I began to feel very conscious that it was just the two of us out in public.

"Do you still think Daniel could be spying on us?" I asked, scanning our surroundings.

"Maybe. But he has already revealed his hand to you. I don't think he'll bug you again before we leave."

"But do you think it's okay if we're seen together? After what Daniel said about us—"

"That is inconsequential. Besides, the crowds will offer us a sense of anonymity. I doubt anyone could keep a close watch on us, even if they tried."

"Hmm. I guess so."

Neil slowed his walking pace to match mine. "You'll be safe with me."

I perked up, his reassurance putting a spring back in my step. "Which way are we going?"

"This way."

He led me through winding streets and back alleys, the sounds of laughter, sizzling food, and clinking utensils growing louder with each step. The smell of frying food wafted through the air, drawing us closer. We turned a corner, and a bustling open-air food court came into view. I scanned the stalls around the perimeter as we weaved through crowds speaking multiple languages. The clattering sounds of woks and the rhythmic chopping of ingredients filled the atmosphere.

"Anything catch your eye?" Neil asked.

"How about that one?" I gestured to a stall with pictures of noodle and rice dishes on its signage. The fragrance of spices drifted from its open kitchen, beckoning us closer.

"What would you like?"

"I don't know the first thing about Singaporean cuisine. I'll just get whatever you're having."

"Are you sure?"

I nodded.

We joined the queue. It moved quickly, despite its length. When we got to the front, the hawker man behind the counter greeted us with a wide, toothy grin. "What can I get for you today, young couple?"

A rush of embarrassment scorched my cheeks, but I didn't bother to correct him. Neither did Neil.

"What's a vegetarian dish you recommend?" Neil asked.

"Ah, for our vegetarian friends, how about some vegetable dumplings and fried rice? Both are very good."

"Does that sound okay to you?" Neil asked me.

"Sounds perfect."

"Yes. We'll take it. Enough for the two of us." Neil handed a wad of cash to the hawker. "Keep the change."

"Thank you, sir."

We stepped out of the queue and watched from the sidelines as a cook prepared our order, folding dumpling wrappers filled with veggies and spices, then adding them to a bamboo steamer. Meanwhile, a wok sizzled with a medley of colourful veggies, the scent of garlic and onions filling the air.

A few minutes later, loaded with plates piled high, Neil and I searched for a vacant table.

"Here." Neil pointed out a lone empty table surrounded by a cluster of occupied ones.

As soon as we sat down, I noticed the table was wonky on the uneven pavement, but somehow that only added to the rustic charm of the experience.

"Go ahead." Neil said, breaking apart a pair of disposable chopsticks and passing them to me.

The first bite offered a powerful burst of flavour, with a blend of crunchy vegetables, savoury seasonings, and delicate dumpling wrapper. The fried rice proved equally satisfying. Each mouthful brought together the nuttiness of the jasmine rice, the sweetness of fresh vegetables, and the umami of soy sauce.

"What do you think?" Neil asked.

"Delicious," I mumbled with my mouth half-stuffed.

Neil seemed more interested in watching me eat than his own meal. I tried to pace myself, matching his controlled tempo, savouring each morsel.

"You used to eat here often?" I asked.

"Yes. It hasn't changed much." Neil glanced around. "Maybe a few new vendors."

"When I was cleaning your house, I got the impression you don't cook very often."

"You'd be correct. Cooking isn't my strong suit. I'd like to learn how, but I don't have the time. What about you?"

"It's too expensive to eat out. I cook my own meals."

"Commendable."

I shrugged. "Not really. I just do what I have to do."

"Trust me, in my position, you start to long for the taste of home cooking."

"I'll bring you my leftovers."

"You're being facetious, but I would seriously take you up on that offer."

I pushed my food around on its plate. "Maybe I will, maybe I won't."

Neil huffed with theatrical indignation. I smiled to myself, adoring how receptive he was to my teasing.

"You must be looking forward to going home tomorrow," Neil said, his tone shifting to a more serious note.

I paused, my chopsticks hovering over my plate. "Why do you say that?"

"This trip turned out to be more… *eventful* than I expected. I'm questioning if bringing you here was the right decision."

I reflected on the whirlwind of events we had experienced. "Well, it's been an interesting few days, to say the least. It was challenging, but I feel I rose to the occasion. I'm just glad I could be here to support you."

"You're much more capable than I sometimes give you credit for."

"You know, I think this trip was worth it just for this moment, sharing a meal like this." As soon as I said it, I worried I had overstepped my mark and wished I could reel my words back in and lock them away, but to my surprise, Neil leaned in, appearing to mirror my sentiment.

"I agree."

By the time we finished eating, the hawker centre was even more packed than when we had arrived. As we navigated the sea of people, I was worried I'd get separated from Neil and get lost. I instinctively clung to his arm. Then, realising what I had done, I dropped it, conscious about crossing the strict bounds of our relationship. To my surprise, Neil reached out, took my hand in his, then placed it back on his arm where it had been. "It's crowded. Stay close."

I held on to him, the gentle bulge of his bicep evident through the thin fabric of his shirt. He was warm beneath my fingertips.

We emerged from the heart of the hawker centre and into an open space with thinned-out crowds. I let go of him.

"Are you ready to go back? Or do you want to walk around a bit?" Neil asked.

An opportunity to prolong the evening was more than welcome. "Let's go for a walk."

We walked side by side along the picturesque Singapore River, its shimmering waters reflecting the multicoloured hues of the city lights. I relished the long periods of comfortable silence between us, the sounds of the city, and the lapping river in the background.

"Do you go for walks much in Auckland?" Neil asked, hands in his pockets as he strolled along.

"No. Not much. It's not very pleasant to walk around the area where I live. Sometimes I make it out to the Domain, though. You?"

"Every day. I usually alternate. Running one day, walking the next day."

"Sounds like a good routine."

"The Viaduct and Wynyard Quarter are perfect for it. Once you move, you'll be able to make the most of it."

I had been so caught up in the trip and all it entailed that I hadn't given much thought to my impending move, but now that Neil had brought it up, I felt a rush of anticipation. "I can't wait."

"Are you still aiming to move next weekend?"

"Yes. Saturday morning."

"Do you have much stuff to move?"

"No. Not really. I've already sold as much as I can. But I'll maybe need to rent a car for a couple of hours. I haven't sorted that part out yet."

"You can borrow mine, if you like."

"The Tesla?"

Neil nodded.

"I wouldn't know how to drive it." The prospect of operating a top-of-the-line electric vehicle was more than a little daunting when I had only driven petrol-chugging clunkers in the past.

"I could give you a quick lesson. Or, if it's not going to take more than one trip, I could pick you up from your place. It wouldn't be much trouble."

His suggestion sparked hope in me. I clasped my hands together in front of my chest. "Could you? That would be so helpful. I don't think it'll take more than one trip. There's nothing big to move."

"Just let me know what time you need me, and I'll be there."

"Thank you so much!"

We reverted to comfortable silence until a glowing structure in the distance caught my attention. "What's that?"

"Ah. That's the Merlion statue. A fountain with the head of a lion and the body of a fish. It's quite famous. Do you want to take a look?"

"Sure!"

We approached the statue. The majestic figure stood perched on a platform, its eyes gazing into the distance, and a gentle stream of water cascading from its mouth. The statue was lit up, making it appear almost mystical. I grappled for my phone to take a picture. I snapped a couple of shots, then thought it would be better if I could be in the photo. "Would you mind taking a photo of me? I want something as a memento of this trip."

"Of course."

I passed him my phone, then I posed in front of the statue with a cheesy grin plastered on my face. Neil watched on with clear amusement that made me smile even harder. As he took the photo, a passing elderly couple saw us and approached, speaking an unfamiliar language between themselves. The man tapped Neil on the shoulder. In a mixture of broken English and miming, he offered to take a picture of us as a couple. Neil was shaking his head, but the man was insistent. He grabbed my phone and herded a slightly bewildered Neil next to me. The woman motioned for us to stand closer together. No longer having the will to fight the friendly old couple's instructions, we obliged, moving closer to each other. The woman wasn't satisfied until we had fully closed the gap between us, the sides of our bodies touching all the way down.

Snap, snap, snap.

At last, the couple returned my phone and went on their way.

"Thank you!" I called as they left.

The man turned back to give me a thumbs-up before they disappeared down the winding path into the trees.

I grimaced. "That's the second time tonight we've been mistaken for a couple."

Neil smirked. "We must look good together."

His flirty remark rendered me gobsmacked. He was full of surprises tonight. I tried to gather myself to think of something equally flirty, or at least vaguely witty, to say in return, but the moment slipped away.

Dark clouds gathered overhead.

"Do you feel that?" Neil asked, raising a palm up towards the air.

"Yes."

The humidity was almost oppressive

"We should go back now. It's going to rain any minute."

We turned around and hastened our pace, knowing that time was against us. The air grew heavier with moisture by the second. Thunder rumbled in the distance. Fast walking became sprinting, the hotel within sight further down the street.

Almost there.

The sky opened up, releasing a torrential downpour upon us. We dashed down the rain-soaked path and ducked under the shelter at the front of the hotel, drenched to the bone. I puffed, clutching at the stitch in my side from running. The exertion mixed with exhilaration heightened my senses even more to Neil's presence beside me.

"Are you all right?" he asked.

"Yes," I gasped.

His shirt had turned slightly transparent, and it was clinging to his sculpted torso in all the right places. Not to mention his white shorts…

Neil bit his lip, and his eyes were looking everywhere but directly at me. I realised he must have noticed about me what I had just noticed about him, and I folded my arms across my chest.

Neil cleared his throat. "Let's go inside," he said, his voice a shade huskier than usual.

I wiped my shoes on the mat by the door and squeezed the

water out of my hair before we entered. When my wet skin met the cool air-conditioning, I broke out in goosebumps. Neil led the way to the lift and pressed the buttons for our separate floors. We didn't say another word to each other until the door opened.

"Good night, Milly."

"Night."

"See you at seven tomorrow."

I didn't catch another breath until I was safely in my room with the door shut behind me. Once I had calmed down, I changed into dry clothing and climbed onto the bed, clutching my phone tightly in my eager hands. As the rain continued to drum against the windowpanes, I swiped through my phone to look at the photographs of Neil and me together.

My heart swelled with hope and longing as soon as I saw them.

In all three photographs, Neil wasn't looking at the camera, he was looking at me, and with such a fond and wistful expression that anyone who didn't know any better would think he was in love with me. He even had me fooled for a minute.

Before I could talk myself out of it, I sent my favourite of the three pictures to Neil. No caption. Just the photo. I wanted to see how he would respond—If he would at all.

Anticipation gripped me as the message turned from unread to read, and a heart reaction popped up.

Chapter Forty-Three

I was still puzzling over the heart reaction the next morning when I bumped into Neil at breakfast in the hotel restaurant. Was it intentional, or had his finger slipped? The mystery nagged at me, but I wasn't about to bring it up with him.

After we had eaten, we collected our luggage, checked out, then took a taxi to the airport.

Passing through check-in and security was seamless, but instead of heading straight to the business lounge, Neil steered us towards a customer service desk.

"Is there a problem?" I asked.

Neil's demeanour remained cool and composed. "There's no problem. This is all part of the plan."

Plan? What plan?

Before I could enquire further, the customer service agent greeted us with a smile. "How can I help you?"

"I'd like to change my flight to a later one," Neil said.

A barrage of questions flooded my mind, but Neil's prior assurance kept them at bay. I watched as he exchanged his ticket for a flight more than twelve hours later. The agent then turned her attention to me. "Will you be changing your ticket too, ma'am?"

I looked at Neil for guidance.

"You have two options," he said. "Take your scheduled flight as planned, or else change your ticket to join me on the later flight. If it's the latter, I ask that you stay in the airport and don't go back through customs. My advice would be to stick with your current flight. It will be a very long time to wait otherwise, and with nothing to gain for it."

"Are you going somewhere?"

Neil tensed. "Yes, but you can't come with me."

However much I wanted to help him, I knew better than to argue with him. Whatever he had to do, it seemed important.

An impatient-looking man joined the queue behind us, and I became conscious of holding him up if I didn't decide soon. "I'll stick to my current flight, thank you," I said.

I respected Neil's advice enough to take it, even if it meant we had to embark on separate journeys.

With that settled, we stepped away from the desk, finding a more secluded spot to continue our discussion in private.

"I'm going to leave the airport soon," Neil said. "Take care on your own. Winston will pick you up and take you home from Auckland airport, as arranged."

I nodded, comfortable with the logistics of my return.

Neil looked around, then lowered his voice. "You know what this is about, don't you?"

I pieced together the fragments of information at hand. The clandestine nature of his actions hinted that there must be something secretive he had to do—or someone he had to see. Business he couldn't attend to with all the work commitments and potential spying in the mix. Now that he was through airport security and en route to Auckland, no one would be watching his movements anymore. Was he going to meet Veronica? The chairman? Both?

"I think I understand. You have unfinished business to attend to. People you have to meet."

"Yes." He paused for a moment, his gaze lingering on me. "I'll be leaving in a minute. Don't contact me until tomorrow, okay? Not unless there's some kind of emergency."

I nodded.

"Have a good flight," he said.

With that, he swept away and disappeared into the crowd. I fixated on the space he had occupied moments before. There was still so much I didn't understand.

* * *

My mind was more turbulent than the flight itself, wondering how Neil was faring with his secretive business. What dangers lurked in the shadows? Trapped in a metal tube in the sky, there was nothing I could do to help him except hope he would return unscathed.

As I emerged through the arrivals gate at Auckland Airport, the sight of Winston standing there filled me with relief. I found comfort in his familiar face and the knowledge I could depend on him. His bushy eyebrows and bristly moustache couldn't hide the warmth of his smile when he laid eyes on me.

A reciprocal grin spread across my face as I approached him, rolling my suitcase behind me. "Winston, you're here!"

He chuckled. "Of course I am. Couldn't leave you to fend for yourself, could I? Welcome back, Miss Cross. How was your flight?"

"It was fine. I'm sorry you had to come all the way here and pick me up in the middle of the night."

Winston waved off my concerns. "No problem at all. Nothing a strong cup of coffee couldn't help. What matters is getting you home safe and sound." He scanned the surroundings. "Where's Mr. Kingston?"

His lack of awareness about Neil's plan surprised me, even though it made sense that Neil wouldn't wish to involve him.

"He had some business to attend to. He's coming in on the next flight."

"Ah." Winston shook his head. "That man is always up to something. I should be used to it by now." He reached for my suitcase. "Let me take your bag for you."

We made our way out of the airport and into the parking lot. Winston stowed my luggage in the car boot, and I settled into the front passenger seat, just as I had done the first time Winston drove me home all those months ago. Memories of that eventful day resurfaced. The presentation, getting fired, going to the hospital... I had been so furious and upset with Neil, but as Winston drove me back that night, he tried to assure me of Neil's underlying kindness. At the time, I didn't believe him. Now I knew exactly what he meant. I remembered something else as well. Winston had mentioned Neil helping him out when he was in a bad situation. I never got around to asking him what happened, but now seemed like a good opportunity. "Winston, can I ask you something?"

"Of course." He cast a glance in my direction as he drove out of the airport grounds.

"One time, you mentioned how Neil helped you by offering you your job when you were struggling."

A glimmer danced in Winston's brown eyes as he reflected on the past. "Ah, that story. Did you want to hear it?"

"Yes, if you're okay with telling me."

"I don't see why not." His voice wavered as he began. "It was over a year ago now. My wife and I were dealing with money struggles and looking after our grandchildren newly in our care. Things were tough. One day I went to the supermarket, and at the checkout, I realised I didn't have enough money to pay for the groceries. I was deciding what to put back when a kind-hearted man stepped in and offered to pay."

"Neil?"

Winston nodded. "I have my pride, so I refused. But he insisted. What could I do? Afterwards, we had a chat outside. He gave me his business card and made me promise to call him. So I worked up the courage to make the call. Mr. Kingston asked about my skills and said he would help me get a job. I was so shocked, I couldn't think what to say. I never went to university, never worked in an office before… He asked if I could drive. I said yes. He offered me a trial run as his driver, right then and there."

"And it worked out."

"He pays me so well that my wife doesn't have to work, and she can stay home full-time with our grandchildren."

"That's wonderful!"

"I turned my life around, and it was all thanks to him."

As the road droned on, Winston's story cemented what I already knew—Neil was pure-hearted, and nothing could taint that for me. Nothing.

Chapter Forty-Four

Upon Neil's return, he wouldn't discuss anything which had occurred during his last hours in Singapore, leaving the events shrouded in mystery. I was too relieved to have him back safe and sound to push for answers.

Over the next few days, we had several big meetings with senior staff, then we settled back into the rhythm of our familiar routines. I brought Neil his coffee on Friday morning, knocking on the half-open door of his office, then stepping inside. Sunlight filtered through the blinds, casting patterns on the floor. Neil sat behind his desk, engrossed in his work, an air of quiet contemplation surrounding him. Not wanting to disturb his focus, I silently placed the cup on his desk between stacks of papers.

He looked up and acknowledged my presence with a nod. "Thank you."

"Let me know if you need help with anything."

Neil's gaze held mine for a moment before he spoke again. "There is something you can do for me."

"Sure. What is it?"

He swallowed a swig of coffee. "Draft an email to all staff. Everyone is allowed one day off work before the end of the year to engage in community service work."

The idea intrigued me. "What kind of community service work?"

"Anything that makes a positive impact. Volunteering, picking up litter, donating blood. It will not be monitored or enforced. If staff want to use the day to relax or spend time with family, that's fine too. Make that clear in the email. I want to ensure no one feels obligated or judged."

I admired his thoughtfulness. He seemed to have genuine concern for the wellbeing of the staff.

"This will be a pleasant surprise for everyone," I said, trying to envision how the staff would react.

Neil leaned back in his chair. "It has been a tough year. Now that things have settled, morale has improved, and the petition to have me sacked is a distant memory, I think everyone could do with a change of pace—an opportunity to do something more fulfilling, or just take a break. You're included in this too, by the way. Let me know when you want to take a day off."

"Me? I'll think about it."

"Good."

It seemed like Neil had said all he wanted to say, but as I turned to leave, he interjected, drawing me back. "Milly… What time do you want me to come over to help you tomorrow?"

The prospect of the move and spending time with Neil outside the office filled me with anticipation. "Ten thirty would be great if possible."

"I'll be there." A hint of a smile graced Neil's lips as he returned to his work.

* * *

The next morning, I watched as Neil lifted a heavy suitcase into the back of his car, my eyes drawn to the way his arm muscles flexed under the strain.

"We should be able to fit everything in here," he said, surveying the remaining space.

"Yes. Looks like it."

I had whittled down my belongings to the few things I needed or couldn't bear to part with: my clothes, bedding and towels, my favourite books, sentimental childhood items, and things which reminded me of my parents.

It was a sunny spring day. Fluffy white clouds drifted across the light blue sky like puffs of polyester stuffing. Though the air was a touch cool, the exertion of carrying my bags and boxes warmed me up.

My hands and body grazed Neil's several times in the process of loading the car. The electric thrill of our contact made me tingle each time. Neil was dressed in a thin, faded black cotton t-shirt and a pair of blue jeans which might have been the best fitting jeans I'd ever seen on a person—but maybe that was just because it was him wearing them. He had that sexy facial scruff which so rarely made an appearance, and I often found my eyes drifting to take it in.

Neil waited in the car while I did one last check around my apartment, making sure I hadn't left anything behind and that all the power switches were turned off. The sound of my footsteps echoed in the now-empty rooms stripped of their warmth and personality. Satisfied, I locked up for the final time, then slid my keys and access card through the letterbox slot for my landlord. The metallic clink as they landed accentuated the sense of closure.

"All sorted?" Neil asked as I opened the passenger side door.

"Yep!"

The car came to life as Neil took the wheel.

"Thank you for taking the time out of your morning to do this for me," I said.

"Don't mention it. I'm happy to help."

I pondered how far our relationship had come. We were friends now, that much was clear, and from time to time, I sensed a deeper level of affection from him... but maybe it was just my imagination. He was nice to me because we worked together. Reciprocation of my feelings seemed unlikely.

We didn't talk much during the drive, except for some logistics around the apartment and the building amenities. Upon arrival, Neil parked in his designated spot in the underground carpark. He handed me a key card, our fingers brushing in the exchange. "Here. This is yours. For the building doors and the lift."

"Thanks."

We took as much as we could carry up to the apartment. Neil shared the door code with me and showed me how to change it. Upon entry, I smelled fresh flowers. An extravagant bouquet adorned the centre of the glass dining table—peonies with big ruffled petals.

I clasped my hands under my chin. "Flowers!"

"A welcome gift," Neil said.

I punched him in a playful manner without thinking. "You didn't need to do that!"

"I wanted to." His words hung heavy until he quickly added, "I bought flowers for Christine when she moved into her house too. It's simple etiquette."

"Still, you've already done so much for me. I'm in your debt."

Neil brushed me off with a non-committal grunt. My attention turned from the flowers to the apartment at large, marvelling at its resemblance to a high-end hotel suite. I knew I was going to be very comfortable here.

We dumped the first load of my stuff on the floor, then made one more trip to the car, taking the rest of my things.

"Do you need my help with anything else?" Neil asked once we had brought everything inside.

I shook my head. "I think I can manage."

"Any questions?"

"You've already covered everything."

As much as I enjoyed Neil's presence, I was eager to start unpacking and getting the place set up how I wanted.

"Okay." Neil shifted on his feet. "Well, call me if you have any problems."

"I will. Thank you."

He lingered for a second as if he didn't know how to say good-bye. "I'll leave you to settle in, then."

I nodded, displaying my gratitude with a bright smile. Neil exited, leaving me standing in the middle of the room, absorbing my surroundings. This beautiful, lavish, spacious apartment was mine… For a little while, at least.

Chapter Forty-Five

I spent the rest of the day unpacking and arranging the furniture in my new apartment. Though I had few possessions to fill the space, I enjoyed adding little touches like books on the coffee table and a throw on the armchair. I also visited the supermarket to stock the pantry and fridge with the basics I'd need over the next couple of days.

The hours slipped away, and exhaustion set in. I decided to have an early night and retreated to the bedroom. I crawled under the warm covers. As I drifted to sleep, the knowledge that Neil was so close by, in the very same building as me, fuelled my fantasies.

In the morning, I ventured into the bathroom to shower. My bare feet felt the shock of the cool, slick tiles in contrast to the soft bedroom carpet. I turned on the shower, and as the water flowed, I sensed something was amiss. The pressure was weaker than I expected it to be. Undeterred, I shed my pyjamas and stepped under the stream of water. The temperature was fine at first, not hot, but warm enough. As I lathered coconut-scented body wash on my wet skin, the temperature dropped, leaving me shivering in a cold spray. I quickly finished washing, my teeth chattering, and emerged from the bathroom, wrapped in a towel. I tested all the taps in the apartment, confirming the issue was not isolated to the shower. Then I checked the water heater in the utility cupboard. All the settings looked fine, so I didn't know what the problem was. Not knowing what else to do, I texted Neil, hoping he could assess the situation.

> Hi, Neil. There's a problem with the hot water and pressure.

Neil acknowledged my text and said he'd pop by later to take a look.

He arrived in the afternoon, looking effortlessly handsome in a lightweight button-down shirt and jeans.

"Thanks for coming," I said, daring to meet his eyes.

Neil said nothing, and he didn't move from the doorway to enter. He just stared at me with a look of shy fascination. I wondered what he found so mesmerising, then I looked at myself and realised what it was. I was wearing his sweater. The one which had shrunk and he had told me to keep.

The heart-stopping moment in his car came to my mind.

"It suits you."

I suddenly felt way too warm to be wearing it, but knew taking it off now would draw even more attention to it. We stood in awkward silence for a second before Neil dragged his eyes away, clearing his throat. "I'm sorry you're having issues with the water. Can you show me what the problem is?"

I led him to the bathroom, a room now filled with a sense of femininity because of all my products. Neil rolled up his shirt-sleeves, revealing the toned arms I couldn't help but imagine wrapped around me. He turned the shower on.

"At first it's not too bad, but after a few minutes, the pressure and temperature drop," I explained.

He let the water run for a while, and the stream died down. "I see what you mean." He checked the water heater, his brows furrowing as he tried to decipher the issue. "I'm afraid I lack skills as a handyman. I'll have to get a plumber in. Hopefully tomorrow. Will that be okay?"

"Yeah. There are showers downstairs at the gym, right?"

"I'm afraid those showers are undergoing maintenance."

"Never mind. I can just take cold showers in the meantime. It's fine."

Neil shook his head. "I have a perfectly good shower at my place. You're welcome to use it. I'm usually out of the house by half-past six on weekday mornings, so you would have the place to yourself."

I considered Neil's suggestion and decided that it made sense, since I was already familiar with his apartment, and it was just a lift ride away. "That's a good idea. Thank you."

"I'll send you my door code. Sorry for the inconvenience."

* * *

At eight o'clock the next morning, I made my way up to Neil's apartment, clutching a tote bag stuffed with my work clothes, a towel, and a toiletries bag containing my body and hair products. I had thrown on a pair of sweatpants and a t-shirt over the underwear I had slept in, covering myself as I made the short journey.

Anticipation mounted as I ascended the floors. I was going to shower in Neil's bathroom. The place where he got naked. The mental image of him showering, water glistening on his body, made my heart race.

When I reached his apartment, I pressed the doorbell, just in case he was still home. I half hoped he would be. But several seconds passed with no response, so I entered the door code and let myself in.

The interior of Neil's apartment hadn't changed since the last time I saw it. His space was tidy, minimalist, and sophisticated, yet it possessed a lived-in quality with the scratched-up rug on the floor and the clutter of game controllers, DVDs, and books in the living area. Both of the cats came padding up to me. Chichi wove in and out between my legs, and Bowey nudged my feet. I smothered them with affection until I couldn't delay the task at hand any longer.

There were two bathrooms in the apartment, but the one downstairs had no shower. I would have to use the ensuite upstairs. I walked through Neil's bedroom to access it, noting his crumpled duvet on the bed, reminding me he had slept there. The room smelled like his cologne, mixed with the faint musk of his natural scent.

I entered the bathroom, looking around with a newfound appreciation. Cologne and aftershave bottles lined the shelf, and a safety razor rested beside the sink.

I turned on the shower and undressed, my heart pounding with the knowledge that I was naked in Neil's personal space. My thoughts continued in a similar vein as I stepped under the hot spray. The temperature and pressure were perfect. I washed myself, hands against my skin, taking my time. Neil had said he wouldn't come back home this morning, but I indulged in a fantasy that he did come back, and he walked in on me naked and vulnerable, and one thing led to another.

But Neil didn't come back. Of course he didn't.

I turned off the water and dried myself off with my towel before changing into my clean work clothes and gathering my belongings. I felt like I was running late, and checking my phone validated that feeling, so I left in a hurry.

* * *

On my way to work, I mentally rehearsed my apology for being late, but when I arrived, my office door was locked, which meant Neil hadn't arrived yet. I checked his schedule, in case there was a meeting I had forgotten about. But no, he was late. That was unlike him, but I was sure he had his reasons. In the meantime, I unlocked the door, settled at my desk, and got down to work.

Neil arrived twenty minutes later, and as soon as I saw him, I flashed back to the vivid fantasies from the morning shower. Cheeks flaming, I wiped my mind blank to greet him. "Morning."

"Good morning," he said, straight-faced as usual.

He offered no explanation for his late arrival. Instead, he asked me to determine the best day for him to take off.

I looked over his calendar. "The next few weeks are pretty packed. This Friday is quiet, though. I would only have to shift one meeting."

"Lock in this Friday then."

"Sure. Do you have something planned?"

"I'm going to take my community service break."

"You're doing that as well?" For some reason, I hadn't considered the prospect of his participation.

"Yes."

"So, where will you be volunteering?"

"There's an animal shelter out west."

"You're going to work with animals? How fun! Maybe that's what I should do too." I smiled, envisioning myself surrounded by adorable, furry creatures.

We looked at each other. I wondered if he was going to invite me to join him, or if I would have to ask. Then we both spoke at once.

"Would I—" I said.

"Do you—" Neil cleared his throat. "Go ahead."

"Could I come with you on Friday? I'd like to help at the animal shelter too."

"Yes, but are you sure? We spend so much time together as it is. Don't you want to get away from me on your day off?"

"No, I don't. Do you want to get away from me? Because I don't have to—"

"Not at all. I would like you to be there."

"Then I'd be happy to join you."

"Okay, but I must warn you it's hard work." He cracked a slight smile. "I was about to say, 'It's not a walk in the park,' but you do get to walk dogs in the park."

I chuckled. Neil's smile intensified, matched by a fondness in his eyes as he watched me laugh.

"But seriously, you'll have to pick up dog doo and clean dirty kennels," he said.

I crossed my arms. "I know that! I'm not afraid to get my hands dirty."

"Good. Then it's settled. We'll both go. I'm sure they'll be happy to have an extra pair of hands. I'll let them know."

"And I'll move that meeting and inform the team we're on leave on Friday."

"Yes. Please do."

He had a chuffed look on his face as he retreated to his office.

I daydreamed about what our animal shelter trip could have in store for us while I worked. Just the thought of Neil caring for animals was cuteness overload. I couldn't wait.

As the day progressed, my excitement for Friday tapered off, replaced by a strange sensation tugging at the back of my mind. A feeling like I had forgotten something. I tried to dismiss it, but it wouldn't go away. My thoughts returned to the shower in Neil's apartment. I had been in such a rush to leave this morning… Did I forget something?

Suddenly, it hit me.

I gasped.

Chapter Forty-Six

M*y underwear.*

I had left a pair of undies in Neil's bathroom. At least, that's what I worried had happened, because I couldn't recall seeing them again after I returned home this morning.

I chewed my nails as I pondered what to do.

I'll check my laundry basket when I get home. If they're there, then good. If not, then I'll have time to sneak back to Neil's apartment and grab them before he gets home.

I was working through some of the finer details of my plan when Neil emerged from his office, making me jump. "I've just been on the phone to the plumber," he said. "He can come over in an hour. Will that be okay? You can leave early to meet him."

I agreed without giving it any thought, realising too late that a plumber being around would interfere with my schemes. Hopefully, he would be in and out quickly.

I left work at four o'clock and made the short journey home. While I waited for the plumber to arrive, I checked my laundry basket for the undies I had been wearing that morning—a plain white pair of bikini-cut briefs with a tiny bow just below the centre of the waistband. I groped through the small pile of clothing that had built up since I moved in two days ago, but couldn't find them. I tipped the contents onto the bed and went through each item individually. They weren't there. I searched every corner of my bedroom, then the rest of my apartment. They were nowhere to be found. I had to face the truth. My initial hunch was right; I had left them in Neil's bathroom. The plumber still hadn't arrived. Did I have time to go to Neil's apartment and grab the errant underwear now?

My doorbell rang.

No. Obviously not.

I greeted the plumber, who arrived wearing a pair of dirty jeans and black work boots, the faint scent of grease and metal accompanying him. I explained the problem with the water, even though I was sure Neil had already briefed him on the situation. His heavy boots thudded on the floor, and the contents of his toolbox clanged as I showed him to the relevant areas of the apartment. While he worked, I mentally hurried him along, praying he would finish quickly so I could leave and sort out the underwear conundrum.

All up, the plumber spent more than an hour tinkering with the water heater and testing the taps. He had to come and go from his vehicle multiple times, and also took several long phone calls during the job, making it take even longer. I was beginning to wonder if I should just nip out and leave him there alone for a few minutes, but each time that thought crossed my mind, I told myself he'd finish soon.

At last, he approached me. "I think I've solved the problem, But I've discovered a separate issue with the shower that needs fixing. It shouldn't take too long."

It turned out that his version of not taking too long was far longer than my version. By the time he finally left, it was past six o'clock in the evening, and my determination for the underwear recovery mission was waning. What if Neil came home earlier than usual and caught me in the act? I'd be mortified beyond words. But what were the alternatives? Text him and tell him what happened? Wait for him to come home and confront him in person? Every option I could think of would cause more embarrassment than I could handle. No. I had to go through with it. The idea of Neil knowing anything about the underwear incident was too mortifying not to.

Having made up my mind, I crept from my apartment to Neil's. I rang the doorbell to ensure he wasn't home, rehearsing a story in my head in case he was. I buzzed once more, waited, then entered the code to unlock the door. An error sound played. My hands were shaking so much, I must have typed it in wrong. I tried it again, the door clicked open, I pushed it open a crack—

"Amelia, what are you doing?"

My soul just about left my body.

That was Neil's voice. In my anxious state, I hadn't heard the lift open or his footsteps approach me. Nothing left to do except face up to him. I turned around. Neil looked down his nose at me, his dark eyes gleaming. The world seemed to narrow around us.

"Sorry," I stammered, unable to look at him.

I braced myself for anger and disappointment, but instead, he seemed a mite amused, his lips twitching to form a smile but resisting. "Please explain yourself."

"You know how I had to use your shower this morning? Well, I accidentally left something here. Sorry. I should have let you know instead of just sneaking in to get it, but I thought I'd be in and out in two seconds, and I was too embarrassed to say anything."

Neil seemed unfazed. "Wait right here. What did you leave? I can go in and get it for you."

I bit my lip. "I'd rather get it myself, if that's okay. It's, uh, something *personal*." I flinched at my own words, wondering if I had said too much.

No more questions. Please.

Neil relinquished with a sigh. "All right." He pushed open his door and stood aside to let me in.

I slipped inside and bolted to the bathroom. There they were.

My white undies, lying right in the middle of the white-tiled floor. I grabbed them and scanned the bathroom to see if there was anything else I had left there, the details of the room coming into sharp focus, and the sensation of being in Neil's personal space reigniting. All clear. I was just about to leave when it occurred to me that I had nowhere to conceal the underwear. I couldn't just walk out with them scrunched up in my hand, could I? Neil would notice. Perish the thought. I patted my body, searching for a pocket, but I had none.

Damn, women's clothing and their lack of pockets!

Not wanting to linger another second, all I could think to do was to stuff them in my bra. So that's what I did, the folded up cotton fabric nestling against my breasts. It wasn't too noticeable unless you really scrutinised my chest, and I didn't think Neil was going to scrutinise my chest anytime soon, even if I wanted him to.

I emerged, flustered, yet relieved to be done with the ordeal.

Neil stood behind the kitchen island, pouring himself a glass of water. "Did you find what you left?" he asked.

"Yes. Thank you. I'm sorry for trying to sneak in."

"Forget about it. I know you didn't mean any harm. Did the plumber sort out the water issue?"

"Yes. All fixed."

"Good. Apart from that, how are you settling in?"

"I'm fully unpacked now, and I went grocery shopping yesterday. It's so nice. I don't think I'll ever want to leave."

"If there are any more problems, let me know."

"I will. Thank you. Well, I'll be going then. Good night." I started towards the door, feeling a stab of desperation to extricate myself.

"Milly," Neil said, stopping me. He was back to using my nickname again. "About Friday. I've let the animal shelter know we're both coming. Wear suitable clothing and meet me in the carpark on Friday morning, okay?"

"Okay. I will. Good night."

"Good night."

With that, I extracted myself to safety, hoping he hadn't noticed how flustered I was.

Chapter Forty-Seven

"It's not too late to back out now," Neil said as I approached him in the apartment building carpark on Friday morning.

I screwed up my face in mock disdain. "What makes you think I'd want to back out?"

Neil just smirked in that cocky way of his. "Get in," he said, opening the car door.

I had dressed in old jeans with a hole in one knee, sneakers, and a baggy black t-shirt tucked in at the waist. I wore my hair pulled back in a messy pony. Neil sported a similar ensemble: jeans and a t-shirt. His usual luxury watch was absent from his wrist, and he lugged a backpack over one shoulder. He hadn't shaved for the occasion, the greying stubble on his chin, throat, and cheeks eliciting a thrill in me.

I flung a bag containing wet-weather gear and a packed lunch into the car, then slid into the passenger seat. As Neil drove me to the animal shelter, he ran through what to expect. His confidence on the subject made it clear he knew what he was talking about.

"You've done this before," I said.

"I adopted Bowey and Chichi from the shelter not long after I arrived in New Zealand. Since then, I've volunteered a few times."

"So, this is how you spend your days off..."

"I wouldn't go that far. I just help out occasionally."

"You must really love animals."

"I do."

Of course, I already knew that. His affection for his two cats was evidence enough.

As we entered the motorway, the sky turned a deeper shade of grey, and raindrops began to batter the windscreen.

"Great day for it," Neil said.

The wipers squeaked against the windscreen as I watched city high-rises give way to suburban sprawl.

When we arrived at the facility—an austere building on the outskirts of the western suburb of Henderson—Neil ushered me inside, the smell of wet dog wafting over me. An elderly woman emerged from a room behind the counter. Her greying hair was pulled back in a low bun, and she wore a polo shirt embroidered with the shelter's logo.

Her wrinkled face lit up when she saw us. "Neil! So wonderful to see you again."

Neil returned a polite smile. "Good morning, Margaret."

I made the connection at once. This was the lady who had sent Neil the dog plush toy.

"Thank you so much for volunteering today. You already do so much with your generous donations."

"It's my pleasure."

Donations? So he donates as well...

My heart fluttered at yet more evidence of Neil's kindness and generosity.

Margaret turned her attention to me. "And this must be—" She drew a blank and looked at Neil for support.

"My..." Neil started. "Amelia." His face coloured.

My Amelia.

It sounded nice, even if he hadn't intended it to come out that way.

"Nice to meet you, Margaret," I said.

"Nice to meet you too." Margaret clasped her veiny hands together. "Right. Let me take you through."

She led us down a dim corridor lined with locked doors. Faint barks and whimpers emitted from behind them. A young woman with short hair and a side-swept fringe sat at a table, reading an old magazine. She had fair skin, a smattering of freckles across her nose, and bright green eyes.

"This is Jade, one of our longest serving team members," Margaret said. "Jade, this is Amelia, and of course, you already know Neil."

Jade stood to greet us. "Hey." She beamed.

"Jade will show you around and assign your tasks for the day," Margaret said before retreating back to reception.

"Let's get you started," Jade said. "I'm going to put you both on canine today, since that's what Neil has the most experience with, and we need a lot of help. We'll start with a tour, then I'll introduce you to some of our dogs. They'll be excited to get some attention."

Jade showed us around the kennels, infirmary, grooming room, and indoor and outdoor play areas. The shelter housed around thirty dogs, mostly larger, mixed breeds.

Jade led us to a row of kennels. The dogs erupted into eager barks and whimpers at our arrival. I cooed at a dog with a fluffy coat as it strained against the gate of its pen. Neil watched on with a hint of a smile.

"Let's take a few of them out to the field so you can get acquainted," Jade said.

Neil and I put on our rain jackets and gumboots before going outside. In the grassy field, moist with continued drizzle, Jade released six dogs of various sizes and breeds. They frolicked around us, vying for head pats and belly rubs. A black Labrador nuzzled at my hands until I gave her the attention she desired. Meanwhile, Neil stood back, allowing the dogs to come to him. A pair of pit bulls arrived at his feet, tails wagging. Neil rewarded them with gentle strokes along their backs.

While the dogs familiarised themselves with us, Jade fetched a bunch of leads.

"Time for the fun part," she said upon her return. "Walking the dogs. Do you have any experience with walking dogs, Amelia?"

"No, I must admit I don't."

"Don't worry." She clipped leads onto the collars of two terriers with perky ears and button noses. "I'm sure you can handle these little ones."

I felt the excited dogs yank the leads as she passed them to me. I tightened my grip.

Next, she leashed the four largest dogs and passed the reins to Neil. "Since you have more experience, you can take this rowdy group."

Neil nodded. "Not a problem."

"There are doggy-doo bags on the leads and rubbish bins situated around the track. Give the small dogs at least two laps around the trail, and the big dogs will need at least three."

Jade flicked up the latch on the gate and opened it, revealing a walking trail which looped around the perimeter of the property. I wrangled my yappy pair through the gate, Neil and his pack following behind me.

"Have fun!" Jade said as she closed the gate behind us.

The rain continued, dusting my jacket with glistening beads of water. The ground was slick with mud under my boots. Neil's group of large dogs dragged him along with boisterous energy. Within seconds, they were far ahead, disappearing from view into the trees. I took my time with the small dogs, letting them sniff and explore at their own meandering pace, their paws leaving dainty prints in the mud.

I completed one lap of the track with no issues apart from the expected task of having to pick up and dispose of dog poo. But on my second lap, I came into trouble.

One dog veered from the path, nose to the ground. I stepped sideways to follow its lead, my foot landing in a patch of sloppy mud. My boot sank in up to the ankle. I tried to take another step but lost my balance, toppling backwards into the mud. My clothes soaked through in an instant.

The cheeky dog stared at me, head cocked. Its shiny coat was pristine compared to my muddy state.

"Why, you little…" I muttered, scrambling to stand.

The other dog let out a sneeze, as if laughing at my mishap. I grimaced.

Squelching footsteps approached. Neil emerged through the trees, the dogs at the ends of his leads tugging him along. He surveyed me up and down, eyes gleaming with mirth. "What happened to you?"

"Oh, shut up," I snapped, cheeks burning. "One of these dogs led me off the path."

Neil bit his lip, holding back a grin. "Do you want me to take over with these two?"

"No, I'm fine."

Neil stepped closer. "You know, it's not too late to admit defeat, call it quits—"

"Absolutely not!" I huffed.

His lips twitched. "If you insist."

We finished up the walk, then left the dogs in the enclosed field for the staff to attend to before heading back inside the shelter. I ditched my muddy gumboots by the door and hung my wet jacket on a coat hook. My clothes underneath were soaked as well, clinging to my body and dripping dirty water on the lino floor. I shivered, my teeth chattering.

Neil tsked. "Look at you."

I brushed off his teasing remark. "I think I'm gonna need some time to dry off."

Jade caught up with us momentarily. She took one look at me and chuckled. "Rookie mistake. It gets real slippery out there in the rain. Did you bring a spare change of clothes?"

I frowned. "No. I didn't."

"I did," Neil said. He took his backpack off its hook, unzipped it, and pulled out a pair of sweatpants, a t-shirt, and a towel. He offered them to me with a smug look on his face.

"Thanks."

It struck me that this was my second time engaging in the intimate act of borrowing clothes from him, but I was too grateful to be embarrassed about it.

With my arms loaded with the dry clothes and towel, I made my way to the restroom to clean up. The sight of a shower stall drew a sigh of relief from me. I peeled off my dirty, wet clothes, then submerged myself under the shower's hot spray. In a matter of minutes, I was clean, warm, and dry. I left my dirty clothes hanging over the shower door as I changed into Neil's sweatpants and t-shirt. The clothes were ill-fitting, but far better than the alternative. I pulled the draw cord of the pants tight around my waist and tucked the loose t-shirt in to control the excess fabric. The result was serviceable, though unstylish. If I squinted at my reflection in the mirror, I did look *kind of* cute, in a "boyfriend's clothes" type of way—ignoring the fact that Neil wasn't my boyfriend.

"Knock, knock," Jade said, tapping on the bathroom door.

"Come in."

Jade entered, brandishing a bucket full of water. "Chuck your dirty clothes in here to soak."

"Good idea. Thanks."

She looked me up and down. "Good thing your man came prepared, eh?"

I choked. "My *man?*"

"Neil, of course. You're together, aren't you?" She bit her tongue. "Wait, am I wrong?"

"He's my boss! This is a work thing. A volunteering day. I'm his secretary."

Jade's eyebrows shot up. "Really? I'm sorry, I just assumed it from the way you two look at each other and interact. You seem so close." She eyed me sceptically. "And you're wearing his clothes right now."

She had a point, but still...

"Plus, you bicker and tease each other like an old married couple. It's very cute."

"C-cute?"

Jade chuckled. "Don't worry. I won't say anything in front of Neil. But are you sure there's nothing going on between you?"

"There's nothing going on between us."

"If you say so," she singsonged as she sauntered out.

I finished up in the bathroom, Jade's words echoing in my head as I dropped my dirty outfit in the bucket to soak.

Do we really look like a couple?

I reminded myself that it wasn't the first time we had been mistaken as such. We looked good together—even Neil had said so. I stared dreamily into the mirror, imagining what it would be like if we really were a couple. Walking hand in hand with him, kissing him, waking up next to him...

My daydream came to an abrupt halt when the door scraped open behind me, and a staff member entered the restroom. I took that as my cue to leave and get back to work.

I found Neil waiting for me in the break room, two mugs of tea prepared on the table. His eyes widened almost imperceptibly when he saw me swimming in his oversized sweatpants and t-shirt. "I see the spare clothes worked out," he said, his voice sounding slightly strained.

"I would have brought my own change of clothes if you had warned me to, you know."

"I thought that would have been common sense."

I huffed, then sighed, my shoulders slackening. "Well, thank you. I don't know what I would have done without them."

I tucked my still-damp hair behind my ears self-consciously as Neil's gaze drifted over me. Something unreadable flickered in his eyes before he seemed to catch himself staring and looked away. "Of course," he said. "I'm glad I could help."

He busied himself adding milk to the mugs of tea, though he couldn't seem to suppress a faint grin. Seeing me dressed in his clothes always seemed to rattle him. I wondered if he found it attractive. Now there was an interesting thought…

My face grew warm, exacerbated by the recent exchange with Jade and my little girlfriend-and-boyfriend fantasy.

"Here. This will warm you up," Neil said, nudging one of the mugs towards me.

"Thanks."

I wrapped my cold hands around the hot surface, absorbing its warmth. The heat spread through me with each sip of sweet, milky tea.

"I'm glad you've recovered," Neil said. "That was quite a fall you took back there."

I shot him a glare for bringing it up again. "Don't pretend like you weren't two seconds from falling in the mud yourself with those dogs dragging you every which way."

Neil laughed. "Fair point."

His hearty laugh made my insides turn to mush. I grinned stupidly back at him, feeling like falling in the mud had been worth it just to hear that laugh. Neil's eyes locked with mine. He bit his lip. I almost forgot to breathe.

Caught in the moment, I didn't notice Jade poke her head into the room. She cleared her throat. "Am I interrupting something?"

I broke eye contact with Neil.

"Not at all," Neil said smoothly.

"Just wanted to let you know the kennels are ready to be cleaned whenever you're done with your tea." Jade looked between us, an impish grin on her face. "But take your time!"

She disappeared from the doorway with a wink. I avoided Neil's eyes, suddenly very interested in my mug of tea.

The pungent smell of ammonia stung my nostrils when we returned to the kennels. Jade demonstrated the cleaning process, spraying down the concrete floors and scrubbing them, then replacing the bedding with fresh blankets.

Armed with buckets, hoses, and sponges, Neil and I got to work. I took my time, ensuring every speck of grime was erased. Meanwhile, Neil rushed through the task with broad strokes, finishing each kennel in half the time it took me. We didn't talk much, except when we took a moment to inspect each other's work.

"You missed a spot," I teased.

"Done is better than perfect," Neil retorted.

When Jade came by to survey our efforts, she nodded in satisfaction at my spotless kennel floors but shook her head at the corners Neil had neglected. "Next time, be a bit more thorough."

"My mistake," Neil said. "I'll try harder."

I shot him a triumphant look, and he eyed me back like, *"Don't push it."*

We took a break to eat lunch, then returned to clean more kennels. I was exhausted by the end of it, but I wasn't about to let Neil know it.

"You two have worked so hard today," Jade said. "But I hope you'll stay and play with the dogs a while before you leave."

"Of course we will," I said, without consulting with Neil. Even though I was tired, this was the part I had most been looking forward to, so I wasn't going to pass it up.

Jade beamed, pumping her fist. "All right. It's play time!"

With her arms full of toys and treats, she led us to a wide open area with indoor and outdoor sections, where several dogs were relaxing, including some we had walked earlier. The rain had stopped, and sunbeams extended from gaps between the clouds.

I settled on the floor inside. The two small dogs from earlier approached tentatively before recognition sparked in their beady eyes. Their tails wagged, thumping against the floor. I offered them treats, and they nibbled from my palm, their warm tongues tickling my skin.

Meanwhile, Neil played ball with a couple of German shepherds. They scampered after the ball, returning it dutifully to

Neil's feet each time, gazing up at him with wide, adoring eyes. Neil ruffled their pointed ears, eliciting contented tail wags. I couldn't decide which was more adorable—Neil, or the dogs.

Over the course of the afternoon, I received my fair share of sniffs and licks, but one dog stayed slumped in the corner, ignoring all the treats and toys. He was a sad-looking dog with scruffy salt-and-pepper fur, droopy ears, and mournful brown eyes. While the other dogs vied for my affection, this one kept to himself, resigned to his solitude.

Drawn to the lonely dog, I cautiously approached him. "Hey there, little fella," I said, offering a pat.

He wearily accepted my hand with a soft grunt. I thought maybe he wanted to be left alone, but when I moved away from him, he trailed after me, and when I sat down, he rested his head in my lap.

Jade came up beside me. "Awww. I see you've made friends with Archibald. He's one of our longest residents. Been here for over a year now."

"How come he hasn't been adopted?"

Jade's expression turned sombre. "He's an old dog, and he has some health issues."

"But he's such a sweetheart." I stroked my hand through his short, dark fur, slightly coarse to the touch.

Jade smiled. "He's taken a liking to you. He's usually very shy and reserved."

Neil walked over to us, joining in our conversation and fuss over Archibald.

"Good boy," Neil said, scratching him behind his ears.

"Gosh. He likes you too," Jade said. "Two friends for Archibald in one day. It's a new record."

"What's his story?" Neil asked.

"It's a sad one. His owner was an elderly man who passed away in his home and wasn't discovered for several days. During this time, Archibald was left with no access to food or water. He was starving and dehydrated when someone finally found him. His owner had no family who could take him, so he was sent here."

"The poor thing," I said. "No wonder he's so timid and withdrawn."

"I hope someone will come along and offer him a forever home soon. There's only so much we can do for him here."

Archibald nuzzled against my palm, looking up at me with his big, forlorn eyes.

Ouch. My heart.

"I so wish I could adopt you," I told him. "But I'm going overseas soon, so I can't."

"What breed is he?" Neil asked Jade.

"He's a mix, but we think he must be part basset hound, wouldn't you agree?"

Neil nodded. "He reminds me of a childhood pet."

"Oh, really? What was your pet like?"

"He—" Neil hesitated, suddenly tense. His next words were strained. "It's a painful subject. I'd rather not talk about it."

The sudden display of fragility from him caught me off guard. Before I knew what I was doing, my hand was on his arm. To my surprise, I felt him lean in to my touch.

"I understand. Childhood memories can be a touchy subject." Jade got to her feet. "Oh well. I better get back to the kennels now. It's nearly feeding time. Come find me and say goodbye before you leave, won't you?"

I nodded, then realising I was still touching Neil's arm, I dropped my hand, embarrassment catching up with me.

Jade left. Beside me, Neil turned rigid and unemotional again. I wondered what had happened to his childhood pet to upset him so much. A heavy silence descended between us, unbroken until a yawn escaped my mouth.

"You're tired," Neil said. "We should get going soon."

I gave Archibald one last rub between his ears and down his

back before attempting to gently shift him from my lap. He let out a heart-wrenching whine in response.

"He knows we're leaving him," I said, pouting. "Poor old Archie… Oh! Neil, I just realised. His name—it matches. Archie, Bowey, Chichi. Isn't that funny?"

Neil laughed. "I think that settles it. I'm going to adopt him."

Chapter Forty-Eight

I gasped, scarcely believing what I had just heard from Neil's mouth. "Are you serious? You'd do that for me?"

The thought of Neil adopting Archie filled me with pure joy, but I tamped down my expectations before I could get too excited. Neil was a busy man, and this would be a huge commitment. I wouldn't blame him if he decided not to take Archie on after all.

As if sensing my hesitation, Neil looked me straight in the eyes and gave a firm nod. "I'm serious. The moment I saw you with Archie, I just knew. I want to give the old boy the home he deserves. And I'm doing it for me as much as for you. Adopting a dog has always been a part of my grand plan, and he reminds me so much of my childhood dog. This time, things will be different. I know I can give Archie a good life. I'm ready for this."

Archie yelped as I sprang to my feet. Overcome with emotion, I flung my arms around Neil in an enthusiastic hug. Neil let out a surprised huff of air, his body tensing up at the contact. Slowly, he raised his arms, but they hovered around me as if he didn't dare to touch me. I clung to him. Bit by bit, Neil relaxed into it, melding against me. One hand found the dip between my shoulder blades, and the other claimed the inward curve of my waist. A contented sound slipped from my lips. Then Neil turned rigid again. We broke apart.

An awkward beat passed between us before I worked up the courage to meet his eyes. His guarded exterior cracked, his impassive mask giving way to a fond smile and a soft crinkle around the eyes. He smoothed his shirt. "Well, I'm glad you approve of the idea."

I beamed. "More than approve! But how are you going to properly look after a dog with all the work and travel you do?"

"Fair question. He's an old dog. He won't require too much exercise. Since I live so close to work, I can come home throughout the day to check up on him, or even bring him in to work with me. During trips, I can afford to get a dogsitter. An apartment might not be the best place to house a dog, but there's plenty of space and an outdoor area."

"Don't forget that I can help too. While I'm still here."

"Thank you. I have no expectations of you, but if you're happy to do it, I'll gladly accept your help."

"Looks like you've got all your bases covered, then."

"Let's find Jade and tell her the good news, shall we?"

We located Jade in the kennels, filling dog bowls from sacks of food. Her green eyes widened, and she clapped her hands together when Neil told her the plan.

"Amazing news! I had hoped you'd come around. I'm so happy for Archibald. Let's go tell Margaret and get the adoption process started."

She led us to the front counter where Margaret was tapping away at a desktop computer. Her leathery face lit up when she saw us approaching. "Are we all done for the day?"

"Neil wants to adopt Archibald," Jade said.

"Oh, that's wonderful!" Margaret turned misty-eyed. "That poor old boy has been here far too long."

"When will I be able to take him home?" Neil asked.

"Since we know you well here, and you're such a generous

donor, I think we can wrap this up pretty quickly. You can have him as soon as you've signed the forms and paid the fee. Archibald has been ready for a long time, so let's not leave him waiting any longer. I'll print the adoption form for you to sign."

She clacked away on her keyboard, then the printer screeched as it churned out the documents. She passed a pen and the forms to Neil across the counter. As Neil filled in his details, she prattled on about Archie's medication and specific care needs.

Meanwhile, I bounced on my toes in anticipation, unable to contain my excitement. I felt almost as pleased as if I were adopting Archie myself.

Neil signed the last page with a flourish and slid the paperwork back to Margaret. Next, he handed over his credit card. Margaret swiped it through the machine. "All done," she said. "Jade has already gone to fetch Archibald for you."

While we waited, Margaret prepared an adoption gift pack containing food, toys, medicine, and other essentials.

Soon enough, Jade emerged with Archie on a leash. His tail thumped from side to side, and he let out a happy bark, straining to get to us.

"I have never seen him so happy and full of beans. I think he knows he's going home with you," Jade said.

Neil knelt down and ruffled Archie's ears. "That's right, old boy. You're coming home with me."

Jade and Margaret sent us on our way with a request that Neil send a photo and an update once Archie had settled in. He readily agreed, then we said our goodbyes. Archie hopped into the back seat of the Tesla without any fuss. I sat next to him to keep him company.

We stopped by a pet store on the way home to stock up on everything Archie would need: a bed, a crate, bowls, more toys, treats, and grooming tools.

When we pulled into Neil's spot in the apartment building carpark, I immediately began gathering up the supplies. "Let me help you carry some of this."

Neil raised an eyebrow. "You don't have to do that."

"I want to!"

"Well, if you insist."

Together, we carried it all up in one go, while Archie charged ahead on his lead in all kinds of directions. I put the haul down in the entryway of Neil's apartment. Neil set Archie loose around the living room. Though hesitant, Archie sniffed around, acclimatising to his new surroundings. The cats were nowhere to be seen. They were probably hiding somewhere. I watched on in amusement.

Neil approached. "Thanks," he said. "For today. For everything."

I shook my head, brushing off his gratitude like there was no need for it. "I had fun."

"Me too."

I swallowed the lump in my throat, knowing it was time to say good night. "Well, I guess I should get going…"

"I suppose so."

I reluctantly reached for my tote and the plastic bag containing my wet clothing, then we lingered by the door in tense silence, neither of us making a move. Neil stared down at me with intense eyes and a tight jaw. He looked dishevelled in the sexiest way possible, his hair tousled, shirt wrinkled. I felt the air shift as he moved towards me. My breath hitched. He reached out. His arm grazed my side as his hand made contact with the doorhandle behind me.

I exhaled with an acute sense of disappointment. Of course Neil wasn't going to make a move on me. He wasn't that kind of man.

His fingers clasped the handle, but he didn't turn it. After a loaded moment, he released his grip and let his hand drop back to his side. He gave a self-conscious cough. "Look, I, uh… This is somewhat…" He sighed, raking a hand through his hair. "Do you want to stay awhile? Spend some time with Archie while he settles in for his first night. We could have dinner. I'm asking you as a friend, Milly, not as your boss. What do you think?"

My eyes widened. "Are you sure?"

"Yes. If you want to."

"I'd *love* to."

Neil's lips curved into a faint smile. "Okay."

I smiled back at him.

Neil shyly averted his gaze, then stood aside, inviting me back in. But as I stepped forward, my awareness shifted to the heavy plastic bag I clutched in my hands. "Actually, I better go home and put these clothes in the washing machine first. And have a shower. And get changed. Can I come back in half an hour?"

Neil nodded. "Sure. Take your time. I could do with a shower and a change of clothes myself. I'll see you later."

Archie appeared at my feet and whined as I tried to exit. I bent down to give him a parting cuddle. "I'll be back soon, Arch."

* * *

The prospect of spending one-on-one time with Neil in his home had me fussing over every detail of my outfit. I wanted to appear cute, yet casual, not overly done up—a difficult balance to achieve. I spent far longer than I'd ever admit trying on outfits and scrutinising myself from every angle in the mirror.

At last, I returned to Neil's apartment, freshly showered and dressed in light-wash jeans, a chunky cardigan, and white sneakers. A touch of mascara and tinted lip balm polished off the look.

I still couldn't get over it. He had invited me to have dinner with him. Alone. In his apartment. Okay, technically it was so I could play with Archie, but Neil wouldn't have asked if he didn't want me there.

My pulse quickened as I reached for Neil's doorbell, wondering what the night had in store for us. I knew he would never initiate anything romantic with me, yet a simmering sense of anticipation set my nerves on edge.

I heard Neil's footsteps, then he opened the door. He had also freshened up, his hair damp and his face shaven. Even though I liked his stubble, the fact he had groomed himself for my sake tickled my fancy. He looked unfairly handsome in jeans and a snug henley top that seemed to accentuate all the finely tuned muscles hiding underneath. He smelled like his dark floral cologne and the vanilla-scented body wash I had sniffed in his bathroom.

"Come in," Neil said, waving me through.

After all this time, the timbre of his voice still made me shiver with delight.

"Thanks." I stepped inside. "I put the clothes you lent me in the wash, by the way. They were too dirty not to."

"As long as you didn't shrink them."

"I hope not!"

Neil chuckled. "They're old clothes, anyway. And once again, they look better on you than they do on me."

"I bet that's not true."

I had meant my words to be self-deprecating, not a compliment towards Neil, but the way they came out sounded like flirting.

Neil's eyes widened a fraction, and I caught a fleeting look of curiosity as he tried to interpret my remark. A hint of colour edged up his neck, then he broke eye contact. The silence was thick until Archie scurried over to greet me, his nails clicking on the floorboards. I lavished him with pats and baby talk while Neil looked on, his demeanour relaxing.

"Are you hungry?" Neil asked.

"Very," I replied.

"Pizza?"

"Good idea."

"I'll put an order in. Do you want to look at the menu?"

"Yes, please."

He pulled it up on his phone and passed it across to me. I scanned the list. "Vegetarian?" I asked.

"Yes, for me. But you can get whatever you like."

"I'm fine with vegetarian too. What about the hot chilli pizza? Do you like spice?"

"I love spice."

His smooth assertion made me forget myself for a second, then I handed his phone back, flustered. "Then that's my choice."

Neil finished making the order, then something caught his attention. "Ah. There she is."

Chichi had emerged to suss out the new arrival. She approached Archie with her head held high and her tail in the air. Archie tried to get a good sniff as she circled him. Meanwhile, I spied Bowey keeping his distance, watching the unfolding situation warily from atop a bookshelf.

"Looks like Bowey's still not ready to introduce himself," I said.

Neil grimaced. "He's a big scaredy cat. It will take some adjustment, but I'm sure they'll warm up to each other, eventually."

Chichi flicked her tail with indifference, returning to her napping spot on the rug, while Archie gave a hoarse whine and flopped onto the floor.

As we waited for the pizza, Neil and I sat crossed-legged, playing with Archie. Neil cradled the dog's head in his hands with tender affection. "This is the first time I've owned a dog since Rufus," he murmured, a distant look in his eyes.

"Was Rufus your childhood dog?"

Neil gave a solemn nod.

I sensed he had a lot of difficult emotions tied up with the memory of this dog. It would explain why he hadn't wanted to talk about it back at the shelter. But now he had brought the subject up again, I wondered if he'd be willing to confide in me. "Do you want to talk about him?"

Neil inhaled a sharp breath. He stared down at his hand as he stroked Archie's fur, gathering himself before speaking. "Well,

Rufus was like my best friend. I turned to him for comfort whenever my father got abusive towards me or my mother."

A knot tightened in my stomach as I pictured Neil's younger self, lonely and scared.

"One day—I must have been about ten at the time—I did something to upset my father. I don't even remember what it was. He said, 'You're going to pay for that.' The next day, Rufus was gone, and I never saw him again." His voice cracked. "My father knew I loved that dog. I think he killed him or dumped him somewhere as punishment for whatever I did. That's the kind of man he was." He turned his face away, but not before I caught a heart-shattering glimpse of tears in his eyes.

"Oh, Neil. I'm so sorry. That's awful."

On instinct, I reached out and pulled him into a fierce hug. There was no resistance from him this time. He buried his head in my shoulder and shuddered a ragged rhythm against me, silently weeping. I held him until the shudders subsided.

Neil lifted his head, his eyes rimmed red. "I'm sorry for laying this on you and getting overly sentimental."

"You don't have to say sorry."

He wiped his face. "I've never told anyone that before."

My breath caught, the magnitude of his trust in me sinking in. "Thank you for telling me. That wasn't an easy thing to say."

"We all have our demons."

"Yes." I thought of my own father, a barrage of memories flickering before my eyes. "We do." My voice was faint.

Neil's phone dinged. He didn't check it. "Is there something you want to say?" he asked.

Just like him, there were parts of my history I hadn't shared with anyone, not even my closest friends. It was easier to exist with them bottled up, locked away where they couldn't hurt me, or worse, be judged. But with Neil... I felt safe. "I... I do have something I want to say." Where to even begin? I took a shaky breath. "It's just... difficult."

Neil's eyes held mine, a silent reassurance that he was there, he was listening, and he would understand. It gave me the strength to continue.

"My father was also abusive."

The sheer look of utter pain on Neil's face was heart-rending. "Oh, Milly…"

"Not in the same way as yours," I felt the need to clarify. "He was never violent."

"But he still hurt you?"

I shook my head, the gesture more of a reflection of my internal struggle than a denial. "I don't know. I didn't even consider it to be abuse until after he died. He killed himself."

"I'm so sorry."

A bitter laugh escaped my lips. "The counsellor I saw said my dad had neglected me. I was so angry, I walked out of the session. But looking back… he was right." The memories surfaced, sharp and painful, of a childhood spent navigating loneliness and responsibility beyond my years. "Ever since my mum died when I was just a little kid, my dad was depressed, and he did the bare minimum to raise me. I basically had to do everything by myself. Cook, clean, get myself where I needed to go… Maybe he was doing his best, but it wasn't good enough." The tears I'd held back for so long spilled over, hot tracks down my cheeks. "I know it sounds stupid. It's nowhere near the same level as what you went through—"

Neil took my hand in his. "It's not stupid. Not at all. He didn't look after you the way he should have. Yes, that was abusive. You deserved better."

Just hearing him acknowledge my trauma felt cathartic. It wasn't all in my head, or an overreaction as I'd sometimes feared. "Thank you, Neil. I really needed to hear that." I wiped the tears from my eyes.

"I think we both got something off our chest today. I'm glad we had this talk."

"Me too."

Neil let my hand go like he'd only just realised he had been holding it. The warmth of him lingered like an imprint.

"You and your mother—what happened? Did you get away from your dad?" I asked.

Neil nodded. "We escaped when I was twelve, and I've never heard from him since. I don't even know if he's alive or dead. Nor do I care."

Just then, an eruption of squeaks rang out. Both of us turned to see Archie sprawled on his back, gleefully gnawing on one of his new toys—a squeaky pizza slice.

I couldn't help but laugh at the absurd juxtaposition of Archie's joy and the seriousness of the situation. Neil chuckled too, the hearty sound warming me up from the inside.

"Looks like that pizza slice is his new favourite toy," I said.

"Speaking of pizza..." Neil checked his phone. "It's ready. I'll go pick it up. You just stay here and look after Archie, okay? I'll be back in a minute."

While Neil was gone, I played with Archie until he got drowsy, then I coaxed him into his dog bed. He circled a few times before flopping down with a contented sigh. I stroked his back until his eyes drifted shut, feeling grateful he was here and not cooped up in a cage at the shelter. I knew Neil would provide him with all the love and care in the world.

By the time Neil returned with two pizza boxes stacked in his arms, Archie was fast asleep.

"He's all tuckered out," I said.

Neil smiled. "It's no wonder, with all the excitement." He placed the boxes on the coffee table.

I approached, feeling sensitive to the fact we no longer had Archie to use as a buffer between us. Neil must have felt the tension too, his hand darting to fidget with the neckline of his shirt. "Feeling better now?" he asked.

"Yes. You?"

"The walk and fresh air helped." He shifted, his arms crossing and uncrossing. "If you'd rather not hang around, you can take a pizza home if you like."

I appreciated his offer, but the way he looked at me, his dark eyes soft and imploring, suggested he really wanted me to stay. And so did I. "Are you trying to get rid of me?" I asked.

"Believe me, that's not the case."

"Then I'll stay, if you don't mind."

"Very well."

Neither of us could pretend this was about Archie anymore. We had opened up to each other in a way that had blurred the line between us into something beyond recognition. I didn't know what we were to each other now, but I wanted to find out.

Neil grabbed plates from the kitchen, then joined me in the living room. I dared to take a seat next to him on the couch, rather than on a separate armchair. He flipped the TV to a game show and opened the pizza boxes. The aroma of melted cheese and charred crust rose up. I helped myself to a slice.

"It's so good," I said, relishing my first bite of tangy sauce on crispy crust.

"Have as much as you want," Neil said.

We ate without the need for small talk, the lively game show providing a comfortable backdrop. I pretended to watch, but paid much more attention to Neil's sharp profile in my peripheral vision, acutely aware that he was just a few centimetres away from me. Now and again, our elbows bumped.

When I had finished eating and the game show credits rolled, I searched for something else to occupy myself with. A basket full of video games under the side table caught my eye. I leaned over and rifled through it. "I never would have guessed you're a gamer," I said, running a finger across the spines.

"Why not? Do you still get the impression I'm not a fun person?"

"No. I know you're fun."

And cute. And dreamy.

"Do you want to play something with me?" Neil asked.

I perked up at his proposal. "Sure! Which game?"

He selected a racing game and popped it into the console. He passed me a controller and explained the buttons as the game loaded.

"I have to warn you, I'm terrible at video games," I said.

"That's all right. I'll go easy on you." Neil grinned.

We started racing, Neil's red sports car overtaking my bulky blue hatchback. I gripped the controller hard as I struggled to steer around turns. Neil offered instructions, but it was hopeless. I just couldn't get the hang of it. Before long, we both dissolved into laughter at my lack of coordination.

"This is ridiculous!" I said, as I crashed my car for the tenth time.

Neil's shoulders shook with mirth.

We played several more rounds. Without realising it, we had drifted closer together on the couch until our arms and legs brushed with every movement and laugh.

"I give up! This game is impossible," I said as my car veered off the track yet again.

Neil laughed, his eyes crinkling at the corners. "You can't quit now. We still have two more tracks to go."

I sighed in exaggerated annoyance. "Fine. But when I come last again, don't laugh at me."

"I make no promises."

With renewed determination, I pressed on the accelerator button at the start of the next race. As expected, Neil's car zoomed ahead while I struggled to even stay on course. My tongue poked out in concentration as I wrestled with the controls.

On the winding coastal route, I misjudged a turn and crashed headfirst into a guardrail. "Ugh!"

Neil bit back a smile. "You're getting better, though. Look, you just passed two cars."

"By pure luck," I grumbled, though I did feel a glimmer of pride.

The final track was set in a busy city with tricky shortcuts.

Vehicles careened and smashed around me, but I managed to avoid any collisions through cautious driving. I was so focused I didn't even realise it was the last lap when I crossed the finish line.

"Melia," Neil said.

I almost dropped the controller. What did he just say? *Melia?*

I recalled him using that name for me once before. He had groaned it in his sleep in my hotel room in Singapore.

"Melia," he repeated.

Now I knew it was intended and not a slip of the tongue. So, was this a new pet name he had for me?

"Look at your placing," he said.

"Hmm?" I glanced at the screen and saw my name in fifth place out of nine.

I gasped in astonishment, then I threw up my arms. "Hooray! I didn't come last!"

"Congratulations."

I did a little victory dance in my seat, much to his amusement.

Meanwhile, a box popped up on the screen saying my controller had a low battery.

"Looks like we'll have to stop there," Neil said. He checked his watch. "Anyway, it's getting late."

"Yeah. It's probably time I should head home."

I wanted him to protest, but he did not. I grabbed my bag from beside the couch and stood up.

Neil started gathering the plates and pizza boxes. As I rummaged through my bag for my phone, I realised it wasn't there. "Um, have you seen my phone anywhere?"

Neil stopped what he was doing and glanced around. "No—" His eyes landed on a dark object wedged between the couch cushions. "Is that it?"

We both leaned in to grasp it at the same time. Our hands collided, and we froze, faces inches apart. Time seemed to stop as we hovered in tense proximity. Neil was close enough that I could see flecks of amber in his dark eyes and feel his warm breath fan across my cheek. All of my nerve endings were alive from his knee brushing mine, his fingers still pressing against my hand. My gaze slid from his eyes to his lips, and I saw his throat bob as he swallowed.

In that suspended moment, I knew nothing would happen unless I made the first move. I steeled myself. I closed in and pressed my lips to his.

Chapter Forty-Nine

Neil's lips parted ever so slightly beneath mine… Then he clamped them shut. He grabbed my shoulders and pushed me away. "Milly," he rasped. "We shouldn't."

He dropped his hands like I had burned him, and his jaw clenched and unclenched as if he were cycling through conflicting thoughts and emotions.

My face broke out in a flush of heat. How could I have misread the signs so badly? "I'm sorry, I—"

No excuse came to mind. I had to get out of there. I grabbed my things and charged towards the exit.

"Milly, wait!" Neil called after me. "Can we talk about this?"

But I was already stumbling through the door, unable to so much as look at him. "I really should just go. I'm sorry."

Ignoring Neil's protests, I slipped out of the apartment and hurried to the lift. Tears stung my eyes. How could I ever face him again after being so reckless? I had ruined everything between us.

I mashed the down button but gave up waiting and took the fire escape stairs instead. My mind raced as I descended the steps, analysing every excruciating detail of what had just happened. I couldn't believe I had kissed him. What on earth had possessed me to do something so foolish?

I thought he liked me. That's why.

Was I deluded? Maybe. But the way he looked at me, the tension between us… I couldn't have imagined it. Could I?

He had pushed me away, but why did he look pained afterwards? Was it because he was my boss? Did he think it was inappropriate? Or did he just not have those kinds of feelings for me at all?

My head spun with questions as I agonised over each minuscule interaction we shared, searching for clues I had missed. But the truth was, I had no idea what Neil was thinking.

Back in my apartment, I collapsed in a heap on the bed. I tried to meditate to mute the barrage of thoughts swirling through my mind.

Gradually, my breathing evened out, and I started to relax, but just as I neared a sense of calm, my phone buzzed on the nightstand, jolting me. My stomach dropped, knowing it was likely Neil trying to contact me. I didn't want to hear from him, but I couldn't stop myself from looking.

With a deep breath, I grabbed the phone. As expected, a new text message from Neil awaited me.

Please talk to me when you're ready.

I chewed my lip, uncertain how to even begin responding. My fingers hovered over the keypad until I gave up. I just couldn't face him yet. I turned my phone off and curled up under the blankets. I needed time to nurse my bruises in private before letting him back in. Whenever that would be. I knew one thing for sure; nothing would ever be the same between us.

Chapter Fifty

I considered calling in sick on Monday, but I knew Neil would see straight through me. Besides, I couldn't avoid him forever. Better to get it over with.

My heart thumped as I entered my office. The room was quiet. Neil's door was ajar, but I didn't dare peek inside. I tiptoed to my desk, hoping to delay the inevitable confrontation a little longer.

Just when I had convinced myself Neil hadn't heard me enter, he emerged. He was dressed and groomed to perfection as usual, yet something about his demeanour seemed frayed. He looked at me with hard eyes, his mouth set in a stern line. "Good morning, Amelia. Can we speak in my office?"

So, we're back to Amelia again.

I tried to stall. "We're meeting with finance in fifteen minutes—"

"This won't take long."

His stony expression said he wasn't going to take no for an answer. He made a head-jerking action that told me to come with him. *Now.*

I suppressed a shudder as I followed him into his office. He closed the door with a deliberate click. "Take a seat."

I obeyed, perching on the edge of the couch. Neil continued to stand. I opened my mouth to explain my side of the story before he had a chance to reprimand me, but my tongue felt thick and clumsy, making me stumble over my words. "Look, I'm sorry about what happened. I just felt close to you… I don't know what came over me."

Neil remained shuttered. "I crossed a line. I invited you into my home—more than once. I invited you for dinner. That was negligent and an abuse of my position as your employer. If you want to report this to HR, please do so. I will accept any punishment that's handed to me."

I gaped. "What? No, that's absurd! You did nothing wrong."

Neil frowned, his forehead creasing. "Don't make excuses for me. I manipulated you."

"No, you didn't. Why are you acting like I had no agency in this?"

"Amelia, please—"

"I *wanted* to kiss you!" I blurted. It came out louder and more forceful than I had intended, and I slapped my hand over my mouth in shock.

Neil appeared to consider my outburst for a second before dismissing it with a shake of his head. "Regardless, whatever this is, it has to stop now. It just can't happen. Even if I wasn't your boss, it can't happen."

His rejection stung, but I pressed my case. "Why not? What would be stopping us? Hypothetically speaking."

Neil sighed, touching his forehead as if warding off an oncoming headache. "I'm not a good man, Amelia."

"Why would you say that?"

"Oh, please. Don't be so naïve. I've done things. Terrible things. You don't get to be as rich as I am while being a good person." His voice was bitter, laced with self-loathing.

"But you *are* good! What does money have to do with anything?"

"Everything. Money, power, and control. I should never have

allowed you to get so close to me. I've already endangered you enough as it is."

I strained to understand where this was coming from. "Are you talking about what happened in Singapore? Is that what you mean? Because Daniel hasn't contacted me or done anything since then. I think he's given up on me."

Neil said nothing, but every bone and muscle in his body seemed to strain.

I wished I could see into his mind, know what he was thinking and feeling. I rose and moved closer. "Look, I know you're not perfect. None of us are. But I also know you have a good heart. I've seen it."

"You don't know me as well as you think you do."

"Maybe not, but I'd like to get the chance to know you better. As a friend, at least. Can't we move on from this and go back to how things were before?"

"We can't be friends." Neil drew his brows together, eyes full of regret. "I thought we could be, but I was mistaken."

"Neil…" I reached out to touch his arm, but he flinched and turned his back on me.

"I need to get to the meeting."

"What about me?"

"I don't need you. Spend some time thinking about whether you'd like to resign or change roles within the company. I think it would be for the best if we didn't work together anymore."

* * *

Neil's words replayed in an endless loop inside my head, tormenting me.

"I'm not a good man, Amelia. I've done things. Terrible things."

What did he mean by that? What sort of "terrible things" could he have possibly done? I tossed and turned beneath the twisted sheets, analysing every detail of our exchange. Why did he blame himself for the kiss when I was the one who initiated it?

He said he had manipulated me, but I didn't feel that way at all. I wanted to kiss him. It was my choice as a grown woman who knew my own mind.

"It just can't happen. Even if I wasn't your boss, it can't happen."

If it wasn't about the ethics of our working relationship, then why did he insist we couldn't be together? Was it about me going away? Or did he just not like me?

My thoughts circled back to Singapore. The way he tensed up when I asked if his rejection had to do with what happened there. Was I getting close to something he didn't want me to know?

I groaned, burying my face in the pillow. This endless guessing game was getting me nowhere. I tried to go to sleep, but whenever I closed my eyes, I was back in Neil's office, in the midst of our confrontation.

The first rays of light peeked through the curtains by the time exhaustion claimed me. I had barely slipped under when I jolted awake to the screeching alarm. My head throbbed as though someone was drilling a hole into it. My joints ached, my nose was congested, and my throat felt raw. I couldn't tell if it was the start of a cold or if stress had done me in. Either way, I knew I was in no state to go to work.

I called James, since I didn't have the nerve to speak to Neil directly. "Hi James, it's Milly. I don't think I can make it into work today. I'm sick. Could you let Neil know?"

"Sure, no problem. Rest up."

I thanked him and hung up, then swallowed a couple of painkillers before crawling back under the covers. Neil would probably think I was faking illness to avoid him, but so be it.

One day off stretched into two, then three, as I battled with sinus congestion, aches, chills, and fatigue. My doctor confirmed it was a virus, likely brought on by stress.

On the fourth day, I called the office again. My voice came out strained and hoarse. "Hey, James, it's Milly again. Still not feeling well."

"Yikes, you sound terrible!"

I let out a pathetic half-laugh, half-cough. "I guess this bug is really doing a number on me."

"Don't worry about it, just focus on getting better. I'll pass it along."

I shuffled to the kitchen and prepared a coffee, hoping the caffeine might help clear my brain fog. Since falling ill, I hadn't had the mental clarity to think about Neil's rejection and what to do about his order to resign or change positions. Cradling the warm mug, I curled up on the couch and tried to think things through again. Did Neil seriously want to get rid of me, or did he say that in the heat of the moment? If I made it clear that I wanted to keep working with him, would he let me, or would he fire me? A job loss now meant I'd have to take up cleaning again to fill in the gap before going overseas.

I lay down, feeling another headache coming on. The leather cushions squeaked beneath me as I shifted, trying to get comfortable. At some point, I must have drifted asleep, because I stirred sometime later to the shrill tone of my phone ringing. I fumbled to grab it off the coffee table, but missed the last ring. My heart constricted at the sight of Neil's name on the missed-call message. I wondered what he wanted to say to me, but I didn't have the courage to call him back, so I just left it. This wasn't the first time I had ignored a call from him either.

In the afternoon, I found the energy to clean the house, put on a load of laundry, and restock the barren pantry from a grocery delivery. Bit by bit, I started to feel like myself again.

I was in the middle of preparing an afternoon snack of crackers and cheese when my phone rang. I tensed, expecting it to be Neil again, but saw an unexpected name instead: Christine Liu.

That's weird. Why would she call me?

I picked up. "Hello?"

"Hi, Milly. It's Christine. How are you? Neil said you've been unwell."

Hearing her voice lifted my spirits. "Oh, hi, Christine. I had a bad sinus thing going on, but I'm feeling a bit better now. I think I'll be able to go back to work on Monday."

"Neil will be relieved. He sounded so worried about you on the phone. He asked me to check in and see how you're doing."

I blinked, unable to fathom Neil fretting over my absence when he had been so cold the last time we spoke. "Did he?"

"He sounded quite distraught, actually." A teasing lilt crept into her tone. "Did something happen between you two? He seemed to have the impression you'd be more likely to answer a call from me than from him."

I hesitated, weighing how much to confide in her.

"You can vent to me," Christine said. "I won't tell on you."

I supposed if anyone could help me decode Neil's behaviour, it would be Christine. "Well, actually… Yes. Something did happen. I… made a mistake, and now Neil is upset and wants me to leave my job."

"What?" She sounded genuinely shocked. "But I thought you two were getting along really well."

"We were."

"What happened?"

I shuffled my feet. "I don't want to say. It's kinda embarrassing."

"Oh really? Well, I'm sure Neil has his reasons. He can be stubborn at the best of times. What did he say exactly?"

"He told me he's not a good man, he's done terrible things, we can't be friends…"

Christine let out a soft sigh, as if Neil's reasoning didn't surprise her at all.

"Do you know what he meant by that?" I asked.

"I think he has a guilty conscience. Zelthia's not exactly known for good working conditions across their companies. Not to mention all the blackmail and bribery and corruption. He's tried to keep his hands clean throughout the years, but that hasn't always been possible."

I reeled, struggling to reconcile this darker version of Neil with the man I knew. Of course, I was aware he couldn't have achieved his success through wholly ethical means. Cutthroat tactics were par for the course in the corporate world, especially at his level, but hearing the stark reality laid bare still came as a shock. "So when he said those awful things about himself, that's what he meant?"

"Most likely."

"That's quite a lot to take in."

"You deserve to know who you're dealing with."

"But he doesn't seem to be a bad person. Not anymore, right?"

"I don't know how much he's told you, but he's doing the best he can behind the scenes to reform the business."

"I have some idea. I just wish he'd let me support him instead of pushing me away."

"Milly, you know what I think?" Christine's voice took on a conspiratorial hush. "I've heard the way Neil talks about you, seen the way he looks at you… I think he cares an awful lot about you—even more than he lets on. If he's pushing you away, it's because he's trying to do what he thinks is best for you."

I frowned. "Why would pushing me away be what's best for me?"

"Because he's trying to protect you."

"From what?"

Christine paused, then her tone turned serious. "Neil is involved in something very dangerous right now. If the wrong people were to find out about his plans… Well, look what happened to Alex Patterson."

I shuddered. "So you also think his death was orchestrated?"

"I don't know. But I do know Neil is worried."

"That he could meet the same fate as Alex?"

"No. He accepted that possibility a long time ago."

"Then what?"

"I think he's afraid of what could happen to *you*, Milly. He's afraid you could become a target."

Chapter Fifty-One

I had a lot to discuss with Neil, but before that, I needed time to process everything Christine had revealed.

The breeze stirred my hair as I ventured outside for the first time in days. I hoped a walk would help me organise my thoughts.

The harbourside promenade was busy with couples strolling hand in hand, groups of friends bar-hopping, and families eating alfresco. I wove between them, inhaling the salty sea air. In the distance, the harbour bridge sparkled from the stream of car headlights as the sun descended.

Despite feeling better physically, my mind felt like a tangled mess. Christine's words had validated my instincts about Neil while simultaneously adding new layers of confusion. Was she right? Did his rejection stem from a desire to protect me rather than a lack of interest? The more I mulled it over, the more it made sense. His hot-and-cold behaviour, the way he dismissed me yet looked pained as he did so—it aligned with someone who cared for me but felt he had to cut ties for self-sacrificing reasons.

And this dangerous succession scheme Neil was involved in… Why did it suddenly matter how close we were now, but not back in Singapore when Daniel literally thought Neil and I were sleeping together? Was it my attempted kiss which triggered Neil into defensive mode?

And what about the theory I could become a target? My life had never been smooth sailing, but never before had I faced such a threat. I frowned, chewing my lip. Maybe distancing myself from Neil was the wiser choice, no matter how much it hurt.

But then again, Neil was the closest person I had in my life right now. Maybe ever. I'd confided in him, opened up to him in ways I'd never imagined I could with another person. Was I willing to walk away from that because of some perceived threat that might never materialise?

I ambled along with my head down, lost in my thoughts. At some point, I wandered off the main stretch. My surroundings grew quieter as I found myself on a footpath running alongside the marina. Gleaming yachts bobbed in their moorings, their towering masts swaying like metronomes in the breeze. I stared out at the rippling water.

A familiar bark put a pin in my ruminations, then I felt something rough and tickly on the back of my leg. I looked down and saw Archie's scruffy face nuzzling my leg, his tongue licking me, tail wagging. My gaze lifted, following Archie's leash to the man holding it. Our eyes locked. In that charged moment, my internal debate crystallised into a single, resolute thought: No matter what dangers or difficulties lay ahead, I knew with utter certainty that I could never walk away from him. I was going to fight for him, for us—whatever that meant—no matter what it took.

He was dressed in dark shorts that showed off his toned, lightly tanned legs. A fitted t-shirt hugged his broad shoulders and athletic frame, the short sleeves emphasising the bulge of his biceps. The fading sunlight lit the harsh angles of his face. I was entranced.

Archie let out a low, grumbly whine, begging for my attention.

"He's missed you," Neil said, eyes crinkling with a fond look directed more at me than the dog.

"Have *you* missed me?" I asked, emboldened by the strength of my desire for him.

"Yes, I have." His voice was raw, making my stomach flip.

"Me too. I've missed you too."

Neil stepped closer, searching my face with lingering concern. "How are you feeling?"

"Much better now, thanks. I have a doctor's note if you need it."

"That won't be necessary. I'm glad to hear you're okay."

I bit my lip. "Were you worried about me?"

Christine had told me as much, but I yearned to hear it directly from him.

"I had to stop myself from going to your apartment to check on you. I didn't want to invade your privacy."

I imagined him showing up at my door, his concern laid bare for me to witness. I almost wished he had done so. "It's probably for the best you didn't. You could have caught my bug."

"I thought you might have been avoiding me on purpose."

"Maybe I wanted to avoid you so much that I physically manifested an illness."

I meant it as a light-hearted jab, but Neil seemed to take it seriously. He tensed. "I'm sorry. The other day… I was too harsh with you." He touched his face. "I guess I'm not doing a very good job at keeping my feelings in check. The last thing I wanted to do was to hurt you. It was never my intention—"

"Are you trying to protect me?"

Neil recoiled. "Did Christine say that?"

"She might have. Is it true?"

Neil looked around, then he leaned in. "We've become… *close*. Certain people could use that knowledge to their advantage."

"You mean Daniel? He's in Singapore, and we're here. How could he know anything? Even a spy in the company wouldn't know how we've been spending time together outside of work. The very fact he thought we were sleeping with each other when we weren't proves he doesn't know what's really going on."

"Yes, well, maybe I am being a touch paranoid—but all the same, you don't know what he's capable of."

"Then help me understand." I lifted my chin and faced him eye to eye, gathering my courage. "I want to keep working with you. I want to stay here, and I want to help you as much as I can, both with Luxmore and Zelthia business. Whatever you need. Whatever the risk."

Neil's pupils flared. "You don't know what you're asking—"

"Yes, I do. I've played it safe my whole life, and I don't want to be that person anymore. Even if it could put my life at stake, I want to stay by your side and help you achieve your goals, for my sake, as much as yours."

Neil searched my eyes, as if trying to verify the truth of my words.

I held his gaze. "Besides, won't it look suspicious if you suddenly fired your new secretary, who you used to get along so well with, without a good explanation? It might draw unwanted attention."

Neil rubbed his chin. "That thought has crossed my mind."

Sensing his weakening resistance, I pressed on. "Wouldn't it be better if I stayed close to you so you can watch over me?"

"I shouldn't. We shouldn't..." His voice lacked conviction. His will was crumbling.

"I've made up my mind. This is what I want."

After a weighted pause, Neil let out a ragged sigh and nodded. "Very well. If that's what you truly want, I won't stand in your way."

"Thank you."

"But if you ever want to back out, I won't blame you."

"Don't worry. I'm not going to back down."

"And I swear to God, I won't let anything happen to you." The intensity of his voice gave me chills.

"I know."

We stayed locked in each other's sight, the significance of our exchange sinking in. I suddenly felt very conscious of how I had tried to kiss him, how I had felt him on the verge of yielding to my lips and mouth before he pulled away… I turned my attention to Archie to distract myself, scratching his floppy ears and patting his back. "You're such a good boy, Archie. Has Neil been looking after you well?"

"I took him in to work today. He loved it."

"He's looking so much healthier and more energetic than he did at the shelter."

Neil watched on with a tender look while I doted on Archie. Meanwhile, the last rays of sunlight slipped away, leaving us bathed in the soft glow of street lamps and lit windows.

"Let's head back," Neil said.

Archie trotted along in front of us as we walked towards our apartment building in the distance.

"Did Christine mention the work dinner to you when she called?" Neil asked.

"No, she didn't."

"I've invited a few people out to a restaurant next Friday. Christine and Ed, James, Winston and Carol. You're invited too, of course. If you would like to attend."

I perked up at the prospect of a fancy dinner shared with my work family. "I'd love to come!"

"Great."

We fell silent again until we passed through the lobby. Riding up in the lift, I snuck glances at Neil in my peripheral vision, still hardly believing I had broken through his defences. When we stopped at my floor, Archie yanked Neil towards me as I stepped out.

"He's quite attached," Neil said, trying to rein him in. "He doesn't want to leave you."

"Then why don't you walk me to my door? Or is that off-limits?"

Neil's exasperated sigh didn't cover up his amusement. "I suppose I can manage that."

We walked down the hall. Outside my door, I stooped to give

Archie one last ruffle of his fur. When I straightened up, I saw Neil staring at me with heated intensity. He opened his mouth as if to say something, then seemed to think better of it.

I took an uneven breath. "Well… good night."

"Good night, Milly."

We lingered, neither of us making a move to part ways, almost like we had forgotten what to do next.

At last, Neil turned to leave, but he hesitated and faced me again. "Just so you know, if things were different… If I wasn't…" He huffed, raking a hand through his hair. "Well, I wouldn't even have to think about it."

With that cryptic remark, he strode back to the lift, tugging Archie along in his wake.

Chapter Fifty-Two

When I returned to work, Neil and I carried on business as usual, yet the subtle shift in our dynamic was palpable. Every shared glance and fleeting brush of contact felt loaded with unresolved tension. Surely it wasn't my imagination. Neil had to feel it too.

On Friday afternoon, we emerged from a meeting on the fourth floor to head back to our office on the twentieth floor. One lift was out of order, and the other one taking its sweet time to arrive. When the door finally opened, the interior was packed to the brim. Everyone shuffled to make a sliver of space for us. I squeezed in first, while Neil hesitated on the periphery until someone said, "You can get in. There's room."

Neil reluctantly jammed up to me. My breath hitched as I noticed every point our bodies made contact: my arm against his, my hip grazing his thigh, his chest centimetres from my face. I dared to glance up at him. He stared straight ahead, jaw clenched. Meanwhile, my whole body was on fire, painfully attuned to his proximity. The lift stopped at nearly every floor on the way up. When enough people exited to create some distance between us, I could breathe again. Neil fidgeted with his tie and watch, avoiding eye contact, until we arrived on our floor.

Once we were both seated at our desks, I tried to re-focus my attention on work, but I couldn't stop thinking about the way Neil felt against me, and how good it would feel if he pressed me up against the wall in his office...

I shook the fantasy out of my head. If I had any hope of maintaining a sense of professionalism, I had to restrain myself. I sighed and forced my eyes back to the computer screen, determined to get some work done.

Sometime later, a private message from Neil popped up on the work chat.

> Can you please take a final look at the strategy document for me? Then print it out. I need sex

What did I just read?

I did a double take, peering close at the last sentence to make sure I hadn't hallucinated it. Nope. It was there, all right. S... E... X. I responded with a question mark, then Neil typed three messages in quick succession.

> Sex copies

> 6 copies

> Sorry

After I had dislodged my left eyebrow from the top of my forehead, I proceeded with the task at hand. *It was just a typo,* I told myself. Still, it wasn't like Neil to make such an egregious error.

The full read and review of the complex document took me over an hour. As the papers came through warm on the printer tray, the sound of Neil's voice on the phone drifted from his office. He had a consoling tone, and he mentioned the dinner tonight. I figured he must be speaking to either Christine or Winston. I hoped nothing had derailed the dinner plans. James had already dropped out due to a scheduling conflict.

With the document pages collated and stacked, I carried them through to Neil. He had already finished his phone call. He thanked me with a nod and reached for the papers, but as they exchanged hands, he winced, dropping them on his desk.

"Are you okay?" I asked.

"It's nothing. Just a paper cut." He examined his index finger.

"Here, let me see." On instinct, I grasped his hand in both of mine, turning his palm upwards to inspect the minor injury. Neil did not resist. The implicit affection of my action struck me too late, and by then I couldn't bring myself to let go. His hand was warm and a little clammy, the rough pads of his fingers pressing into my smooth palms. I traced my gaze along his veins, exploring every groove and contour. Neither of us moved. At last, I regained control of my faculties. I released Neil's hand and took a step back, a furious blush bursting onto my cheeks. "Sorry. It's not even bleeding."

Neil blinked hard and shook his head. "It's fine."

"Is everything okay for tonight?" I asked, changing the subject. "I heard you on the phone before."

"Winston is unwell and won't be able to make it."

"Oh, that's a shame. Is he okay?"

"He has a headache and a runny nose. I told him to go home early."

"I wonder if it's the same bug I had."

"Possibly." Neil pinched the bridge of his nose. "That makes three drop-outs. James, and Winston and his wife."

"Maybe we should reschedule."

Neil shook his head. "Christine has already arranged for her nanny to babysit, so I wouldn't want to make her change plans this late. She and Ed are still coming. I'll call the restaurant and let them know there will be fewer people."

"Good idea."

Before leaving his office, I paused. "What should I wear tonight?"

Neil's eyes widened. He seemed lost for words.

I rushed to correct myself. "I mean, how formal is the dress code at the restaurant?"

"R-right. It's, uh, reasonably upmarket. I'll wear the same thing I'm wearing now, but you can wear whatever you're comfortable in. There will be plenty of time to go home and get changed if you need to."

"Thanks for clearing that up."

Why, oh why, did I feel the need to get his opinion on such a matter? I tucked a loose strand of hair behind my ear, suddenly finding my shoes very interesting as I made my exit.

* * *

I stood in front of my bedroom mirror, smoothing my hands over the cotton sundress I had chosen for the evening. The silhouette was feminine, with a shirred bodice and a mid-length skirt. A delicate blue-and-white floral pattern adorned the fabric. Pretty, but there was a problem: the whisper-thin straps were slightly loose and kept falling down. I also didn't have a suitable bra to wear underneath, so had to go without one. I considered adding a cardigan or light jacket, just in case it got cold later, but decided against it. Carrying an extra layer seemed like a hassle. No, this outfit would do. I slipped on a pair of heeled sandals, spritzed myself with perfume, then headed out the door.

The sun remained high in the sky as I walked to the restaurant, its rays beating down and reflecting off the harbour. People lounged on the benches lining the waterfront, chatting and eating ice creams, basking in the early evening sunshine.

The restaurant was on the upper level of the downtown ferry building. I entered a spacious foyer lit by a chandelier resembling a cluster of floating candles. A host greeted me. "Do you have a reservation?"

"It should be under Neil Kingston."

"Please, go on through."

"Thank you."

I climbed the stairs. The restaurant interior was modern and elegant with a black-and-white colour scheme. On one side of the room, a glass wine rack extended from floor to ceiling, backlit with yellow light, housing a vast collection of wine. On the other side of the room, large windows and French doors faced a balcony over the harbour and ferry terminal. I saw Neil, seated by himself at a table indoors. He wore his white shirt with one button open at the collar, his suit jacket flung over the chair behind him. With fluttering anticipation, I approached. He glanced up, his mouth falling open a fraction. Appreciation flitted in his eyes. I lifted the fallen right strap of my dress while his stare lingered on my shoulders and loose hair.

"Hello." I pulled out the chair opposite him.

"You look…" he swallowed, hesitating over how to finish the sentence he had started, "lovely."

"Thank you. So do you. I mean, you look good. As always." I cringed inwardly as I stumbled over my words.

"Christine and Ed are running late."

I nodded along, trying my best to act casual. Even though we had just spent the day together, I felt nervous tonight.

"Would you like a drink while we wait?" Neil asked.

"Yes, please."

He passed me the drinks menu. I scanned the list, weighing my options, until a waiter approached the table. "Can I take your drinks order?" the young woman asked.

"I'll have a lychee cosmopolitan, please," I said.

"And for you, sir?"

"A bottle of San Pellegrino, thank you," Neil said.

"Anything else?"

Neil looked to me. I shook my head.

"That's all," Neil said.

After the server left, I distracted myself from the awkwardness of the situation by glancing around the sophisticated dining space. My focus drifted to the French doors and the balcony beyond. The doors had been propped open, allowing the murmur of conversation and clinking of glasses to reach my ears. Sheer curtains billowed in the breeze. Through the gauzy panels, I could make out intimate round tables dotted across the balcony. Diners laughed and chatted, soaking up the last rays of golden-hour sunlight as they sipped wine and picked at shared plates. The atmosphere was much more casual than the formality indoors.

"I'm afraid I couldn't get a table outside," Neil said.

I waved him off. "This is perfect."

Our drinks arrived. Condensation dripped down the chilled glass as I brought the light pink cocktail to my lips. The sweet taste of lychee and kick of vodka made me sigh. Meanwhile, Neil's phone buzzed. He swiped at the screen. "It's Christine," he said. "Her babysitter has fallen through."

"Oh no. Does that mean she can't come?"

"She's still coming. Ed's staying home with Rosie."

"Ah. Poor Ed. So, it'll just be the three of us now."

Neil glanced at his watch. "It might be awhile before she gets here. Shall we order an appetiser in the meantime?"

"Good idea. I'm getting hungry already."

We ordered some bread with dips. As we waited for the food, we talked about work to fill in the time. Somehow—maybe it was the alcohol kicking in—I felt bold enough to bring the conversation to Zelthia and Neil's schemes. "How are things progressing in Singapore?" I asked.

Neil stiffened. "You shouldn't concern yourself with any of that."

"I thought we agreed I was going to help you."

"You would help me the most by staying out of it as much as possible. Besides, it's a waiting game now. I've already set things in motion. Now we'll see if the right dominoes fall."

The bread arrived. We nibbled in silence until Neil's phone rang. He answered the call. "Everything okay?" After a pause, his frown deepened. "I see… That's too bad… Well, some other time, then. Have a good night. Bye." He hung up. "That was Christine. I'm afraid she won't be joining us after all. Car trouble on top of the babysitter issue."

"Oh dear."

An awkward pause followed as the reality of our situation sank in. We were well and truly alone now for this intimate dinner.

I spoke up. "So, now that it's just the two of us… Are we still having dinner, or…?"

Neil rubbed the back of his neck. "It seems like the universe has conspired for this to happen."

"I agree."

He sighed. "Well, I suppose it would be a shame to waste the reservation. If you're happy to stay…"

"Yes, of course. I'm happy if you are."

"All right, then." He caught the waiter's attention and informed her the other two wouldn't be coming after all. "Is there any chance we could move to a table outside on the balcony instead?" he asked.

The waiter nodded and showed us to a secluded little table down at the far end of the balcony. The sun was melting into pink and orange hues on the horizon. Strings of lights twinkled on the balcony railing, and boats drifted across the shimmering harbour. Neil held my chair out for me. Our bodies brushed as I moved to sit down. Neil settled opposite me, menu in hand. "Order whatever you'd like," he said.

"Even the caviar?"

"Yes."

"What about a bottle of Château Lafite Rothschild Pauillac?"

Neil's eyes crinkled. "Now I know you're just teasing me."

I chuckled. "Yeah. I probably didn't even say it right. My tastes are much simpler than that. I wouldn't know how to appreciate it."

We decided on our orders—a salmon dish for me and mushroom risotto for Neil.

By the time our meals arrived, the sun had slipped below the horizon, and a fresh chill laced the air. I hugged myself for warmth.

"Getting cold?" Neil asked.

"A little."

"I thought by now you would have learned to dress appropriately for the weather." His teasing tone took the sting from his words.

I shot him a mock glare. "It was hot before."

The waiter must have overheard our exchange, because she returned with a woollen throw and offered it to me.

"Thank you so much!"

"You're welcome." She lit the tea light candle on our table before retreating.

I met Neil's eyes through the golden glow of candlelight. Shadows danced across his face, accentuating his sharp features—the cut of his jawline, the intensity of his deep-set eyes. Those eyes softened as they settled on me, taking in my blanket-clad form.

"What?" I asked sheepishly.

"You look cosy."

"I am. Turns out I didn't need to dress warmer, after all."

His lips quirked. "Or were you just relying on wearing something from me again?"

"No. Well, maybe subconsciously…" I fiddled with the blanket's tasselled edge, avoiding his stare.

When I chanced a glance back at him, he wore a look of smug satisfaction. I felt sure my racing heart was visible on my face. I sipped water, then busied myself with my meal, spearing a flaky piece of salmon on my fork. The fish was cooked to perfection, the pearly pink flesh giving way to the prongs. As I took a bite, the tender meat melted on my tongue, imbued with the flavours of lemon and herbs.

"How is it?" Neil asked.

"Delicious."

After the main course came dessert. Crème brûlée for me and an espresso for Neil. By then, our conversation had drifted into personal territory.

"How are your travel plans coming along?" Neil asked, putting his cup down.

The question felt like a lead weight dropping in my stomach, but I forced a tight smile. "I've got my visa all sorted for the UK, and my friend Hannah said I can crash at her place in London until I get settled." I paused, pushing the crème brûlée around in its dish with my spoon. "Then I plan to do some backpacking around Europe for a few months before trying to find a more permanent job and living situation over there."

"Looking forward to it?" Neil's voice was carefully neutral, giving no hint of his own feelings on the matter.

I hesitated, my growing doubts taking root. Did I really want to leave this all behind—my job, my home, *him*? Mucking around in Europe seemed hollow now compared to the path my life was taking here.

"To be honest…" I dragged my spoon across the caramelised sugar topping, watching it splinter and crack. "I've been having some second thoughts lately. I'm not as excited as I used to be."

Neil raised an eyebrow. "Oh? Why is that?"

"I booked the trip because I wanted to escape my life, but now…" I met Neil's eyes in the flickering candlelight. "I no longer have such a strong desire to escape."

Neil held my gaze for a heated moment before asking carefully, "I hope you're not reconsidering because of me?"

I broke eye contact, my face warming at his presumption. But he wasn't entirely wrong. "I suppose you're one factor," I admitted, twisting the spoon between my fingers.

"You should still go. I wouldn't want you to miss out on your trip for my sake. You can always come back if it doesn't work out."

"Will I still have a job when I get back?"

"Yes, provided I'm still CEO."

"Then what about the apartment?"

"It's yours, Milly. I might rent it out in your absence, but you can have it back when you return."

I gawped, stunned. I hadn't expected Neil to let me stay in the lavish apartment long-term, since we had always framed it as a temporary measure. "Are you sure?"

"Yes."

"But it's worth so much more than I'm paying you—"

"It's not a selfless act by any means. I want you to live somewhere I know is secure, and I want you close by so I can keep an eye on you."

"Keep an eye on me?" I questioned, though his possessiveness secretly thrilled me.

"I got you involved in dangerous business. It's my responsibility to keep you safe. I don't think I could live with myself if I let something happen to you."

His solemn declaration struck me deeply. Throughout my life, I had always fended for myself. But with Neil, I felt protected and cared for in a way I never had before. "Nothing is going to happen to me," I assured him.

He nodded. "I'll make sure of it."

He brought his coffee cup to his lips, reminding me of the neglected crème brûlée in the china ramekin on my plate. The custard was smooth and rich, eliciting a little whimper from me.

Neil watched on with a look of amusement. I paused, wondering if I had got some on my face. I dabbed at my mouth with a serviette.

"You're clearly enjoying that," he said.

"It's divine. Want to try some?"

"No, thank you. I don't care much for sweet things."

"Oh, that's right."

As I savoured the last few bites, Neil's expression turned thoughtful.

"Something on your mind?" I asked.

He rubbed his neck. "Are you sure you want to keep working for me when—*if*—you return?"

I stopped eating. "You don't want me to?"

"It's not that," he said quickly, seeming flustered. "I mean, you have so much potential. Why not finish your medical degree?"

I shook my head without needing to consider his question. "The only reason I went to med school was because that's what people with good grades do. My life revolved around trying to make my dad proud of me; be the top student in school, get into medicine on a scholarship, become a brain surgeon or something equally impressive. Even after he died, I've always been striving towards something. It would be nice to slow down, live life day by day, and appreciate what I have. I don't know. Maybe I'm not wired for that."

"You won't know until you try."

Just sharing those thoughts with him was a weight off my chest. I set my spoon down in the empty ramekin. "What about you? What do you plan to do when all this is over? If your plans succeed—or if they fail—will you go back to Singapore?"

Neil shook his head. "I'd like to stay here. I'd like to leave Zelthia behind me and do something else."

"What will you do?"

He shrugged. "Move to the countryside, live in a big house with my pets, grow vegetables, learn to cook, maybe start a non-profit..."

His ideas resonated, aligning with my own dream of a simpler, more meaningful life. "That sounds *perfect*. But what about..." I faltered, losing my nerve.

"Hmm?"

"Any plans to share your life with someone else?"

His dark eyes burned into me. "That remains to be seen."

Under the table, our knees bumped, sending tremors up my leg. I thought of all the signs over recent weeks and months pointing to his affection for me. His playful banter, his protectiveness, his lingering gazes… It gave me the courage to keep my knee pressed against his.

Neil tensed, but he didn't pull away. He pinned me with a smouldering look instead.

"Is there someone you like?" I dared to ask.

His voice dropped low. "I think you know the answer to that."

A shuddering thrill coursed through my veins. I leaned a tad closer to him, but before I could say or do anything else, the waiter approached to collect our empty dishes. I retracted to the back of my seat.

"How was everything?" she asked. "Did you enjoy your meal?"

"Yes," I said, a little breathless. "It was perfect. Thank you."

Neil nodded in agreement as he produced his wallet. "Here. This is for you."

He discreetly slipped her some cash, causing her eyes to widen. "Thank you!"

I didn't see how much the tip was, but judging by her reaction, it must have been generous. She walked away without clearing the dishes, but she turned back and quickly gathered them before scurrying off with a mumbled apology.

My attention returned to Neil. He drank me in with unconcealed longing. His lips were parted, and I could see the rapid rise and fall of his chest beneath his slightly rumpled shirt. On the tablecloth between us, the dying tea light candle flickered, then extinguished.

"Shall we go home?" Neil asked, his voice steady.

"Yes," I replied, my stomach swooping with anticipation. "Let's go."

I couldn't decipher what he intended for the rest of the evening, but I was ready to find out.

I folded the blanket into a neat square and placed it on my seat. Neil paid the bill. As we left the restaurant, I shivered, the cold breeze whipping my bare shoulders and arms. Neil's suit jacket was around me before I could protest. His body heat lingered in the fabric as I slipped my arms through the oversized sleeves. We fell into step side by side.

"So, you're lending me your clothes after all," I said.

"I never said I wouldn't," Neil replied.

I couldn't hide the giddy smile which burst onto my face. Neil smiled too.

We passed shops, restaurants, hotels, and offices before reaching our apartment building. Neil held the door for me as we entered the lobby. No one joined us in the lift. Neil pressed the buttons for both my floor and his, clarifying that he wasn't about to invite me back to his place. I was too overwhelmed to feel disappointed.

The door opened on my floor.

"Good night, Milly," Neil murmured.

"Good night," I said, biting my lip. "Thank you so much for dinner. I had a lovely time."

"Me too."

I was about to step out into the corridor when I realised I was still wearing Neil's suit jacket. I stood in the door's path to keep it from closing as I shrugged the jacket off. "Wait. Before I forget. Here. Or else I'll probably try to wash it and ruin it like your sweater."

Neil accepted his jacket, his fingers grazing mine. He guided it back onto his broad shoulders. As he smoothed the lapels, his gaze fell upon my collarbone, exposed where my dress strap had slipped down yet again. Before I could fix it, he reached out and hooked his fingers under the thin strap. He painstakingly slid it back into place, his touch scorching my skin as it trailed over my bare shoulder and collarbone. I trembled in response.

Neil seemed hypnotised throughout the action. Then he suddenly snapped out of it. He started to pull his hand away, but like an automatic reflex, I covered his hand with my own, pressing it flush to my shoulder.

He did not resist.

I looked into his eyes, and I knew I had broken him.

Chapter Fifty-Three

Neil rubbed his thumb back and forth against my collarbone. "Melia," he breathed. "This might come as a surprise to you, but there's a limit to my willpower. You're making this very hard for me. Do you understand?"

The seductive quality of his voice reverberated in my bones. I couldn't back down now. I was too far gone. "There's something I need you to fix in my apartment," I said.

Neil's lips curved into a devilish smirk that made my insides clench. "Then I better take a look."

I led him to my door on shaky legs, my heart pounding an erratic beat. I fumbled trying to enter the code, inputting it wrong twice before the lock released.

As soon as we entered, the first thing Neil did was push the strap of my dress aside and sink his lips onto the spot still sensitive from his touch. I threw my head back in unbridled rapture as he moaned into my flesh, causing vibrations down my spine. He held my waist while he nipped and sucked a path to the crook of my neck, then the bottom of my ear. He trailed rough kisses along my jaw before claiming my lips. My knees buckled. I clung to him for support. Our mouths moved together, slowly at first, then gaining fervour, the silky slide of his tongue against mine igniting a hot ache in me. My fingers twisted in his hair while his hands roamed my body, tracing every curve and contour through the thin fabric of my dress. I nibbled his lower lip and felt him smile against my mouth before pulling back to look at me. His eyes burned with unconcealed desire as they lingered on my lips, my chest, my hips—all the parts of me he couldn't openly admire under normal circumstances. "You're so beautiful, Melia. I've wanted you for so long."

He closed in on me again, his hands resuming their exploration, gliding up and down my sides, over my backside, hips, waist, and stomach. I matched his movements with my own, gripping his shoulders, feeling his muscular chest and arms, relishing his solid form pressed against me.

He let up only to take my hand and tug me towards my bedroom. I followed him, powerless to resist his magnetic pull. We stood beside the bed, foreheads pressed together, his ragged breaths mingling with mine. He pushed the other strap of my dress down, both shoulders fully exposed now. He massaged them and dusted them with kisses.

"Do you have a shoulder fetish?" I asked.

"I have a fetish for every part of your body. Especially here." He brushed my hair back and pressed a tender kiss behind my earlobe. "You have the most delicious little freckle… I only see it when you wear your hair up. I always look for it."

"I didn't even know I had it."

"It's incredibly sexy." He nuzzled the spot while he toyed with the hem of my dress, then slipped his hands underneath, running them up my bare outer thighs, alighting all my nerve endings in his wake. "Are you wearing them?" he murmured in my ear.

"What?"

"Those white panties."

"White…?" I gasped. "You mean…?"

The only time he could have seen my underwear was when I accidentally left them on his bathroom floor. But he hadn't been home then. Had he?

"You saw them? How?"

He looked at me like I should very well know the answer. "You left them in my bathroom."

"But you weren't home."

"I didn't intend to come home, but I had to grab something I'd forgotten. You were already gone."

"I left them by accident—"

"I know. You wouldn't have been so forward as to leave them there on purpose—as erotic as that would have been."

My gut twisted, wondering if he had done anything unsavoury upon discovering my errant underwear. "Did you... um..." I trailed off, too embarrassed to finish the question.

Neil lifted my chin. "Do you really want to know the answer to that?"

I nodded, holding his darkened gaze.

"Well..." He shifted his hand from my outer to inner thigh. "I couldn't keep my eyes off that perfect little pair of white panties lying on my bathroom floor." He slowly ran his hand up my leg. "I got so aroused, Melia, I was so hard. Thinking of you in your panties, sliding them down your thighs... I was so fucking aroused."

I had never heard him swear before. It gave me a thrill that went straight to my core. "Did you...? Ah!"

His fingers reached the edge of my underwear, and he lightly flicked his thumb over me. "I got in the shower. I jerked off and came so hard to the sight of them... So much. All over the shower door."

I shuddered at the graphic mental image as Neil swiped his thumb over me again.

"Are you disgusted?" he asked. "Do you think I'm a dirty old man?"

"No, not at all," I assured him. "I've had similarly... *vivid* thoughts about you."

"Do tell."

"When you called me at home one time, I... I..."

"Yes?"

"I'm so embarrassed."

"Tell me."

"I had been, uh, pleasuring myself, before you interrupted me. Hearing your voice… It made me even more turned on, so I…"

"Go on."

"I used my vibrator, thinking about you. Just the memory of the sound of your voice was enough."

"Did you come?"

I nodded.

"Good girl."

"Neil?"

"Hmm?"

"I'm wearing them." I lifted my dress and showed them to him. Plain white cotton bikini briefs with a tiny bow below the waistband. They might not have been the exact same pair since I owned multiples, but they were identical.

"Fuck, Melia," Neil said with a guttural quality that had me quaking.

He dropped to his knees, his hands coming up to cup my backside and pull me close as he pressed a kiss to the bow. I gasped, my head falling back, as I threaded my fingers through his hair, urging him on. He trailed kisses along the edges of my underwear. My skin burned everywhere his mouth made contact. Just when I thought I might combust from the exquisite torture, he hooked his arms under my knees and stood swiftly, lifting me up. I let out a surprised yelp which melted into a needy moan as I wrapped my legs around his waist, feeling his blatant arousal pressing hard against me.

He set me down on the bed, and he captured my lips again in a searing kiss. Our mouths moved together with unrelenting urgency, tongues sliding and caressing. He kissed me deeply, fiercely, like a man starved, his stubble scraping my chin. I returned the intensity, pouring all of my pent-up longing into the connection of our lips. He pinned me on my back, my dress bunched up around my hips. He shrugged off his suit jacket and discarded it on the floor. His chest was heaving. His crotch was tight at the seams. He bent over me and yanked the bodice of my dress down, my breasts spilling free. "Gorgeous tits," he grunted, before burying his face in them.

I cried out, my back arching as he lavished attention on my breasts. His hands, mouth, and tongue had me panting and writhing beneath him, my hands gripping and twisting the sheets. This was killing me. I wanted more. I bucked my hips and ground on him, to which he rewarded me with a luscious groan in response.

Breaking away from my breasts, he shoved a hand in between us to unbuckle his belt, then slide it out of the loops. The friction of the action almost had me in pieces.

"Take off your dress," he said, his voice raw with need.

"Mr. Kingston—" I protested.

It had the desired effect. He snarled and wrested my dress down my hips, then onto the floor. Hovering over me on his hands and knees, he stared down with a look of pure reverence. "Beautiful. So beautiful."

I reached up to catch him by his shirt collar. "Your turn."

From there I attacked his shirt buttons, my shaky hands fumbling, unable to keep up with my desperation.

"Allow me." Neil leaned back and took over, freeing each button until his shirt hung all the way open, revealing a tantalising glimpse of the taut body underneath.

Frantic to see even more of him, I pulled off his shirt and drank in his glorious physique. He was toned and sculpted in a way that showed off his efforts to stay in peak physical condition. He had none of the boyish lankiness of my former boyfriends. He was broad and sturdy, with muscles that were strong but not over-inflated. A light smattering of dark hair covered his pecs and trailed down his stomach. I ran my hands over him, tracing each ridge and valley down his chest and abs, down to his hips, his pubic bone…

He took a sharp intake of breath as I stroked my hand down the bulge in his pants, then back up again. Now it was his turn to fumble, his fingers tangling in mine as he tried to undo his fly. He eased his zipper down at last, then removed his trousers. He wore a pair of black boxer shorts underneath, tented by the force of his straining hard-on. He pulled me up to meet him on his knees in the middle of the bed and kissed me again, my bare breasts pressed to his chest, his hand down my panties, palming my backside. I closed my eyes and gave in to the sensation of his tongue, his skin, and the mounting pressure where our hips moulded together.

Neil punctuated his deep kiss with a soft, shallow one pressed gently to my lips, then he lay back on the pillows and guided me down with him. We settled on our sides, face to face. He brushed a strand of hair from my cheek and tucked it behind my ear. "Are you still sure you want to do this?"

"Yes. Don't stop." I had never been more sure of anything.

Neil traced my bottom lip with the pad of his thumb. "You want me?"

"Please."

I hoisted my leg over him and drew him close. He rutted in response, driving his erection deep between my thighs, rubbing hard against my aching core. I stifled a moan by latching on to his throat, kissing that alluring expanse of skin I'd always wanted to kiss so badly. Neil whimpered and slapped my arse. I dug my fingers into his back.

Our movements became more and more frenzied. Amidst the mess of our tangled limbs, I felt Neil slip a hand between my legs. He stroked his way up my inner thigh in light, incremental motions. I bit my lip, the tension in me coiling like a spring. When he reached the top of my leg, he toyed with the elastic of my underwear between his fingertips. He dipped, then retreated, dipped, then retreated, making me squirm and clench with antici-pation. Finally, he slid his hand further, his fingertips grazing my twitching pussy through the crotch of my underwear. He teased me with light, languid strokes, up and down, around and round. I gripped his shoulders hard, my body crying out for more. Just when I couldn't take it anymore, he slipped two fingers underneath and swirled them in my slick folds. "So wet for me," he murmured.

I was coming undone, panting, a mess. "Please… please…"

"Yes?"

"I need you."

"That sounds so good, Milly. Say it again for me."

"I need you. Please."

"Yes… Yes…"

He withdrew his hand and tugged down his boxer shorts. I couldn't help but gape at the impressive sight of him. He tossed his boxers on the pile of discarded clothing on the floor, then paused, looming above me. "Before we do this, any infections I should know about?" he asked.

I blinked up at him, his unexpected seriousness throwing me off balance.

He smoothed my hair back. "Don't take offence. I just want to keep you safe."

My surprise faded. Of course, he'd be the responsible adult in this situation. It was one of the many facets of his personality I admired so much. "Sorry. I didn't mean to seem shocked. You're absolutely right to ask. And I'm clean. You?"

"Clean. Do you have a condom?"

"I'm on birth control."

"I'd prefer to use a second form of protection, just in case."

His caution struck me as so very different from previous partners, but I appreciated him even more for it. "I think there's one in my bedside drawer. I'll get it."

Neil rested his hand on my back as I leaned over to rummage in the drawer. My fingers made contact with the distinctive packaging. I passed it to him. He inspected the expiry date before he tore it open and rolled the condom on with practised ease.

"Now, where were we?" He hooked his thumbs in the waistband of my underwear then peeled them down my thighs and off my feet.

I opened my legs for him. In return, he gazed upon me with a look of sheer longing and devotion. "Oh, Milly," he rasped.

He climbed on top of me and positioned himself between my thighs. I felt the tip of him push and drag along my tender, swollen lips.

"Are you ready for me?" he asked, his voice husky with desire.

I nodded, my body quivering in anticipation.

He pushed in slowly, his eyes locked with mine, watching my every reaction as he entered me inch by inch. I gasped at the pressure and fullness of him.

"Tell me if I'm hurting you," he said.

"I will. Keep going."

He grasped my hips, pulling me closer, easing further inside me, slowly, slowly…

He let out a deep, satisfied groan. "Wow. You have all of me. Can you feel that?"

I trembled at the sensation of him. "Yes. I feel it."

He cradled my cheek and pressed his forehead to mine. "You're divine. You're heaven."

I lifted my chin and met his warm, eager lips. He kept the rest of his body still while we kissed, as if he were savouring the feeling of being inside me. I endured it for as long as possible, but the buildup of pressure was getting too much for me. I tore away from his mouth and bucked my hips, urging him to move. He began to roll in a slow, steady rhythm. The friction of his every ridge and throbbing vein dragging up and down my inner walls had me grasping the sheets. Each of his thrusts was controlled and drawn out to an agonising degree, paired by a look of immense concentration on his face. He was driving me crazy. I rutted against him, desperate to pick up the pace. "Faster."

Neil gritted his teeth as he indulged my request, his movements getting quicker and shallower. A new angle spurred an all-consuming ripple of pleasure through me. "That feels so good."

Neil thrust hard into the same precise spot. "Right there?"

"Yes!"

He turned up the pace, hitting me over and over again. I grabbed on to his back. He was all smooth flesh and hard muscle under my hands. I felt those muscles tighten with each thrust, while my little whimpers and his luxurious, vibrating groans filled the room.

The look of strain on Neil's face showed how hard he was trying to keep himself in check. His breathing was laboured, and he had broken out in a thin sheen of sweat. But he didn't let up. His hand moved to my clit, his fingers seeking and finding the sensitive nub. I cried out, my hips bucking wildly at the new sensation. He worked with varied speed and pressure as he continued to drive into me, pushing me towards the edge.

"I'm close," I stammered.

"Let go," Neil growled.

His hips slammed into mine as I wriggled and writhed beneath him, the heat in my core building to breaking point.

"I'm... Ah!" I clenched hard around him, over and over.

"Oh, fuck, Milly. Are you coming?"

"Mmm. Yes. Ahh."

I quaked from aftershocks as Neil moved in frantic little bursts, skin slapping against skin, until he twitched and pulsed inside me. He grunted, his body tensing and shuddering. He rode out his orgasm until the very end, then collapsed on top of me, his chest heaving as he tried to catch his breath. "Damn," he said, voice ragged. He rolled off me, fixed himself up, then drew me back into his arms. "Melia..." He nuzzled the crook of my neck. "You're incredible."

Though my head and body were still reeling, I somehow managed to reply, "You too. I've never... No one has ever made me feel so good. You were perfect."

"You deserve nothing less."

Chapter Fifty-Four

The room I awoke in was familiar and foreign at the same time. I clutched the bedcovers to my chest as I scanned my surroundings, getting my bearings. The room was large, dark, and moody. Beyond sheer curtains, floor-to-ceiling windows framed a decadent view of the city.

This was Neil's bed, in Neil's bedroom.

The memories of last night came flooding back all at once, my body tingling with the echoes of Neil's passion. After our tryst in my apartment, we had relocated here because Neil didn't want to leave his pets home alone all night.

I drew in a stunned breath as I turned my view to the man beside me. He lay on his stomach, face half-mashed into a pillow, one arm curled beneath his head. The other arm was slung over my hips in a possessive hold. His bare, muscular back rose and fell with each breath. I smiled, drinking in the rare, unguarded sight of him. I stroked my fingertips over his shoulder blade, which made him grunt, eyelids fluttering. For a second, I wondered if I had woken him, but he nuzzled further into his pillow without opening his eyes.

As much as I wanted to stay and snooze next to him, my

bladder had other ideas. I extricated myself from under Neil's heavy arm and slid from the bed, then padded to the ensuite. I caught my reflection in the mirror as I entered. *Oof.* Limp hair, smudged mascara, blotchy complexion. A far cry from alluring. I splashed cool water on my face and raked my fingers through my messy hair to revive myself.

When I left the bathroom, I paused at the sound of scratching coming from the bedroom door. *Huh? What is that?* I hurried over to investigate. As I cracked open the door, two inquisitive feline faces peered up at me.

I should have known.

"Shhh," I whispered, slipping into the hallway and pulling the door almost closed behind me. But it was too late. The cats darted between my ankles and into the bedroom before I could stop them. I grimaced as Chichi leapt onto the bed and strutted up Neil's body, meowing in his ear.

"No, Chichi!" I tried to shoo her away. "Let Daddy sleep."

Neil stirred with a sleepy grunt. Dark lashes flitted open, blinking up at the cat now kneading his pillow. "Attention seeker," he huffed, giving Chichi's ears an affectionate scratch. Then his gaze settled on me. The unrestrained tenderness in those inky irises made my muscles feel weak. Suddenly shy, I hugged my arms around myself.

"Good morning," Neil said, his voice gravelly from sleep.

I climbed into bed next to him and pulled the sheet up to cover myself, sitting up against the headboard. "I tried to keep her out. Sorry she woke you."

"Don't be. This is my preferred wake-up call—and with you here, all the better." He sidled up to me. "You're not a dream, are you?"

"Definitely not a dream. My bedhead and morning breath couldn't be more real."

Neil chuckled. "I think you're gorgeous. However..." His gaze dropped to my sheet-covered chest. "I would prefer you without the modesty act."

I gave his shoulder a playful swat. "Neil! Your children are watching."

He bellowed an even heartier laugh, scrubbing a hand through his dishevelled hair. Next to him, Chichi continued to knead the pillow. At the foot of the bed, Bowey stared balefully up at us.

"I think they want breakfast," I said.

"Yes, apologies, Your Highness," Neil said to Chichi. He glanced at the glowing digits of the bedside clock. "It's past their usual mealtime."

"I'll feed them."

"Are you sure?"

I nodded. "I'm fully awake now. You can have a snooze."

Neil acquiesced with a sigh, sinking back against the pillows.

I pulled on the change of clothes I had brought with me the night before, then headed to the kitchen. Both cats twined figure-eights around my ankles, their mews growing more insistent.

I poured cat biscuits into two bowls decorated with paw prints. Chichi and Bowey immediately attacked the food, their crunching filling the silence. Smiling to myself, I peeked inside the cupboard by the fridge until I located the dog kibble.

Now, where's Archie?

I found the old dog curled up in his plaid dog bed, snoring gently. He lifted his grizzled head at my approach, tail sweeping back and forth across the tiles.

"There you are," I crooned, giving him a good scratch behind the ears. "Are you hungry too?"

He gave a throaty woof, his back end rising to stand. I refilled his water and food bowls, then gave him belly rubs as he munched away.

When I straightened, strong arms encircled me from behind. I yelped, then melted back against Neil's bare chest, my heartbeat galloping. He pressed a smiling kiss below my ear. "The bed got cold," he murmured into the crook of my neck.

"Well, we can't have that…"

He was wearing nothing but his boxers, his body warm

against my back. Archie gave a disgruntled huff around his mouthful of kibble. Neil turned me in his arms until I faced him. Desire simmered in his heavy-lidded gaze as he studied my face. Then he dipped his head and caught my lips in a long, lush kiss that curled my toes. I looped both arms around his neck, heat swooping low in my stomach. We stumbled backwards until my tail bone hit the kitchen bench. I could feel his arousal pressing against me.

"Let's go back to bed," he said.

I nodded, my mouth too dry to respond.

He led me to the bedroom, lowered me onto the bed, then his lips were on mine, hard and impassioned. I wrapped my legs around his waist, pulling him close. He reached a hand under me, squeezing my backside as he lifted my hips to press even closer. We moved together, mashing and grinding through the building heat and friction between us. Neil's movements became increasingly frenetic. He attacked my waistband, pulled down my pants, then tugged at my underwear. He only got them halfway down my thighs before he was fumbling to put a condom on, then burrowing into me with desperate little thrusts. I wriggled and rutted, urging him on.

"Slow down," Neil whimpered.

But I couldn't. "No. Please, don't stop."

His grip on my hips tightened, fingers digging in. I felt him swell inside me, then he spasmed hard, groaning. He kept going for as long as he could before rolling off me, heaving deep breaths. "Sorry," he said, grimacing. "I'm out of practice. Easily excitable and overstimulated."

That I could have such an effect on him pleased me more than anything. "Don't be sorry. I loved it."

"C'mere."

He beckoned me into his open arms. I lay my cheek against his chest while his hands trailed patterns over my back and sides, tracing every dip and curve as if committing my shape to memory. I still couldn't quite believe this was real.

"How long have you liked me?" I asked through a haze of sleepy contentment.

"Since I first met you. Though I didn't realise quite how much until I caught you in my home, and I wanted you to belong here. With me."

"I thought you couldn't stand me—"

"Never. I was just angry at myself for wanting you."

I recalled our early interactions and his prickly demeanour. The thought of him secretly pining for me that whole time gave me a thrill.

"What about you?" he asked, stroking my hair. "When did you start liking me?"

I had a think for a second. It was difficult to pinpoint a precise moment. "When you pulled me out of the way of the splash from the bus going past. But you've always intrigued me. I just couldn't admit it to myself."

"Intrigued? Tell me more."

"You know what I mean. You can be quite charming some-times—when you're not being an insufferable tyrant."

Neil chuckled, his chest rumbling beneath me.

"And your laugh is the best laugh I've ever heard in my life."

"I didn't know it was anything special."

"Oh, it is."

"Then feel free to make me laugh more often."

"I will."

I sighed, his steady heartbeat thrumming under my ear. If only we could stay suspended in this perfect bubble of intimacy forever, shut away from the outside world. But reality beckoned.

Neil drew back, his eyes crinkling. "What would you like for breakfast? I can pick something up."

My stomach rumbled at the suggestion of food. "Oooh. Yes, please. Anything's fine."

"Are you sure?"

"I'll come with you—"

"No, you won't."

His short reply was a stark reminder that there would be stipulations to this relationship. He clearly didn't want to be seen buying breakfast with me on a Saturday morning. I understood why.

"Of course. Sorry. I wasn't thinking."

He pressed a kiss to my lips in lieu of an apology before sliding out of bed. I propped myself up on one elbow, admiring the view as he walked to the ensuite.

After Neil had showered and dressed, he kissed me goodbye. "Make yourself at home while I'm gone. I'm taking Archie with me for a walk, but he gets tired quickly, so I won't be long."

"Take your time."

I heard the click of paws on the floorboards, excited doggy whimpers, and the jangling of a leash on Neil's way out of the apartment.

While Neil was gone, I hopped in the shower. The rainfall fixture felt heavenly beating on my shoulders. As I lathered up with soap, I recalled what Neil had confessed to doing in this very shower. Just thinking about it made me flush all over. I had to run the cold water for a second to recover.

Freshly scrubbed and wrapped in a robe I found hanging on the back of the door, I made my way to the kitchen. I had just figured out Neil's high-tech coffee machine when the front door opened. Archie trotted inside panting, his leash trailing behind him. Right on his heels, Neil strode in, holding a fragrant white paper bag. My mouth watered at the scent.

Neil's eyes trailed over me. "Wearing my robe?"

I tightened the tie across my waist. "You don't mind, do you?"

"I might as well give you free rein of my wardrobe at this point."

"Yes, please."

Neil huffed but couldn't hide his amusement.

"What did you get?" I asked. "Smells amazing."

"See for yourself."

He slid the bag across the counter. I eagerly opened it to reveal two glossy bagels—one loaded with egg and melted cheese, the other glistening with sweet cinnamon cream cheese and fresh strawberry slices. My stomach gave an impatient rumble as I reached for two plates from the cupboard.

"I'll hazard a guess that you would prefer the sweet one," Neil said.

"Correct," I said, plating both bagels. "Good guess."

Neil grinned. "Oh yes, terribly difficult to deduce."

I stuck my tongue out at him and took an enormous bite, closing my eyes to savour the burst of flavours—the doughy bagel base, the sweet and tangy cream cheese, the ripe juicy strawberries… "Oh wow. This is incredible."

"Don't talk with your mouth full."

I cracked one eye open to find Neil regarding me with undisguised affection beneath the stern reprimand.

"Yes, sir," I said.

Neil just shook his head.

We settled at the dining table with our bagels and coffee. As much as I enjoyed chowing down on breakfast, Neil's increasing solemnity didn't escape my notice. He cleared his throat as if gearing up to say something serious. I stiffened.

"I think we should discuss the, er, *developments* between us," he said.

My stomach dropped. I always knew this was coming—I wasn't stupid. But still…

I fidgeted with my almost-empty coffee mug, unsure how to respond.

Neil must have noticed my dejected body language, because he placed his hand over mine. "Don't worry. I know my situation is complicated, but I want this to work. More than anything. Okay? This isn't just a fling to me."

I turned my palm up beneath his, lacing our fingers. "I want this to work too."

His thumb stroked my knuckles. "But if we're going to keep seeing each other, discretion is key. I'm sure you understand why."

"Because you're still my boss, and because you don't want Daniel to find out about us in case it puts me in danger."

Neil's jaw tightened at the mention of his nemesis's name. "Yes. So we have to keep this a secret, at least until the Zelthia situation reaches its endgame."

"There's something I don't understand. Daniel already thought we were sleeping together, and it didn't matter then, so why does it matter now?"

"Because for a man like Daniel, you can fuck someone without having feelings for them. In other words, I'm not concerned if he thinks we're sleeping together. What I don't want him to know is how much I care about you."

The reason was more simple than I thought it would be, and it made complete sense. *And Neil cares about me…*

"Okay, I think I get it. But none of this matters if Daniel doesn't find out that you're scheming to oust him, does it?"

Neil nodded. "He's definitely suspicious that something's going on, but beyond that, I don't think he has anything concrete against me. I just want to be cautious. Once the dust settles on the succession, that's when we can tell people about us."

"Any idea how long that might take?"

Neil exhaled through his nose. "Could be months, a year… longer. There are a lot of moving pieces."

My heart sank, but I tried not to let the disappointment show on my face. I understood Neil's need for discretion, but the thought of sneaking around for ages, only catching fleeting moments with him, twisted my insides in knots. Then there was my impending trip to Europe, throwing further complications into the mix.

"Trust me, Milly, it kills me to have to act like you're some kind of dirty little secret. You deserve so much better than this. I wouldn't blame you for backing out right now. Do you want to?"

I shook my head. "I'm prepared to go through with this."

"I know it's not much of a consolation, but we can still see each other freely within this building. We can trust my security team here."

I nodded, buoyed by this compromise. "Oh, good. But what about work? You're not going to make me quit, are you?"

Neil shook his head. "You were right before. You leaving will look more suspicious than not, plus I'd prefer to keep you within arm's length. But we'll have to be careful. I ask that you keep your conduct strictly professional. I'll do the same."

"Even when we're alone in your office?"

"Even then. After the spying incident, I won't risk anything."

"Good point."

"And soon enough, you'll be leaving, anyway. Off on your big OE."

I nibbled my lip. Given the changed circumstances of our relationship, I hated the thought of putting an ocean between us so soon. "About that. Are you still sure you want me to go?"

"Yes. It will give me peace of mind knowing you're far from Daniel's reach. I'll rest easier at night."

"And you'll wait for me to come back?"

He squeezed my hand. "Yes, I will. And when that happens, hopefully all of this will have blown over. But if you can't wait that long, I'd understand. Or if you meet someone else—"

"I can wait! I'll wait however long it takes. And there's no one except you. I can't even comprehend wanting to be with anyone else but you."

Neil's posture relaxed, his hunched shoulders deflating. "As tough as it was, I'm glad we had this talk."

"Me too."

"Good. Because I don't ever want to upset you." He clasped my hand between both of his.

I looked up at him through my eyelashes. "You said we can still see each other here in this building…"

"Yes, as long as we don't make a show of ourselves in the corridors and lobby."

"I wouldn't dream of it! Well, actually, I would, but I'll refrain."

"You were saying?"

"Right. So... Can I stay here with you this weekend?"

Neil grinned. "I was hoping you'd ask that."

Chapter Fifty-Five

Just act normal. How hard can it be?

I plastered on my best poker face and strode into the boardroom for the first scheduled appointment of the day. A handful of colleagues had already assembled, chatting over coffee cups and notebooks splayed across the long table. I plunked down on my usual seat. No sign of Neil yet.

"Hi, Amelia." Sharon, from sales, dropped into the neighbouring chair with a smile. "How was your weekend?"

My mind reeled with snippets from the last two days. Neil's fingertips digging into my waist, the scrape of stubble against my cheek, his low voice whispering fevered praise in my ear... My throat constricted as I scrambled for a neutral response. "Oh, you know, uneventful. I didn't get out much. Just stayed at home. What about you?"

Sharon launched into a detailed account of an unexpected visit from her in-laws. I nodded along until the boardroom door creaked open. Neil strode in with his arresting air of authority. My heart stumbled as we made eye contact. The memory of those eyes burning into mine last night filled my mind. Clenching my thighs, I tried to peel my gaze off him, but it snagged on a reddish-purple mark peeking from his shirt collar.

Oh. My. God.

My stomach plunged. Right there, for all to see, was the blatant evidence of our passion.

A hickey.

I thought of gesturing to Neil to tighten his tie, but quickly abandoned the idea for fear of drawing more attention to it.

Blood pounded in my ears as Neil took his seat at the head of the table. The sooner this meeting got underway, the sooner I could confront Neil in private. I squirmed, trying to look anywhere but at the glaring love bite.

The presentation kicked off, the speaker sharing insights from the latest competitor-analysis document. I scribbled notes, trying in vain to keep my treacherous eyes from drifting back to Neil. He sat relaxed, radiating total composure. Either he didn't know about the hickey, or he didn't care. My guess was the former.

After what felt like an eternity, the meeting adjourned. I wanted to tell Neil straight away, but he lagged behind, stuck in a conversation with Sharon. I went to the bathroom. That was where I ran into Kate—a colleague who had also just come from the meeting. She was reapplying lipstick in the mirror.

"Oh, Amelia." She paused, giving me a wicked look through her long eyelashes. "You saw it too, right?"

My heart jumped. "Saw what?"

"I noticed you staring at Neil. Don't deny it. That was a monster of a hickey on his neck, right? Wonder who gave him that?"

I gave an airy shrug. "Maybe it's not what it seems. He could have just got a bug bite or allergic reaction or something."

Kate rolled her eyes. "*Sure.*" She blotted her lips. "He must be seeing someone…"

"I don't know about that. It's his private life."

"Oh yes, very private. Parading *that* around."

"I'll have a word with him. He should at least cover something like that up."

"Heh, heh. How embarrassing."

Kate flounced out of the bathroom, smirking to herself. I watched the door swing shut.

Does she know something? Or was that just her usual gossipy self?

Neil had already returned to his desk by the time I got there. He was fixated on his computer screen when I barged through his door without knocking. He glanced up, one eyebrow raised. "Everything okay?"

"No, it bloody well isn't!" I hissed.

His eyes widened. "What's the matter?"

"Have you looked in a mirror lately?"

"No…"

I pointed to my neck. "You have a…"

Neil's hand flew up to the spot I was gesturing to. His eyes went wide again. "I didn't think it was visible."

"Well, think again. And people have definitely noticed. I just got confronted by Kate. She knew exactly what it was. I had to say it was a bug bite, but I don't think she bought it."

Neil's throat bobbed. For once, the man who always had it together looked a tad bewildered. He tightened the knot of his tie, pulling his collar up higher. "Better?"

"A little." I leaned in and whispered, "Sorry. It won't happen again."

Neil gripped the edge of his desk, his voice dropping. "Pity. Because I wouldn't mind if it did. Just make sure you aim lower next time."

I pursed my lips, mustering my composure.

Neil sat back, loosening his grip on the desk. "I want that report proofed by the end of the day, Amelia."

"Yes. I'll get right on it."

My legs felt like jelly as I backed away. Once settled in my chair, I dropped my forehead into my hands and exhaled a shaky sigh. That was a close call back there. We couldn't afford to let our guards down. Not with so much at stake if anyone discovered us.

Ten minutes into my workload, the shrill ring of my desk

phone broke out. I grabbed the receiver. "Hello, Neil Kingston's office, Amelia Cross speaking."

"Hi, Amelia, it's Clara from Human Resources."

My shoulders bunched at the HR manager's clipped tone. "Clara, hi," I forced myself to chirp. "What can I do for you?"

"Could you please pop over to my office when you get a moment? I'd like to have a chat with you."

My mouth went dry. *What's this about?* "Of course. I'm a bit busy right now, though. Later this morning?"

"How about eleven o'clock?"

"Okay. Eleven. That works. See you then."

"Thank you, Amelia. Bye."

"Bye."

I slammed the phone down. Could this have to do with me and Neil? Not the hickey, surely? Maybe it was just about paperwork, but that would be a strange coincidence, given the timing.

I marched straight back into Neil's office and told him about Clara's request to see me. "Do you know what it's about?" I asked.

"No." He rubbed his chin, frowning. "Why don't you listen to what she has to say? See what she wants before you worry."

His relative calmness helped soothe my frazzled nerves. "You're right. I shouldn't overthink this."

* * *

Clara Evans sat ramrod straight behind her spotless glass desk. Two ceramic pen holders shaped like cats guarded the corners by her monitor. Their sightless blue gazes seemed to track my every jerky movement. I wiped my clammy palms on my thighs.

"Thank you for coming in so promptly, Amelia," Clara said.

I slid into the seat opposite her. "No problem. What was it you wanted to talk about?"

She leaned forward, steepling her manicured fingers under her chin. "The reason I asked you here is that a staff member informed me they saw you out to dinner with Neil Kingston on Friday evening. They were concerned it didn't look... work-related. Would you care to comment on what happened?"

Cold sweat bloomed across my shoulder blades beneath my blouse. I resisted the urge to tug at my collar. "Thanks for your concern, but it was a coincidence that Neil and I ended up dining alone. It was supposed to be a work dinner. A few other people were meant to attend, but they all had last-minute cancellations. Ask Winston Ramsey or James Campbell. Both of them could back this up."

Clara's narrow eyes fixed unblinkingly to mine. "Even so, this staff member said you and Neil looked rather close."

I shrugged, feigning nonchalance even as my heartbeat thundered in my ears. "Well, Neil and I have developed a more casual relationship since we work so closely together. Plus, we live in the same apartment building now. It's easy for things to get misconstrued."

Clara regarded me a moment longer before she sank back into her ergonomic chair with a creak of caster wheels across the carpet. "I see. Well, that does help explain the context, and Neil did already inform me about your living arrangements, so I was aware of that." Her slender shoulders slumped beneath her blazer. "But I'm sure you understand why I had to address such concerns."

"Of course. Thanks for looking out for me."

Clara rummaged in her drawer before sliding a glossy brochure across the desktop. I scanned the serif font heading. *Sexual Harassment in the Workplace.*

"I want every woman at Luxmore to feel safe and empowered here. So if you ever feel coerced or pressured by a superior, you can come forward in confidence."

"That's reassuring to know."

We exchanged a few more pleasantries before Clara sent me on my way. The pamphlet crinkled in my white-knuckled grip as I power-walked back to the lift. When I rounded the corner, I nearly collided with a mail trolley. "Oh! Excuse me," I yelped, jumping aside.

The mail clerk shot me an odd look before continuing down the corridor. I punched the button until the lift door lurched open.

When I stepped into Neil's office, he was standing in front of a window, his hands clasped behind his back. At my approach, he turned, face impassive. "Well?"

I gave him the rundown without stopping for breath. His expression remained fixed throughout.

"We can discuss this later," he said.

Later. My insides performed a backflip. I knew he must mean tonight.

* * *

I stood on tiptoes to greet Neil with a kiss at his apartment door. But my lips grazed air. Neil pulled away from me. "Let's talk first," he said, an undertone of steel in his voice.

My stomach knotted. Neil strode inside and braced himself against the back of the couch. I followed him. "What's wrong?"

He turned, dragging a hand over his jaw. "I've been thinking. Maybe continuing a physical relationship isn't wise right now. Not while we're under so much scrutiny."

My pulse stuttered. I sank onto the other couch, hands twisting together in my lap. "You want us to stop?"

Neil shook his head, then began to pace in front of the fireplace. "Not permanently. Just until things settle down. It will make maintaining professionalism easier if we... detach emotionally."

Detach emotionally? I understood Neil's need for discretion, but the thought of losing our newfound intimacy wrenched my heart into my throat. I couldn't let this happen without a fight—not after the bliss we'd shared these past few nights.

I perched on the edge of the cushion, fighting the quaver in my voice. "Not even here in your apartment?"

"It's for the best."

There had to be some way to make him reconsider, some flaw in his logic I could seize upon. I chose my next words carefully. "We've tried that kind of restraint in the past and look where it got us." I rose from the couch and crossed the short distance between us. I placed a hand on Neil's forearm, feeling the heat of his skin rise through his shirt. "Don't you think keeping it all bottled up will increase the tension and make it more obvious to everyone around us?"

Neil swallowed. After a long pause, he took my hand, thumb tracing the veins on my inner wrist. "You raise a good point. I suppose fully cutting things off would only increase temptation..."

I stepped closer, tilting my chin to look up at him. "So, you'll reconsider?"

He toyed with my fingers, his eyes darkening. "Perhaps we can find an alternative solution. Something that will reduce the scrutiny while allowing us to meet freely. I'll give the matter more thought."

I sagged against him, my chest unclenching. "Thank you."

His eyelids lowered. "I think I'd do anything for you."

"Then what about tonight?"

He drew back a fraction and cocked an eyebrow.

I flirted with his shirt collar, running my fingers back and forth over the sharp crease. "We've agreed it's better to get it all out of our systems, right?"

Neil cradled my cheek in his large hand. "You're going to be the death of me."

He descended on my mouth.

Chapter Fifty-Six

A few days later, I waltzed into the office with a spring in my step. Humming an upbeat tune under my breath, I deposited my purse under my desk with a flick of my wrist. As the bag left my grip, the click-clack of computer keys reached my ears. I swivelled towards the sound. A familiar face glanced up over the monitor of the spare desk on the opposite side of the room. Her light brown hair was plaited in a thin, limp braid.

"Petra!" I blinked, taking in her beige cardigan and sensible black slacks. "What are you doing here?"

She offered a weak smile. "Oh, hi, Milly. Mr. Kingston asked me to fill in again for a bit. I hope you don't mind sharing your space with me."

I shook my head, moving towards her desk with slow steps, buying time to school my expression. "Of course not. You just caught me by surprise. That's all." I held back a frown. When had Neil organised this, and why hadn't he mentioned it to me? "I didn't know you would be here."

Petra nodded, her braid bobbing. "It all happened quite suddenly. Mr. Kingston called me first thing this morning and asked if I could come in straight away."

"I didn't even realise we needed extra admin support right now."

"I think he wants me here for the next few weeks or so."

Weeks? What's this all about?

"It will be nice to have you here," I said with forced brightness.

"I'm thankful for the opportunity. It makes a change from my usual work."

I turned on my heel. "Well, I'll just go and make Neil's coffee."

"Oh! There's no need. I've already made him one."

"You have? Great. Thank you."

I grabbed my diary off my desk and strode towards Neil's office before I could dwell on the tickle of irritation from being left out of the loop.

Neil was thumbing through a sheaf of papers when I entered.

"Morning." I waved my diary. "I just wanted to touch base about our schedule for the week."

Neil's mouth edged up at one corner. "Straight to business, then?"

I shut the door behind me with a snap. "What's going on? Why did you bring in Petra all of a sudden?"

Neil laid his pen down, linking his fingers atop the stack of paperwork. "No need for alarm. Petra will provide some temporary assistance. I have a trip to Singapore coming up. While I'm away, it will lessen your workload to have someone helping with admin tasks."

"What trip? It's not in the calendar."

"It's personal, not business-related."

"We haven't talked about it."

His eyes bored into mine. "We can talk about it later."

I crossed my arms, tension winding through my muscles. After everything we had been through, he was still keeping me at a distance. "You could have mentioned you were bringing Petra back."

Neil arched an eyebrow. "I wasn't aware I needed to clear every business decision past my secretary."

Ouch.

He might've been my superior at work, but I thought we were a team now we were dating. *Dating?* Whatever our arrangement was supposed to be.

Neil's demeanour relaxed slightly. "It was a spur-of-the-moment decision. I didn't think it would bother you."

I knew I was being petty, questioning his executive decisions. But I couldn't shake the niggling sense he was keeping something from me about Petra's role. I shuffled on my feet. "I guess I just don't see why you think I need help. I'm perfectly capable of holding down the fort solo for a few days."

"I know you are." Neil rounded his desk with slow strides until he stood before me. His dark floral cologne flooded my senses, reminding me of time spent wrapped in his arms. "But there's another reason I thought it prudent to have Petra here." He inclined his head closer, dropping his voice. "I considered what you said before. If others grow suspicious of the time we spend alone, it will invite more speculation and accusations. I thought bringing in a third party could help dispel some of the rumours. Think of her as a buffer for propriety's sake."

"A buffer?" I exhaled a long breath as his meaning crystallised. He intended Petra as some kind of chaperone figure. Not ideal, but compared to the alternative he originally had in mind, I had no complaints. "Well, okay. When you put it like that, I guess I don't mind having her around. It will be nice to have some company."

Neil stepped back, clearing his throat and adjusting his cuff-links. He returned to his chair.

I noticed the untouched cup of coffee on his desk. "Petra's coffee not up to your standards?"

Neil regarded the mug with a flicker of distaste. "Hmm, yes." He met my gaze. "I suppose you'll have to show her how to make it."

"I will."

Petra perked up as I emerged from Neil's office. Her wide eyes tracked me all the way to my desk. I gestured her over with a sweep of my arm. "Come sit next to me, and I'll show you the ropes for the day-to-day."

She rolled her chair over to me, then sat hands folded in her lap like an attentive student as I walked her through my typical routines

At half past ten, Neil came out, straightening his already perfect tie. "Are you ready?"

I had almost forgotten about the meeting with Polonia Electronics. No matter. I closed out of what I was doing and readied myself.

Petra popped up from her chair, clutching her notebook to her chest. "Oh, should I come along?"

I blinked at her. Surely she didn't expect Neil to ferry her along to corporate meetings?

"Yes, you may join us," Neil said.

I shook off my surprise and swallowed back the bitter tang of accommodating a third wheel. Like Neil said, having Petra in tow would bolster the guise of normalcy.

We went down to the lobby and exited through the double doors. Parked at the curb, Winston straightened from buffing a smear off the gleaming vehicle and trotted around to open Neil's door. His liver-spotted face creased into its usual genial smile beneath his cap. "Morning, Mr. Kingston, Miss Cross." His gaze shifted to Petra hovering behind me. "Oh, hello there."

"This is Petra Browne," I said.

"A pleasure, Ms. Browne." Winston swept off his hat. "Winston Ramsey, at your service."

"Nice to meet you," Petra said.

Neil seated himself in the backseat of the car. As I meandered towards the opposite door, Petra slipped past and got to it first, securing the spot next to Neil.

Recoiling, I stalled for a second, then yanked open the front passenger door and plopped myself down, smoothing my skirt over my thighs.

Winston clambered behind the wheel, catching my eyes with a knowing look. I crossed my arms, biting the inside of my cheek. Neil seemed unfazed by the seating switch-up, engrossed in something on his phone screen.

Is this going to be how things are from now on?

Chapter Fifty-Seven

I tapped my knuckles against Neil's open door before entering. Petra was out running an errand, and this was my last opportunity to spend a moment alone with him before he departed on his trip to Singapore.

He stood behind his cluttered desk, adjusting a row of folders on his bookcase. His black suitcase waited by the door. He'd be gone for five days. All he had told me about the trip was that he planned to visit the chairman with Veronica and her newborn child—the chairman's grandson. He said he'd tell me more upon his return.

Neil turned at my approach. "Yes, Milly?"

I clasped my hands to keep from fidgeting. "I just wanted to double-check you have everything in order for your trip."

"Thanks to the extensive packing list you prepared, I believe I'm accounted for on all fronts."

I drifted closer. "Good. So… five whole days, huh?"

"You almost sound like you'll miss me."

"The office won't feel the same without you."

"I hope you'll find ways to fill your time without me cracking the whip."

I sidled a measured half step closer. "I'm sure I could find some trouble to get into."

Neil's face hovered inches from mine now, his voice dipping lower. "Just try not to burn the place down, will you?"

I chewed my lip. Neil tracked the movement like a man possessed.

"You'll need to leave soon," I said.

He checked his watch. "I still have a minute to spare." He scanned the doorway, appeared satisfied the coast was clear, then turned back to me.

I froze as he inched nearer.

What is he doing? Is he actually going to break his rule? No, it can't be.

I thought I must be mistaken right up until he inclined his head, his breath wisping along my cheek. My hands clenched at my sides, pulse thrumming as his mouth hovered over my skin. I squeezed my eyes shut, awaiting the firm press of his lips.

The floor creaked.

My eyes flew open, and Neil yanked himself away from me just as Petra appeared in the doorway.

How did she get back so fast? She didn't see anything... did she?

Petra's vacant eyes slid right over us. Her thin lips pressed into a flat line, arms locked in place at her sides. "Um, we're out of printer toner. Do we have more stocked anywhere?"

I caught my breath before answering. "Check with James. He handles office supplies."

"Ah, James. Got it." She retreated.

I sagged, clutching my chest. It didn't seem like she had noticed anything amiss.

Once we had recovered from the interruption, I braced for Neil's next move. But the moment had passed. His buzzing phone diverted his attention. "Winston is waiting outside," he said. "I should get going."

I nodded. "Have a smooth flight."

He glanced at the door again, then brought his hand up to

briefly cup my cheek. "Thanks again for offering your pet-sitting services. They'll be much more comfortable with you than a stranger."

"It's no problem, honestly. I'm happy to help."

"I know they'll be in good hands, but let me know if you have any issues at all."

"I will. So…" I shuffled my feet, "you'll be in touch?"

"Of course."

We lingered for another moment. Then he tore himself away, striding over to collect his suitcase.

As we stepped out into my office, Petra returned holding a new toner cartridge. "Are you going now?" she asked.

"Yes. Winston's waiting," Neil said.

"Goodbye, then. Have a good trip. See you in a few days!"

"Goodbye, Petra." He turned his focus to me. "Amelia." He favoured us both with a perfunctory nod.

And then he was gone—off to pursue whatever mysterious machinations awaited him on the other side of the world. With my sight still fixed on the empty corridor, I settled behind my desk while Petra fiddled with the printer. As the printer roared back to life, she scooted her chair over to mine, heaving a theatrical sigh. "Whew. The big boss man is gone. I feel like I can stop holding my breath now."

I swivelled towards her. "Is he really that bad?"

She tilted her head. "Well, now that you mention it, he does seem a bit more… easygoing than he used to be."

I blinked. "Easygoing? I wouldn't use that word to describe him."

"Okay, poor choice of words. I just meant he seems less… harsh than before. Less prone to yell or put people down over tiny mistakes." She picked at a hangnail, avoiding my gaze. "I don't know. Maybe I'm imagining things."

I leaned back in my chair, considering her words. I supposed Neil had been less caustic since… whatever this thing was between us. "You could be right."

Petra sat up straighter. "Right? It's like he's actually *happy* sometimes. I swear yesterday I spotted him whistling."

I concealed a snort of laughter behind the act of clearing my throat. The image of Neil wandering the corridors whistling a jaunty tune was too much. Though, come to think of it, I had caught him smiling a lot more than usual, especially when he must have thought no one was looking.

Petra squinted. "Do you think maybe he's seeing someone?"

I jerked so fast my mug of pens toppled with a clatter, rolling every which way across my desk. "I really doubt that!"

I quickly gathered them all up.

Petra nibbled her lip. "Yeah, no. You're probably right. I mean, who would ever want to date him?"

I gave an airy laugh, which Petra echoed after a beat.

"True." I spun my chair towards my computer. "Can you imagine?"

"I'd rather not."

She rolled away, leaving me stewing. *That was a close one.* As oblivious as she seemed, Petra had an uncanny knack for stumbling uncomfortably close to the mark. Neil and I would have to watch ourselves once he returned.

Chapter Fifty-Eight

Milly—please make yourself comfortable while I'm away. And yes, you may borrow my clothes if you wish. Yours, Neil. x.

The note was stuck to Neil's fridge with a magnet. It made me smile every time I looked at it, easing the sting of his departure, the secrecy, and my powerlessness.

Without the privilege of accompanying him on his trip, the most I could do to help was look after his pets to the best of my ability—a role I was more than willing to fulfil.

"Who wants treats?"

I shook the bag, and Bowey and Chichi materialised at my feet, tails swaying in anticipation. I sprinkled their favourite snacks into their bowls. They tucked in while Archie watched on. He gave a breathy whine.

"Not for you, bud."

Jowls drooping, Archie whimpered again, looking at me with those mournful eyes.

"Okay, okay. How about walkies instead?"

I located his leash and clipped it to his collar. A quick ride down, then we emerged into the Viaduct. Archie stopped every few paces to sniff each pole and rubbish bin as we ambled along the waterfront promenade towards Silo Park. I tilted my face up to catch the breeze off the sparkling blue water, squinting against the glare of sunlight on gentle swells. White sails and clumsy seagulls dotted the scene. My thoughts circled to Neil, wondering how he was getting on in Singapore. Contact from him had been sparse over the last few days and provided little insight. Whatever his mysterious dealings entailed, I still nurtured a shred of unease. I sighed, dropping onto a bench facing the marina, watching luxury yachts bob at their moorings. My life had been flipped upside-down in the past year. And it was about to flip again. Soon, I'd be heading off to backpack around Europe while Neil carried on without me…

The ding of a new text message snapped me from my pensiveness. I peered at the screen. What was Hannah doing texting me at some ungodly hour in her time zone?

Do you know what's happening with Nicole?

I shot her a reply.

About her wedding postponement?

It's all called off now.

I gawped at the message. Nicole's perfect romance had seemed like something out of a magazine spread—well, up until the postponement. I recalled the last conversation I had with her, and how hard she must have been trying to keep it together.

Nicole's been quiet, but I've heard rumours she cheated.

Any sympathy I had for her dried up in an instant.

Damn. Poor Paul if it's true.

Maybe this makes me a bad friend, but I think it's true.

You know her better than me, so I have to agree.

Archie lumbered over and flopped at my feet with a groan of protest that echoed my own sigh. I gave his belly a sympathetic rub. "Getting tired, bud?"

He grunted.

"Let's head back."

I had no reason to dwell on the news about Nicole. To think I used to envy her life. How times had changed.

After returning to Neil's apartment, Archie made a beeline straight for his dog bed, snuffling and turning a few times before he settled with a snore. Now that I had taken care of the pets' needs, I had time to kill before making dinner.

Maybe I'll read something.

I wandered over to the packed bookcase. As my fingers trailed along a row of battered paperbacks, I noticed the fine layer of dust coating the topmost shelf. I clucked my tongue, my inner neat freak waking from dormancy. Neil's new cleaner obviously didn't share my meticulous approach. But that was easily remedied. I rolled up my sleeves. Neil kept most of his limited cleaning supplies stowed under the kitchen sink. I gathered everything into a bucket along with a few microfibre cloths, then set to work dusting and wiping every surface.

Once I had eliminated every trace of grime, I changed the cats' litter boxes and refreshed their water bowls. After one last survey to ensure everything was immaculate, I shucked my rubber gloves and sank onto the couch. Chichi leapt up to drape herself across my legs while Bowey hopped onto the back cushion, peering down at me with lamp-like eyes. Archie continued to snore nearby, curled up with his favourite squeaky pizza toy.

I leaned back and admired the view through the floor-to-ceiling windows. Boats drifted across the harbour, and daydreams floated in my head. I pictured Neil hovering above me, his eyes burning with lust, my fingers tangled in his hair as our mouths met again and again. I shivered, recalling his hands roving my body, his breath hot against my neck…

A noise coming from the door startled me out of my daydream. I glanced up just as the door clattered open. Neil's dark frame filled the entryway, his carry-on luggage bumping over the threshold behind him. He was dressed in business casual, his hard jaw peppered with stubble. My heart launched into my throat at the sight of him. I swung forward and off the couch. "You're back! I thought you were coming tomorrow?"

"Change of plans." Neil kicked off his shoes. "My flight got cancelled, so I made a split decision to take an earlier one. I wanted to surprise you."

"Mission accomplished!"

Archie stirred, lifting his grizzled head. At the sight of Neil, he lumbered over to greet him with a flurry of sniffs and grumbling woofs.

"Have you been a good boy while I was away?" Neil asked, stooping closer to Archie's level.

"He's been very well-behaved."

"Thank you for looking after him. And the cats."

"No problem at all."

Once man and man's best friend had been properly reacquainted, Neil steered me back to the couch. We sat down beside each other with his arm slung behind my shoulders. He drew me close and kissed my forehead. "I've missed you," he said.

"I missed you too." I tucked my head in the crook of his neck, his chest beneath my cheek. "How was your trip?"

"Everything went smoothly." Neil nuzzled me. "What about you? How did you manage without me?"

As much as I'd missed having him near, a part of me still smarted from being left out of the loop about his clandestine dealings in Singapore. "I managed just fine. But tell me more about your trip. I want to know the details." I levelled my gaze at him. I wasn't going to let him deflect my question again.

For a beat, his expression went carefully neutral. Then his shoulders sagged. "Yes. I suppose I owe you that much." He reached over and took my hand, his thumb tracing patterns across my knuckles. "Veronica recently gave birth to her son, Benjamin. My trip to Singapore was to facilitate a secret visit between Veronica, the chairman, and Ben."

"Why secret? Can't the chairman just meet his grandson normally? They're family, after all."

"Because Daniel doesn't know Ben exists. Not yet. If he did, Ben could be in danger. You see, Daniel only has two legitimate children—both daughters. And his son from a past relationship has special needs that make him ill-suited to take over the reins of the company someday. With the arrival of Ben, the chairman has a new viable successor, one that could sway succession talks in Veronica's favour."

As the full extent of Neil's intricate gambit became clear, my scepticism and hurt faded. "You could have told me all of this before you left."

"Yes, I could have—but if someone were to get their hands on you because they think you have information..." Neil shook his head. "It's over now, so I can tell you. But not a word of this to anyone."

"Of course. I wouldn't dream of it."

"I'm sorry I can't be more forthcoming with you."

"It's okay. I know you have your reasons. I'm just glad you're back." I glanced at his luggage. "How about I help you unpack?"

"It can wait. This is more important." He traced the curve of my jaw to cup my face and kissed me.

*** * ***

I peered over the top of my book, admiring the view as Neil emerged from the ensuite in a plume of steam. His hair was damp, and his bathrobe gaped, clinging to the sharp lines of his collarbone and offering a tantalising peek of toned chest and stomach. An errant water droplet trickled down his forearm, catching the light as it traced a prominent vein before disappearing beneath his sleeve. I bit my lip, suppressing a smile. "Good shower?" I asked, trying to keep my voice even.

"Yes," Neil said. "Much needed."

With a satisfied exhale, he crossed the room to his side of the bed while towelling off his hair. He dropped onto the mattress, then immediately sprang up with a wince. He reached under the duvet and extracted a bubblegum-pink silicone object.

My vibrator.

"Well, well, well..." Gripping his discovery between thumb and forefinger, he lifted his eyebrows at me. "What do we have here? Don't think this belongs to me." He dangled the toy in front of me. I made a hapless grab for it, but he whisked it out of reach, chortling.

"I can explain," I stammered.

"No need. The evidence speaks for itself." He switched the toy on and off for an experimental buzz, eyebrows leaping even higher.

I covered my face behind my book. "I can't believe I left that there."

"Now, now." Neil leaned in close enough for his warm breath to graze my earlobe. "Don't be ashamed. I'm just glad you were able to take care of your needs in my absence."

A fresh wave of heat suffused my body.

Neil trailed his hand down my side. "How many times did you use it?"

"I don't know."

"You must have some idea."

"Maybe once a day. I can't remember."

The mattress dipped, and I uncovered my eyes to see Neil

above me, an arm braced either side, caging me in. He plucked the book from my hands and set it aside. All my nerve endings sparked to attention.

I crossed my arms and shot him a venomous glare. "You're loving this, aren't you?"

"I can't help it." He grinned. "You're just so fun to tease."

"Enough." I grasped the back of his neck and pulled him down. Our mouths met in a blistering kiss that obliterated conscious thought. Neil gathered me against his body, his skin still flushed and damp from the shower. I sank deeper into the kiss, feeling the wet-hot sensation of his lips and tongue exploring my mouth. Neil groaned as I squeezed my legs tighter around him. He pulled away to murmur, "Show me," pressing the vibrator into my hand. "Show me how you pleasure yourself."

I hesitated, startled by the request. "I'm not sure—"

"Trust me, Melia, nothing in the world would be sexier to me."

I let the idea sink in, taking a moment to get comfortable with it.

"You don't have to," Neil said.

But I had already made up my mind. "I'll do it."

If it would drive him wild, it would be worth any potential embarrassment. He gave my shoulders a squeeze, then backed away from me.

"What are you doing?" I asked, watching him get up from the bed.

"Getting into position." He pulled up the chair from the corner of the room to sit at the foot of the bed.

"I didn't think I'd be putting on a show."

"I want to put some distance between us so I'm not tempted to interfere." He placed his elbows on the armrests and intertwined his fingers under his chin. "Go on."

I sat on the bed in front of him, unsure where to begin.

"Open your legs," he said.

I complied, exposing the crotch of my underwear beneath the oversized t-shirt I was wearing as a nightgown. Neil's gaze followed the movement. I could sense his anticipation, and it gave me a surge of confidence. I brought the vibrator between my thighs and began to trace it over myself in slow patterns.

Neil watched with rapt attention. Emboldened, I turned it on, its hum filling the room. Neil's breath hitched, and he adjusted his position in the chair. I moved in circles, hips rocking in time with the motion.

"That's it," Neil said. "Just like that."

I opened my legs even wider, giving him a better view. I moved faster, more erratically. Neil was fixated, his hands clamping the arm rests. I pressed hard, moving side to side, up, down. Faster. Harder.

"Take off your underwear," Neil begged, voice ragged. "Please. I want to see all of you."

I obeyed, tugging them down my legs and kicking them onto the floor.

"F-fuck," Neil whimpered.

The vibrations felt even more intense this way. Pressure built up as I stroked myself into a frenzy. "I'm… I'm… Ah!" I gasped, my body convulsing.

"Good," Neil said. "That's so good."

As I ground through each crashing wave, the vibrator sputtered, then died. "It's had it," I said, breathless. "Piece of junk."

Neil undid the tie of his robe as he stood up, revealing just how hard he was for me. He dragged my discarded underwear closer with his foot. A few frenetic pumps, then he came with a groan, spilling himself on my underwear. He stood there until he caught his breath. Then he was on the bed, arms around me, pressing a kiss to my forehead. We lay in silence for a moment, recovering. Neil reached down and fished the busted vibrator from the blankets. "Well, it served its purpose," he said.

"It certainly did."

"I'll buy you a new one. A decent one."

"I'm going to hold you to that. I'll need one while I'm away."

While I'm away.

A shadow flickered across Neil's face at my words, there and gone. He drew me closer to him. "We should make the most of the time we have left together before you leave."

"And how do you plan on achieving that?"

"I know all this secrecy has been hard on you. It's been hard on me too. I want to take you out on a proper date."

I blinked at him. As much as I had daydreamed about going out and showing him off as my boyfriend, I had already resigned myself to our covert meetups being the closest he could offer me for the foreseeable future. "But how? People would see us."

"So we go out of town. Far away enough we won't run into anyone who could recognise us."

"Like where?"

"Somewhere quaint, quiet… We could have dinner, stay at a bed-and-breakfast, make love all night, sleep in all morning."

"Sounds perfect. When are we going?"

"Soon. As soon as possible."

I couldn't tell if he was being serious, or if this was just a flight of fancy, but I let myself believe it could be a reality.

Chapter Fifty-Nine

I poured the dregs of tea from the teapot into my cup. Across from me in the cafeteria, Neil sipped from his espresso mug with economical movements. To my right, Petra nibbled her almond croissant. I swept stray crumbs off the table into a serviette, then adjusted my legs under the table, accidentally knocking my knee against Neil's. His stern expression didn't change, but I felt him tense at the contact. I suppressed a smile.

Neil had suggested regrouping over morning refreshments to discuss work matters that arose during his absence. After the recap, he placed his cup down on his saucer with a decisive clunk. "I think that about catches me up on what I missed over the past week. Unless there's anything else?"

He raised his eyebrows at Petra and me. I shook my head, but Petra jolted upright. "Oh! Um, well..." She fiddled with her scrunched-up serviette. "I'm not sure if this matters, but we did get an odd call asking for you on Friday."

Odd call? She hadn't told me anything about this.

Neil leaned forward. "Go on."

"So this man—Daniel Ling, I think he said his name was—rang asking to speak with you. Well, I told him you were away on personal business. Then he started asking all these questions about where you'd gone and why." Petra's voice climbed in pitch as she spoke faster. "I tried not to give him any details, but he was very persuasive. He said he was your boss."

Neil massaged his temples. "I see."

Petra's eyes rounded. "Sorry, was that wrong? Should I have refused to talk to him?"

"Don't worry. Daniel Ling is the president of Zelthia Group. Thank you for telling me he called."

Petra nodded, placated.

Neil sipped the rest of his coffee in thoughtful silence, a vein on his forehead throbbing.

"I'm just going to nip to the restroom," Petra said, getting to her feet. "Back in a sec."

I watched her depart, then angled myself towards Neil. "So, I'm assuming it's a problem that Daniel was sniffing around for information on your whereabouts?"

Neil pinched the bridge of his nose. "It's certainly not ideal."

"I wonder what Petra told him."

"I dare say not much. She can't tell what she doesn't know."

As Petra returned, Neil rose. "We'd best get back. Lots of work piled up over the week, I'm sure."

Murmuring our agreement, Petra and I gathered our belongings.

We arrived on the twentieth floor to the sight of a massive bouquet dominating James's desk. Blue hydrangeas, white roses, and baby's breath burst from blue wrapping paper with a teddy bear attached, and a metallic blue helium balloon proclaiming "It's a Boy!" in silver cursive lettering.

I wondered who on earth that was for. Then I noticed Neil's reaction. He turned rigid, the colour draining from his face. My stomach dropped like I'd missed a step. Something was wrong. Very wrong.

Neil shouldered past me. "What is that?" he asked James, who was hidden behind the bouquet.

James beamed. "They just got delivered for you, Mr. Kingston.

Aren't they lovely? I didn't realise you're a new dad. Congratulations!"

My jaw unhinged. Since when was Neil a father? Was this somehow connected to Veronica's baby? Wait. Was Veronica's baby *his* baby?

Petra crowded up to Neil, practically fizzing. "Oh! Is that what the trip to Singapore was about? Did your partner give birth there? Wow, congratulations, sir!"

Neil stood motionless. Silence congealed in the space where denial should have been.

I must have the wrong end of the stick. There's no way he'd keep something so monumental from me.

"Neil?" I managed in a strangled tone.

He seemed to register my presence again, his eyes flitting over to me. A heavy pause draped over us.

Please say something. Say it was someone's idea of a cruel prank. Say there's been a mistake...

Neil licked his lips, eyes drifting back to the bouquet. Each passing second of silence twisted the knife in my gut further. I swallowed through a constricted throat, the hot sting of unshed tears welling behind my lashes.

"Thank you," Neil said. "I'll take them to my office." He reached for the bouquet and cradled the blooms against his shirt. Then he was off down the corridor.

Petra exchanged a confused look with me. I shrugged at her, keeping my tears held back.

If the baby was his, did that mean Veronica and Neil were a couple this whole time, and I was the other woman? Or was this all some kind of misunderstanding?

I trailed after Neil into his office, closing the door behind me with a snick.

Neil plunked the bouquet onto the coffee table. The teddy bear toppled over, grinning vacantly at us with its embroidered smile and glass bead eyes.

"Neil... What's going on?"

He didn't answer me. He searched the bouquet and teddy bear thoroughly, then shoved them inside a cabinet.

"Neil?" I asked again.

He dragged a hand over his face. "Someone's just sent me a clear message that they know about Ben."

"Are you… Are you Ben's father?"

Neil hesitated, then replied bluntly, "Yes."

The admission detonated inside me with the force of a bomb. I nearly lost my footing.

So, it's true.

More questions shuddered past my quivering lips. "A-Are you two… together? Have we been having an affair this whole time?"

"No. I promise you. There are reasons for everything."

I scoffed. "Like what?"

Neil took a step towards me. "Amelia, please…"

I shrank away, shaking my head vehemently. Tears spilled free at last, blazing paths down my cheeks.

"It's not what you think. Allow me to explain."

But what explanation could there possibly be? He had been messing around with me while the mother of his child fended for herself in Singapore. Whichever way you looked at it, that wasn't good.

Neil said something, but I didn't hear it over the blood rushing in my ears. Then the shrill ring of his phone cut through the room. He swore under his breath as he plucked the device from his suit jacket and squinted at the caller ID. "It's Ruby," he said.

A.k.a Veronica. The mother of his child.

I crossed my arms. What was he going to say to her?

Neil shakily picked up the call. "Hello?" As he listened, his expression turned grave. "Understood," he said. Then he faced me. "The chairman is dead. We have to leave. Right now."

* * *

Winston drove Neil and me to our apartment building. In the basement carpark, Neil rounded the car and wrenched open my door before I'd finished fumbling with my seatbelt. His hand closed over my elbow, propelling me from the vehicle. "Hurry. Time is of the essence."

In a daze, I allowed him to steer me towards the lift. "What's happening?"

"The shit has officially hit the fan, and if Daniel wants to punish me, his best course of action would be to harm you."

"I'm in danger?"

"I don't know how much Daniel knows about us, but we have to play it safe. My priority is getting you as far away from him and his cronies as possible."

"How?"

"You're going to London."

"But my flight's still weeks away—"

Neil shook his head. "Change of plans. You're leaving today."

"You want me to drop everything and flee the country?"

"Yes."

"And if I disagree?"

"That would be very unwise indeed."

My head swam. I swiped a shaking hand down my face.

"Pack your luggage and go straight to the airport," Neil instructed as we rode up to my floor. "Winston will drive you there. Get on the next available flight to London—one without a stopover in Singapore." He rummaged in his pocket, extracted his wallet, then slipped out a credit card. "Use this." He pressed the card into my limp hand.

I stared at his name embossed on black plastic.

"And this." He gave me another card—a business card. "I want you to contact this man—Alan Dixon—once you're in London. Tell him you want to apply for a job. He'll ask you to come in for an interview—"

Neil continued to speak, but the words blurred together. I swayed on my feet.

"Whoa." Neil caught my shoulders, steadying me.

The door lurched open, and we stepped out.

"Are you okay?" Neil asked. "I know this is a lot to take in."

I didn't answer.

"Hey, look at me."

I raised my eyes to meet his. The hard lines of his face had smoothed into an expression that was tender and earnest. He cupped my cheek. "I don't want to send you away, but I have to, to ensure you're as far from danger as possible. Do you understand? I need you to trust me, Milly. Please. You're everything to me, and I..." His throat worked. "I want to protect you. This is hard for me. The hardest thing I've ever had to do. Believe me. If I lost you, I—I couldn't live with myself." Tears had gathered in his eyes.

My heart stirred. But how could I trust him when he had concealed the truth about Veronica's baby from me?

I remembered that day months ago on the roof, when Neil had warned me, "Trust no one." His cynical advice had struck me as extreme—even sad. But I was starting to comprehend the hard lessons that had ingrained those words within him.

"Trust no one," I said.

"What?"

"A few months ago, you told me to trust no one."

"Do you still think I'm a good man?"

I hesitated. "I... I'm not sure anymore."

Neil clasped my hands in his. "You have every reason to doubt me. I haven't been the partner you deserve, and I wouldn't blame you if you no longer wanted anything to do with me. But if you can find it within yourself to offer me one thing, it would be this: Stay safe. Get away from me and stay safe until I can come back for you—if you still want me to."

I searched those fathomless eyes of his, reflecting my own scared, lost expression back at me. Behind his mask, glimpses of the real Neil shone through. The Neil who had opened himself up to me, and who was now trying to protect me, even as it gutted him inside.

"You said everything has a reason. Is that true? Because I don't understand why you'd have a child with your ex."

"I know it's hard to believe—"

"Will you tell me everything once you're finished doing what you've set out to do?"

"Yes. I promise."

I stood on a precipice. Everyone important to me in my life had abandoned me. Maybe Neil would too. I couldn't control that. But I could control whether I'd fight for him or give up. So, in that moment, even though the odds were stacked against me, I decided to trust him.

"Okay," I said through the lump in my throat. "I'll go."

Chapter Sixty

Compulsively checking the news from Singapore was a bad habit since arriving in London. I scrolled through article after article, hungry for any new twist in the Zelthia succession battle. But mainly, I hoped for reassurance that Neil remained unharmed. So far, so good.

I had done a lot of thinking over the past weeks. While the articles stated Neil and Veronica were an engaged couple, I realised this didn't add up. I remembered meeting Veronica in Singapore, her smile in reaction to seeing Neil's shirt on my bed, and her claim that she was in a relationship which wasn't public knowledge. With that evidence in mind, I could believe Neil had told me the truth.

As for the baby, could it be a pawn in the inheritance game? The theory left a bitter taste in my mouth. If true, then Neil wasn't as pure-hearted as I thought. But he had never pretended he was.

"Taxi will be here in five," Hannah said, poking her head into my bedroom. "You almost ready?"

"Yep! Just about." I tucked my phone away in my bag.

In the three weeks since I'd arrived in London, there had been no evident threats to my safety, and I felt ready to let my guard down for once. I was determined to enjoy this afternoon at the Christmas market, regardless of my circumstances.

I swapped my hoodie for a chunky cable-knit sweater and wrapped a tartan scarf around my neck. A black wool coat and a pair of fleece-lined gloves completed the look.

"Taxi's here!" Hannah called as I emerged from my room.

I hurried to meet her by the front door, where we pulled on waterproof boots. She wore all black—leggings, leather jacket, fingerless gloves, and earmuffs. Her dark hair was tied back. She hooked her arm through mine. "Ready to get into the Christmas spirit, Grinch?"

I rolled my eyes. "Oh please, I am so not a Grinch."

Hannah grinned. "Could've fooled me."

"I've just been distracted. That's all."

"I know. It's not an easy situation to be in, but at least *try* to enjoy yourself."

"Don't worry. I plan to enjoy the hell out of this."

"That's the spirit!"

"You'll stay with me the whole time, though. Won't you?"

"Of course. I won't leave your side. Now, let's not keep the driver waiting." Hannah opened the door, a blast of chilly air sweeping in.

We stepped into the courtyard shared by all the flats in the block, security cameras hidden in every corner of the perimeter. Hannah locked the door behind us. We then proceeded through the tall wrought-iron gate separating the courtyard from the pavement. Specks of icy rain needled my cheeks, and I burrowed into my scarf as we dashed across the pavement. A black cab idled by the curb, yellow headlights beckoning through the gloom. I scanned the busy street before letting Hannah climb inside ahead of me.

The interior smelled of stale coffee and air freshener. Hannah reminded the driver of our destination. Rain pattered against the windows as we eased into traffic. I fiddled with my bag strap, excitement kindling as I watched festive shopfronts slide past. The closest I'd come to a real Christmas was back when Dad was alive. Most years it had just been the two of us. Not much effort or festivity. This year, all things going to plan, I'd spend Christmas with a group of old friends who were staying in London.

I looked out the window, losing myself in the steady drum of rain and the swish of passing cars as we wound deeper into the city. Vibrant holiday lights, storefronts, and pedestrians blurred into Impressionistic smears of colour. But gradually, the shop displays faded, giving way to warehouses, chain-link fences, and loading bays. I blinked hard. This didn't seem right. Were we still heading towards Hyde Park?

I shot Hannah a questioning look. She returned my gaze, lips pinched tight, eyes round. My chest squeezed. No words needed. Her tense look mirrored the unease now sitting like a stone in my gut.

"Excuse me," Hannah ventured, artificially bright. "I think you may have taken a wrong turn back there. Hyde Park is the other way. Could you turn around, please?"

No response came from the driver. Just the steady rumble of tyres over wet pavement. We continued gliding deeper into nowhere.

This wasn't the first time I'd been in a taxi heading to the wrong destination against my will. Last time, it was Daniel Ling's doing. I whipped my head towards Hannah. She gave an almost imperceptible nod.

Chapter Sixty-One

Panic engulfed me as the taxi continued farther from the intended destination. I had mentally prepared for this kind of situation, but now that it was actually happening, all my preparation was out the window. "Stop the car!" I yelled.

The driver ignored me. I jostled the door lock, but it was stuck fast. The child safety lock was engaged. I checked my phone, but it mysteriously had no signal. Something must have been blocking it. I sent an emergency SMS anyway, hoping it would still transmit.

Hannah shouted and pounded on the back window of the car, but the window was foggy, and there were no cars close enough for anyone to see.

The driver's hunched shoulders tightened further as he turned down a narrow alley leading towards a dilapidated warehouse surrounded by a barbed-wire fence. My pulse crashed loud in my ears. I clutched Hannah's arm as we slowed towards the ragged chain-link gate barring our way. A suited man bearing a neck tattoo stepped into position to open the gate. Hannah hammered on the car window to get his attention, but his deadened eyes skated over us, unmoved.

We bumped across a forecourt overgrown with weeds poking

through cracks in the concrete, then into the warehouse's gaping entrance. The car slowed to a stop. The man with the neck tattoo, and a shorter, stockier man, approached either side of the vehicle. The driver rolled his window down slightly, and the neck-tattoo man slipped a thick envelope through the gap. As the driver counted the cash in the envelope with grubby fingers, the ominous men yanked open both rear doors in jarring unison.

"Get out," the brute at my side barked, fetid breath billowing as he dragged me from the taxi with enough force to nearly rip my arm from its socket. Hannah yelped as the other man wrestled her out with equal violence. They forced us to our knees on the freezing, wet concrete.

Hannah locked eyes with me, communicating wordless reassurance as the men bound our hands behind us with zip ties. I didn't know whether she had a plan to get us out of this, or if she thought we'd get rescued soon. I was doubtful on both counts.

The men frisked our pockets and bags for phones and cash and confiscated them, so even if we could somehow escape, we'd have no resources to depend on. The driver drove the car away, and with a metallic rumble, the warehouse roller door descended behind us, encaging us in musty darkness.

I sucked in a deep breath, willing my frantic mind to think. I had to stay calm. If the men planned to use me as leverage in a bargaining situation, then my life wasn't in immediate danger since I'd be no use to them dead. If I could keep my wits about me, maybe I could get information. Anything that could help bring Daniel Ling and his people down.

"What do you want from us?" I managed.

The stocky one shrugged. "Just following orders."

"Whose orders?" I pressed.

He scoffed. "Need-to-know basis, love."

His lanky partner with the tattoo curling up his neck studied me closely. "Which one of you is Amelia Cross?"

Before I could respond, Hannah piped up. "I am."

I blinked in surprise. The neck-tattooed man narrowed his

eyes, scrutinising Hannah's features. "Funny," he said. "Our photograph looks more like this one." He grabbed my jaw, his yellow teeth bared inches from my face. "Did you really think we'd fall for that?"

He yanked me to my feet and dragged me towards a chair set behind a tripod and video camera. My knees quaked, but I locked them rigidly. I had to cooperate, buy time, and if worse came to worst, I just hoped Hannah could get out of her zip ties.

One man guarded Hannah, while the other one tied me to the chair. I took stock of my surroundings as the rope tightened around me, seeking anything to help me formulate an escape. The warehouse was large and empty, with a concrete floor of chipped grey squares and rusty pipes snaking along the walls. Above, skeletal trusses weaved across the ceiling and broken skylights let the cold seep in. A few grimy bulbs hung from exposed wires, providing a hazy light source. A double door at the back of the warehouse was barred, chained, and padlocked. The only other way out was the roller door we came in through. There had to be a switch for it somewhere, but we wouldn't be able to activate it with our hands bound behind our backs.

I turned my focus to the camera in front of me. "Are you going to video me?" I asked my captor.

Neck Tattoo leaned down, his hot, sour breath on my face. "Obviously."

"So, how does this work? Do I have to say anything? Do I get a script or something?"

"Bit of pleading for your life will do the trick."

"You want to show someone my life's in danger... to force them to comply with your boss's demands?"

"Clever girl."

"So, do you get paid well for doing stuff like this?"

"Not well enough. Anyways, enough chitchat. I'll have to gag you if you keep running your mouth."

"Sorry. I'm just interested, that's all. It's not every day you get to pick the brains of paid criminals."

He gave an amused grunt in response as he pointed the lens at me.

The man guarding Hannah spoke up. "Hey, Gaz. D'you know what we're s'posed to do with this one? Didn't realise there'd be two of 'em."

"We'll have to ask the boss."

"Reckon boss man wouldn't mind if we had a lil fun?"

A cold weight sank through me. They couldn't hurt me, but they had no reason not to harm Hannah. I jerked against the restraints.

The neck-tattoo man, Gaz, shot his partner a warning look. "No funny stuff till he gets what he wants."

I exhaled. She was safe. For now.

Gaz fiddled with the camera settings, brows pinching together.

"Need some help?" I asked.

"Not a chance." Gaz called for his partner. "Oi, Jono, know how to work this thing? You're the tech wiz."

Hannah's guard left his post to assist Gaz.

My hands strained against the unforgiving plastic biting into my wrists while every second dragged like wading through quicksand. Backup had to be coming… right?

Between the two goons, they figured out what was wrong with the camera settings, and I saw a red light switch on. It was recording. My nerves hitched. Just what exactly were they planning to shoot?

"Right then, girlie. Time for your star turn," Gaz said.

"W-what should I do?"

"Getting scared now, eh?" His grin made my stomach turn. "Good. We're just getting started."

Chapter Sixty-Two

I peered up at the imposing glass edifice, its facade reflecting the surrounding skyscrapers of Canary Wharf. Was this the right place? I double-checked the address on the business card clutched in my gloved hand and cross-referenced it with the Maps app and the number etched above the building's revolving door. The biting air made me shiver as I stood on the pavement, mustering my resolve. This had to be it. Time to go in.

I hitched my bag higher on my shoulder and stepped through the revolving door into the lobby. The sheer scale of the place was overwhelming. Men and women dressed in corporate attire strode purposefully across the vast floor. I lingered just inside the entrance, struggling to get my bearings. The business card said Avenex Holdings was on level ten, but a row of steel security gates cut off the way to the bank of lifts. I needed a visitor pass.

I approached the wide, arched desk positioned in front of a backdrop of wooden panels. Two workers manned the desk, typing away on computers. I stepped up to the male receptionist on the right. "Excuse me. I have an appointment on level ten with Alan Dixon from Avenex Holdings."

The man flicked his eyes over me. "ID, please."

I fumbled in my bag for my New Zealand driver's licence and

handed it over. The man typed my details into the computer, then took my photo with a small webcam mounted to his monitor. Moments later, a plastic visitor badge printed out. He attached it to a lanyard and passed it over along with my licence. "Wear this at all times. It will get you through the gates to the lifts and grant access to level ten." His bored tone made it clear he issued hundreds of these passes each day.

"Thank you."

I slipped the lanyard over my head, the badge dangling across my chest. Now properly credentialed, I headed for the gates, nerves rising with each step.

Another security check awaited me on the tenth floor. A guard inspected my pass and ID before nodding me through. I supposed these big financial institutions had to take their security seriously. London was a different world compared to Auckland.

"Please take a seat, Amelia. Alan will be with you shortly," the blonde woman at reception said.

I settled onto a couch along the wall, clutching my bag in my lap. My knee bounced with excess adrenaline as I scanned the waiting area—all gleaming surfaces and minimalist sophistication.

I had no idea what to expect with this meeting. Neil had given me Alan Dixon's business card and told me to contact him as soon as I arrived in London. To arrange a job interview, he said, but I knew that had to be a cover for something else. What, I did not know. Alan had revealed little on the phone.

Minutes later, a man strode towards me, hand extended. Recognition stirred, but I couldn't quite grasp where I had seen him before. He looked to be in his early sixties, with grey hair, a neatly groomed beard, and black-framed glasses perched on the bridge of his nose. His tailored suit was reminiscent of Neil's impeccable style, and he possessed a gentlemanly air, with ambiguous features which were somehow menacing and benevolent in equal measure. "Amelia, how lovely to see you again!"

I shook his proffered hand, still struggling to place him. "Mr.

Dixon, I'm so sorry. I recognise you, but I don't quite remember—"

"Understandable. We met briefly in Singapore."

It suddenly clicked. "Oh, of course! At the shareholder meeting."

I retraced my memory. Avenex was one of the largest shareholders in Zelthia after the chairman. Neil had introduced me to Alan Dixon, along with several other important people.

"That's right." Dixon's eyes crinkled behind his glasses. "I must say, you handled yourself admirably that day, stepping in for Neil's presentation on such short notice."

"Oh, thank you."

"You made it here okay?"

"Yes. Now I know why everyone raves about the public transit here."

"It's a convenient system. I'm glad you were able to figure it out. Shall we?" He gestured towards the frosted glass door through which he had emerged.

Since Neil had asked me to meet with Dixon, that meant I could trust him, right? Either way, it was too late to back out now.

Dixon unlocked the door with his access card, and I followed him inside. Five smartly dressed employees populated the open-plan office within, but we bypassed them to enter a private inner room. As we stepped inside, a young woman glanced up from her seat at the table within. She had an oval-shaped face framed by long dark hair tied back in a low ponytail. An air of quiet capability surrounded her, along with a poise that struck me as almost military. She looked different from the other employees here. Who was she?

Dixon secured the door behind us with a resounding click. "Take a seat."

I lowered myself onto a chair as Dixon rounded the table to sit beside the unknown woman.

"I'll get right to business, Amelia," Dixon said, lacing his fingers on the table top. "Neil has informed me of certain… developments between you two, and the implications those developments may have for your safety. He arranged this meeting so I could oversee your security during your time here and facilitate contact between you."

Neil had set this all up so Dixon could take care of me in London?

"I think I understand. So, you're working with Neil?"

Dixon inclined his head. "For some time now. Our sights have been set on problematic figures at the helm of Zelthia. Daniel Ling chief among them." He shifted in his seat. "With the chairman's recent passing, the will reading is imminent. Neil believes he is named as a beneficiary. We can expect Daniel to fight to maintain complete control over the company."

My mind spun, struggling to absorb all the implications. "Neil is… I thought Veronica…"

"Neil and the chairman had a special relationship. Neil was his protégé, superior to Daniel in every way, apart from blood."

"What about Veronica?"

"Neil and Veronica are united in their cause. His share is as good as hers."

"Is Neil going to be okay?"

"I should think so. It would look very suspicious if he suddenly died or disappeared at this point. Daniel wouldn't be stupid enough. No, the person who is in the most danger right now is *you*."

I recoiled. Neil had warned me I could be in danger, but Dixon's words still came as a shock.

"I'm afraid Daniel either knows, or has guessed, that you are Neil's weak point." Alan's eyes drilled into mine. "Neil thought you would be safe here, but he was wrong. An inside source has informed me that Daniel knows your whereabouts, and he intends to use you as a means of leverage against Neil. If Daniel's thugs capture you, he could coerce Neil into relinquishing his stake. You are now an active target."

My mouth went dry. This was the kind of danger Neil had

warned me about, the reason he was so adamant we couldn't be together. My tongue prodded the inside of my numb lips, urging words to form, but none came. A cold sweat bloomed across my neck.

"I know this is a lot to take in," Dixon said.

"What should I do?"

"Neil would advise you to vanish. Go underground until the danger passes. I could assist you with that."

I pictured an existence in hiding, paralysed by powerlessness, while my dream trip passed me by. How long would I need to stay in hiding? Weeks, months, years?

"But I have an alternative proposition," Alan continued. "One I believe you are uniquely poised to assist with, if you'll lend your courage."

I hitched in a sharp breath. My next words emerged faintly. "I'm listening."

Dixon motioned to the unknown woman who had been so silent I had almost forgotten she was present. "Do you recognise her?" Dixon asked me.

I looked the woman up and down, searching for clues. "No. Should I?"

"Not exactly, but she has been with you since you arrived in London."

"What do you mean?"

"She has been keeping a lookout for threats. While I don't expect Daniel to strike so soon, we can't be too careful."

"I had no idea."

"Her name is Hannah Frank."

My neurons fired, making connections. "But that's the name of my friend I'm going to stay with…"

Hannah inclined her head.

"…You're going to impersonate my friend?" I asked.

"Bingo," Dixon said. "I want you to stay with this Hannah, not your friend, and she will be your bodyguard."

"And I won't have to go into hiding?"

"If it all works out."

"What about the real Hannah? Will I have to tell her I can't stay with her anymore?"

"I'm afraid so. We have a story prepared that you can use as cover."

I bit my lip. I hated to stand up my friend, but it seemed deception was part of this cloak-and-dagger game. "Okay. I think I get it. But what's the catch?"

Dixon leaned forward, planting his elbows on the table. His eyes locked onto mine. "You will be bait."

I started. "Bait?"

"We put you out there, let Daniel's agents catch your scent. When they inevitably strike, we'll be waiting to intercept them."

Out there? Out where?

The fake Hannah took over explaining, her voice as cool and smooth as glass. "We would set you up in a safe house. You'd continue your travels as planned—within reason—while I accompanied you as protection detail under the cover of being your friend. Behind the scenes, my team would monitor you at all times. You would, ostensibly, serve as bait to draw out Daniel's men, but the moment things get hairy, I'll extract you."

I tried to unscramble this information in my frazzled brain. If I had it right, they wanted to dangle me in front of the enemy to lure them out. "It sounds dangerous."

"There's no denying that," Dixon said. "But it's potentially very high reward. If Daniel takes the bait, we will be able to build a stronger criminal case against him, adding to the file of evidence we already have, ready to release at the most advantageous moment."

His unflinching confidence made me shiver. This wasn't just speculation. Dixon fully expected me to be targeted and attacked. My head reeled. "Does Neil know about this… bait tactic?"

Dixon grimaced. "No. He doesn't know anything about any of this. And he cannot find out. He would never allow us to put you at risk, despite the potential upsides."

"So I'd be going behind Neil's back."

"Indeed."

"And the other option is hiding?"

Dixon nodded. "It's your choice, Amelia. So, which will it be?"

I sucked a thin breath through my constricting throat. The blood roared in my ears, drowning out all other sounds. I could practically feel Daniel's spidery hands closing around my neck, his rancid breath hot on my cheek…

I jerked back to the present moment. Dixon watched me closely, awaiting my response while my heart ricocheted in my chest. I could play it safe, or I could be brave. Hide away, or help. Was I willing to gamble with my own life in order to help Neil's cause?

But I had already made this decision when I accepted the dangers of loving Neil. I wanted to stand shoulder to shoulder with him in this fight, not languish on the sidelines. This was my opportunity to act. Neil wouldn't approve, but I was done with seeking other people's approval, including Neil's. For once, I was going to do the thing that I felt was the right thing to do.

I steeled my nerves and met Dixon's gaze. "I'll do it. I'll be your bait."

Chapter Sixty-Three

Gaz drew a gun from beneath his jacket. Stark fear rooted me in place as he waggled it in my direction. My vision tunnelled. I couldn't tear my gaze from the dark eye of the barrel. This wasn't supposed to happen. I should have been rescued by now. What was taking so long? Had the plan failed? Why wasn't Hannah doing anything to get us out of this?

"Go on then," Gaz said. "Start begging."

I pictured Neil seeing this footage, forced to bargain for my life. Ice spread through my veins.

Gaz moved closer, shoving the gun under my chin. The metal burned cold against my skin. Behind him, Jono watched, beefy arms crossed, a smug grin on his face. My heart battered my ribs. I focused on keeping my breathing steady. In and out. *Don't lose hope now. Help will come.*

"I said, beg!" Gaz jabbed the gun harder against me.

I faced the camera lens through a blur of tears. Summoning my voice took every scrap of courage. "P-please." The word scraped my dry throat.

A metallic rumble reverberated through the warehouse as the roller door jerked into motion, rattling open. I flinched in surprise.

Gaz lowered the gun, brow furrowed as he turned on Jono. "The hell? What'd you do that for?"

Jono threw his hands up. "I didn't do nothin'!"

"Where's the remote?" Gaz's eyes were wild, spittle flying from his stained teeth.

Jono patted his pockets. "I dunno."

"What d'you mean, you don't know?" Gaz went up to Jono and grabbed him by the lapels, his face turning a deep crimson.

"I had it a minute ago!"

The door continued grinding open at a crawl, but there was nothing outside except darkness. Even if I screamed with everything in me, no one would hear.

Gaz released Jono and shoved him away. "Fuck's sake. Get that door back down. Now!" He jerked his gun towards the switch on the far wall.

As Jono lumbered away, Gaz rounded on me again, his eyes holding a crazed glint. "Now, where were we?"

I shrank away, ready to choke out another plea, but a flash of motion over Gaz's shoulder caught my eye.

Hannah.

She was creeping up behind Gaz, her restraints nowhere to be seen. How did she get free? No time to wonder. This was our chance!

Gaz noticed me looking past him. He spun around just as Hannah grabbed his wrist. With a deft twist, she pointed the weapon away from us. Before Gaz could react, she struck his thumb with a sharp elbow blow. His hand spasmed open, and she snatched the gun, flipping it to aim at his chest in one smooth motion. "Don't move."

Gaz froze, eyes bulging. "Who the hell *are* you?"

I sagged against my bonds, dizzy with delayed panic and relief. Hannah had seized back control of the situation. But we still had to get out of this alive.

As the roller door descended, Jono spun around by the wall, confusion twisting his features. "What the?"

As understanding dawned on his face, his hand flew to his hip. But Hannah was faster. She swung her aim towards him, blocking his draw. "Don't," she warned.

My peripheral vision picked up a movement from Gaz. "Watch out!" I yelled, just as he lunged at Hannah.

She side-stepped him in the nick of time, and his own momentum sent him stumbling past. A backhanded blow from Hannah was all it took to make him fall over. He smacked his head against the concrete and lay still. Hannah pinned him down with her boot on his neck, all the while keeping the gun trained on Jono.

"Okay, okay! Don't shoot me!" Jono said, hands in the air.

With that, Hannah slipped the remote control out of her pocket and pressed the button with her spare hand. The door ascended again. This time, a bar of light shone through. Tyres crunched outside on the cracked concrete. Car doors slammed, and voices called back and forth. The widening gap revealed several police cars and other vehicles surrounding the building. Then the warehouse flooded with uniformed officers.

* * *

Bone-deep exhaustion weighed on me as Dixon drove Hannah and me away from the police station. Over twenty-four hours had passed since our rescue, and I was running on fumes. The previous night at the private hospital being treated for shock and mild hypothermia had afforded little rest. Today was consumed by police statements as I recounted my capture and everything leading up to it, forced to relive the experience over and over. My mind was ready to shut down. Questions could wait. All I wanted was the oblivion of sleep.

Dixon navigated the evening traffic while Hannah typed away on her phone in the seat beside him. I yawned. The passing city lights became blurs across my vision, and I let my temple rest against the chilled glass of the car window. I began to drift off.

Dixon turned down a ramp into an underground parking garage, jolting me alert.

"Where are we?" I asked, looking around at the cars and concrete pillars. I thought we had been heading back to the safe house, but this was somewhere totally different.

"We're on our way to operations headquarters. You won't be staying at the safe house anymore," Dixon replied over his shoulder.

I straightened. "Operations…? What's that?"

"You'll see soon enough."

"What about all my stuff? It's still—"

"Don't worry. All your belongings have already been moved to the new location."

We pulled into a space and stepped out into the concrete stillness. Dixon led the way through a door into a brightly lit stairwell. At the top of the stairs, we entered the main lobby, and I realised we were back in the Canary Wharf office building where Avenex was located, only now, it was a little after hours, the former buzz of energy now a subdued hum.

A security guard took one look at Dixon and opened a gate for us. In the lift, Dixon pressed the button for the tenth floor. I leaned against the handrail, confused. Was the Avenex office the operations headquarters?

When the doors slid open, we bypassed the dark, empty reception area and entered a room which looked like a supply closet. Metal shelves laden with boxes of copier paper and various office supplies filled the space. Dust tickled my nose. Dixon walked past the clutter to a section of wall that appeared seamless. He opened an electrical circuit breaker box, inside of which was a hidden keypad behind a false back. He typed a code. The wall emitted a gentle clunk. It swung inwards with a firm push. A secret door.

"This way," Dixon said, motioning for us to follow him into the room beyond.

I shot a questioning glance at Hannah, but she just nodded,

smiling calmly. We stepped across the threshold together, into a dark and dank passage. Through a second locked door, we emerged in a room that looked like some kind of control centre. Along the left wall, a mosaic of screens displayed surveillance footage of various locations. Along the right wall stood whiteboards scrawled with notes and complex flow charts, alongside pinboards cluttered with newspaper clippings, printed articles, and glossy photographs. Red string connected items in elaborate spiderwebs.

I turned to Dixon. "What is this place?"

"Welcome to headquarters. This is the nerve centre of our operation to bring down Daniel Ling and seize control of Zelthia Group."

Dixon wasted no time, steering me through a nondescript door on the back wall into a small attached suite. The windowless bedroom contained a neatly made single bed, a wooden desk and chair, and a navy armchair. My suitcase and backpack waited next to the bed.

"This will be your room now," Dixon said.

I stood there awkwardly, taking it all in. This was meant to be the place I disappeared to, I realised. The alternative to the bait plan. Despite everything, I had still ended up here.

Dixon gave me a sympathetic look. "I know it's not much, but try to make yourself comfortable."

"How long will I have to stay here?"

"Until we've deemed the threat level low enough. We don't expect Ling to be a free man for much longer, so just hold tight. This is the safest place for you in the meantime."

I chewed my lip, contemplating my new reality. A tense silence stretched between us until Dixon shifted his weight between his feet. "Get some rest. I expect you need it. I'll be back with food later. We can debrief over dinner."

My stomach rumbled at the promise of a hot meal, but my eyelids drooped. "If I fall asleep, I'm not sure I'll be able to wake up in time for dinner."

"If that happens, I'll leave leftovers for you in the kitchen, and I'll come back tomorrow. Any food preferences?"

I thought of the bland soup and sandwiches from the hospital. "Honestly, I'll eat anything."

"Noted."

With that, Dixon stepped out and closed the door behind him. I switched off the bedside light and collapsed onto the mattress without even taking my shoes off. Sleep hit me hard and fast.

I awoke after an unknown passage of time, the savoury smell of takeaway curry drifting under the door, making my stomach cramp with hunger. I was still tired, but I was also hungry as hell. With the resolution to eat, then come back to bed straight after, I forced myself up and out of the room.

"Ah, you decided to join us, after all," Dixon said.

He sat with Hannah at the central table, food piled up on plates in front of them. I slid into the empty seat beside Hannah. "The smell was too tempting."

"You're just in time to hear the good news," Hannah said. "We've had word of Daniel's arrest in Singapore."

I blinked, taking a second to process the new development through my brain fog. "They've got him?"

"That's right," Dixon said.

"So, the plan worked?"

"Indeed. Because of your courage, the police were able to extract concrete proof from those criminals, linking Daniel to an organised crime outfit here in the UK, leading to his arrest."

I slumped forward, relief hitting me on top of the hunger and exhaustion. "Thank God."

Hannah served me a heaped plate of food, along with a tall glass of water. I wasted no time tucking in, the flavours bursting on my dry tongue. Dixon debriefed me on the situation while I ate, the food and drink reviving me enough to grasp the significance of what we had accomplished.

I sat up straight. "So what happens now?"

"Now?" Dixon's smile held a hint of menace. "With the UK

and Singapore cooperating in this case, we will be able to bury Daniel Ling beneath the mountain of evidence we've accumulated against him. With him behind bars, contesting his father's will becomes exponentially more difficult for him. Checkmate."

I exhaled, picturing Daniel finally getting his due after years of evading consequences. One chapter was ending, but the rest of the story remained unwritten. I still had no idea what the coming days and weeks held. But for now, I took comfort in this victory, even at the huge personal cost.

Just then, a cell phone buzzed to life, breaking the pensive spell. Dixon answered the call, looking uneasy. "Yes? ... Understood. Thank you." He hung up. "Brace yourselves. We're about to have an unexpected guest."

Chapter Sixty-Four

A few minutes later, the door to the operations room burst open with such force that it slammed against the wall. Neil stormed in, eyes blazing, jaw clenched so tight the tendons in his neck strained. He swept towards Dixon. "You fucking bastard!" Each syllable was a lash of venom. "How could you put her in danger like that?"

Dixon rose calmly to his feet. "It was the only way to—"

"Bullshit! She could have been killed!"

I'd seen Neil angry before, but never like this—never with such unrestrained, primal fury. The sheer potency of his anger caused the hairs on my arms to rise. If I didn't intervene, I thought he might actually attack Dixon.

I rose from my seat, palms up in a pacifying gesture. "Neil, wait. Let me explain..."

He whipped towards me. "Are you all right?" His eyes roved over me as if checking for injuries.

"I'm fine. Really."

Some of the rigid tension leeched from his shoulders, but his hands remained bunched into fists at his sides.

With cautious steps, I moved towards him until I stood just within arm's reach. Up close, I could see the storm still simmering in those dark eyes. "Alan didn't force me into anything. He gave me a choice, and I chose to go along with the plan. It was my decision."

Neil's nostrils flared, his scowl deepening. "You were coerced."

"No." I surprised myself with the vehemence in my voice. "I wasn't."

For a long, fraught moment, he stared at me. The war of emotion waging within him was palpable—the anger and betrayal, the petrified terror of potentially losing me, the desperate yearning to shield me from harm even as his rationality reminded him I was my own woman, free to make my own choices.

A muscle twitched in Neil's neck, and the vein in his forehead throbbed as his anger swelled once more. "How could you put yourself in harm's way like that?"

I opened my mouth, but Hannah spoke up first. "It was my job to protect her. The fault lies with me."

Neil turned his thunderous glare on Hannah. She met him head-on, chin raised, brown eyes steady.

"I don't blame you," Neil said. "You were just following orders." He shot another withering look at Dixon. "But *you*... I can't stand the sight of you. I never thought... of all people..."

"Don't forget that it was your emotional entanglements that got us into this mess in the first place," Dixon said.

Neil shook with barely contained rage. "Go. Before I do something I might regret."

Dixon hesitated for a split second before relenting with a curt nod. "Very well."

As the older man disappeared through the door, Hannah followed suit. "I'll give you two some space," she said on her way out.

In the wake of their departure, Neil slumped like he had exerted himself from all his rage. "Come here," he said gruffly.

I wasted no time closing the distance between us. Neil gathered me into his arms, pulling me flush against his body. I let out a soft sigh, drawing comfort from the safety of his embrace after the hellish ordeal I had endured.

"I hopped on the first flight as soon as I heard," Neil murmured into my hair. "Thank God you're safe."

A profound sense of relief washed over me at having him here, holding me close. But it was quickly followed by a stab of guilt over the fear and anguish I must have put him through. I drew back enough to look up at him. "Neil, I'm so sorry. I know I went behind your back, did the exact thing you asked me not to do." I swallowed hard against the burgeoning knot in my throat. "If you want to break things off with me, I–I'd understand."

He studied me, a crease etched deep between his brows, letting out a long, weary sigh as his thumb stroked over the arch of my cheekbone. "Is that what you want?"

I recoiled sharply. "No! But I betrayed your trust by putting myself in danger, after you made it clear—"

"I would never break up with you. Christ, when I got that call…" He shook his head, eyes squeezing shut. "I've never been so terrified in my life. But you're here, you're alive. That's all that matters now."

Tears filled my eyes. I swiped at them before they could trickle down my cheeks. I had to keep my guard up. "What about Veronica and Benjamin? They're your family. You should be with them, not here with me."

Neil grasped my shoulders, meeting my gaze intently. "I'm going to tell you the whole truth now, okay?"

I stiffened, bracing myself for the devastation I knew was forthcoming. "Okay."

"It's true that Benjamin is my son—biologically speaking. But Veronica and I have been separated for a long time. Years. We only kept up a pretence of a relationship in front of her father, so that he'd continue to treat me like a son, for the purpose of gaining from the inheritance."

"But you slept with her—"

Neil shook his head. "Not since we broke up. The baby was conceived via sperm donation."

My mouth dropped agape. This was not what I had expected. "W-what? Why?"

"Veronica has had a new partner for a number of years now. Her name's Natasha."

"She... Huh?"

"Veronica and Natasha genuinely wanted to have a child. Giving the chairman his long-wished-for grandson was just a side effect. We didn't even know the child would be a boy."

The puzzle pieces slotted into place until I felt a visceral snap of comprehension. "So what you're saying is, you donated sperm so Veronica could have a child with her same-sex partner, and that's why you're the father of her child? Not because you're still in love with her? And not because you wanted to manipulate the chairman?"

Neil nodded.

Tears sprang unbidden to my eyes. Neil was right all along. There was a good reason for everything. Sure, it wasn't a perfect scenario, but it was one I could live with. I could forgive him. I could be with him after all.

Neil pulled me close, letting me cry into his shirt. "Veronica and Natasha will parent Ben, not me. That was part of the deal. But I still want to have a relationship with him to some extent. I know it's not fair on you. You never signed up for this. I should have told you the full truth from the start."

I shook my head against his shirt, sobbing.

"Shhh." He ran his hand up and down my back. "You're trembling."

"I'm just... I'm so glad. When I thought you were with her and having a baby together... I was so scared of losing you."

Neil pulled back to cradle my face between his palms, brushing away the tears trailing down my cheeks with his thumbs. "You could never lose me."

I hiccupped another sob. Neil wrapped me in his arms again,

stroking his hand through my hair. "If I could go back, I never would have attempted to take down Daniel. None of it has been worth putting you in danger."

Sniffling, I shook my head in fervent denial. "Don't say that. What you're doing, taking a stand, striving to make a difference— it matters. I knew getting involved with you came with risks, I knew who you were up against, and I made my choice. I have no regrets."

"You deserve better than being caught in the crossfire, Melia. A life of peace and safety, not one spent constantly looking over your shoulder."

"Could you live in peace without fighting for what you believe in?"

Neil's throat worked, his eyes boring into mine. "No."

"Well, neither can I. You don't have to fight this fight alone anymore. I'm with you."

Something inside Neil seemed to shatter in that moment, like a dam bursting after years of relentless pressure. I felt the rigidity leave his body, the last of his defensive walls crumbling away. He sought my lips. I opened to him without hesitation. His kiss was deep, tender, and passionate. I matched it with everything I had.

When we finally surfaced, I was tingling down to my toes. Neil rested his forehead against mine and traced the curve of my kiss-swollen lips with his thumb. "I love you," he rasped. "God help me, I love you so bloody much."

The sheer conviction in those words made my heart feel like it might burst. "I love you too."

Chapter Sixty-Five

Fragments of memories haunted me—rough plastic biting into my wrists, the dank mustiness of the warehouse choking my lungs, the void-like darkness of a gun barrel. I jolted awake with a strangled gasp, heart thundering.

Where am I?

As my eyes adjusted to the shadowy room, I registered Neil's form curled around me, his arm draped over my waist.

Neil is here. I'm okay.

The tension seeped from my muscles as his deep, even breaths and the steady rise and fall of his chest lulled me back into a sense of security.

The single bed was cramped, too small for the both of us, but I didn't care. After everything, having him near was the greatest comfort I could ask for. I shifted, nestling deeper under the covers. Neil reflexively tightened his embrace with a soft murmur, and I allowed my eyelids to drift shut.

The next time I woke up, Neil was gone.

Before I had time to panic, the hinges of the door creaked. Neil slipped back inside, a fond smile gracing his lips as our eyes met. He crossed to the bedside table and set down a tray laden with a full English breakfast—sausages, eggs, beans, toast, the whole shebang—along with a mug steaming with the promise of a decent cuppa. "Morning, Sleeping Beauty," he crooned. "I was starting to think you might hibernate right through until next Christmas."

My stomach rumbled with blatant, traitorous need. Just how late had I slept in?

Neil dragged the desk chair over to the bedside with a screech and sat, watching me expectantly.

"What time is it?" I asked, yawning.

"Just after eleven."

I rubbed grit from my eyes. "Wow. I slept in."

"You needed it. Now, eat up. If you can get your energy back, I'll take you out this afternoon."

I snapped upright. "Out? Like, outside? Isn't that dangerous?"

Neil shook his head. "While Daniel's in custody, and his criminal contacts in the UK are under close police scrutiny, no one will dare make a move against you or me. We're free to stop hiding."

In a rush of emotion, I threw my arms around Neil. He held me for a long stretch, stroking my hair.

"Does that mean it's finally over?" I asked.

Neil's smile faded to something more sombre. "Yes. It's over. I don't think Daniel's going to worm his way out of this."

"That's a relief."

Neil nudged a fork towards me. "Now, eat."

I dug into the pile of fluffy scrambled eggs and ate a mouthful to appease him. "So, where did you want to take me?" I asked, loading the fork again.

Neil grinned. "I heard your Christmas plans got rudely interrupted. Let me make it up to you."

I dropped the fork and flung my arms around him again.

* * *

The crisp air nipped at my cheeks as Neil and I strolled hand in hand along a path lined with wooden stalls decked in strings of fairy lights. Cinnamon, mulled wine, roasting nuts, and ginger-bread perfumed the air. All around me, the Winter Wonderland hummed with an infectious energy. Christmas music played, and crowds flocked at food vendors, amusement park rides, and an ice rink. It was like something plucked straight from the pages of a storybook. It was everything I had imagined and more.

Neil led me away from the main thoroughfare towards a quiet alcove housing a quaint little cafe strung with twinkling icicle lights. We ordered piping-hot mulled wine—his the classic blend, mine a tart Bramley-apple flavour laced with cinnamon. I inhaled the heady scent as we settled across from each other at the rustic wooden table.

As idyllic as this moment was, the cold knot deep in my stomach refused to unwind. I traced patterns through the conden-sation on the tabletop, reluctant to shatter the magical ambiance with questions and insecurities. Neil's eyes met mine over the rims of our steaming mugs, a knowing look in his eyes. "What's on your mind?" he asked.

Curling my fingers around the warm mug, I mustered my words. "So, now that Daniel is out of the picture for the time being, what comes next?"

Neil took a slow sip of his mulled wine. "We wait. Even uncontested, the will could take a year to process."

"That long?"

"Maybe even longer."

"And then?"

"Daniel will own eight percent of Zelthia, I will own four percent, and Veronica one percent."

"But that means Daniel would still be the majority shareholder…"

Neil smirked, the corners of his eyes crinkling. "I still have one card left up my sleeve."

I arched an eyebrow. "Oh?"

"Avenex owns a three point five percent stake."

"Dixon—"

Neil shook his head. "Dixon is just the manager. Avenex is my company. I own its shareholdings—unbeknownst to Daniel. When the time is right, I will reveal my hand. Veronica and I will pool our shares into Avenex, which will give us the majority."

I shook my head, dumbfounded. "You had this all planned out from the very beginning."

"Not quite. A lot of pieces fell into place through sheer dumb luck along the way. But yes, things are lining up as I envisioned."

A pensive silence fell between us as I digested everything. It was happening. Soon, Daniel would be relegated to the sidelines while Neil and Veronica took control and began their reforms to turn Zelthia into an ethical, sustainable business. After years of plotting, Neil was on the cusp of achieving his goal. My heart swelled with awe, pride, and exhilaration on his behalf. But through the euphoria, a twinge of melancholy pricked at me. Now that his end game was in sight, what did that mean for us? The thought of him slipping from my grasp made my chest ache. I forced the worries down and lifted my chin. "Once you've taken control, what will happen?"

"My job is done. I'll be handing the reins to Veronica. She's the one who will lead the new era of Zelthia."

"And what will *you* do?"

Neil reached across the table and took my hand in his. "I want you to have as much say in that as I do."

The knot in my stomach came undone. He wanted to be with me. He wanted us to shape our future together.

His expression turned serious. "But before all that, I need to tie up loose ends in Singapore and in Auckland. I can't leave everything up in the air. Ronnie needs me, Luxmore needs me... unless... unless you want me to stay with you? Because I'd do it. I'd turn my back on it all for you, if that's what you wish."

His voice was so raw, so earnest, I knew he meant it. In that moment, part of me was tempted to take him up on the offer. But I couldn't ask that of him. Not after he'd already come so far. To throw away years of work and sacrifice now would be a betrayal, not just of the mission, but of the person Neil had fought to become. And truth be told, that was the person I had fallen in love with.

Swallowing hard, I entwined my fingers through his. "I want you to see this through to the end. No matter how long it takes."

Neil's eyes widened a fraction, brows lifting. Then, all at once, his features relaxed and settled into a look of pure gratitude and adoration. "I'll make it up to you, I promise."

I shook my head, squeezing his hand. "Just come back to me in one piece, that's all I ask. Oh, and look after Archie. He needs you just as much as Ronnie and Luxmore need you."

Neil grinned. "He's in good hands with a capable dogsitter. But you're right. I need to get back to him."

The tension between us eased, a comfortable understanding blossoming in its place. When it came to the important things, we were aligned. Even if our respective paths diverged for a while, they would eventually converge once more.

"I'll have Europe to keep me occupied while you're busy finishing what you started," I said.

Neil sighed. "After what happened to you, I'm going to have a hard time with the knowledge you're out on your own. I doubt Daniel would be capable of sending anyone after you anymore, but still... It would ease my fears if you had Lana as a chaperone."

"Lana?"

"The woman you referred to as Hannah. Lana is her real name. She'll need a new assignment now."

"Lana..." Even though she had been paid to act as my best friend, I liked to think we had become real friends in the process, and I wouldn't mind spending more time with her. Besides, if having her along to watch my back would grant Neil some peace of mind, I could allow him that. "If she agrees, then yes. At least for a couple of months until I find my footing."

Neil's shoulders eased, some of his worry lines smoothing out. "Good. I'll arrange it."

I brought my hands back to cradle my hot drink. "When are you going to leave London?"

"The police wish to talk to me, but once that's taken care of, I should go."

"Stay with me until Christmas." The words sprang to my lips before I could even think them through.

Smiling, Neil leaned across the table. "Your wish is my command." He sealed the deal with a chaste kiss pressed to my lips.

"Thank you."

"I wouldn't want to spend Christmas with anyone else."

"Me either."

When we had finished our mulled wine, Neil stood and offered his arm. "Shall we?"

I rose and slipped my hand into the crook of his elbow. As we walked side by side, faint white flecks began to drift through the air.

Chapter Sixty-Six

A swarm of buzzing nerves built to a frenzy inside me as I rocked on the balls of my feet, scanning the street outside the hotel entrance.

Any second now…

A black cab emerged from the line of traffic rounding the corner. I held my breath as the driver pulled up in front of the hotel. Even before the door opened, I recognised the familiar shape and movements of Neil unfolding from the backseat.

For a heartbeat, time seemed to stand still.

Neil got out and straightened to his full height on the pavement, those dark eyes seeking me out and locking onto me with laser focus. He rolled his shoulders to work out the kinks. His hair was longer and more tousled than usual, the tips brushing the collar of his black wool coat. He looked good. Really good. I'd forgotten just how gorgeous he was. So much better in the flesh than in my memories and on screens.

For a second, we just stared at each other. The faint crinkles at the corners of his eyes deepened as a smile tugged at his mouth. He moved towards me, rolling his carry-on over the cobblestones. "Hi," he said.

His voice! That soft yet deep, velvety baritone.

"Hey. Welcome to Vienna."

Neil closed the remaining distance between us, enveloping me in his arms. "Missed you," he murmured against my temple, sending a delicious shiver skittering down my spine.

"Missed you too."

When he released me, I seized his hand and intertwined our fingers, electricity thrumming through every point of contact. Neil squeezed gently as we strolled through the opulent lobby and into the lift.

"How was the flight?" I asked.

"Endless. All I could think about was getting back to you."

"Not too busy thinking of me to get some sleep, I hope? I've got quite the itinerary planned for us."

"What's on the agenda?"

"Museums, galleries, parks, restaurants… The usual."

"I thought you'd be all travelled out by now. I thought we'd spend most of our time… in private." His voice carried a sinful note.

Heat prickled up the back of my neck and into my cheeks. "In that case, I promise we won't spend too much time sightseeing."

We paused outside the door to the suite as I dug through my purse for the key card. After I swiped the card and pushed inside, Neil rolled his luggage to a stop beside the closet door. His gaze roamed around the room, sweeping over the king-sized bed with its sumptuous linens, before flicking to the windows showcasing a view over Vienna's frosty rooftops. One brow inched upward as he took in the details. "You really went all out."

"You booked this place, remember?"

"I suppose you're worth it."

I swatted at him in faux indignation before turning my attention back to the pretty view. "It's certainly a big step above everywhere else I've stayed."

"If you weren't so bloody stubborn, maybe you could have stayed in places like this more often."

"If I stayed in places like this, then I wouldn't want to leave my room, and what's the point of that? Besides, I don't want to have to rely on you all the time."

"It's okay to rely on me."

"If it's any consolation, I'm prepared to let you spoil me rotten for the rest of the time we're here."

With a firm tug, Neil hauled me flush against his body. "Good, because I plan on doing exactly that."

He slanted his mouth over mine. My eyelids drifted shut as I surrendered to him, but he offered just a taste before he broke away, stroking my cheek. "How have you been?"

"Apart from missing you? I've had a wonderful time. Where do I even start? Paris was amazing, so was Lisbon, Florence…" Words failed me as a rush of memories resurfaced—winding, ancient streets; stunning art and architectural treasures at every turn; cafes overflowing into sun-dappled piazzas. A brilliant, breathtaking world which made all my anxieties feel insignificant in the grand scheme of life.

"You looked gorgeous in your photos. Radiant. Happy."

Averting my gaze, I blinked against the unexpected sting of tears. "The first couple of months were hard. I was constantly looking over my shoulder. If it hadn't been for Lana… She was amazing. Kept me occupied, kept me laughing so the anxiety and fear wouldn't get to me. My other friends helped too." I shook my head in silent awe of my resilience. "Eventually, things got easier."

Neil tilted his head down, brows knitted. "I'm sorry I couldn't be there to take care of you myself."

"No. This was the way it had to be, and it was exactly what I needed. I'm glad I did it. But now, I can confidently say I'm ready to go back home and start our lives together."

Neil squeezed my shoulders. "We can still have holidays. Romantic getaways."

"I'll hold you to that."

"Be my guest."

An unbidden smile burst onto my lips as I discarded my coat and scarf. "Fancy a cup of hot chocolate?" I asked, moving towards an area for preparing drinks.

"Sounds… indulgent." Neil shrugged free of his suit jacket and tossed it over the arm of a couch.

"I'll take that as a yes. Don't worry, it's bittersweet." I filled the electric kettle with water and switched it on. "So, how's Veronica getting on as the new leader of Zelthia?" I asked as I rummaged through the wooden case of complimentary drink sachets and tea bags.

Neil removed his shoes before sitting on the couch. "She's taking it in her stride. Her first order of business has been to dissolve the partnership with Magnium Oil. Even that has been a challenge. It's lucky Natasha's so supportive of her career and stays home and looks after Benjamin."

"And the Luxmore handover?"

"As smooth as I could hope for. Petra has returned to the admin department with a promotion, Winston is driving for the new CEO, and James is… well, carrying on as usual. Christine is also looking to get back to work. She'll do great wherever she ends up."

"So, you're officially unemployed now?"

"As unemployed as you are."

"And Daniel Ling."

"Yes. His first trial was cut and dry. He's languishing in a prison cell as we speak."

"Will the police restart the investigation into Alex Patterson's death now that Daniel is a confirmed criminal?"

Neil shook his head. "His family doesn't want to, and I don't blame them. Why reopen old wounds? It won't change anything."

"I agree."

"I stand by my original conclusion that Alex was scared of Daniel, and that played a prominent factor in his death. The file I put together backed this theory. It helped build the case against Daniel when we submitted all our evidence."

"I suppose that's a worthwhile outcome."

"Yes. I think so."

The kettle came to a boil. I warmed a small pitcher of milk in hot water, then poured the contents of two hot chocolate sachets into mugs. I brought our drinks over to the couch, the rich, comforting aroma of cocoa wafting in the air. Neil accepted a mug, letting the whorls of steam kiss his face.

I sank into this moment, the two of us together, all the worries and dangers of the past behind us, with nothing but the promise of our future ahead. Watching Neil, I thought I saw the same sentiment reflected back at me.

"What?" Neil asked, smile widening.

I shook my head, unable to wipe the matching grin off my face. "Nothing. I'm just… happy."

He draped an arm around my shoulders, pulling me snug against his side. I laid my head against his collarbone.

"Me too," he said. "More than you could possibly know."

He lifted his cup to his lips before taking a reverent sip. I followed suit, closing my eyes as the decadent beverage warmed a trail down my throat.

Neil let out a murmur of contentment. "Almost as delicious as you."

I cocked an eyebrow. "But not quite?"

"Not quite."

His eyes darkened with a molten intensity that made my stomach swoop. I set my drink down before he leaned in to claim my parted lips in a deep, luscious kiss. I flung my arms around his neck, my fingers tangling in his hair, as I met his ardent passion with my own. His mouth was warm and sweet. His tongue, imploring and insistent.

Our kiss broke just long enough for him to murmur against my lips, "God, I've missed you…" before his mouth ravaged mine again. He twisted to press me against the arm of the couch, and his thigh nudged between mine, making my back arch.

Neil unknotted my hair from its ponytail, letting it tumble

loose around my shoulders. He parted from the kiss to mouth his way to the freckle behind my ear. His palm slid under my shirt, fingers mapping the rise and dip of my ribs before cradling the swell of my breast. My head tipped back against the cushions as I let out a trembling gasp. I pulled him closer, needing to feel more of him against me. He clutched my hips as he dipped his head to lap at the hollow of my throat, stubble rough against my skin. I bucked against him.

"Getting impatient?" he growled.

"I've waited months."

"Don't worry. I won't make you wait much longer."

He scooped me off the couch, my legs wrapped around him, then carried me to the bed. As soon as he set me down, we divested each other of our clothing. Neil quickly took care of protection, then he dove back to me, our naked bodies crushing together, mouths meeting, devouring. I ground on him, aching for him.

"Want me?"

I nodded, biting my lower lip in anticipation.

In gentle, fluid motions, we rocked into position.

"How's that?" Neil asked.

"Amazing."

I moved, letting my body dictate what it wanted, chasing what felt good.

"Yes. Take what you want from me," Neil groaned.

I clung to him, nails digging into his back. I felt his muscles ripple and strain beneath my touch. Pressure built in me, every nerve ending screaming for release. I didn't let up until I teetered on the edge. One more ragged thrust, and I tipped over, head spinning.

I collapsed with a languid sigh.

We lay there, bodies entangled, hearts thumping. My head rested against Neil's chest, rising and falling with his deep breaths. His fingers toyed with the ends of my hair while I traced idle patterns over the ridges of his abdomen. "I love you," I said against his skin, pressing a soft kiss over his heartbeat. "So much."

Neil tilted my chin up to meet me eye to eye. "I love you too. And I'll never stop loving you."

Epilogue

"**A**gnes! You rascal."

That girl was going to give me a heart attack one of these days. Her frenzied clucks rang out across the yard as I gave chase, gumboots squelching in the mud. She flapped and squawked, zigging and zagging out of reach.

"Get back here!"

She ducked around the corner of the toolshed, and I scrambled after her. When I rounded the bend, she was trapped against the wire fence, clucking in distress.

"Gotcha!"

With a dive, I seized her flapping body and clutched her to my chest, cooing to settle her nerves. "Silly girl." I stroked her glossy feathers. "You know you can't be out running amok. Dexter plays rough."

Speak of the devil.

A flash of gold streaked by, followed by a dark blur—Dexter and Evie. Those two loved tormenting the chickens whenever they got the chance.

"Dexy, Evie, settle down! You're scaring Agnes."

The golden retriever puppy and black kitten glanced at me, eyes sparkling with mischief, before scampering off.

With a sigh, I trudged towards the chicken coop. After depositing Agnes inside, I stood back with hands on my hips and stared across the grounds. Twilight always made our little slice of paradise look even more enchanting. The lush greenery took on an indigo tone, while the first faint pinpricks of starlight winked into view above the horizon. I drew in a long breath, filling my lungs with the fresh, salt-tinged air. Despite living here for almost two years now, the tranquil beauty of the place never failed to give me pause. I still couldn't believe this was my home.

Muffled clanking from the house interrupted my peaceful interlude.

I wonder how dinner's coming along.

Warm light poured from the open French doors, a gauzy curtain floating in the gentle breeze. I kicked off my boots on the stone patio before heading inside.

The herby, garlicky aroma of Neil's lentil Bolognese greeted me as soon as I stepped into the kitchen. He stood at the stove, an apron tied at his waist, stirring the bubbling pot. "Did you detain the escapee?" he asked, not looking up.

"I swear that hen has a death wish," I huffed.

Neil angled a wry look over his shoulder. "But she's your favourite."

I rolled my eyes. "Just because she's adorable, it doesn't make up for her bad behaviour."

Chuckling under his breath, Neil went back to tending the sauce.

Across the threshold into the living room, Archie let out a wheezy snore from his dog bed by the stone fireplace. The old mutt didn't let much rouse him these days. Meanwhile, Chichi and Bowey squabbled over the last scraps in their food bowls.

"Hey." I nudged Neil's hip. "You seem to be in a good mood. Did the call go well after all?"

A crease formed between his brows. "Actually, I have good news and bad news."

I tensed. "Give me the bad news first."

"The call didn't exactly go well. They're still dragging their heels on approving that contract. I was hoping they'd green-light it today so we could move forward, but..." He let out a frustrated sigh.

"Hey, let me deal with them tomorrow. I'll call them and see if I can smooth things over. You don't have to handle this on your own. We're partners, remember?"

"Thank you, my love. What would I do without you?"

"And the good news?"

Neil's face lit up. "I've had word from Ronnie—She and Tash are coming for a visit, and they're bringing Ben with them!"

My heart leapt. We had been talking about this possibility for ages, and now it was happening. "Oh, that's wonderful!" I launched myself at him, wrapping my arms around his waist and burying my face in the soft fabric of his shirt. "When are they coming?"

"November. So, we'll have another little troublemaker to keep away from the chickens."

I swatted his chest, though I couldn't keep the grin from my face. "Yeah, right. That boy's an angel. The chickens will have nothing to fear."

"That's what you think."

I shook my head in disbelief.

Neil smoothed my dishevelled hair behind my ear, gaze softening into something tender and profound. After all this time, he could still unravel me with the slightest glance or touch.

"What?" I asked, suddenly breathless.

Rather than answering, he guided me back against the kitchen counter and sealed his mouth over mine. My body hummed with sheer contentment as I surrendered to his kiss.

Author's Note

Dear reader,

Thank you from the bottom of my heart for making it to the end of Milly and Neil's story. I hope you enjoyed reading it as much as I enjoyed writing it!

This book came about because I adore the grumpy boss trope, and I wanted to contribute to the underserved niche of single-POV, slow-burn romance.

Fun fact: Bowey and Chichi were inspired by real-life cats, Bryan and Lily. While they're not my own pets, I'm kind of like their godmother!

Writing this book wasn't easy. I faced many personal challenges along the way, but Milly and Neil's story offered me refuge. Their world became a place I could escape to, and I hope it provided you with some comfort or joy as well.

If you'd like to stay connected, the best way is through my newsletter. I'm not big on social media, but I do send consistent emails. You'll get life and writing updates from me, plus new release alerts and exclusive content. It's my favourite way to keep in touch with readers. You can subscribe by visiting my website.

Thanks again for reading this story. Your support means everything, and I'm grateful you chose to spend time with my characters.

-Sara

saramartinauthor.com